A Refugee in Switzerland

Atther W. Qureshi

iUniverse, Inc.
Bloomington

A Refugee in Switzerland

iUniverse books may be ordered through booksellers or by contacting:

iUniverse
1663 Liberty Drive
Bloomington, IN 47403
www.iuniverse.com
1-800-Authors (1-800-288-4677)

Because of the dynamic nature of the Internet, any web addresses or links contained in this book may have changed since publication and may no longer be valid. The views expressed in this work are solely those of the author and do not necessarily reflect the views of the publisher, and the publisher hereby disclaims any responsibility for them.

Any people depicted in stock imagery provided by Thinkstock are models, and such images are being used for illustrative purposes only.

Certain stock imagery © Thinkstock.

ISBN: 978-1-4759-3864-7 (s)
ISBN: 978-1-4759-3865-4 (hc)

Library of Congress Control Number: 2012912884

Printed in the United States of America

iUniverse rev. date: 12/03/2012

Firstly I would like to thank Professor Nabila Kyani, Badar Alam, Tariq Sultan and Mr. Muhammad Ahmad for their support

In the early nineties of the last century something extraordinary happened with me. I moved to Lahore to study in the university. I met new people and made a lot of new friends. Luckily, most of those people were very much enlightened. They introduced me to the world of books in general and reading in particular. Every writer is a reader but every reader is not a writer. So I'm taking my chance and climbing the ladder. Here, I would also like to address a potential misunderstanding. This book is not an autobiography rather a work of fiction. However, after living so many years in Switzerland, I too find some of the events quite resembling.

During the Spanish Civil War, German bombers, in support of General Franco, destroyed the city of Guernica. Picasso, shocked at the destruction of the historic Spanish city, painted his famous work titled *Guernica*. In occupied Paris, once a German officer asked Picasso in his studio, pointing to that painting:

"You did this?"

"No, you did," Picasso responded.

So I didn't write this book, Switzerland did.

Elie Wiesel had once said: "I believe it important to emphasize how strongly I feel that books, just like people, have a destiny. Some invite sorrow, others joy, some both."

As this is my first effort, I remain on the mercy of my reader.

Atther W. Qureshi
atther2001@yahoo.com

To Switzerland

"But in all circumstances of life, in obscurity or temporary fame, cast in the irons of tyranny or for a time free to express himself, the writer can win the heart of a living community that will justify him, on the one condition that he will accept to the limit of his abilities the two tasks that constitute the greatness of his craft: the service of truth and the service of liberty."

Albert Camus, at the Nobel Banquet in Stockholm, December 10, 1957

"You know what the fellow said – in Italy, for 30 years under the Borgias, they had warfare, terror, murder and bloodshed, but they produced Michelangelo, Leonardo da Vinci and the Renaissance. In Switzerland, they had brotherly love, they had five hundred years of democracy and peace – and what did that produce? The cuckoo clock."

From the movie – The Third Man

P.S: Cuckoo clock is not Swiss rather German.

The train that brought Jawad to the station left after a brief stop for its next destination, leaving him empty-handed and alone. He glanced at the platform and saw the name of the town, *Kreuzlingen*, written on a signboard. It was the second largest town in the Canton of Thurgau, which was one of the twenty six Cantons of Switzerland. People were busy buying tickets from the counter, while others occupying the grey benches on the platform waited for their trains. A kiosk in the corner sold hot snacks and sundry items. The station was small but beautifully designed, unlike the ones in Pakistan which were dirty and crammed. Jawad felt hungry but he had no time for breakfast. As he stepped outside the train station, he saw a row of taxis lined up against the curb, ready for hire by those who could afford the fare. The taxi-drivers were either smoking in a circle or perusing the day's paper. Across the road, the signboards guided passers-byes to various hotels and restaurants located within the vicinity. He walked the road along the railway line, looking for the crossing. It was not far. He could see it from a distance. He crossed the track and looked to his left for a signboard but found none. He noticed a *kebab* shop in the corner, which a mustached Turk was busy cleaning with an old, soapy mop. He nervously approached the man.

"Asyl (Asylum in German)?" the Turk called out, before Jawad could say a word.

"Yes," he responded.

Neither knew the other's language. The Turk put his right arm forward and gestured him to cross the road and walk westwards. Without a word, Jawad moved on. He started walking in the direction prompted, and the Turk returned to his mop.

After a short walk, Jawad saw a large, grey, army-style building surrounded on all sides by a fence. It was the premises of the "Refugees Reception and Registration Center." There were three more centers like this in other parts of the country. At the main entrance stood a long queue of almost 40 people; conversing in an array of languages. Africans, Asians, Arabs, even Europeans. Most of them were young but Jawad could see a few old men. Few families were also there, with children swirling around their knees. They all seemed to have one thing in common, helplessness and a need for shelter. Finally, a guard in a blue uniform opened the main gate that created a sharp noise and the crowd huddled together to enter. The guard signaled the crowd to straighten the queue. He took about 10 people inside, waving back the left-out crowd and locked the gate. An hour passed and the door reopened, same guard took more people inside. Jawad was bit hungry; it was 10.30 in the morning and there was no sign of any food available. He stood his ground because there was nothing else he could do but wait for his turn. More people arrived and line grew longer.

His turn came at 11 am, the guard counted every person entering the gate. As Jawad stepped inside the gate, the guard halted the queue and locked the gate again. The main building was located a few yards away from the main entrance. The guard asked them to form a line and beckoned them inside. He spoke in English as well as native French and German, but some people could still not understand what he was saying. Giving up, he used his hands to explain what he wanted them to do. As they entered the building, Jawad saw more people inside. Two computers placed at a counter stood protected by glass windows along with four small cabins. To his right was a recreation hall with doors on every side. Opposite to the hall was an information counter. To his left, he could see a row of small rooms with silver nameplates, mentioning a number and the function each occupant provided. Residential area was in the back side of the premises. The group settled on benches in the corridor. The guard appeared with a couple of documents in his hands and asked all of them their mother tongue, handing each a form. Some spoke Albanian, some French, and some Arabic. When it was his turn, he asked:

"Could I have the form in English or Urdu please?"

'English' the guard nodded and handed over a form in English. Pencils and cardboards were at the counter. The form was like a small questionnaire with empty boxes to be filled in with the applicant's particulars. Name, parent's names, nationality, age, and questions like, "Have you ever been in Switzerland or any other European country before as a refugee? Do you have relatives or friends in Switzerland?" Jawad filled out the form and waited like others.

After 15 minutes, the guard collected the forms and disappeared in one of the rooms. It was his routine duty. He took them individually in the cabin. Some had small suitcases or bags which were searched. Jawad hardly had anything with him except for his clothes and a wallet with approximately 20 Swiss Francs. When his turn came, he entered the cabin and the guard politely asked him to remove his jacket. The guard carefully searched all his pockets and pulled out the wallet for a quick check. He counted the money, mentioned the amount on a sheet with Jawad's name on it and asked him to wait outside.

A woman came to the group and took them to the next cabin, larger than the previous one. She took their photographs with a Polaroid camera and attached them to some papers. Then they were escorted to another room. One by one, a man in a sky blue jumper washed their hands with a fragrant liquid soap and cleansed them carefully. He took out a stamp pad and carefully took their fingerprints on a plastic paper. The paper resembled a camera film.

The clock struck noon and it soon became evident that everyone was ravished by hunger. Finally, they were taken to the main corridor that led them to the main gate. It was then that Jawad noticed a white van entering the Reception Center. The guard brought them their temporary identity cards that had their names, nationalities and pictures on them. They were now enlisted as refugees in Switzerland. They were supposed to keep it with them at all times. The newly identified refugees were taken to the recreation hall for lunch, large enough to comfortably serve more than a hundred people. At the door and on the surrounding walls of the hall hung pictures of pig marked with a red cross. These mentioned, in several different languages, including English, that none of the meals served there contains pork. Jawad was pleasantly surprised to see that meals were cooked without pork to accommodate different religions.

The lunch was served soon. They moved slowly but in order, each holding a tray with a plate, a fork and a knife towards the counter. Three male cooks served the meal. Jawad put forward his tray and one of the men put a piece of roasted chicken, the next one filled it with fried potatoes and the third handed him a salad. He hurriedly looked for a place to sit and feed his empty stomach. Each table had bottles of water with glasses. In one corner, there was a vending machine which sold non-alcoholic drinks. Some refugees used their coins to get a coke or other drinks rather than drinking water. Once finished, they threw their garbage in a blue dustbin. There was a wagon in the corner for empty trays and plates. A guard stood in one corner monitoring their movements.

Some people stepped out in to the compound for a smoke. Jawad looked around the place and the people. He could see Kurds, Albanians from Kosovo, a renegade province of Yugoslavia, a few Africans and a group of Arabic speaking youth. He also caught sight of a few Tamils huddled together in a group, talking. *Must be from Sri Lanka.* Jawad felt lonely because he can't find anyone from his homeland or speaking his mother tongue. Suddenly, a young man approached him from behind. His jet-black hair and brown complexion soothed Jawad's eyes.

"May I ask where you come from?" He asked in English, accompanied with two other boys of similar complexion.

"I'm from Pakistan. Where did you come from?"

"Bangladesh."

"Are you Muslim?" asked the eager young man.

"Yes."

"We're also Muslims," he pronounced as if this was an added quality they shared. "Come, join us."

Together they exited the hallway and sat on the grass outside.

"I'm Rehman. These are my colleagues, Roni and Azhar," he introduced his group

"I'm Jawad."

"You speak Urdu?" asked Rehman hesitantly.

"Yes, I do."

"I also know Urdu, but very little," Rehman told him.

"Where did you learn it from?" Asked Jawad, surprised to see a Bengali knowing their former national language.

"I learned it from Bollywood movies." Rehman confessed with a wink.

"Did you come here together?" Jawad asked in Urdu this time.

"No, we just met here."

"Ok."

"Have you eaten?" Rehman asked.

"Yes, haven't you?"

"We did, but my friends had a problem."

"What problem?"

"They couldn't eat the chicken because it was not *halal*. I just recited "Allah u Akbar" and ate it. They looked at me in surprise. I told them they should've gone for asylum to a country where they could be served *halal* food. The trouble is there is none available."

The issue of *halal* food stirred Jawad's conscience too. He was not a strictly practicing Muslim, but still it troubled him. He knew that eating something which was not *halal*, could become a daily routine very soon. It was an issue he would have to learn to live with or else he could become a vegetarian. "Compromise", he said to himself. Was this the way his life was to proceed here on?

"What are we supposed to do now?" Jawad asked Rehman.

"Look brother, we don't know much either. However, before I arrived here, I called a friend who was here a few months ago and now lives in Zurich. He told me that we'll be interviewed. Then there is a medical check-up. Afterwards, we'll be transferred around the country where we'll be given proper housing."

"I see."

"But I pray to God that they send me to Zurich."

"Why do you want to go Zurich?" Jawad inquired.

"It's a nice city. You are permitted to work after six months. Jobs are available and the pay is handsome," Rehman replied.

It seemed he had done some homework and was not that ignorant. He did most of the talking and other two only nodded. Soon the guard beckoned the newly arrived refugees back to the hall. He carried a list of names and he called out 10 names at a time, telling them to board the white van outside. Jawad's name was among those.

"Where are we going?" Jawad asked the guard.

"This place is full. You're being transferred to the hostel in downtown."

The list also included two families with children. None of the Bengali boys were in Jawad's group. The driver started the wagon after a recount of the group. He drove less than 10 minutes in the sloppy streets of downtown Kreuzlingen then stopped in front of a huge building. Everyone got off the van and entered in the new premises. In the corner office, a white-haired man sat behind a table loaded with different stuff. One by one, he called out the names, providing each with a blanket and towel. He asked if they needed other things, like razor, toothbrush or toothpaste. Jawad took a sigh of relief. He picked a razor, a toothbrush and toothpaste. To the families with children, he gave enough diapers to last a whole week.

As they were being taken upstairs to allocate beds, Jawad noticed that this place too, like the previous one, was full of refugees. He was taken to a large room full of bunk beds. He was allotted the top bed, easily accessible by ladder. Men and women were allotted separate rooms. He felt tired and sleepy and immediately jumped onto the bed and nodded off. After sleeping soundly for almost three hours, he woke up to find himself alone in the room. The weather outside was cloudy but it hadn't rained so far. That house was built on a hill and through the window one could have a pretty good view of downtown alleys and lush green meadows. It was a picturesque town; the kind one sees on postcards. At the far end of the town there was a blue strip, probably a river or a lake. He later found out it was Lake Constance.

He cleaned his teeth. Afterward Jawad stepped out and looked around eagerly for company. He walked downstairs. The dining hall in that house was larger than the last one. It had space for almost 200 people. There was a TV in the corner. A soccer game was being shown which attracted a large audience. There were sliding doors opening to a beautiful terrace, currently occupied by some African boys huddled together, sharing a smoke. Jawad took a chair and watched the sunset. Dinner was served soon. Tonight's menu was spaghetti. Jawad, with no prior experience of Italian food, dreaded the meal. He silently observed the people around his table using a fork and spoon simultaneously, rolling the spaghetti around their forks supported by the spoon and devouring it. Jawad tried his best to do likewise, without much luck. To compensate for the plain meal, everyone was then given a pudding. When dinner was over, few of them went to the kitchen to help with the washing and cleaning. Later in the night, the hall buzzed with people watching television. Jawad joined them but the program was in German, a language he did not understand.

Jawad knew that house was a temporary shelter for the newcomers. They were housed here because they had not received their transfer orders yet. It had rules and the warden of the house, a man in his fifties, had an efficient staff. All the residents had to participate in household chores, such as cleaning and helping in the kitchen. They had fixed hours for meals and for going out. Smoking was strictly banned inside the rooms. The place had always two security guards in case of any trouble.

Every morning a transfer list arrived for people who had completed their process and were supposed to move on to their next destination. There was also a list of people who had appointments at the hospital for medical check-ups and another list for people who had to help around in the house, doing chores. It was common practice to check the list every morning.

Next morning, he took a bath, shaved and felt energized. After a light breakfast, he checked the soft board and saw his name in the list for medical check-up. Everyone had to go for that twice. Van soon picked them up and within minutes they reached the hospital which was being run by the Red Cross. There were headphones at the hospital which informed each individual about the medical test. They all submitted their blood samples in the lab and got vaccinated. Chest X-rays followed. After the check-up, they were given a card with their medical conditions and vaccination. It was noon when they finished the check-up. Van did not return to their residence rather it took them to the Reception Center where they had lunch. They were allowed to visit town, but before the allotted time of 4:30. Jawed did not see his Bengali mates he had met earlier at the Center.

Unable to find company, he decided to take a walk downtown on his own. The streets were lined up with multiple shops but Jaw ad's thoughts were far away. At the end of the street he saw a lush, green park. He entered the park and occupied a bench beside the road, noticing people strolling with their pets and children cycling. He sat there almost an hour. Suddenly, someone called out his name. He turned around to the sight of Rehman, Roni and Azhar. Rehman had a large packet of chips in his hand. They all settled on a bench.

"How are you?" Rehman initiated.

"I'm fine. What about you guys?"

"We're okay brother. Have you been to the hospital earlier?" Rehman asked.

"Yes."

"You'll have to go there again."

"Yes, I know."

"Let us take a walk in the town." Roni suggested. They walked in the streets to kill time. Rehman stopped in front of a sex shop; perhaps this was the first time he had seen one. He started commenting on the synthetic substitutes of human love. But Jawed didn't like it. He forced everyone to move. They reached the Reception Center on time. From there Jawad had to return to the hostel, while Rehman and his friends stayed at the Reception Center. At the hostel Jawad went straight to the dining hall. He saw a man in the hall. His features told Jawad that he was either from Pakistan or India. He noticed Jawad too and approached him.

"Are you from Pakistan?" he asked.

"Yes, I am."

"Me too either."

"Which part of Pakistan?" Jawad inquired.

"Faisalabad".

"I'm from Lahore."

"So we're from the same province."

"Yes, indeed. Did you arrive today?"

"Yes, but when did you come?"

"I came here yesterday."

"By the way, I'm Kamal Khan. What's your name?"

"My name is Jawad."

It was almost sunset and gradually the weather around became colder.

"Well, how is it coming along?" Jawad asked to Khan.

"Fine, I've to go through a medical examination."

"Well, you're not the only one. It's the standard procedure for everyone. But the living conditions aren't so bad here."

"But, they aren't so good either."

"That may be true but people stay here for only a few days. As soon as their process is complete, they are transferred immediately to other parts of the country."

"Do they give a choice in terms of transfer? I mean if anyone wants to go to a certain place?"

"I've no idea. But where do you wish to go?"

"I want to go to Canton Zurich," Khan replied.

"Why does everybody want to go to Zurich?" Jawad asked curiously.

"I've an acquaintance there from my hometown. I phoned him before I came here. He told me that it's good to be transferred to Zurich. Because once someone is transferred to a Canton, he is not allowed to change it. There are many Cantons where you're not allowed to work and only provided for basic necessities. If you're not allowed to work, it means one is penniless and have no money to send back home," Khan explained the whole situation.

Jawad felt Khan was more informed than Rehman. Soon they heard the dinner bell. Both settled for dinner together. Finally, he had someone with whom he could share his thoughts. After dinner Khan went to the vending machine and brought two cups of coffee. They settled on the chairs. People were busy watching television. Jawad wanted to go out but it was prohibited. It was too early to go to bed and there was nothing else to do. He felt little depressed. Khan too felt the same way. He pulled a pack of cigarettes and offered one to Jawad. They went to the terrace for a smoke. Smoking relaxed him a little. He was not a regular smoker.

Khan talked profusely about his future while Jawad knew nothing as to what may happen next. Before coming to Switzerland, he was unaware of his fate that lay before him, hidden from his sight.

"How did you come to Europe?" Jawad asked Kamal Khan. It was difficult to kill time and a little story telling might help.

"I came to Turkey from Pakistan. I stayed there for about six months as I could not find a reliable agent who could help me reach Europe. Then I heard about a Pakistani guy who was working with human traffickers, smuggling people from Turkey to Europe. You see Turkey is a hub for people like me. Those people had just transported a group of people to Italy via sea. I met him and he told me that they were again leaving with a large group. I had no choice but to trust him. We agreed on $3,500. I met him on the appointed day and he handed me over to another person who was responsible for the transportation of the people to the ship. They used small boats as the ship was still far away from the shore. It was an old ship. We were kept in the lower part of the ship. There were Tamils from Sri Lanka, Afghans, Kurds from Iraq and Turkey, people from African countries and also a couple of Pakistanis. It was an assembly of misery. We stayed in the ship as it wandered for days before it reached the Italian shores."

"And how were the living conditions on the ship?" Jawad asked out of curiosity.

"Terrible, the crew was very harsh." Khan lit another cigarette and started speaking again. "We were almost 100 in count; women, children and the young. From the moment the ship started sailing, people started vomiting. This made a huge mess. The crew gave us plastic bags but the foul smell had spread around the ship. Children got sick and cried all the time. The food was bad and inadequate and worst of all the toilet conditions were unimaginable."

"And still you think that living conditions here aren't good?" Jawad asked teasingly..

Khan was at a loss for words, pondering over his earlier comment, but he continued.

"As the ship arrived in the Italian waters, the crew got harsher. One night they came near the shore and ordered us to leave the ship. There was a small launch available and they were in a big hurry. They packed us in the launch like potatoes in a sack and then brought us to the shore in two turns. We were left in knee deep water. Everybody struggled to reach the shore. It was a dark night. While on ship, a Pakistani told me that his brother lived in Italy and was in contact with the people who brought us here. He hoped that he would be searching for him. People dispersed in groups. I was with two other Pakistanis. We walked in the night without any idea where we were. At the crack of dawn, we passed through a jungle and found a road. We started walking on the road. There was little traffic when suddenly a police van appeared. We had neither the strength nor the desire to run and it was of no use. The policemen locked us up in their van. As we reached the police station, we found many people from the ship gathered in the compound, guarded by the police. It was a small town so everybody found out what was going on. The children cried with hunger. Thank god, someone from the village informed the local church that came to our help. They brought food for us. They even brought milk and clothes for the children."

Jawad listened to the whole story with keen interest. He sympathized with Khan's situation because he understood exactly what he went through. Khan continued his heart-rending tale.

"I don't know whether it was pressure from the church that halted the police to take further action against us or the police decided to leave us themselves. They merely wrote down our names, took our fingerprints, and let us go. They handed us written orders to leave Italy within the next 30 days. They had our data in their computers, and we could get caught any time. The brother of my Pakistani colleague had also heard about the incident and arrived to help. He only made a move when we left the police station. He asked me where I wanted to go. I told him I want to go to Milan where I had some friends waiting for me. They helped me to buy a ticket at the nearest train station. I reached Milan and stayed there for a month. Afterwards it was decided that I should try my luck in Switzerland, so they found someone to smuggle me here."

"But why did you really come here?"

"What if I ask you the same question?" Khan shot back.

"I've been sent here. I'm not the captain of my soul to sail at my own free will."

"Look Jawad, we've all come here to make our lives better," Khan confessed.

They chatted away till the clock struck eleven. Jawad wished Khan good night and both went upstairs to their rooms. Jawad desperately missed his family. He pondered over Khan's words. Better life. He was not even sure whether there was a future for him here. However meeting Khan had satisfied Jawad as it showed that he was not the only fortune hunter there. But the question that kept nagging him was whether this tiny country had the solutions to the problems which hounded them in their native countries.

Jawad was born in Lahore, second largest city in Pakistan. A city engulfed by the charm of its culture, and the legacy of its bejeweled history. Since ancient times it had been the center of art, music and literature. In the middle of this great city passes a small canal. The eastern side of the canal houses luxurious colonies of the mighty rich, all leading lavish lives. The streets are lined up with state-of-the-art shopping malls and restaurants providing the world's finest cuisine. The western side of the canal houses people dreaming of the day they would move on the eastern side. Jawad's family belonged to the lower-middle class. Not particularly hand-to-mouth, but still unable to live a life according to their wishes. They had to compete to maintain a certain status in society. He was the eldest of four children. Next there was Faraz, his younger brother and two sisters Amna and Rabia. Both his parents were teachers and they resided in a middle class colony.

After the birth of his youngest sister, Rabia, his mother, Rasheeda Begum gave up her job at school to care for her family. However, she did not stop teaching students at home. A group of children from the neighborhood would come to their house every afternoon. His father, Mohammad Alam, was a lecturer and taught English literature at a government college. He also worked as a private tutor to make ends meet. He taught children of rich families at their homes in the evenings. Each evening, he would ride his old scooter to the bungalow of a rich family to teach their children studying at the most expensive private schools in town. He also prepared his students for various exams, to help them study abroad. With his hard work, he had acquired a good reputation. Most rich families had one aim in common for their boys; to send them abroad for higher studies. All his private students lived on the eastern side of the canal. At times, Jawad would accompany his father to one of those mansions. He was always appalled by the grandeur and splendor of the wealthy owners. He dreamt large about his future but was aware that he might not be able to attain all this because of his middle-class status.

Just like his neighborhood friends, Jawad also went to the local government school. After school, he was always under the watchful eyes of his mother. He shattered his parents' dreams when he selected Arts over Science for his matriculation. This choice left no chance for him to ever become an engineer or a doctor, two professions with the highest demand in Pakistan. As time passed, he attended the college where his father taught. After college, he joined the University of Punjab for his Masters in English as his father had done.

His favorite hobby was to read books and his father made plenty available to him. From the very beginning, his parents made the atmosphere in the house quite literary. Always bringing new books and encouraging their children to share their ideas. While at University, Jawad got the membership of the British Council Library. He became a bookworm, reading books on various topics outside of his curriculum. Going through books in the library one day, he grabbed a book on world famous inventions. The book intrigued him; he wanted to know about those fantastic inventions. He brought the book home for a thorough study. But what amazed him most in the book was the association of every scientific invention with the West.

The term "West" was not used in geographical terms. It represented the first world or the developed world.

He knew well that it wasn't only the inventions that were adopted from the West but also the basic concepts of life of the last decade of the 20th century. Concepts such as, democracy, freedom of speech, and respect for human rights, all came from the west. He pondered over the fact that even the ideological aspect of the modern world is taken from great thinkers from the West. His entire childhood, Jawad had heard that the West also had its demons and shortfalls, such as colonialism. Then there were autocratic ideologies like Fascism and Communism. He had read how the colonizers maltreated and subjugated the weaker nations by enslaving them and later heralded themselves as champions of democracy and strong supporters of human rights. But today he could see that inside his own country, the courts still used the laws promulgated by the British during their colonial rule. He considered it ironic.

He also became a huge fan of Hollywood movies especially action-packed ones. He and his college friends would slip from home on the pretext of playing cricket and rush towards the cinema. The advent of the heroine on the big screen would leave the boys in the hall awe-struck. Each of them would fantasize about the blonde, blue-eyed creature and simultaneously let out a sigh on watching her kiss the hero. Bollywood movies were always there on his list but ones he would rather watch on videocassettes at a friend's place because his mother disapproved of VCR. "That could have a bad effect on your morals," she would say. However, when he joined the university, he begged his parents to buy him a VCR so he could watch Shakespeare's plays to understand them better.

Jawad watched film adaptations of Shakespeare's famous plays which he could easily get from the British Council Library. He'll visit the library every other day to bring something new and exciting. His perception about himself and the world took a new turn. He soon realized that it was the West from where *brave new world* actually originated. From injected vaccines to launching a spaceship to the moon, the West had given a whole new meaning to this world. Their progress, led his fellow countrymen to follow their path of success. They would line up in long queues at various western embassies to get a visa to migrate. But one thing made Jawad uncomfortable and sad. Seeing his country not progressing filled him with disgust for the rulers who ran after power, while the *mullahs* preached religion. The classes were divided on the basis of how much money they had instead of their intellectual and progressive contribution towards their country. The middle and lower classes were left to survive on hand-to-mouth incomes and hardly given their basic rights. They were the most subjugated classes who were made to work more than the upper class did and still weren't provided enough to live a comfortable life.

Another of Jawad's newly adopted hobby, apart from watching movies, was alcohol. He disliked the taste but liked the effect it had. He tried it at a friend's wedding for the first time and savored it on rare occasions with his friends. Once he managed to drink heavily at his friend's farmhouse and returned home only after becoming sober. Another habit he picked up from his friends was smoking, but just like drinking, it wasn't an addiction. He'll only smoke when he was outdoors with friends.

He inherited a good physique from his parents: fair skin, brown eyes, black hair and a height of five feet ten. He had a reserved demeanor with a slight inclination towards oratory. He was a young, good-looking university student. One who would indulge in good poetry and had an eccentric taste in literature, culture and arts. But he hardly ever thought of having an affair with one of his classmates because he was well aware of the consequences in the conservative society he lived in. He had seen one of his friends flirt with a classmate and had to deal with severe consequences. Having a girlfriend was seen as unsocial and immoral. His society did not encourage dissent; any opinion against the wishes of society's established norms was discouraged. Whether is it a political matter, a social matter or even a personal matter. They were supposed to follow the norms. All members of the community were supposed to stay within limits. Under normal circumstance even an inquisitive question could be considered blasphemous, and penalty for such a crime would be high. One had to hide such thoughts and they were doing a lot of hiding themselves. To enjoy a drink, to meet a girl or to have an open discussion they had to hide somewhere.

Immediately after his Masters, he applied for the Civil Services Exam to get a good, secure job in the government. Some of his friends were also following the same path. It took him a year and a half to take the exam. He tried hard but failed. His failure brought huge disappointment to his family and great distress to himself. It almost devastated him. With all his education, he could not find a well-paid job to support his family. Jawad gradually started losing hope. He felt helpless at the hands of destiny. Being the eldest son, he was supposed to share his father's burden but circumstances around him did not allow that. He could not stay happy when he hung out with his friends or even when he was at home. He tried to reappear in the exams but did not have the courage to go through it again and face another failure.

He wondered hopelessly whether he would ever be able to earn enough to support his family. He saw his mother saving money for the marriages of his sisters. The dowry custom was a huge burden put on the parents of a girl as a condition for marriage into a good family. Although Jawad's father had managed to provide a good education to all his children, they did not have enough money to better their house. Both his parents worked harder but they were getting old and Jawad knew well that there was no other source of income left. His siblings were studying, which too required a lot of money.

To make some money, Jawad started giving tuitions in his neighborhood instead of sitting idle and waiting for a good opportunity to arise. His father had always stood by him, understanding the difficulty of him being unemployed. But he never underestimated Jawad; he had been his support system. He always encouraged Jawad to find work that would suit him, work that he would enjoy. His mother was also worried about him. She had a habit of visiting the shrines in the city. There were plenty of them around. Like every mother she had high hopes for her son but she could see him going nowhere. Disappointed from the living, she turned to the dead. On her regular visits she would pray to the saints of the shrines, those who had died hundreds of years ago, to secure a job for her beloved son. Sometime Jawad would also accompany her at her insistence. Those shrines received a lot of visitors. Lovers, jobless, destitute, visa seekers, businessmen, all would come there and put the authenticity of the saint to a new test. Some people permanently lived there, indulging in meditation or even lecturing the attendees. On one occasion his mother went inside the tomb of a saint while Jawad went to listen to a man who was speaking in a circle. Jawad knew it would be a while till his mother would return. She had a list of demands to utter after some recitation from the Quran. The speaker took no notice of Jawad and kept talking.

"People do everything for love these days and some even kill themselves. But what do they get? If a woman is kind to someone she could only offer her body but if a saint is kind to someone he could lead him to heaven. We should try to get the affection of a saint and through that of God so we could be saved."

On that the people surrounding him shouted some slogans and became emotional. Jawad moved away as he had some serious doubts to the philosophy being taught. In his view, humanity needed scientific knowledge to fight poverty, disease and famine. He wondered how those saints could help in such matters.

His father had a friend named Agha Ihsan Elahi who lived on the eastern side of the canal. Though he was very rich, he always met his father on equal terms, never assuming a superior position due to his status in society. Everybody called him 'Agha Sahib' for respect. Jawad proposed that his father should speak to his friend for a job. At first, he was hesitant, but eventually agreed. One evening they went to meet him. Agha welcomed them at the gate with his bodyguard.

"Why do you need a gunman?" Jawad's father inquired.

"For security reasons, yesterday a child got kidnapped in the neighborhood. My wife and I are worried for our children."

Jawad's father was shocked to hear about the incident. Soon they were enjoying tea with snacks. His father explained the purpose of their visit.

"I'll see what I can do," Agha replied in response.

Two days later, Agha called in the evening and talked to his father. He wrote something down on a paper.

"This is the address and the name of the person you'll meet for your job tomorrow. Agha Sahib had arranged everything."

"What kind of a job is it?"

"It's a currency exchange job. Normally, those people don't trust strangers but he had given them your guarantee. I hope you won't break his trust."

"What about my evening students? Will I be able to teach them once I start working?"

"You'll have to manage your time, son."

Jawad took the address and the next morning left home to visit his potential employer. It was called Money World Currency Exchange and was situated at the heart of Lahore's commercial district. An armed guard stood at the gate. He asked for Mr. Nadeem Malik at the counter, referring to the note his father had given him.

"Mr. Malik is not here yet but he'll be arriving shortly. Can I do anything for you?" the man behind the counter asked Jawad.

"No thanks. I'll wait here."

After around 30 minutes, a bald man in his fifties entered the office, busy swinging his car keys. His arrival stiffened the staff around. The guard saluted him and the work force became serious and active. He opened the door to his room and disappeared inside. The man at the counter also went inside. Minutes later, Mr. Malik, as they called him came out of his room and greeted Jawad.

"I'm Nadeem Malik, are you looking for me?" he said extending his hand.

"Sir, my name is Jawad. Agha Sahib sent me here."

"Oh, so it's you. Come with me."

Malik took him to his office. Inside, Jawad saw staircase leading upwards. He climbed upstairs and Jawad followed. It was a comfortable office.

There were lockers on the right and to the left were monitors. The whole place had cameras.

"Would you like cold drink or may be tea?"

"No thanks," Jawad responded politely.

"Agha Sahib told me you have done Masters in English."

"That's right."

"He speaks very high of you."

"That is very kind of him."

"Now about this job, we deal in currency exchange from across the globe. It's imperative that we should have trustworthy staff. We've many trade secrets that are to remain under wraps. I've a brother in England and we both work together. For me Agha Sahib's words are good enough and I've complete faith in him. Now you tell me, when could you start?"

"Well, it depends. I also work as a private tutor and parents of my pupils might be informed to arrange a new tutor."

"The timings here are from ten in the morning to eight in the evening, with a lunch break. Lunch is on us. You'll be paid 6,000 Rupees in the beginning and then we'll see. You can start from next month. You'll work at the counter with two others. It's not tough, just multiplying and paying the customers and I'm sure you would learn it fast."

"I'll think about it and inform you as soon as possible."

"I'll wait for your answer. People working here are good, but none of them is with a Masters in English." Jawad thanked Mr. Malik and returned home.

The money was not bad to start with; it was more than he earned from tuitions. He heard that Master degree holders were working as traffic constables and taxi drivers due to the unavailability of good jobs. His parents did not force him to make a decision and told him to decide for himself. Jawad felt confident that he could do the job till a better one came along. He wished he could acquire a job as a lecturer but presently there was a restriction on hiring. The following day he called Malik to inform that he'll join next month. That was the last month he taught his pupils.

The day arrived when Jawad, with his knowledge of Shakespearian prose and Victorian-era poetry, went to work as a clerk at the Money World Currency Exchange. Malik had not arrived, but his co-workers welcomed him warmly. At the counter he was given a bundle of US dollars to count. A wet sponge was placed at the left corner of the desk to lubricate his fingers for counting cash smoothly. Malik arrived at his usual time. The company mostly dealt in British pounds, Dollars, and Gulf region currencies as the majority of the ex-pats resided in these countries.

Jawad gradually got better at his job. Every morning there was a new currency list when he arrived at the counter. All they had to do was to multiply the amount of the foreign currency in Pakistani rupees, make a receipt and pay it to the customer. Some customers obtained foreign currency by exchanging Pakistani rupees. At the end of the day, Malik would collect all the cash from the counters and take it upstairs to store it in the lockers. What he was doing with all that money, nobody knew.

At times Jawad would get an opportunity to speak English when a foreign customer arrived for currency exchange. His customers as well as his co-workers were impressed by his fluency every time they heard him speak. Mr. Malik would always pass a smile, his way to show his appreciation. Jawad soon became friends his co-workers, especially one of them, called Ahmad, became very close to him. They were of the same age and background. He'll pick Jawad every morning from his home and they would both ride to the office on his bike. After work, sometimes they'll go to the cinema. Ahmad was smart and knew how to get things done. He dreamt of going abroad one day and making a successful life of his own. He was learning English for this very purpose and often sought help from Jawad. He wanted to study at a foreign university and get a well-paying job.

At work Jawad made a discovery. His boss Mr. Malik was a regular drinker. On any given evening, Malik could be found drinking whisky in his office. There was always a bottle of imported Scotch hidden away in his drawer. Jawad did not hide his drinking habit from him though it was risky. One day after work, he invited Jawad to his office for a drink.

"Don't worry, I won't tell Agha Sahib," he assured Jawad with a smile.

Jawad drank with him for the first time that evening. Malik was in a good mood. He talked about his family with Jawad. He told him about his father and how he used to have a newspaper stand and lived in a poor neighborhood. But their fortune changed when his elder brother went to England where he worked hard day and night. His in-laws were already settled there and they helped him start up a business. Soon after, their father opened a general store in Lahore. On his brother's suggestion, Malik started dealing in foreign currency and the family had never looked back. They lead a prosperous life. His children were attending good schools and his house was located in one of Lahore's most expensive areas. Jawad enjoyed listening to his story and hoped that one day he could do the same for his family.

Jawad contributed as much as he could to the family with his earnings. But his frustration increased day by day. At work he would exchange dollars and pounds for rupees, noticing the joy of the lucky customers. They were all well off, riding their luxury cars to Money World with their women clad in gold jewelry. He wondered whether he'll ever be able to enjoy the same luxuries in his life. This was the state of affairs when he reached his 24th birthday. He felt his life was going nowhere. He often saw Ahmad, carrying brochures of different international universities, where he would apply for admissions. He'd cleared the necessary exams but what he needed most was a handful of cash. He hardly had the money to pay the huge admission fee. Even if he could manage the initial fee, he still had to show that his parents in Pakistan were rich enough to support his studies abroad. For this he needed to present various documents, such as property deeds and bank accounts of the family that would prove his sound financial background. However, he had none. Ahmad sometimes proclaimed to acquire fake documents to get the visa and admission, but was afraid of the legal action if he got caught.

One of Jawad's distant cousins, Nasir lived in Munich, Germany. Brought up in Lahore, he had been settled in Germany. He was married to a German woman. Through his earnings abroad, he was able to provide a new house and a brand new car for his family in Lahore. Nasir was over the moon when he at last acquired his German citizenship. He was considered the pride of the family as he had been able to pull them from poverty. Jawad's family was on good terms with his family and Nasir too visited them whenever he was in Pakistan.

Jawad knew that he won't be able to improve the condition of his family if he stayed at Money World. He had to break this deadlock and get a well-paid job. The currencies that switched from his hands every single day made him realize their value. He thought about his possibility of going abroad. But it required a huge amount of money, which he was sure his parents did not have. Jawad was hesitant to ask his parents for the money they had been saving for the weddings of his sisters. But he knew once he reached Europe, he might be able to earn enough for all his family's needs beyond providing for his sisters. In a way he saw it as a kind of investment on his parent's part.

One day he talked to Ahmad about this issue.

"Ahmad," Jawad spoke in a desperate tone. "I need to get out of here."

"What are you saying Jawad? I don't understand."

"I want to go abroad to start a new life. I need money to meet my obligations. Here it's difficult."

"I know what you mean, my friend. But where do you want to go?"

"I think England might be a good option, because I know the language."

"I agree with you. Mr. Malik's brother is settled there and he might help you. Your Master's degree can get you an admission at any good university."

"Why should I go on a student visa? Aren't there any other visas?"

"Yes, you can get a business visa or a visit visa, but you're not allowed to stay more than a specified duration. However, a student visa gives you the opportunity to stay there for a couple of years and if you get a good job, you can settle there permanently."

"But there are people who have been living abroad for years without any legal status."

"Yes, you're right. They live illegally and do odd jobs."

"But they still manage to earn better than us." Jawad argued.

"Not all of them."

"Do you know anyone who could arrange a visa for me, any kind of visa?"

"Well, Lahore is full of agencies providing visa service, but they are mostly frauds. My father works at the passport office. He has a friend, Mr. Sheikh, who helps people with visa-related matters."

"I see. Why didn't you ask him about yourself?"

"I knew you'll say that. The thing is, I'm the only son of my parents and they don't want me to go abroad. So if I really want to go, I'll have to do it on my own."

"Do you have any idea how much money is required to go to England?"

"I've no idea. I heard from my father that Sheikh does these kinds of things as a side business and not on regular basis. But have you got the money for such a venture?"

"That is my biggest problem. My parents have savings, but they are for the girls."

"I understand that but I think you should cut a deal with your parents."

"What kind of a deal?"

"Ask them to support you with their savings to go aboard and once you get there, you can take care of everything. Believe me it'll be beneficial for you as well as for your family."

"But are you sure about this Mr. Sheikh?"

"Let me talk to my father about this issue first. But the important thing is my father's willingness to do so."

"You think he could refuse?"

"Well, he is my father, not my son. So far he had refused to do it for me."

That day Jawad returned home pondering over his conversation with Ahmad and hoping he could find a way. At dinner, he ate quietly. His mother asked him if there was something that was bothering him. He told her it was just work stress. In his mind, he thought of a good opportunity to talk to his parents. On that weekend after lunch, Jawad told his parents that he wanted to talk to them about an important issue. He noticed a strange smile on their lips. Jawad realized the smile belonged to the impending news of Jawad's decision of getting married, but that wasn't on his mind. They settled in the drawing room to listen to him. He asked his younger brother, Faraz to join them as well. His parents settled on the sofa as Jawad took a chair and sat in the middle, while his brother perched himself on a cushion.

Gradually, he started with acknowledging his failure in securing a reasonable job, but his parents intervened and told him it wasn't his fault. Jawad told them that being parents they knew that for anything positive to happen in the future, something needed to be done. The girls had to be married; their house needed a full renovation. If God forbid someone in the family got fatally ill, they would have to find a private hospital as the facilities provided by the government hospitals were poor. He, being the eldest son, shouldered the responsibility of providing these comforts to his family. His parents were surprised to realize that it was not about a girl or him getting married; their son was worried about the future of their family.

"We understand your concerns my son, but I think the situation is under control. You're not unemployed and your sisters are still studying and there is no immediate cause of concern as such," explained his father.

"You're right father. But still, I think that the prospects are not that bright either."

"What do you suggest then?" his father asked in an inquisitive tone.

"I've decided to try my luck abroad."

There was a pin drop silence in the room for a while.

"What do you mean by abroad?"

"England may be."

His parents watched him disapprovingly, while his brother could not cover his smile. His father took a deep breath and said:

"And how're you going to get there?"

"I'm working on it; there is someone who might help me to get a visa."

"But that might cost a lot of money and it could be risky," his father spoke skeptically.

"There is always a risk involved in whatever we do."

They discussed the matter for hours. He told them about Ahmad and Mr. Sheikh. His mother was instantly against the whole idea. For her, Jawad was her boy. She can't bear his absence, which she made very clear during their discussion. Jawad told them that he had dreams of earning good money, of being rich and moving forward in his life. He made it clear to his parents that he needed money from them but once he had a job abroad, he'll more than pay them back.

As far money was concerned Jawad had a good record. His parents never had any complaint against him. Since he started working at Money World, he gave all his salary to his mother. Whenever he needed anything, he asked her for it. He liked it that way and his mother was always careful with the money. His father asked about the cost required for attaining a visa but Jawad did not know for sure. He told Jawad that he would talk to Jawad's cousin, Nasir in Germany. Jawad felt that his father was not fully against the idea of going abroad. He felt satisfied talking about his feelings with his family.

Next day, he decided to ask Ahmad to arrange a meeting with Mr. Sheikh through his father.

"But are you sure that you can arrange the money?" Ahmad asked to make sure.

"Not yet. But hopefully my parents would agree eventually. I think we should meet your father's friend as soon as possible."

Next morning Jawad asked Ahmad again whether he had spoken to his father. Ahmad started laughing.

"Patience my friend, in matters like these it is very important that one should have a lot of patience. Look at me, I've been trying for years and there is still no hope. I'll talk to him soon and let you know," Ahmad spoke like an elder.

Meanwhile his father told him that he had spoken with Nasir in Munich, who assured his father that Jawad's decision was good. However Nasir showed his concern over the traps Jawad might fall in spread by fraudulent agencies. Jawad assured his father that he won't take any step unless he was completely satisfied. Still his father promised him nothing. On Thursday, Ahmad told him that his father had a long conversation with his friend on the phone. Mr. Sheikh would see them at his place next Friday evening. It was their day off.

Friday evening, Ahmad picked Jawad from home. They crossed the canal and entered the posh residential area of Lahore. Ahmad stopped his bike at the gate of a finely built mansion and rang the bell. A teenager boy opened the door and led them to the drawing room. Couple of minutes later a man appeared, probably in his fifties; Jawad and Ahmad stood up and greeted him. This was Mr. Sheikh, the man who had the power to alter the course of Jawad's life, forever. Mr. Sheikh did not look like a businessman; in fact, he resembled a retired boxing champion with strong muscles and a tall stature. He greeted them warmly and offered them a seat.

"So, this is your friend who wants to go abroad?" Sheikh asked, once Ahmad introduced Jawad.

"Yes uncle and we are like brothers," Ahmad emphasized.

"I see. Then he is as dear to me as you are," Sheikh responded with a smile.

Sheikh turned to Jawad and asked him about his background, his education, and his future plans. Jawad laid forward everything in black and white. He mentioned his desire to go to England and start a new life. Sheikh listened to him patiently. He stayed quiet for a while and after thinking things over spoke in a decisive tone.

"I can't arrange a visa for England, but I can try for a Schengen visa."

"Which visa?" Jawad had no knowledge of that.

"A Schengen visa, Oh probably you don't know about that. Schengen visa allows you to travel to a number of countries in Europe, for instance Germany, France, Holland, Belgium, Spain and a few more. These countries have an agreement among themselves, known as The Schengen Agreement. Visas issued by any of these countries are valid for all the member countries."

Jawad was a little disappointed on hearing that he could not go to England, but he stayed positive. *At least he is offering something rather than a blunt 'No'.* An opportunity to go to Germany presented him with a chance to seek help from his cousin. The offer excited Jawad's nerves and he knew that the German economy was a whole lot stronger than England's.

"And how much will it cost?" Ahmad spoke before Jawad.

"Look son, your father is my friend and I'm doing it as a favor. It's a pity that this country could not provide a reasonable living for a talented young man like him. The problem is that I'll have to prepare a lot of documents for him."

"What kind of documents?" Jawad interrupted.

"I'll have to show you as an employee of my company. For that we need tax documents, salary slips, bank statement and a job agreement from a previous date. All those fake documents will help you to get a visa."

Jawad felt a sudden dryness in his throat. The teenager reappeared and brought two bottles of coke. Jawad did not hesitate to pick one from the tray.

"But this will all be illegal. What if we got caught?" he asked Sheikh.

"Well there are certain risks one has to take and if you're not ready, then go home and forget everything," Sheikh commented.

Jawad realized that he had annoyed Sheikh by his questions and he must make a move to repair the damage.

"Forgive me, sir," Jawad spoke to Sheikh apologetically. "I'm just a little worried about the consequences."

"What consequences? The worst thing that could happen is that your visa application might get rejected and that's all. Nobody is going to hang you."

"I understand that but how long will this whole process take?"

"Around 2 to 3 months, after starting the process."

Jawad was afraid to talk about the money; Ahmad noticed the worry on Jawad's face and came to his rescue. He told Sheikh about the financial position of Jawad's family.

"How much is it all going to cost?" Ahmad asked again.

"I'll charge 150,000 Rupees and then you'll have to arrange traveler's check for one thousand American Dollars, along with a return ticket. The traveler's check and the plane ticket are part of the process. Once you reach at your destination, you can reimburse the checks and the return ticket. That's the maximum I can do for you. When you arrange this, just tell me and give me a photocopy of your passport. The whole transaction may cost approximately 270,000 Rupees and it'll be spent in installments. There is no advance but I trust you and I hope you won't disappoint me," Sheikh concluded.

Jawad realized that further questioning may annoy Sheikh. They warmly thanked him for his time with a promise to see him soon. On their way home, Ahmad felt Jawad's silence.

"Why are you so quiet Jawad?" Ahmad finally asked.

"Nothing, I don't know how to break this to my parents."

"I can understand how you feel," Ahmad commented.

At home, he told his father about the meeting with Sheikh.

"Mr. Sheikh is not asking anything in advance father, but once he has done his job he expects to be paid."

"That's a lot of money, my son. I'm scared because there are so many risks involved. You know the position of our family. It takes years to save that much."

"But there are no risks involved. Ahmad's father had spoken with Mr. Sheikh himself and we are satisfied."

Jawad did not want to argue with his father, but he was not ready to give up either. He thought about arranging a meeting between his father and Sheikh to prove the latter's trustworthiness.

"Why don't you meet Sheikh yourself? Then you can decide whether he is a trustworthy person or not." Jawad said, showing Sheikh's business card to him.

"All right, I think we should do that. It sounds appropriate."

Next day, Jawad called Mr. Sheikh and asked for an appointment. It was decided that they could meet next Thursday evening. On that evening Jawad and his father went to see him. His son opened the door and escorted them to the drawing room. Sheikh arrived immediately and shook hands with them warmly. He knew why Jawad's father was there so he wasted no time in bringing the issue to the table.

"Being a father I understand your concerns but I encourage Jawad's decision to go abroad. I'll do my utmost to turn Jawad's dream into reality."

His father questioned him if there were any other possibilities. Sheikh answered his questions politely. He informed him about the process and the documents that must be prepared to obtain a visa. He did not exaggerate the matter or give them false hope. His answers were short, but solid. He made his position clear, indicating that it won't harm him if they were to back off from the deal.

Next few days after the meeting, Jawad's father made sure if Sheikh was indeed true to his words. He also met with Ahmad's father, who assured him of Sheikh's fidelity. He called Nasir in Germany once more and discussed the process that Sheikh advised. Jawad waited patiently for his father's decision. At work he would often get lost in his thoughts. Ahmad could see Jawad was always worried and he tried to cheer him up. He'll tell him that if Jawad got the visa, he would also renew his efforts and try to convince his parents to allow him to go abroad. One evening after returning home, Jawad's father summoned him to his room. His mother was also present. He sat on his desk with his notebook open on the table with a pen, evidently exhausted by the endless calculations. The notebook appeared to be the family ledger. Jawad instantly realized the gravity of that moment for him and his father.

"My son, I know that you've been expecting an answer from me and I appreciate your patience. I've given the matter much thought. I've also spoken to every person who could guide me with the issue. And today, your mother and I've decided to support you with your dream. You can call Mr. Sheikh and tell him to start the process. I know he did not ask for an advance, but all those documents cost money. So I want you to give him some money to show our confidence in him. Tomorrow you can go to the passport office and arrange for your passport."

Jawad's ecstasy knew no bounds. He saw his mother and father smiling and fully supporting his dream of earning a livelihood abroad. For Jawad, the hardest part of his ordeal was over; getting a visa and going abroad to him seemed minor issues. He immediately called Ahmad at his home. He also asked if his father could help him in the passport office.

To get a passport was a tricky business and there were a lot of formalities and red tape. The applicant first had to fill out a form and then provide all kinds of supporting documents. Outside the passport office a lot of agents had established their makeshift offices under the pretext of selling application forms. They charged an extra fee to save the applicants from red tape. It was a place where corruption was rampant. With the assistance of Ahmad's father, Jawad could avoid this hazard. It'll also give Jawad an opportunity to meet the man who was closer to Sheikh than anyone else. The passport office was located in an old colonial-era building, a symbol of the country's bitter past. It seemed that the government did not have funds to build a better infrastructure. It was a sordid place crammed with people. They would line up from the wee hours of the day to submit their applications. To Jawad it seemed like every one was bent on leaving the country. It was not difficult to find Superintendent Masood Ahmad. He sat behind a table in a small room, occupying half of it. The table was stacked with files. Jawad introduced himself. He offered him a chair. From his drawer he gave Jawad a passport application form and a slip to pay the fee at the bank.

"First, you'll deposit the fee in the assigned bank and then fill the form, attach all the required documents and give it to Ahmad. I'll take care of the rest. Once your passport is ready, Ahmad will bring it to you."

It seemed that Ahmad's father had a lot of influence in the office; the usual procedure was lengthy but Jawad didn't have to go through the regulations. Jawad asked a few questions and turned the conversation towards Sheikh.

"Don't worry. We've been friends for many years and I've never seen him failing. I'm glad that he agreed to help you because he is usually very busy with his other businesses."

Jawad thanked him for his help and told him that he respected him like his own father.

"For me you are like my own son. I wish you the best of luck," Ahmad's father blessed him warmly.

Jawad made his way to the bank, where he paid the necessary fees. Within two days, he handed his passport application to Ahmad, complete with all the necessary documents. He was satisfied with the proceedings concerning his passport. He kept his father informed about all the developments. After two weeks Ahmad gave him an envelope, which contained his freshly issued passport.

"Wow!" he exclaimed with joy, "Thanks to your father it all went smoothly."

Jawad immediately called Sheikh and asked for an appointment.

"Have you got the passport?"

"Yes sir."

"You can come to my office tomorrow morning at ten, along with your passport and National ID."

In the evening, he showed the passport to his father. He informed him about his upcoming meeting with Sheikh. His father went to his safe and came back with an envelope.

"Here, count them. These are 30, 000 Rupees. Give it to Mr. Sheikh tomorrow. It'll show him that we mean business. "

Next morning Jawad went to the address mentioned on the visiting card. Sheikh's office was on the 5th floor of a multi-story building. At the entrance 'Sheikh Enterprises, Importers and Exporters' was written on a golden plate. Inside was a large hall, with nicely partitioned cubicles. At the reception he asked for Mr. Sheikh. Receptionist guided him to his room. Sheikh was in the office, busy talking on the phone. He indicated Jawad to have a seat. When he was finished talking, he acknowledges Jawad.

"Did you bring your passport and ID?"

Jawad gave him his newly issued passport. Sheikh rang the bell and a man appeared. He asked to make a photocopy of the passport and ID card. The man returned soon and presented the freshly made photocopies to Sheikh. He put them in a file and took Jawad's signature.

"What are you going to do now?" Jawad asked him.

"I do have business relations with a Dutch company. I used to buy wallpaper form them. I'll contact them and ask for an invitation for you. From now on you are my, shall we say "Marketing Manager". But it could take some time as any impatience may arouse the suspicions. One has to play with these people. I'll mention that I'm about to get a big contract to renovate an entire university campus here. Most of the correspondence will be done with your name, to make things look official. In the meanwhile, I'll prepare other documents for you, but you need to be calm. I don't like people pressing me."

Jawad took out the envelope and handed it to Sheikh. He shot Jawad a surprised look.

"My father gave me some money for you. He thought that there might be some initial expenses."

Sheikh took the envelope, counted the money and placed it in his drawer.

"Well, in the beginning there is not much need for money. But anyhow thank your father for being so courteous. I'll keep in touch with you if something comes up. You can also call me on my cell phone if there is something you need to ask," he added.

After six weeks, Jawad received a phone call from Sheikh. He invited him to his office the next day. When Jawad entered Sheikh gave him a file.

"Have a look at this".

Jawad opened it. The contents shocked him. The file contained a bank statement in his name, a tax return showing how much tax he had paid and a letter of recommendation from The Chamber of Commerce and Industry. Few visiting cards showing his name and designation and also some salary slips for the past two years. They all looked authentic. The documents were duly signed and stamped by relevant authorities. There were also the copies of the documents showing past dealings between the Dutch company and Sheikh Enterprises. There was a complete record of the fax communication between "Jawad" and a certain lady in the Dutch company. He wondered what might happen if the lady came to know that it wasn't Jawad who had actually written and sent those faxes. The quality of his copied signatures was not bad either. Sheikh advised him to go through it and memorize all the details. He showed him the fax copy of a request letter from the Dutch company asking the Netherlands Embassy in Islamabad to issue Mr. Muhammad Jawad, Marketing Manager of Sheikh Enterprises, a short term visit visa so that he could travel to the Netherlands to negotiate a business deal with his Dutch counterpart in Amsterdam.

"They've sent the same copy to their embassy in Islamabad," Sheikh told him.

"What's the next step?" Jawad asked with excitement.

"We'll go to the Dutch embassy in Islamabad next week to apply for a Schengen Visa. But before that you've got to do certain things."

"What things?"

"First, you'll go to the travel agency and buy a return ticket for Amsterdam on these dates," he said handing him a piece of paper.

"Here is the address of the travel agent. Go there and mention my name and everything will be fine. Then go to American Express and purchase traveler's check worth $1000 by showing them your ticket and passport," Sheikh concluded.

At home, he informed his father that he needed to purchase a ticket and traveler's check. His father decided to draw more cash from the bank. Jawad realized there was no risk involved in buying the ticket and the checks as both things were to stay in his possession. His father gave him the required money next day. He bought the ticket and the traveler's check as advised. Then he went to visit Mr. Sheikh again.

"Have you got the ticket and the traveler's check?" Sheikh asked him immediately.

"Yes, I did exactly as you told me to do," he put the ticket and traveler's check on the table.

"Keep these things in your custody, on Sunday we would leave for Islamabad. Monday morning we'll visit the Dutch Embassy," Sheikh informed him while returning the ticket to Jawed.

Together they planned the journey to Islamabad. It was agreed that they would meet at the train station on Sunday at 4 pm. Sheikh would make their reservation on phone. They would reach Islamabad at precisely 10 pm and get a room in a hotel. Early morning both would leave for the

Dutch Embassy. That evening Jawad disclosed the news to his parents. Everybody was excited to know that he was finally going to the embassy. His father told him that he should take enough money with him to pay for the travel and visa fee. Before leaving for Islamabad, he spoke with Mr. Malik about his plans. He too encouraged Jawad. Sunday afternoon his father drove him to the train station. Sheikh had not yet arrived and Jawad went to the reservation office to get the tickets by mentioning Sheikh's name. As he came out he saw Sheikh talking to his father. They bid farewell to Jawad's father and boarded the train. They reached Rawalpindi, the twin city of Islamabad at expected time. They took a taxi and drove to an average hotel and rented a room. After dinner they went to their room to discuss their course of action.

"Let's check everything once again," Sheikh said pulling a chair.

Jawad opened the yellow file and Sheikh went through everything.

"Jawad, there is something very important for you to know. Due to some reasons I've not told you this before. I already have a multiple Schengen visa. At the embassy, I'll show them my passport and tell them that we are travelling together."

"But why do we have to do that?"

"Because that will increase your chances of getting a visa and they'll think we really mean business."

Jawad knew whatever Sheikh was doing was in his best interest, so he thought it was better that he kept quiet. Jawad switched off the lights and they both went to sleep. They woke up early morning and dressed themselves in business suits, resembling some business executives. They left for the embassy, situated in the diplomatic enclave of Islamabad. There was no time for breakfast. People had already started forming a queue. At 9 am the Dutch embassy was officially open. Jawad and his 'boss went inside along with a number of people. They picked up the visa application form from the counter and started filling it. A tall, white guy sat behind the partition, waiting for the applications to be handed back. On the other side of the waiting hall there were six cabins with their respective numbers on them. Jawad was sure that those cabins were used for the interviews.

Jawad's English skills and Sheikh's assistance helped him at the reception. The receptionist looked puzzled, when he saw two rather than one person standing in front of him for a single application. Jawad realized that the only thing which mattered now was his English. In a voice and dialect suitable for Shakespearian actors, he explained the whole situation. Sheikh recounted that he would also travel with Jawad to Netherlands for which he already had a visa. He showed his passport. Sheikh also had multiple visas for Britain and USA. Jawad presented all his documents and the copy of the invitation letter from the Dutch company. Then he paid him the non-refundable visa fee. The man at the counter went inside a room behind him and came back with the similar fax copy of his invitation. The Dutch company had faxed the same to them. He placed all the documents in a file and asked them to wait in the sitting area.

An hour passed when Jawad heard his name on the small speaker fitted to the pillar, telling him to enter cabin number 5. He opened the door and entered the cabin. The cabin was partitioned with a thick glass. The telephone on the table resembled one he saw in Hollywood movies, used by prison inmates to talk to their visitors. There was a gap in the glass partition through which the documents could be exchanged. Suddenly, a blond lady appeared, first ever he had seen in real life. She placed a file in front of her which contained his particulars. She greeted Jawad and started asking questions. Most of the questions were about the documents he had presented and he found no difficulty in answering them.

"According to my understanding your boss is also travelling with you?" she asked.

"Yes, that's right."

"In my view he should be able to handle the situation himself. Why do you have to go as well?"

"You're right. But he wants my involvement in the selection as well as in price negotiation. So that afterwards if there is a problem, I'll be able to handle it. He had other portfolios to look after." Jawad answered her with unbelievable confidence.

"My boss is in the waiting room and if you like, I can call him," Jawad tried to sell Sheikh's presence.

"That won't be necessary," the lady replied.

She asked a few more questions and folded the file, concluding the meeting. She pushed a receipt through the glass partition.

"This is the receipt for your passport. Come next Thursday and by then we'll have a decision. This is the standard procedure."

Jawad returned to the waiting room to Sheikh.

"Are you done?" he asked while standing up.

"Yes, for the time being," Jawad responded.

On their way to their hotel, Jawad told him the details of his interview. Sheikh seemed satisfied with the proceedings.

"Look Jawad, if they wanted to refuse you, they could have done it today. I don't think that there will be a problem now."

Sheikh also told him that he won't accompany him the next time.

"You must be there before 9 am. Go to the counter and show the receipt. Whatever the outcome is, call me immediately. I'll wait for your call."

They returned to Lahore the same day. Jawad was tired, mentally and physically. He told his parents about the proceedings briefly and went to bed. At work, Ahmad was anxiously waiting for him to know how things went at the embassy. Jawad was finding it hard to wait for Thursday. He felt as if his life was hanging by a thread.

The next week, Jawad started his journey at midnight. It was still dark when he reached Islamabad. There was no point checking in a hotel. He caught sight of a nearby cafeteria and rushed towards it. After breakfast he felt refreshed. He reached the embassy on time. The place was as occupied as before. Some people were waiting in line to collect their passports, other for submitting their visa applications. The door opened in time and people rushed in.

He showed his receipt at the counter. He was told to wait. After an hour, Jawad heard his name with an advice to come to the reception.

"Here is everything that you gave us last week," the same tall guy spoke to Jawad returning him his papers.

"Yes, except the passport," Jawad replied.

"Here is your passport," he pushed his passport through the glass partition. "We're issuing you a one month single entry visa. Have a nice trip to Netherlands."

"Thank you," Jawad responded while picking up his passport.

His happiness knew no bounds. He ran to the nearest phone booth. First, he called his mother and then Sheikh and told them the good news. Everyone congratulated him. Sheikh told him to come to his office the following morning.

"And my dear, don't forget to bring my fee. I've done my bit and now it's your turn."

"Don't you worry Sir; I'll be there tomorrow morning."

His journey back home consumed the rest of the day and on reaching Lahore he was very tired. He showed the passport to his family. For Jawad, that visa was the key to his family's prosperity. He informed his father about the payment he was supposed to make to Sheikh tomorrow.

"I'll also go with you to his office to thank him," his father announced.

Jawad knew it was not easy for Sheikh. It took a lot of courage and experience to do this work. The preparation of fake documents would have been too risky for him. His business relations with the Dutch company in the past were too important as well. No one could have arranged things for him in such a perfect way.

"Handle it with care. It's my hard-earned money," his father told him, giving him the handbag while coming out of the bank next morning.

They hurried to Sheikh's office. He smiled warmly as he welcomed them. He congratulated Jawad on his success. Jawad presented all the documents and the passport to Sheikh. The latter inspected the visa and sorted out some papers and handed them to Jawad.

"These documents prove your authenticity; keep them with you at all times during your journey. In case someone questions your credentials, you can show these documents. The people dealing with immigration often cause trouble and one has to convince them. Just state that you are travelling on a business trip."

"I've a genuine visa, but do you think that there could still be a problem?"

"Well, no one knows for sure but it is better to take all necessary precautions."

His father took out an envelope from his handbag and presented it to Mr. Sheikh.

"A bundle of money with a bundle of thanks," he commented.

Sheikh smiled and put the money in the drawer, without even counting it. It was time for them to leave. Sheikh told Jawad to keep in touch when he reaches abroad. Jawad and his father both went to their respective workplaces.

On his way, Jawad bought sweets for his colleagues. They congratulated Jawad on hearing the news and wished him the best of luck, health and happiness. Ahmad made jokes about his future girlfriends. Malik invited Jawad in his office. He always cooperated with Jawad and ignored his absences and late arrivals. He gave his brother's contact number in England and told Jawad that he could call him, in case he needed help. He also paid him his salary. It was Jawad's last day at work and he wanted to spend the rest of the days with his family. He had mixed feelings when he left his workplace; he wondered what lay in store for him in the future. That evening, Jawad and his father talked to Nasir in Munich who congratulated Jawad. He told him to contact him once he is in Amsterdam. Jawad informed him about his arrival date in Amsterdam.

"That's great! I'll be at home that day. But in any case, call me and I'll tell you what to do next. First you'll have to go to the Amsterdam's main train station. There you can get a train to Munich."

Jawad spent the rest of his days with his family, packing, planning and partying. The day soon arrived when he had to leave. His whole family came to the airport. He saw tears well up in his mother's eyes, as she kissed his forehead before he left to catch the plane. He bid farewell to all and they wished him the best for his journey. He flew from Lahore to Karachi by a domestic airline. It was his first experience in an airplane and it certainly made him nervous. The immigration officer at the Karachi Airport asked him a couple of questions before stamping 'Exit' on his passport. From Karachi, he had a direct flight to Amsterdam. The flight was seven hours long; he watched movies on the small screen and tasted red wine for the first time in his life. He enjoyed his travel; his plane piercing through the clouds on the way. It was early morning when the plane landed in Amsterdam. He went through the immigration where he was questioned about the purpose and duration of his stay. He was allowed to leave when he presented a copy of the invitation sent by the Dutch company. From there he went to a currency exchange counter and changed $200 worth traveler's check and stepped out of the airport.

He could breathe in the fresh morning air of Amsterdam. He noticed workers of coffee shops rolling up their shutters. Suddenly he heard some singing. A group of people passed him and they were all singing. They were the followers of the Hare Krishna movement, heading to India. *Some were coming to Europe to get enlightened and to be rich, some were leaving Europe to stay poor and live in darkness.* He decided to go to the main station. He walked down the stairs and followed the sign for the train. There were a few passengers at the platform waiting. He went to the ticket machine to get the ticket for. Amsterdam Central Railway Station was a beautiful, old building. He got himself freshly brewed coffee, but the sip left a bitter taste. He settled on a wooden bench for a pause and watched life around him with profound interest. He saw parting lovers kissing at early hours of the day. Everything seemed so different and pleasant. *Finally I've reached Europe, the paradise of my dreams.*

He wanted to visit the 165 Canals in Amsterdam he had read about in his guidebook in the airplane. However at the moment he wanted to save money. It was seven in the morning and he decided to call Nasir. He bought a phone card and dialed his number.

"Hello," said Nasir, in a hoarse voice.

"Nasir, Jawad here."

"Hey! How're you? Have you arrived in Amsterdam?"

"Yes, I'm at Amsterdam central train station right now."

"I'm so glad to hear you voice. Now, go to the ticket counter and ask for train to Munich at the earliest. Munich is called *Munchen* in German and Dutch. Once you got the ticket and timetable, call me again and tell me the time of your arrival. I'll be waiting for you at the station."

Jawad went to the counter and asked for a ticket to *Munchen*. The lady in a blue uniform smiled at his pronunciation. She typed the name of the city on her computer and waited for the reply.

"Your train will leave at exactly 8:30 am. But this is not a direct train. The first stop will be Mannheim and from there you'll switch to the train headed to Munich. You'll reach Munich around 5 pm, would you like to buy the ticket?" She spoke in impeccable English.

"Yes, second class please. How much does it cost?"

"Second class ticket will cost 210 Guilders."

Jawad paid the money and got the ticket. Then he called Nasir again to inform the timing.

"Great! See you at the train station then, brother. I've called your family and informed them about your safe arrival. We'll call them again when you're here," Nasir told him.

Train left at the exact time. On Jawad's opposite seat sat a lady in her early forties, reading a newspaper. The weather was sunny outside. Unlike trains in Pakistan, they moved swiftly and without noise. The train passed through lush meadows and fields covered with all the beautiful shades of green. The view outside the window left Jawad speechless; he had never seen a more peaceful and serene countryside. It reminded him of television programs that showed such wonderful views and today he was seeing them in real. The green fields, trees, flowers, in fact everything looked so beautiful. A vendor passed by their compartment holding a trolley full of snacks and drinks. Jawad bought a cheeseburger and a soft drink to satiate his hunger. Train as running along a river and across the river he could see old towns and beautiful churches with their metallic crosses glowing in the sunshine. It reached Mannheim at one in the afternoon. He stepped out of the train with his suitcase and searched for the train headed to Munich but he had to rush to it as it stood at another platform.

Jawad reached Munich around 5 pm. Nasir was waiting for him at the station. They had a big warm hug. Nasir took his suitcase and they went towards the parking lot. He had a blue BMW and they reached Nasir's apartment within 20 minutes.

It was a small flat in a multi-story building with a beautiful balcony decorated with small flowerpots hanging from the railing. Silvia, Nasir's wife, was a typical German girl, tall with golden hair blue eyes. She welcomed him warmly. Their son, Umar was a handsome one year old who looked at the visitor with curiosity. Jawad took the boy in his arms and covered him with kisses. Silvia was delighted to finally meet someone from her in-laws. This also pleased Jawad. He took a bath and caught up with Nasir in the lounge. Silvia went to the kitchen and prepared dinner. In the meantime, Jawad called his family. He felt his heart warm at hearing the voice of his parents on the other end. He didn't make a long call; he didn't want to burden his cousin with his personal expenses. Soon dinner was ready. They all sat in the kitchen where the dining table was placed. It was a delicious meal and everybody enjoyed it. Even little Umar took few bites.

"Jawad," Nasir said to him after dinner. "You look tired, it's better for you to go to sleep. I'm free these days. We'll catch up tomorrow."

Nasir and Silvia had allocated one of their three rooms for Jawad before his arrival. Nasir led Jawad to his room. He helped Jawad arrange his wardrobe. Jawad changed his clothes. There was a window in the room and as he opened it, a cold breeze filled the room. The heater kept the house at a normal temperature. It was a cold early March night, unlike Lahore. He slept soundly and woke up the next morning. He went to the washroom. His movements awoke his cousin.

"Did you sleep well?" Nasir asked.

"Like the dead."

Nasir laughed out loud at the solidness of his answer and went to the kitchen to prepare breakfast. After breakfast, Nasir was excited to talk about Pakistan and their families.

"What am I supposed to do now?" he asked Nasir.

"There are many options. I've a lot of Pakistani friends in this town; we'll go and discuss with them what is best for you at the moment."

"Is it possible for me to go to England?" Jawad shared his intention.

"Not so fast; we'll see what is best for you."

In the evening, Nasir took Jawad to a friend's place. It was a small party and few people were already there. They were all Pakistani expats and were glad to meet Jawad. He too felt comfortable meeting them. All of them had been living there for years and were excited to talk about

Pakistan. They shared their thoughts with him about Pakistan, as if he was their best buddy. He was surprised to see the enthusiasm on their faces, about the very place which they had left at the very first opportunity. Soon the discussion turned to Jawad.

"Listen Nasir," said Haris, their host who was a close friend of Nasir. "You know the only possibility that he can stay in Germany is through applying for political asylum."

Jawad had heard about the term, but didn't exactly know what it meant.

"You already know that the situation is not good for asylum seekers in Germany," he continued, "Asylum seekers are not allowed to travel outside the designated area. They are also not permitted to work, which means they can't support their families. There is also a danger that they might refuse one's asylum application. They had already deported many people once their asylum applications were rejected."

"But I'm not a political person. How could I apply for a political asylum?" Jawad asked in awe.

"That's not a problem," Nasir spoke while lighting a cigarette. "We all applied for political asylum when we first got here and none of us had any political background or other problems in our country. Those were good times, now things have changed. At that time, we were allowed to work and the process of asylum application was slow. We found jobs and started earning but now it's different. The government is hard on asylum seekers, due to their increasing number every year which is a burden on normal German taxpayer."

Jawad was shocked. *Germany, the world's third largest economy, the dream of millions, is unable to provide space for him.*

"Nasir, why don't you try Switzerland?" Haris shot a question. "Switzerland has a relaxed asylum process. Freedom of movement within Switzerland is allowed and certain areas permit the asylum seeker to work."

Jawad was clueless about the suggestion, but it got Nasir thinking. Everyone in the group, except for Jawad shared their knowledge about the place and its matters. It was concluded that the asylum seekers in Switzerland were better off than the ones living in Germany and the best possible option for Jawad would be to go to Switzerland. After the conversation, they all enjoyed dinner. The aroma of the food around the lounge was mesmerizing. It was typical Pakistani food and Haris proved to be an excellent cook. Jawad enjoyed the evening with Nasir's friends. It reminded him of his reunion with his friends back home.

Nasir introduced Jawad to his other acquaintances in town. He and his wife worked part time and they were also getting unemployment allowance from the government. Jawad was confused about the situation. He wished he could go to England but it seemed impossible at the moment. It was like from burning hell in to the frying pan. His visa was expiring soon and still nothing concrete was in sight. Finally, after long discussions and fact findings, they mutually agreed on that Jawad should try his luck in Switzerland. Nasir called a couple of friends to find if there was someone who could help Jawad to reach Switzerland. They soon found a guy named Iqbal. He had been on good terms with one of Nasir's friends. That friend made the connection and introduced them with Iqbal who agreed on helping them. He informed them that he'll be free on Sunday and they could come. Iqbal also told them not to worry as in his view it was not a big deal. But Jawad was not allowed to take his luggage. Carrying a luggage might create suspicions. He was shocked but Nasir assured him that he'll send the necessary stuff through post once Jawad had an address.

"Don't worry; you'll be in safe hands," Nasir tried to raise his spirits.

It was Friday and Jawad had one more day left. After dinner Jawad and Nasir sat in the drawing room to discuss their next move.

"Jawad, you'll have to leave all your documents here as well."

"Why?"

"Because if the German border police arrests you while you are crossing the border, they can't do anything as they will have no proof of your identity. They'll put you in jail for two or three days and then you'll be entitled to apply for political asylum. Same is the case with the Swiss border police, if they arrest you while you're entering Switzerland, they'll hand you over to the German Police because you were entering Switzerland from the German side. But in case you are arrested with your passport, things will be different and won't be in your favor. There is always a threat that the recovery of your passport will make it easier for them to deport you," Nasir concluded.

"Okay, I'll leave them with you," Jawad agreed. "But where shall I go in Switzerland and what am I supposed to do there?"

Nasir took a deep breath and settled himself on the couch.

"When you enter Switzerland, go to the nearest railway station. Memorize the word *Bahnhof*, it means railway station in German. Go there and ask for the train to Kreuzlingen. It won't be a long trip. This is the nearest and the safest place you can apply for political asylum."

"What about the language? I don't speak German."

"That won't be a problem. Most of the people working at public places speak English," Nasir convinced Jawad.

"When you reach Kreuzlingen ask for the Reception Center. All four Reception Centers are located in the border districts and Kreuzlingen is one of them. So when a refugee enters Switzerland, he can easily apply for asylum at the nearest one. You'll be treated very nicely as it has nothing to do with your illegal entrance in Switzerland. However, the biggest issue is the story."

"What story?" Jawad inquired.

"You'll have to explain to the authorities the reason that forced you to seek asylum in Switzerland. You can't tell them that you left your country because there was no job available for you. You'll have to tell them that you were facing political problems in your country, and your life was in danger if you stayed in the country any longer. Fear of persecution forced you to seek asylum abroad. Do not, under any circumstance, mention that you came to Germany first. They can reject your application on the grounds for not taking political asylum in Germany." Nasir spoke like an expert, someone who was giving career advice to a client.

"What did you tell them when you came to Germany?" Jawad shot a question.

"Well, at that time Pakistan People's Party (PPP) was in power and the Pakistan Muslim League (PML) used to be the major opposition party. Many Muslim League workers were either arrested or hid underground because of participation in an anti-government campaign. So when I came to Germany, I presented myself as a member of the PML and told them that my life was in danger so I had to flee to escape arrest."

"But you know the situation is different now. The PML is in power now and PPP is in the opposition block."

"No problem there either. You can just reverse the situation. I know the present Muslim League government is doing the same with the workers of People's Party."

They concocted a fake story to support Jawad's claim for leaving his country. Jawad prepared himself to tell the Swiss authorities every fake detail, from joining the political party in Pakistan to crossing the Swiss border. The story went something like this: He was an active member of Pakistan People's Party, which had lost power and now it was in opposition. He had been involved in politics since he was in college. Local leadership of the Muslim League was against him and he suffered minor injuries due to a clash during a political demonstration. His political opponents filed many false accusations against him and the police tried to arrest him, without sound proof. The local administration, under the pressure of the Muslim League government, launched a campaign against him and his fellow party workers. Under these circumstances he had no choice but to leave the country.

In order to hide one lie, sometime you have to tell a hundred more lies. Jawad realized that he had lied to the Dutch Embassy and it has led him to lie repeatedly.

"What's the matter Jawad? You look sad," Nasir asked without hesitation.

"I'm not good at lying and from the very beginning I've been doing just that. Now it's making me uneasy."

"Jawad, I understand what you're going through. But this is the price we've to pay to get ourselves a living in this part of the world. You've come a long way and turning back won't be easy now. Think of all the money that your father had spent on you. They all depend on you. As your application is phony, you might not have enough time, so finding a job is important. But what is more important for you is to get married, so that you can settle permanently. I might have been deported the very same year when I acquired political asylum, had it not been for my marriage to Silvia. You are young, educated and good-looking. So find yourself a girl and settle there on a permanent basis," Nasir concluded the conversation.

Jawad tried to imagine his next course of action. Entering Switzerland illegally; asking for political asylum on a false pretense. Getting a job and sending the money home; finding someone to marry and settle down in that country for his entire life. And if possible, visiting his homeland for a few weeks and that'll be his life. Achieving this, which he was quite unsure of embracing at the moment, would only be possible after cheating on several people, for which, he would feel guilty his entire life provided he had some conscience left. But there was no other option left for him besides returning to his country empty-handed and this meant failure which he could not afford.

Nasir called Jawad's father to break the news. They spoke vaguely with Mr. Alam as they did not want to create an alarm. He in return, told them to do as they think is suitable. Sunday morning Jawad got ready for the trip. He was wearing jeans, a shirt and leather jacket for his journey. Their first destination was Weingarten. This was the small town where they were supposed to meet Iqbal. Jawad bid farewell to Silvia and the boy and thanked her for the hospitality. They reached Weingarten in two hours. Nasir was on his mobile repeatedly, asking Iqbal for directions. Iqbal was waiting for them in front of the Church where they had decided to meet. They greeted each other and Iqbal told Nasir to let him drive the car because he knew exactly where to go. On their way, Iqbal told them about the route Jawad would take to safely cross the German-Swiss border. He prepared Jawad for his quest in reaching Kreuzlingen.

"In case you get caught, don't mention Nasir or anyone you know in Germany. Give a fake story. Don't carry more than 50 Swiss Francs with you. The train ticket won't cost much and once you are inside the Reception Center, you'll get everything. The more money you have with you, the less you are paid."

Jawad had cashed all the checks. He was carrying a little money in Swiss Francs, rest everything was to stay with Nasir who promised to channel it to his father along with the return ticket. But first they would have to wait as nobody knew how it would go. It was a smooth drive and they reached Bad Sakingen which was their destination. It was located at the Swiss-German border. Jawad saw the river Rhine which was the local border between Switzerland and Germany. On the other side was a small Swiss town called Stein. Iqbal told him that he would walk through the wooden bridge built only for pedestrians. It was not well guarded. The clock struck two and the street was humming with people. Iqbal parked the car in front of a beautiful house.

"Follow me," commanded Iqbal, getting out of the car.

They strolled in the narrow streets like tourists. Iqbal would stop in front of a shop and pretend to be a prospective buyer. They all walked till they reached a point. Iqbal told Nasir to wait in the car for him. Iqbal knew the area well. They immediately crossed the next street and caught sight of the bridge. It was visible from the street. Jawad saw many locals and tourists, walking to and fro on the bridge.

"All right now," Iqbal told Jawad pointing to the bridge. "On your left is Switzerland. First, we'll pass the bridge, pretending as tourists. After covering 30 meters, we'll come back here but you would turn to the bridge and move on. I won't be able to go with you any further."

First they walked close to the bridge and moved in the next street. Iqbal deliberately distanced himself from Jawad after a farewell. Jawad walked in front and once he reached the bridge he hastened to pass it. A tourist group huddled in front of him and he pretended to be a part of it. As he reached the end of the bridge, he saw no policemen patrolling for trespassers. He entered in Stein and desperately searched for a signboard for *Bahnhof* but couldn't find one. Seeing no police on patrol made him feel confident. He felt like a tourist. He passed by the lush green meadows and saw children playing football in one of them. It reminded him of his carefree childhood days, filled with leisure and sport. At the far end of the playground he spotted a signboard in the middle of a roundabout. He hurriedly walked up to it. The signboard indicated different places in an alien language. He frantically looked for the word *Bahnhof*, and finally there it was, at the left corner of the board. He took the street to his left and walked on until the railway tracks became visible. At the end of the road he could see the train station. He hurriedly moved towards it. Only one of the ticket counters was open.

"Is there any train for Kreuzlingen?" Jawad asked in English.

"No, there is no direct train. You'll have to change at the Winterthur."

"What are the timings?"

"The train for Winterthur will arrive at 2:30 and will be there in half an hour. At 3:10 another train will leave for Kreuzlingen and you'll be there in an hour?" She explained, after checking on the computer. Nasir was right. Most of the staff in the public dealing does speak English in these countries. He bought a second-class ticket. There were very few passengers at the station. As the train for Winterthur arrived, he immediately boarded it. It was a double story train with lot of people in it. He sat in the upper story of the train. Ten minutes later, the train stopped at another station. A dark-skinned young man boarded and took a seat opposite to him. Jawad presumed the man to be an Asian in his early thirties. He shot a question at Jawad instantly in English.

"Hi, are you Indian?"

"No, I'm from Pakistan."

"Oh, I see. I'm Chandra from Sri Lanka," he said, shaking Jawad's hand.

"I'm Jawad."

"Are you going to Zurich?"

"No, I'm going to Kreuzlingen," Jawad told him the truth. Chandra seemed quite harmless to him.

"Are you going for asylum?"

"Yes, that's right. How did you know?"

"Just a guess, but that place is closed on weekends. You'll have to wait until tomorrow," interrupted Chandra.

"I didn't know that." Jawad replied nervously.

"Do you have any friends in Switzerland?"

"No, I don't know anybody here." Jawad realized he was in a mess. His face filled with worries. *What should I do now?*

Chandra realized Jawad's predicament.

"I live in Winterthur with my friends. I can help you if you like. You can stay the night with me and early morning you can take the train for Kreuzlingen. If you don't, the police might arrest you for wandering without a legal status. It is considered a crime in Switzerland," Chandra warned him.

"What about the asylum seekers? Do they fall from the sky?" Jawad shot back in a frustrated tone. On that Chandra remained silent.

Jawad thought if Chandra was telling the truth, it meant trouble for him because he'll have to spend a whole night and half a day on the streets until the Reception Center opens. And God forbid he might get caught. He thought it best to accept Chandra's offer.

"Look my friend," Chandra tried to convince him. "When I came to this country I had more or less the same problem and there was no one to help me. Therefore, I know the hardship you are facing at this particular moment. I just want to lend a helping hand because we are from the same continent."

"That is very kind of you. I don't know anyone in this country."

The train's microphone informed them about their arrival in Winterthur. First they changed the ticket for the next day so Jawad didn't have to buy a new one. Chandra took him to the bus station. He checked the bus timetable and got back to Jawad.

"There is no bus available for the next seven minutes and my place isn't far. We can walk if you like," Chandra proposed to which Jawad agreed.

They walked past straight long alleys. After a little walk, Chandra stopped in front of a big building and opened the main door.

"Please do come in," he asked politely.

Both entered the apartment building and took the elevator. Chandra pressed the button for the fourth floor. They entered the corridor of the fourth floor, which had three separate apartments. Chandra opened the one in the middle. His apartment was small, comprising of two rooms, a kitchen and a bathroom.

"How many people live here?"

"There are three of us. One is in Geneva for three days. He'll be back tomorrow evening. The other flat mate is working till midnight."

Chandra showed Jawad his place and brought some snacks and a carton of juice from the refrigerator.

"I'm going to the grocery store. You can just relax and I'll be back soon."

"All right," Jawad answered with a smile.

Jawad stretched himself on the sofa. Chandra returned in an hour with two bags full of food. He went to the kitchen and started transferring its contents to the refrigerator. He took two cans of beer from the fridge and offered one to Jawad. Then he grabbed a packet of potato chips and relaxed on the sofa. They watched an old soccer game between Argentine and England as they chatted. Jawad was a bit hesitant to open up to a complete stranger. Soon Chandra told him his story. He belonged to Jaffna, which mainly comprised Tamil people who had been fighting for a separate homeland from Sri Lanka. The restlessness and civil war in his country, and the bleak future that the situation represented forced him to leave. He decided to take asylum in one of the European countries. He left his country for good and started his voyage, taking the sea. It took him seven months to reach Switzerland. He had been living there for last six years and his asylum application was still held-up for consideration. He was working at a coffee shop. Now, he was quite optimistic about his future in Switzerland, as the civil war back home seemed never-ending. He was not really concerned about the approval of his application. The scenario in his country would never allow the authorities to send him back to Sri Lanka. Sooner or later his asylum application would turn out in his favor.

The evening began to set in and Chandra went to kitchen to prepare the meal.

"Can I help you?" asked Jawad.

"No, I'll manage."

"Then I'll stay in the kitchen to give you company."

"Sure."

Chandra cooked the meal real fast. He boiled some rice. Prepared a white sauce, sautéed the fish and mixed them together. Soon the meal was ready and they dined immediately. After dinner, Chandra made Ceylon tea and offered Jawad a cup. It was time for Jawad to share his story. Jawad told him how bad the situation of jobs was in Pakistan. He had come to Switzerland to earn a living and support his family by working here. They conversed till eleven.

"I've to go to work at seven in the morning. You should get some sleep now." Chandra told him, leading him towards a bedroom. The bed belonged to Chandra's absent flat mate.

"Make yourself comfortable. Tomorrow, before leaving for work, I'll drop you at the train station. Try your best to reach the Reception Center as early as possible. Sometime the place gets too crowded." Chandra said good night and left the room.

He fell asleep as soon as he lay on the bed. The next morning, he was in deep sleep when Chandra shook him.

"Good morning, it's time."

Jawad woke up in a daze, took the towel from Chandra and went for a shower. He used his fingers to clean the teeth as he had no toothbrush. They left without breakfast as the time was short. His mind was preoccupied with difficulties that were about to engulf him. They reached the train station on foot.

"We are almost there," said Chandra pointing at the station. "I've to go to work. Giving you my phone number might be risky. But if you ever want to meet me, come to Winterthur and ask for Café Rio in the old city."

Jawad felt obliged for everything Chandra had done for him. For Jawad he was a mere stranger in an unknown town. He couldn't offer him anything more than a hug and his gratitude for the hospitality. The train station was very busy. He found out about the time of departure for Kreuzlingen; the train was to arrive in the next twenty minutes on platform five. He went to the platform and embarked the train when it arrived.

Rain started in the middle of the night and it seemed that the gates of the heaven had opened. The noise of rain drops on the glass window, sounding like a harsh knocking on the door, woke Jawad up. He covered himself with the blanket and dozed off again. When he woke up in the morning, it was still raining. The world from his window appeared clean and beautiful. He peered out from his window for a long time, taking in nature's beauty.

The recreation hall was full with people having breakfast. As he was entering, the warden was fixing the transfer list on the notice board. Many were delighted to see their names on it. They were to be dropped at the Reception Center for their next journey. He looked around for Khan but could not find him. Jawad wanted to visit the city but was afraid of the consistent cold and rain. He pulled a chair and looked out of the window once again. Rain had enhanced the beauty of the town. A little later, he saw Khan coming downstairs.

"You didn't come for breakfast today?" Jawad asked.

"I could not sleep the whole night. My bed is really close to the window and the rain was so loud."

"Oh, I see. You want some coffee?"

"Yes, very much," consented Khan.

Jawad went to the vending machine and fetched coffee for Khan.

As Jawad sat with Khan who was busy sipping coffee, the warden reappeared with a new list. This was for the people who had to go to the hospital. Jawad went to check the list and his name was also there. He came back to the table and told Khan that his name was on the list but he'll be back soon. The van brought them to the hospital. Jawad showed his medical card like everybody else. He was informed about the results. His blood reports came out clear and he was declared in good health. Once they were all finished, they returned to their hostel with the same transport. Lunch was served at noon, and just when he was finishing he heard someone calling his name.

"I'm here!" he responded.

"Mr. Jawad, you've an interview today."

"At what time and where?"

"At 2 pm and we've an interview room in the house."

At 2 pm Jawad went for his interview escorted by a staff member. The interview room was located at the far end of the corridor. There were two women sitting around a table. One was an Indian, in her fifties and had a *tilk* on her forehead. Sitting next to her was a native of same age with eyes fixed on her computer.

"Have a seat Mr. Jawad," asked the Swiss lady, reading out his name from the computer.

She spoke to the Indian lady in German first who then started talking to Jawad in Urdu. She introduced herself as Rajlate, the translator and the Swiss lady as Natalie Kanel. Madam Natalie represented the *Bundesamt fur Fluchtlinge*, known as BFF which was the Federal Office for Refugees. Rajlata gave Jawad a briefing about the articles of the Geneva Convention under which he had applied for political asylum in Switzerland. Then Natalie asked a number of probing questions and one by one Rajlata translated them for Jawad. She asked Jawad the cause for coming to this far-off land. Jawad had been revising his story all this time and he phrased it all to make it appear real to both of them. The unavailability of any of Jawad's identification documents irritated Natalie.

"How is it possible that you left your country without taking any proper documents along with you?"

Jawad replied that it was not possible for him to carry such documents. Natalie advised him to contact his family in Pakistan and acquire his identification papers. Then there was another round of questioning, targeting his family, his educational career and his duties in the political party. He faced a lot of difficulty answering inquisitive questions like, "Have you ever been in prison? Who was your immediate boss in the party? Why didn't your party save your skin through legal means?" Jawad finely put the blame of his miseries on different people: like the present government of Pakistan and the local police.

"When is it possible for you to return to Pakistan?"

"Not as long as the current government is in power," replied Jawad.

"And how long that might be?"

"The average time span for any civil Government staying in power in Pakistan is three years."

"And how did you come to Switzerland?"

Jawad refreshed in his mind the details he had discussed with Nasir regarding his fictitious journey. He told them that he paid human smugglers. They arranged his flight to Italy on a false British passport. From Rome, someone took him to Milan and there they took away his fake passport. He was handed over to another guy who smuggled him to Switzerland, telling him to go to Kreuzlingen.

"But why didn't you go to Lugano? It's close to the Italian border."

"I don't know. My guide told me it's better here," Jawad felt helpless.

Natalie looked at Rajlata for assurance. Jawad wondered whether his false answers satisfied them. Natalie again started typing on the keyboard. Finally Jawad was reminded to acquire his identification papers as well as proofs of the legal proceedings against him from Pakistan. Natalie got a print out of the interview from the computer and all three parties signed the transcript as per the rule. After that he was allowed to leave. His forehead was damp with sweat. In the last 90 minutes he had done nothing but lied about every single thing. He was ashamed of himself and felt beyond guilty. He cheated whom? Was it Madam Natalie, Switzerland or himself? The last one was the most striking.

Depressed, he went for a stroll alone. Clouds hovered above him, but gladly the rain had ceased. He went to a small café and ordered coffee. He went to the phone both in the café to call Nasir. He told him the whole story, assuring him of his safety. He asked him to inform his family about his safe arrival in Switzerland. Nasir excused for not knowing that the Reception Center was close on Sunday. The coins he inserted didn't last much and soon it was over. He returned to his seat. Never before had he felt as empty as he was feeling at that time. The café was warm and comfortable and he sat there for a while, trying to gather his thoughts. After an hour, he paid for the coffee and returned. He had only ten Francs left in his pocket.

The next morning it was Jawad's turn to help in the cleaning. He hurriedly finished his breakfast and joined the team responsible for cleaning the house. When he was finished, he came downstairs to the recreation hall where he met Khan. They just spoke for a while when the transfer list arrived. Jawad found his name on the list. It was finally his turn to be transferred. The warden entered the recreation hall and called out their names, telling them to return towels and blankets. They were to assemble in front of the door in half an hour. Jawad went to his room to collect things. The storekeeper checked the stuff and put a cross on his name. Jawad returned to the hall to say goodbye to Khan. He was carrying his toothbrush with him while he disposed of the razor.

"You are lucky," spoke Khan.

"Why did you say that?"

"Now you have the opportunity to meet new people and perhaps you may find some work."

The van arrived to pick the group of refugees being transferred. Jawad shook hands with Khan and the house warden. At the Reception Center they were instructed to wait in front of the window. After a few minutes, a lady opened the window and called out their names, one by one. Jawad was the second name she called and he went to her.

"You are being transferred Zurich. This is your train ticket."

"Am I being transferred to Zurich?" Jawad asked with disbelief while picking the ticket.

"Yes, I think I've just said that. This is the address and this map contains the directions for your destination in Zurich. Have a nice trip."

Jawad went to the train station and waited for the train for Frauenfeld. There was no direct train for Zurich and he had to change there. Some of the refugees from his group also joined him at the platform. Five of them boarded the train with him, while the others waited for their trains. One Bosnian group member sat beside him.

"Are you going to Zurich?" Jawad asked him.

"Zurich," he responded, trying to understand the question.

The man showed Jawad his papers. He had the same map of Zurich just like Jawad. They changed the train at Frauenfeld and took the one for Zurich. It was not possible to communicate with each other because of the language barrier. On the way, train stopped at Winterthur where he had spent his first night in Switzerland.

They arrived in Zurich at midday. The train station at Zurich looked more like an airport rather than a train station. It was huge. Jawad and his colleagues walked towards the exit doors as they passed a large hall. The first thing he noticed outside the station was the trams. He heard the distinct noise of tramlines protesting as the trams turned in different directions. A row of shining taxis awaited the passengers. They reached at the tram stop outside the Hotel Gotthard. There were chairs outside the hotel full of people eating, drinking and talking. Jawad looked at the map and they headed according to the directions on the map.

Jawad had seen a glimpse of Zurich in an international magazine, back in his university days. He knew the city was one of the leading financial centers in the world. But its streets resembled a classical city, a mixture of old and modern architecture projecting an image of progression. Jawad did not find any skyscrapers in the city, a trademark of all modern cities. Through the help of a policeman who was also at the tram stop, they reached their destination. It was a small government office. Jawad and his colleagues entered the office. He took out his ID and spoke to the man at counter.

The man checked his name on his computer and took out a print.

"Go to this address, this is the asylum center where you'll be housed," he spoke while handing a new map to Jawad. "At the next crossroad take Bus 72, show this address to the driver and he'll guide you. This is your ticket. Punch it in the machine at the bus stop. At the center, go to the office and show your papers with this printout. They will assign you a place to live in the premises, any questions?"

"Is anyone else coming with me?"

"Rest will be transferred to other places in the city."

Jawad walked to the bus stop not far away from the office. Before boarding the bus, he punched his ticket in the machine at the stop. He showed the driver the address. After about 15 minutes, the driver told Jawad that his destination had arrived. Soon he reached at the given address. The asylum center was a three-story house with full-size glass windows. He entered without knocking as the door was open, looking for office. The office was located downstairs but it was closed till 3 pm. At the end of the corridor, there was a large TV lounge. He went inside and waited for the office to open. Later, he heard someone coming downstairs. Presently a female stood in front of the office.

"Do you work here?" Jawad asked her in English while she was searching her hand bag for keys.

"Yes," she replied politely.

"I'm a new arrival."

"Welcome," she shook hands with him warmly and opened the door.

"My name is Natasha," she introduced herself in a friendly tone in flawless English. "May I have a look at your documents?"

She typed his personal data on her computer and returned the papers to Jawad.

"Okay, Mr. Jawad, I'm going to show you the room now. I'll also give you the things you may need here."

Jawad's room was on the first floor. Upper floors had a number of rooms, with number of toilets and kitchens located opposite to the rooms. Each kitchen had its own dining table. Every two rooms were partitioned from the rest. Jawad's room number was 13. The lady knocked on the door and a young boy opened.

"This is your room, Mr. Jawad. You'll share it with other people."

The room was neat and a big window overlooked the backyard. There were two bunk beds in the room with four wooden closets, four chairs, a table, and a medium-size refrigerator. "This is your room mate Muhammad Abdul from Iraq. He speaks Arabic and French. There is another guy from Pakistan. His name is Ali Akbar but I think he is gone out."

She introduced him with the occupant. Then she took Jawad to the basement. She gave him a new mattress with a blanket and a pillow. She also handed him a toiletry bag with toothbrush, paste, shaving crème, and razor. Along with that she gave him utensils and a pan and a pot. He had almost everything which one requires for a humble boarding.

"Sign this sheet," she handed him a list. He signed the paper and returned it.

Jawad took the mattress and other belongings to his room. Abdul helped him in transferring his stuff. He returned to the office and saw Natasha sitting with two others. She introduced them to him.

"This is Katherine and this is Martin. They both work here. The in-charge of the house is Frau Christina, she is not in today."

Then she pointed at Jawad. "This is Mr. Muhammad Jawad, our new resident."

"*Guten tag* (Good day)," both of them greeted Jawad courteously. Jawad spoke the same in response. *At least he did learn how to greet.*

Martin went to the next room. He returned with a register and a red metallic box.

"All right Mr. Jawad, we give the money for food and other necessities on alternate Tuesdays to all the refugees here. But as a newcomer, you're eligible to receive money from today. Every person is given 304 Francs every month, so I'm going to give you money for the next 12 days."

He picked up a calculator and after calculating, gave Jawad 124 Francs.

"Please sign here," Martin asked him.

It was a list of names with the amount of money written in front. Martin had added Jawad's name and the amount he received at the end of the list. Jawad signed opposite his name. Katherine took Jawad's picture with a Polaroid camera and attached it to his file with a copy of his ID. Jawad was also introduced to the rules and regulations of the house. The residents had to participate in the cleaning of the house. Twice a week they had a compulsory language class. Excessive drinking was not appreciated and there was zero tolerance for dealing in drugs and stolen goods.

"May I go now?" Jawad asked.

"Yes, if you've any problem or if you are sick, please come to the office quickly. We're here to help you," Natasha informed with a smile.

After thanking them all, Jawad returned to his room. Abdul gestured Jawad to follow him, leading him to the kitchen. Jawad put the utensils that were given to him in an empty cabinet and the toiletry bag in a closet. He felt hungry but had nothing to eat. He wanted to wait for his fellow countryman who could guide him regarding food. Meanwhile Abdul brought him bread, cheese and orange juice. Jawad was touched by his act of kindness. He thanked for the food. Jawad was happy with his new residence and the people in the office. The food made him lazy and he soon fell asleep. When he woke up he was alone in the room, it was still day light. The house was not as quiet as it was in the afternoon. He heard children playing in the front lawn. Heading to the kitchen, he saw two young Africans talking to each other in French. He greeted them in English.

"Are you from Pakistan?" one of them asked Jawad.

"Yes. How did you know?"

"Natasha told me."

"What about you?"

"I'm Stephen from Congo and this is John Paul from Ivory Coast."

"Do you speak French?" asked John Paul.

"No," Jawad replied.

"We speak little English," said Stephen.

"No problem, we'll manage," he replied.

Jawad went to the window, looking to the front yard. Some children were playing outside. His eyes caught something. He saw someone go pass the children and in to the house. Jawad was sure he was a Pakistani. He was thin, tall and had brown skin, may be in his mid-twenties. In due course he came to Jawad.

"I'm Ali Akbar. I was informed by the staff that someone from my country came today."

"I'm Jawad."

They shook hands warmly. There were no more language barriers. Both of them spoke the same language. Ali had been living in the center for more than a month. They talked about Pakistan and themselves. Ali had learnt a little German but didn't understand English as he had left school early.

"I want to buy some food. But I don't know where to go." Jawad asked him.

"I'll cook for you today. Tomorrow I'll show you the shop where you can buy groceries. It's not too far."

Ali went in to the kitchen to prepare dinner. He seemed quite an expert. Abdul and others also joined them in the kitchen to prepare their meals. Ali brought a cassette player and put an audiocassette inside. Suddenly, something happened unexpectedly. A very pretty girl walked in to the kitchen and stood in front of him. To him she appeared to be the beauty Shakespeare described in his sonnet, "Shall I compare thee to a summer's day". Jawad thought that he saw sun setting in her eyes. His fluttering heart tried to grasp the unseen beauty in those bright, blue eyes.

She spoke softly. "Good evening. I'm Sonia. I work here as the night supervisor. Are you the new arrival?"

"Yes. My name is Jawad," he replied, catching his breath.

She took a seat next to him on the dining table. Jawad tried hard to find out which book she was reading, but he could not as it was in German.

"I forgot to tell you, Sonia is coming over for dinner," Ali interrupted Jawad's thoughts.

"Okay," said an excited Jawad.

Ali tried his best to attract Sonia towards him. But since Jawad could talk to her, at least in English, she felt more comfortable conversing with him. Sonia told him she was studying sociology. She was working in the center for some extra income. The trio dined together while others were also busy with their meals, chatting and enjoying the food with music playing in the background. Jawad was satisfied with his accommodation and present company. After dinner Sonia returned to the office while Ali followed her. She told Jawad that the people working in the nights had to sleep in the office on a makeshift bed. Stephen and John Paul went out. Jawad decided to watch television. He went downstairs to the lounge. Jawad's fellow housemates were watching an old James Bond movie, dubbed in German. He soon returned to his room as he had already seen the movie. Later, as Ali entered the room, Abdul laughed at him and said something that Jawad didn't understand. But it made Ali laugh out loud.

"Abdul was joking that I'm going to sleep in the office with Sonia tonight," Ali told Jawad.

He stayed silent and drew the curtains of the window.

"Do you need anything Jawad?" Ali asked like an old friend.

"No."

"I think you don't have any clothes."

"Yes, you're right, these are the only clothes that I have presently," he replied.

"No problem. I can give you some. You can take them as a gift from me." He handed Jawad a navy blue t-shirt and a grey trousers.

He thanked Ali for the clothes. Lying in the bed, he couldn't stop thinking about Sonia. In those few moments she had acquired a soft spot in his heart. Her voice resounded in his ears. He had never felt this way before.

Is this love at first sight? But that's a bookish thing, it can't be. He was confused; he couldn't stop thinking about her. *Here you are Jawad; in Switzerland, in Zurich and almost in love*

His first day in Zurich was not that bad and he wondered what the next days would bring his way. Early next morning, a loud knock on the door woke Jawad up from his peaceful sleep. It was time for the language class. Abdul went downstairs to the TV lounge, along with Stephen and John Paul. Half awake, Ali greeted Jawad and went for a shower. Upon returning he prepared breakfast for Jawad and himself. He didn't have a class that day.

"The stores open at 8 am. If you want to buy some food, we can go together whenever you feel like," said Ali.

"Thank you. I really appreciate your help."

"No problem. I'm glad that finally I have someone from my homeland."

"It's my pleasure. Ali, tell me the best way to call Pakistan

"People around here usually call home through prepaid phone cards. They are more affordable."

Ali pulled out his phone card and showed to Jawad.

"This one costs 10 Francs and offers more talk-time than the normal one."

"That sounds great."

"I buy it at an Indian shop in downtown and that gives me around 60 minutes of talk-time. The one at the kiosk hardly lasts ten minutes."

"Can I use your phone card? I'll return the favor later."

"No need for returning the favor, just take it. There is not much balance left anyway."

At 8.30 in the morning they went to the store. Ali helped Jawad in selecting the products. They returned to their room with two paper bags. It was mutually agreed that they will do the cooking together. Jawad was much relieved as he had no prior experience of cooking. In the afternoon they sat together and discussed their future lives in Switzerland. Ali had all the information.

"Switzerland has strict rules regarding asylum. If the authorities are confident about the genuineness of a case, the person is granted political asylum without any delay. But since there are many fake asylum seekers, the Swiss authorities investigate each case very closely. In some cases there are literally no identification provided by the asylum seekers. So there is no guarantee that the applicant is genuine or not."

"I see. What happens when the asylum application is approved?"

"Once the application is approved, that person is issued a Swiss resident permit and provided complete financial help to start a new life. Children and spouse may also join that person. But once the application is rejected, the applicant has no choice but to leave the country or face deportation, which is very humiliating. Asylum seekers are only allowed to work in menial jobs. Other jobs are not allowed unless the application is approved. You may be a doctor or an engineer in your country but no one gives a damn here. People like us, if they get lucky, wash dishes in some restaurant."

"What do you mean by if we get lucky?"

"We are allowed to work after six months only, provided we get a permission to work. In our case we can't be sure we'll get one because an asylum application could be rejected at any time. Even if we get the permission, no one knows how long it will last. Because once the asylum application is rejected, that will automatically terminate the work permit. Here it is difficult to find illegal work though one can try," Ali told Jawad the facts very frankly.

This gave Jawad a jolt. He didn't know what to tell his family. He had promised them he would get a job as soon as he reaches abroad and it had been already a month.

What if, after the entire wait, my application is rejected, what would I do? How would I face my family? All the savings my parents gave me in good faith, what would become of that?

"Hey, don't fret. I knew all this before I arrived here. I assure you still it's worth the risk we are taking." Ali assured him, sensing the worry in Jawad's eyes.

In the evening he called his family for the first time since he arrived in Zurich. They were excited to talk to him. He told his father about the asylum process, hiding the fact that he would have to stay without a job for six months.

"I've got my own room and I'll attend a language class held twice a week. Once I acquire the basic language skills, I can go to work but it might take a few months. Until then the Swiss authorities would provide for my daily expenses." Jawad tried to calm his father and the family, as he knew the speaker would be on.

"How is everyone at home?"

"Everyone is fine here. You take care of yourself, son. Your mother wants to talk to you now."

Jawad's mother was delighted to speak to him. He had tears in his eyes while speaking to her. He had never been away from her so long and lately it had been hard for her. She asked him to take care of himself and inquired about the food. His sisters asked to send snaps as soon as he could. Then she passed the phone on to his brother. Jawad told him about the situation some of which he had already heard.

"Are they crazy? You entered their country illegally and they provided you with everything rather than sending you to prison."

"Don't start that now. I don't have time to tell you all the details now," he disconnected.

Jawad then called Nasir and told him about the latest developments.

"But Jawad, it's unbelievable that they don't allow refugees to work for six months. You need to visit a mosque or a Pakistani shop. People there might help you to find some work." Nasir too seemed disappointed.

"Yes. I think I should consult other Pakistanis here." Soon Jawad hung up and returned to his room.

Jawad soon began to get bored of his routine life. His first language class was due from next week. For four days Jawad would sit by the window and stare outside. He wanted to do something productive and the idea of sitting idle for the next six months frustrated him. He decided to join a library. Monday morning he went to the office to ask about a library. He spoke to Martin about this.

"This is the first time that a resident of this house has come to ask for a library. There is a public library in the local area. I'll write down the address for you."

"Thank you so much."

"However, first there is something else you had to do. You'll have to register yourself at the local *Gemeinde* which means municipal office. This is your certificate of residence, show it there and register yourself."

He then handed him a map of this area, crossing out his destinations.

"I really appreciate your help Martin," Jawad said while taking the ticket from him.

Every resident was entitled to have a ticket for public transport by paying 2 Francs. They could use that ticket for 6 hours. The public library was located close to the local train station. The English section was lined up with bestseller. Jawad wanted to read history books or non-fiction. He was unable to find one. He went to the counter and asked:

"Are there any non-fiction English books available?"

"We only have fiction books in English," replied the girl.

"Where can I get them?"

"They are available in the central library. It's in the down town."

"Could you give me the address please?"

"Sure," she replied, writing down the address.

From there he went to register himself as a resident of that borough. He passed a five star hotel and after crossing two alleys, reached his destination. *Gemeindehaus Oerlikon* was written outside the building. He entered the office, waited in the queue and on his turn handed his ID and certificate. The clerk typed his details on the computer and took a printout. He signed and stamped the paper and handed it back to Jawad.

"What's this?"

"This is a proof that you have been registered as a resident of this area."

The following week Jawad had his first language class. The teacher, Daniel, welcomed him to the class. He gave him an English-to-German dictionary, a notebook and a file. The file contained unsolved exercises, along with illustrations. He was also given a pencil set and a textbook on German. Daniel spoke mostly in German as he knew very little English; Jawad could not grasp the language quickly and the class was mostly unproductive. The language class lasted for three long hours with a 10-minute break after every hour. Those under the age of 18 were sent to regular schools for study on the state's expense. After the class Jawad and Ali had lunch.

"I want to visit the central library sometime today," Jawad told Ali.

"Shall I come with you?"

"No, I'll manage."

"I've never been to a library my entire life," confessed Ali.

Jawad was bit surprised. "Well, I should go and get the ticket now." He left immediately.

"Ok, catch you later." Ali also left.

Jawad went to the office and got the ticket.

"Where do you want to go?" asked Martin.

"I'm going to the central library."

"But be here by 5 pm. There is a house meeting with all the residents and the in-charge of the house is also coming. She is governing three centers simultaneously and is unable to come here every day."

"Ok, I'll be here by that time."

"Do you know the place?"

"No. But I've got the address.

Jawad took a bus to Oerlikon train station then took a direct train to the central station. He crossed the bridge and arrived at the "Central." It was a famous square in Zurich. Central library or '*Zentralbibliothek*' as they called it was a two minutes' walk from there. It was a beautiful 19th century building. Computers were lined up on the ground floor for visitors. Jawad checked the catalogue on one of the computers. He was delighted to see a bulk of English language books available. He selected two books and went to the counter to know the process of borrowing. The woman at the counter asked for his identification.

"We can't issue you a library card because you have a resident permit for refugees."

"But this is a public library."

"Yes. But I didn't formulate the rules."

"This is discrimination."

"You can use someone else's card if you like."

Jawad felt disappointed and insulted. But there was nothing he could do. It didn't seem right to him. The library reminded him of his university days. He decided to sit in the library and read a book on western political thought.

It was a little before 5 pm when he returned. Almost all the residents of the house were assembled in the lounge. Newcomer was introduced to Frau Christina. She was in her fifties and seemed very active. Translators were available for those speaking French, Albanian, Serbian and Arabic. They were asked to put forward any problems they faced living in that house. Most of them were quite comfortable with their lives, but Jawad discussed his inability to borrow books from the library. Frau Christina informed him that she would have a look at the matter. The proceedings of the meeting went smoothly. He liked the assembly atmosphere. The meeting lasted an hour with various suggestions and promises. People dispersed after the meeting quickly as it was time to dine.

"We should try to find some work." Ali spoke to him that evening after dinner.

"But we don't have permission to work. You told me yourself that it is difficult to find illegal work here."

"Yes, but at least we can try. If we find a job right now, we won't have to pay the room rent. We already get our food allowance and health insurance from the government. We'll be saving all the money. Right now all we do is sitting at home or roam around the city, other than the language class twice a week."

"But won't that be illegal?"

"Yes, it sure is. But who cares. It is better for us to make our time here productive. I know a guy who works at a carpet shop and he saves all the money. The employer only pays him half the salary because he is a refugee."

"But where could we find a job? And what if the office people finds out? We'll surely get in to trouble."

"Oh! Come on Jawad. They will never find out. Even if they do, all they could do is just give us a warning and that's all."

"I get your point, Ali. Where should we start?"

"Tomorrow we'll go to the Pakistani shop in the downtown."

"That's a good idea." Jawad consented to that.

That evening the night supervisor was Muller, a young German. He was a student at the University of Zurich, studying European History and

International Affairs. He was fluent in English and Jawad met him in the TV lounge. Jawad had an introduction with him. Soon they were talking amicably.

"Are you a Muslim?" Muller asked.

"Not a practicing one, but why're you asking that?"

"Well, this is my second job as a night supervisor. What I have witnessed is that the majority of problems which force people to become refugees had a religious background. When believers of one religion are in majority, they cause trouble for the minorities and tensions arise. I see religion as a mere accident. I'm a Christian, because my parents are Christians; you are a Muslim because your parents are Muslims. Then what's the big deal man?" Muller made his case.

"But this isn't always the case. You're aware of the fact that about 50 million people perished in Europe half a century ago. Not all of them died because of religious issues."

"We've learnt our lesson but others have not," Muller responded in an apologetic tone.

"Well, we're in a dilemma. You know we were being ruled by the colonial powers and now the same powers have become, after exploiting us for centuries, proxy rulers. They've a simple rule; do as I say and not as I do." Jawad spoke conclusively.

"I agree with you partially but it is not always the fault of outsiders. People are so blinded due to their faith".

"Do you smoke?" Muller suddenly asked him changing the topic.

"It depends."

"Depends on what?"

"On the availability of cigarettes, at the moment, I can't afford."

Muller offered him a cigarette from his pack.

"You see we're living in a world full of hypocrisy. The country who could not control the hand guns in her own background, wants to control the weapons of mass destruction in the whole world." Muller seemed to be referring USA.

On that they both had a good laugh. They spoke for a while and Muller praised Jawad's general knowledge. Their conversation ignited a thought in Jawad's mind. Majority of the refugees he had seen at the asylum center and in Kreuzlingen had one thing in common – they were mostly Muslims.

Next day he and Ali headed to the city for job search. They went to the Pakistani shop which was located in downtown. Mr. Zafar, the owner of the store sold oriental spices, pickles and Basmati rice. He also offered take-away meals for lunch and dinner. Ali went to talk to him while Jawad just browsed the racks.

"What did he say?" Jawad inquired as soon they were out.

"He suggested we should go to the Dry Port. There are a number of warehouses and sometimes they hire extra workers. The port opens at eight in the morning and one may earn 100 Francs for working a few hours."

"Is it dangerous? I mean what if we get caught?" Jawad was always worried.

"No. I asked him and he said the place is big and many immigrants work there."

"You mean asylum seekers."

"Yes, people like you and me."

"So, what's the plan now? We've language class twice a week. We can't go to work every day."

"I know that but this is a daily basis job. Nobody hires you permanently."

"Have you got the address?"

"Yes. We'll go there day after tomorrow because tomorrow we've a language class."

"So what do we do now?"

"Let's go to the lake, I'm sure you'll love it."

Weather was nice and after a pleasant walk of twenty minutes, they reached the lake. Jawad stood breathless for a moment as he caught sight of the lake. It was the second best thing in Zurich, after Sonia. He stood there reveling in its majestic beauty. He wished he could have Sonia with him at that moment. They walked along the lake. It was sunny and a lot of people were sitting on benches along the lake.

"It's a perfect place to read," Jawad commented.

"It's a perfect place to find a woman," Ali said with a wink.

"Can't you think of anything else besides the two W's, work and women?"

"Well, my friend we came to this country for a better life, right?"

"Yes."

"So, for a better life you need to have some money. You can't have money without work. Finding work without a permanent resident permit is difficult. And women are the key to our resident permits."

"What about the work we're looking for?"

"These are temporary provisions, aimed at earning a few bucks. But we need to settle here permanently. This is my second asylum application. The first one was rejected within the first three months so I had to remain underground at a friend's place for six months and then reapply."

"What are your chances now?"

"None, it might get rejected again, but I'm taking my chances because I would rather die than leave this country."

"I wish you luck for the future. Let's get some beer now." Jawad felt thirsty.

"Two beers will cost at least 8 Francs here which we can't afford at the moment."

"Hello there," a man in a black suit, wearing sunglasses and trying to hide a prominent belly greeted Ali. He resembled someone from the Italian mafia.

"Oh! Hello Mian Sahib. It'd been a long time. This is Jawad, my housemate. We're just wandering around the city and enjoying the weather."

"I had an appointment with my dentist and I finished early so I too came here to enjoy the sun. Are you both working?"

"No."

"Have you guys got the permission to work?"

"Not yet."

"It's difficult to find a job without that, but one must keep trying." Mian spoke to them for a while and most of his talk consisted of advice.

"How do you know this guy?" asked Jawad as Mian left.

"I met him at the local mosque couple of times."

"What does he do?"

"He is a salesman of used cars, but he is very sharp. He helps people get a bank loan and supplies prepaid phone cards to different shops. He is always up to something."

They stayed at the lake for a while. Jawad liked it very much. Then it was time to go.

"Should we take a tram?" asked Jawad.

"No, we better take a train to Oerlikon."

Once back home, Jawad went for a quick nap. He got up and found Ali in the kitchen preparing dinner.

"Here is a beer for you," Ali offered him a chilled can at the dinner.

"When did you buy the beer?"

"When we returned, you were sleeping when I went to shop. One beer costs 1 Franc at the store."

After dinner their conversation again turned to their present predicament

"You know what? There is a short cut to settle in this country permanently," Ali told Jawad.

"What's that?"

"One can go for a sham marriage."

Jawad knew that terminology in a vague sense but had no concrete idea.

"How does it work?"

"There are people who work as middlemen for that. They'll find a woman who wants to marry for a price. The average duration of the marriage is five years. The process of getting married and attaining a resident permit may take six months due to strict scrutiny of the documents. The marriage certificate is submitted at the migration office and within weeks you get your Swiss residence permit. All you need to have is a joint address with your wife for future correspondence."

"And how much does it cost?"

"Presently it costs almost 35,000 Francs."

"A lot of people had done it. Every year Switzerland imports thousands of immigrant workers who come here because this country needs labor. So what's wrong if we join their ranks with the help of sham marriage?"

Jawad realized that Ali was bent upon staying in this country no matter what is the price. For Ali, the road to prosperity ran through Switzerland.

"Ali, you're a very optimistic man."

"Why do you say that?"

"Because we can't even afford a beer at the lake and you're thinking about sham marriage worth 35,000 Francs!"

"What? You think I'm kidding? I've seen many people who had a dream to live in this country. And you know what! They actually achieved their dream by working hard, and saving money. Man, I'm ready to make any sacrifice to stay in this country. Moving to yet another country is not an option for me."

"You've a point there but don't you have any morals." Jawad tried to tease Ali.

"Presently I can't afford morals." Ali confessed in an apologetic way. Jawad was not different either. Words like dignity, values, morals and pride were losing their meaning for him. Each new step seemed to be a new compromise, putting another dent on his ego. Pride falls with the fortunes and he knew that. Later that night, Jawad went over their conversation. He realized that the allowance they were given allowed them to live a tad better than a tramp. He thought about Ali and his dreams. It seemed that they were both intertwined in this situation by some divine intervention, but one without a conscience and the other without a vision. Finding a way out was what they had to do.

Being poor gives people a kind of freedom, because not much is expected from a destitute. You may wear what you wish, eat what you like. Nobody objects because they know that you can't help it. But if you tell people you are a refugee, they pity you rather than looking with sympathy. The first victim of poverty is your ego. Even your friends notice your attire. Jawad found this out when they finished the language class next day.

"You need some other shoes," Ali suggested.

"I need a lot of new stuff."

"Yes. But tomorrow we've to go for job hunt and if we get lucky, we might get hired. So you need to buy new shoes as soon as possible. These one are not suitable for work"

"What should I do?"

"You're entitled to receive an allowance for shoes. Go and see Martin and tell him that you need a pair of shoes and he'll give you a check."

"How much does the check worth?"

"Eighty Francs, if he asks what is wrong with the old ones, tell him that they are not good for rain."

At 3 pm the office reopened and Jawad went to see Martin.

"Well, normally we don't give money for shoes this early. What about the shoes you already have?" he asked, looking at Jawad's feet.

"They are not suitable for rain. Every time it rains, they get soaked," Jawad tried to explain.

"Okay. In that case I could make an exception. But you got to be careful because you can only get money for shoes once every six months. What about your clothes?"

"Why do you ask?"

"We've got some used clothes recently given as charity. You can have a look if something suits you. They are almost new."

"In that case I would like to have a look." Jawad had only two pairs of trousers and shirts. His own luggage was still lying in Germany. Ali told him that it was not advisable to give the address of asylum center for abroad. Martin opened the store. There were three closets full of clothes, covered with plastic and recently laundered. Jawad took out a sweater and a shirt of his size. He looked around for some more but could see nothing else. He picked up the clothes and came back to the office. Martin gave him a check with the name of the store on it. Jawad returned to his room and hung the clothes in his closet.

"Have you got the check?" asked Ali.

"Yes. Martin also gave me some clothes."

"Very well, you see your possessions are increasing with the passage of time."

"Oh yes. Thanks to the generosity of the Swiss people. Shall we take bus tickets from the office?"

"No! Why waste 4 Francs on tickets. Shoe store is about two kilometers away. Let's walk instead."

"Okay, let's go."

The shoe store was located in a huge shopping complex. Jawad tried on different shoes and with Ali's help, selected a pair of brown leather boots. He wanted to buy slippers too as he shared Ali's. So he bought a pair of cheap plastic slippers as well. Price for both pairs was 90 Francs. Jawad handed the check to the sales girl and paid the rest in cash.

Early next day Ali awoke Jawad. It was their turn to clean up. Together they cleaned the bathroom, toilet and the kitchen floor of their part of the center. They had breakfast in a hurry and left for the Dry Port. It was a big place with couple of buildings in a restricted area. They passed the gate and went south where many trucks stood by a building.

"This is our destination," Ali told him.

There was a container truck being offloaded by some men. A tall man was supervising and checking the list in his folder. Two of the workers looked Asians which made Ali and Jawad think they could have a chance.

"Sir, we're looking for work," Ali asked hesitantly to the tall man.

"I've no work for you, sorry."

They went to the nearby warehouses and got the same answer. Ali was very disappointed.

"Tomorrow we'll try again," he announced.

"Do you think it'll work?"

"Well, we should keep trying."

Two more days of similar refusals passed. On the third day Jawad grew tired and excused from the further job search. That Saturday, he spent the afternoon in the lawn. The sun was shining. He saw Sonia coming to the house. His heart stopped. He desperately wanted to greet her but at the same time he felt nervous. So he rushed to his room and checked his appearance. He freshened himself up quickly. Ali was also there.

"Are you going out?" Ali asked him.

"Not at all, I felt bored so I decided to freshen up a little. I can't sit idle all day. I'm dying to read some books."

"I think you raised this issue with the people at the office the other day. What did they say?"

"I'm still waiting for their reply."

"You know Jawad you're different from the rest of us."

"Why would you say that?"

"We're in the middle of nowhere. We've no money, no jobs, no women, and no hope for the future and you worry about books."

"Ali, my friend, try to understand. Reading is my passion:"

"I understand. You know I come from a village where education is almost non-existent. There were no industries or work opportunities there. I grew up listening to stories about people going abroad. Once a guy from my neighborhood went abroad and after a few years his family became wealthy and started building a new home. When he returned to the village, he resembled an English gentleman. Clean-shaved and wearing sunglasses, he became the pride of our entire village. People invited him into their homes and some even discretely offered their daughters for marriage. And I thought, 'he made it'. Nobody bothered to ask what his profession was or how much money he really earned abroad. Was he a porter, a cook or a waiter? If lucky enough, may be a taxi driver. People from our countries could do literally anything abroad, from washing dishes to sweeping the streets. You know, it took me eight months to get here. I started my journey on foot. I was imprisoned, beaten, left in the cold in extreme hunger with eleven other guys in a Ukrainian forest. So forgive me brother if the idea of books is so strange to me."

"I know what you mean. Since I've nothing to, why waste time?" Jawad replied clearly annoyed.

Their conversation was interrupted by Sonia's arrival.

"*Guten Abend* (Good evening)," Sonia greeted them in German.

"*Guten Abend*," both responded simultaneously.

She looked as pretty as she did the last time. Her eyes beamed and made Jawad's heartbeat quicken. Sonia's arrival relaxed the atmosphere between Jawad and Ali and both were smiling again. Jawad was eager to find a way to start a conversation with her.

"Where do you study in Zurich?" Jawad initiated once they all settled.

"I'm studying in the School of Sociology. It is about two kilometers from here."

"Do you've a library there?"

"Yes, but it's not big."

"What kind of books do you have there?"

"They are mostly course books and reference books. If we need something other than Sociology, we go to the city's main library."

"I see. I've been there. I love reading so I went there looking for my kind of books."

"Did you like it?"

"It's a wonderful place, except for one thing."

"Oh, what's that?"

"They don't issue books to asylum seekers anymore."

"I didn't know that. But what kind of books do you like?"

"I like the books about history and non-fiction."

"I'm sorry. In our library we don't have such books and most of the stuff we do have is in German."

"Would you like to join us for dinner today?" intruded Ali.

"I'll be here till Monday morning, so I've brought my own food with me."

"No problem. You can bring your stuff along here and we will eat together."

"Okay. I'll be here at six," Sonia replied while leaving for the office.

"Do you think it's a good idea?" Jawad asked Ali once she left.

"What do you mean?"

"Inviting her for dinner because you know there is not much to cook."

"I'll make chicken curry with rice. She will also bring something and there will be plenty."

"Should we go to the market then to buy the chicken?"

"Yes. Since it's a Saturday, grocery stores reduce prices on certain items due to their expiry dates. We might get some chicken at half the price."

"But it's not *halal*?" Jawad tried to tease Ali.

Ali laughed on that. They were regularly eating that stuff without any trouble.

"I don't understand the people. Some people drink Alcohol but when it comes to eating, they go for *halal* food only. Once when I was in another center, my dead-drunk Arab neighbor knocked on the door in the middle of the night and asked me where he could get *halal* food in the area."

On that Jawad could not control his laughter. They went to the store and saw packed chickens in the refrigerator with a 50% off tag. Ali checked the expiry date which was the same day and put one packet in his trolley. They also bought bread and eggs for breakfast. When they returned, Jawad tried to learn from Ali how to cook. Of course they were both having secondary thoughts about Sonia. But for that innocent girl it might be just harmless socializing with those poor asylum seekers. Perhaps they two were the only people whom she felt more deserving for her attention. She came with a packet of pasta and a small bottle of some green sauce.

"What's that?" Ali asked pointing to the sauce. He was finished with cooking.

"It's called Pesto and it's an Italian sauce. It is commonly used with pasta."

"I see, and how do you cook it?"

"It's very simple. One just boils the pasta and then adds the sauce. We students don't have much time to cook, so I prefer food that is ready within minutes."

Ali boiled the pasta and served it into a large bowl, mixing the sauce in it. Soon they were busy eating.

"It tastes really good, especially the green sauce. I thought it might have a minty flavor," commented Ali.

"Chicken curry is also great," Sonia gave her verdict.

"If only she knew that was a 'soon to be expiring' chicken," Jawad thought.

After dinner it was time for Sonia to return to the office downstairs.

"Thanks to both of you," she said before leaving.

"No problem. It was my pleasure," replied Ali, excluding Jawad from his thanksgiving.

"Would you guys like some coffee from the office machine?"

"No thanks, I won't be able to sleep if I drink coffee at this hour," Ali replied.

"I won't mind a cup," Jawad consented and went downstairs with Sonia.

"How is your language class coming along?" she asked, after they had settled with their cups on the sofa.

"Unfortunately, Daniel can't explain in English. So I just sit there and listen to him. I'm not learning much."

"Why don't you learn it yourself? You can go to the local library and get books on German language, or even audiocassettes. One can use the audio system available in the library. I learned Italian like that. It's very convenient."

"That's a good idea. I'll try it."

He couldn't talk to Sonia as much as he wanted to as some other people from the house needed her. He finished the coffee and returned to his room. Ali was still sitting in the kitchen alone.

"Where is Abdul?"

"I think he has friends or relatives here. He spends his most weekends with them."

Sunday mornings were the most peaceful. Stephan and John Paul were mostly at the disco during the weekends and would return in the morning after spending the whole night there. Jawad and Ali stayed in bed as late as they could. That Sunday after breakfast, Ali decided to go to the city.

"Why're you going to the city on a Sunday?"

"The weather is nice and there'll be a lot of people around the lake."

Jawad knew what Ali meant. He wanted to look for an opportunity to get in touch with women. But Jawad wanted to stay at the center and talk to Sonia.

It was customary on Sunday afternoons for visitors to turn up at the center. There was a big board outside the office where the names and the nationalities of the people living in the house were written. Jawad could not wait to see Sonia any more. He chalked out a plan to see her. He decided to ask her help for library card. If she agreed to lend him her card, that might create a way of communication between them. He went downstairs hoping to see her. He glanced at the names at the board, realizing that he was the latest arrival. It was like a small Kreuzlingen with 40 refugees. Suddenly, the office door opened and Sonia appeared at the door. At first there were the customary greetings and inquiries about how they both slept last night. Sonia realized that Jawad was reading something on the board.

"Are you looking for something?" she asked to him.

"No, I was just looking at the number of countries the refugees belong to. It's quite a contrast."

"In what way it's a contrast?"

"This house alone provides for people coming from three different continents."

"Yes, you're right. But we, in Switzerland are used to having refugees. You see during the World Wars, Switzerland was the only country that stayed neutral. So, many war refugees started arriving here. But the problem is many people take advantage of the system and seek fake asylum. It's the Swiss taxpayer who is paying for all these facilities. The xenophobic parties are raising this issue loudly."

A female resident interrupted their conversation. She and Sonia went inside the office. Jawad felt nervous because Sonia knew about the fake asylum seekers. He too came to Switzerland because he wanted a better life. She seemed to be an honest person and this truth about Jawad may annoy her. After five minutes, she emerged from the office.

"I want to ask you a personal favor. Actually I need some help," he spoke in a desperate tone as she turned to him.

"What kind of help?"

"I told you that the central library doesn't issue books to refugees. Is it possible that I could use your library card to borrow books? I know we hardly know each other and you might not want to do this but the boredom is killing me. I assure you I won't cause you any trouble."

"Well, let me think about it. Actually, I'm not a member of the central library and we're also not supposed to grant personal favors while working here."

"I assure you that I would return your card without owing any books to the library before my departure."

"Okay, let me think about it and I'll let you know."

"Thank you so much."

It took Jawad some months to understand the refugee situation in Switzerland. People had been coming here for centuries, all looking for safety. A lot of exiled writers, intellectuals, even members of royal families came here. The advent of the 20th century merely accelerated the number of people seeking asylum. Switzerland's reputation as a neutral country also played a role in it. Jawad also found out that during World War I, so many refugees from Balkan countries came to Zurich that the locals started calling one of the main streets of Zurich *Balkanstrasse* instead of *Bahnhofstrasse*.

Although during World War II, Switzerland was forced to refuse entry to the many Jews trying to enter the country because of German pressure, not a single Jew in the country was harmed. Those who managed to enter the country were allowed to stay. In 1956 a failed uprising in Hungary brought Hungarian refugees, so did the Prague spring of 1968, which brought thousands of Czechoslovakians. The 1979 Iranian Revolution forced many to seek shelter here as well and the Lebanese fleeing from the civil war in the 1980s also joined their ranks. And then there were wars in Afghanistan, Central Asia and Yugoslavia. No matter in which part of the world a war starts, some of the affected would turn up to Switzerland to seek refuge. This was assured and same was the case with many other western countries.

On the other hand to support the booming economy and fulfill increasing labor demands, Switzerland was forced to import labor from many Europeans countries. Lot of people arrived to work and many of them settled in the country permanently. New arrivals meant a large proportion of population comprised of foreigners. Add to that the refugees and the number goes much higher. Almost 20% of the population consisted of foreigners. One may need something but that doesn't mean one also likes that thing.

That day Ali returned at sunset.

"Any luck?" Jawad asked directly.

"No," Ali seemed disappointed. "There were women at the lake with and without company but no one seemed interested. It's a curse when 'refugee' is written all over your face."

"Ali, tell me one thing. If there is a girl sitting on a bench, how would you go and talk to her without even knowing her name?"

"Of course, you can't start a conversation that abruptly. First you sit beside her. Then talk about the weather and stuff like that. If she seems interested, invite her for coffee. After coffee you can tell her that you had a great time with her and would like to meet her again. If she is positive, she might give her phone number and that's it."

"How many have you picked up till now?"

"None, but I'm optimistic, one day I'll find the woman who is waiting for me," Ali claimed, sounding like a Romeo in search of his Juliet.

"What about the rest of the guys here?"

"Well, everyone is trying. You never know my friend, you never know."

Meanwhile, Jawad acted on Sonia's advice and searched for books, audios and DVDs in the local library which may help him understand German. There was a small room with audio-visual systems. To use those facilities, he had to deposit his ID card at the counter. There were lots of movies. All the stuff he had dreamed of. He started with a language learning kit. One of the books also had a CD. It was feasible to read the book and then listen to the CD for the correct pronunciation. This soon became his routine and Jawad was delighted with this new set up. However, in the evenings he still felt sad. All the residents would sit in their kitchens, with misery written on their faces. They would cook whatever they could and discuss their respective situations. Jawad could imagine the feelings of the people with families. What would be the future of their children? If he felt sad about those homeless, stateless children, what about their parents? From Kreuzlingen to the Zurich, Jawad witnessed a strange solidarity among the asylum seekers. One was always willing to assist the other co-unfortunate; brotherhood reigned supreme among the destitute.

Friday evening Sonia came to work again. Although he impatiently waited for a chance to talk to her, he didn't want to make a bad impression on her and decided to wait. His neighbors got ready for their weekly excursion, like hunters looking for the prey. Sonia came for a brief visit. She greeted and smiled and he smiled back. Their brief conversation served as an appetizer with a desire for more. He did not invite her to dinner as supplies were short and he was scared to cook for her. There was no sign of Ali who'd gone to the city. She returned to the office and Jawad took out the dictionary, partly studying, partly napping. He dined alone with some leftovers from the fridge and went to sleep. Abdul was again absent and he was alone in the room.

He had not slept long when Ali woke him from his sleep.

"What's the matter with you?" Jawad asked angrily.

"There is something to tell you, I can't wait till tomorrow?"

"What is it?"

"I did find a job."

"Wow! Congratulations! How did you get it?"

"I met a Pakistani guy, Khadim, at the lake. He is a cook at a restaurant in Letten on the riverside. Every summer, temporary restaurants are set up there for the swimmers. The owner of the restaurant had asked Khadim to bring someone for cleaning and washing. So he asked me."

"What's the pay?"

"A job like this depends completely on the weather. If the weather is good, a lot of people would turn up, especially on the weekends. But if the weather is bad, the restaurant will remain closed. I'll earn 100 Francs for a full day with free food and drinks. I wish for a good summer this year. But promise me that you won't tell anyone about this matter."

"Don't worry, I won't tell anyone?"

"Have you eaten anything?"

"Yes and what about you?

"I'd eaten a kebab. Sorry for disturbing you. I'd also asked Khadim if he could find a job for you as well."

"Thanks, that's very kind of you."

"Don't mention it. Look, I've brought beer to celebrate."

Both came to the dining table and Jawad offered a toast to Ali's success at his job.

"Who is on duty tonight?"

"Sonia. Tell me Ali, what'll be your working hours?"

"I'll start tomorrow at 10 in the morning. I won't be attending the language classes anymore. I know they might fine me or transfer me to another place but I really don't care. I'll have to help with the setting up. I need to be at the restaurant first thing in the morning, before people start to come."

The following day Ali left in the morning for work. Jawad got up and made tea. He was pleasantly surprised to see Sonia as she arrived in their part of the center.

"Good morning Jawad."

"Good morning, how're you?"

"I'm fine and you?"

"Fine as well."

"Did you sleep well?"

"Yes."

"How was your week?"

"I went to the local library and found a lot of stuff to learn German."

"Oh, that's great.

"By the way I'd been thinking about your request. You can use my membership card but first I'll have to get one."

"Oh, thank you so much. I won't forget it," beamed Jawad.

"But keep it between us only."

"Sure, don't worry but can I ask you something?"

"Yes, what is it?"

"Is it possible that we could go together to the central library?

"Yes, that is possible." She left afterwards.

Jawad was delighted. He went out for a walk. Lately he felt a deep connection with Sonia though he knew she could never really be his. She was intelligent, charming and much advanced than him while he came from a third world country. He didn't know how to use the very little supply of charm he had to attract a woman, especially of that caliber. One thing he dreaded the most was that Sonia might have a boyfriend. Always when they talked, he was thinking of a future they may or may not ever have. Engulfed in these thoughts he returned and went to the TV room. He met two men of his age there, one of them walking with a cane.

"Guten Abend," one with the cane greeted him in German. "Sprechen sie Deutsch (Do you speak German)?"

"No, English."

"Where are you from?" the guy switched to English.

"I'm from Pakistan. What about you?"

"We're from Kosovo. I studied English in the school."

"Ok, that's good."

"And I also watched Hollywood movies, lots of them."

"What happened to your leg?"

"I was shot."

Jawad was startled.

"How did that happened?"

"I'm a member of Kosovo Liberation Army. A bullet hit me and I was operated in the hospital in Zurich to remove the bullet. Sorry, I forgot to mention our names. I'm Zavet and this is my friend, Mehmet."

"Glad to meet you guys. I'm Jawad, sorry to hear about your leg."

"Thanks but such things happen when you are in a war zone."

"How is the situation in Kosovo now?"

"It's getting worse. The Serbian Army is ever ready to invade the province. People are fleeing to other countries even on foot. You see, Kosovo Liberation Army is a guerrilla force, not well equipped for regular warfare. We're hoping that NATO will intervene as nobody wants massacres like Bosnia again. We want an independent country of our own and we'll get it." Zavet spoke with zeal.

He was doing all the talking while his friend stayed silent. Perhaps he did not study English in the school. Meanwhile Mehmet went away. He brought three beers and offered one to Jawad.

"Before the war, what did you do?" Jawad asked to Zavet.

"I used to be a car dealer back home."

"How did you come to Switzerland with a bullet in your leg?"

"I was helped by my friends in KLA. They told me I may lose my leg. The bullet was the only reason I came here. I want to go back and fight for my country. I'm just waiting to recover."

Their conversation was interrupted by a knock on the lounge door. Mehmet got up and opened the door. Three men came in. They were all tall and muscular, dressed like businessmen. Zavet and Mehmet took them to their room while Jawad returned to his own. Late in the night, Ali came back from his new job, tired and sleepy.

"How was your first day?"

"It was tough, had to carry a lot of heavy stuff. Then we arranged the kitchen, set the tables and unload dozens of crates in to the refrigerator." Ali slept immediately.

Jawad waited anxiously for Sonia's invitation for the library. On Wednesday he was asked about Ali in the class but he denied about his whereabouts. Jawad returned to his room after the language class. Soon there was a knock at the door. It was Martin with the cordless phone in his hand.

"There is a phone call for you."

"Hello, Jawad speaking."

"It's me, Sonia. How're you?"

Jawad was a little nervous as Martin was still standing at the door.

"I'm fine," he responded hesitantly.

"Listen Jawad; is it possible for you to come to the central library at 4 pm?"

"Yes I'll be there."

"See you then. Ok."

"Ok, see you later." Jawad then handed the phone back to Martin.

It was as if the doors of heaven had opened for him. He was speechless. The first thing he did was to check his pockets. He only had 40 Francs on him. He wondered what he could afford with that money. For few moments his mind went blank. Finally he decided to invite her for a cup of coffee afterwards. He bathed, shaved and got ready to leave for the city. At 4 pm he stood on the stairs of the library and waited for her. He saw her coming with her bag on the shoulders.

"Thanks for coming. I really appreciate your help," Jawad said to her.

"You're welcome."

They went inside the library. She presented her ID card at the counter and within minutes the membership card was issued to her. She in turn gave it to him.

"You can use the card with immediate effect," she informed Jawad.

He checked the electronic catalogue to relocate the two books he had selected other day. He wrote the number and went to the basement to get them from the racks.

"Do you have time?" he asked Sonia after borrowing the books.

"Why?"

"I want to invite you for a cup of coffee?"

"That'll be nice," she consented politely.

They went to the cafeteria which was brimming with students from across Zurich. He bought two cups of coffee and paid for them, although Sonia insisted on paying for her coffee. He felt indebted to her. Soon they came out and walked to the train station. There were a lot of things running in Jawad's mind. Still he didn't know whether she had a boyfriend or not. But he was scared to ask. Suddenly a trick came to his mind.

"Do you live in a student hostel?"

"No, I've rented a room close to Goldbrunnenplatz. It's a 20 minute walk from here."

"Is it expensive?"

"No, it's affordable. Monthly rent is 600 Francs. Before I used to live with my boyfriend there but then we broke up and he left."

"Oh! I'm sorry to hear that," Jawed spoke, hiding his joy.

"It's all right. Life goes on," she said in response.

This is perfect. She is single and living alone in Zurich.

"If you want to go back, we can take the same train because I'm going to meet my mother in Dietlikon." Sonia proposed.

They walked to the station and took the same train. Jawad disembarked at Oerlikon and returned to the center by bus. Before going to his room he returned the ticket at the office. Ali returned at midnight, tired as usual.

"How was your day?" Ali asked while changing.

"I went to the library to borrow some books with Sonia."

"What? She went to the library with you. I can't believe this."

"Why?"

"What surprises me is that I asked her to go out with me a couple of times but she always excused."

"I don't know what you're talking about. Sonia is a good person and she is helping me but that doesn't mean I'll be sleeping with her next week."

"Next year, may be," Ali winked. "Did anyone ask about me?"

"Yes, they asked about you in the class but I denied about your whereabouts." Ali made no remarks on that.

Next morning, Jawad met Zavet in the hall.

"This is for you," Zavet handed him a pack of cigarettes.

"Thanks?"

"You're welcome; let's go outside for a smoke."

"Zavet, is there any news from home?" Jawad asked as a way of showing courtesy.

"Good and bad, both."

"How is KLA doing?"

"They are holding up but we're fighting against the odds, counting on the strength of our people and support from the world community."

Jawad realized from his comments that those people were running on a lot of assumptions. He had no idea whether they had a concrete, viable plan. He thought back of the time when NATO did nothing while thousands of Bosnians were being slaughtered, a fact that Zavet might already knew. Soon Mehmet arrived and joined them.

"I've an appointment with the doctor. We'll catch up later, Goodbye." Zavet left with Mehmet.

"Good bye." Jawad responded.

There were new arrivals in the house. One was from Iraq, other from Congo. Hussein, the Iraqi was to share the room occupied by Jawad and now they were four living together, while Mr. Mumba, the Congolese was attached with the other Africans. Hussein was not new in the country and had lived in another center at Kamptal before. He spoke English with a French accent but was fluent in French and Arabic.

Whenever the money was distributed, which was every fortnight, refugees would run to the desk where Martin distributed the dole money. Their names were called alphabetically to make the payments. Many would then rush to the grocery store to buy supplies. Ali, though busy with his work, always showed up for the money. He was getting warnings and deductions were being made from the cash he was entitled to. He told Jawad that soon they would transfer him to some place far from the city as a punishment for not abiding by their rules.

On the phone Jawad would lie to his family about how comfortable his life was and that very soon he would acquire a job. He felt guilty for lying to his parents. As his frustrations grew, so did his desire to leave Switzerland and live in a place where he could earn some money. He asked Ali about the possibility of going to Canada.

"There are people who will put your picture on someone else's passport, of course at a price. Some get caught while some get through. But it's risky."

He soon dropped the idea. He had no money to undertake such an adventure. To relieve his tensions he started going for long walks in the evenings. He tried his best to stay positive but it was difficult.

Look at these people on the streets, returning home, having meals in their lawns, surrounded by their children, content and happy. They don't know how lucky they are. They don't have to stand in a line to get dole money every second week, alphabetically.

It was not long before Ali's absence was felt. Martin came to see Jawad one afternoon as he was preparing to leave for the library.

"Do you have a moment?" he politely asked.

"Oh sure, what's the matter?"

"Do you know where Ali is? He is not attending his language class and we did warn him couple of times."

"I've no idea at all."

"Ok, I'm sorry but it's time to take disciplinary action. Do tell him that."

"All right, I'll tell him."

That night he told Ali about the matter.

"I don't care what they do. For me this job is the most important thing. They can go to hell."

The weather turned nasty the next day so Ali had to stay home. He went to the office and spoke to Martin. He returned looking disturbed.

"What happened?" Jawad asked.

"I had an argument with that son of a bitch. I told him that I'm suffering from depression and I've no desire to attend the language class. They can send me wherever they like, I don't care."

Jawad knew Ali won't be there for very long. Meanwhile there was a new arrival in the office staff. His name was Peter Perucci. The unemployment office had found him that job. Everyone was introduced to him. Jawad found him very friendly and talkative. He didn't show much interest in his job. Jawad met him alone in the TV lounge one afternoon.

"Hi, Mr. Peter," Jawad greeted him.

"Please call me Perucci," he told Jawad. "I'm Italian from my paternal side and I prefer my Italian name."

"Oh! I see. Do you like here?"

"I don't like working in an office atmosphere. I was unemployed and my counselor at the unemployment office found me this job for six months. This is not my line of work. I'm a journalist."

Jawad was surprised how open Perucci was.

"You seem to be educated?" Perucci tossed a question at Jawad.

"What do you mean by educated?" Jawad replied teasingly at which Perucci laughed.

"You speak good English even though it is not your mother tongue. And your accent tells me you've studied at college level at the least."

"You're right. I've actually done Masters in English."

They spoke for a while and then Perucci left. He seemed to be someone who could be easily befriended and Jawad kind of liked him

The weather improved and sun was out. One day he took his books and went to the lake. There were swans and ducks in the lake being fed by the people. He saw a lot of boats with fishermen and ships with tourists cruising along the beautiful, blue lake. He wished Sonia was there with him. Dreams of long walks and intimate conversation paraded before his eyes. He wanted to hold her hand and go for a stroll. Later they might opt for dinner at a quiet place. The restaurant manager would greet them and a waiter would escort them to their table. They would have *Aperitif*, a glass of champagne or a Martini, saying *Zum wohl*. Then they would enjoy the food and the wine. After the meal he would accompany her. When they would reach her place, she might invite him in warmly. But it was only his imagination; perhaps reality was different. The whole thing had become an ordeal for him.

To lighten his heart, he decided to talk to Ali on the issue of Sonia. They spoke one night when Ali retuned from work early due to the bad weather.

"Ali, there is something very important I want to tell you."

"Go on, I'm listening," said Ali. As always, he was tired from work.

"I think I'm in love with Sonia." Finally he broke the news and felt relieved.

"I'm not surprised because I'm also in love with her. Who isn't?" he joked.

"Don't make fun of me. I'm serious," Jawad said angrily.

"May I ask you when and how this historic event happened? What made you feel this way?"

"I've questioned my heart. I've been searching for a soul mate and I feel Sonia is the one."

"Well, I wish you good luck, brother. What do you want from me?"

"I need your advice because I'm confused. You know our social status. Tell me what shall I do?"

"Talk to her directly and tell her the truth."

"What? I can't go up to her and say that I love her."

"That is exactly what you should do. This is not Pakistan that if you tell her about your feelings there will be a scandal. Things are different here. Buy a red rose and give it to her the next time you meet. Tell her that you are in love with her. That is my honest opinion."

"I'll think over it," but Jawad could not make up his mind.

Mr. Perucci, the new staff member was always nice to him and they often sat together and talked while smoking. Jawad was thankful for the kindness he always showed to him. To show his gratitude, Jawad decided to invite him for dinner. Perucci accepted on one condition that he'll prepare some Italian dish with his own stuff. They agreed on the next Friday evening. That evening Perucci arrived with a bag full of ingredients. He fried the boneless chicken and prepared some pasta with cream sauce. First they had tomato mozzarella salad with fresh basil leaves; they then ate the main course with a bottle of Chianti.

"You are a dark horse," Jawad complimented him after the dinner.

"I like cooking. My father used to say, 'Cooking and singing is in the blood of every Italian'."

"So, are you going to sing now?"

"No. I don't want you to run away. Let's go for a walk," Perucci suggested.

As they crossed the first road, Perucci lit a hand-made cigarette. After taking the first puff, he offered it to Jawad.

"Try this. It's very good."

"What is it?"

"It's a mixture of marijuana and tobacco. It is called 'joint'."

Jawad tried but it was strong for him. This was the first time that he'd tried Cannabis. He returned it to Perucci.

After a moment of silence, Perucci asked, "So, what are your plans?"

"I don't know. I'm waiting for my second interview. I don't have permission to work at the moment. So I spend my time at the center or at the library."

"But do you really want to live in this country forever?"

"I think so. I've no other option. Do you think my decision to stay here is not right? Should I be living somewhere else?"

"I mean to say that you are from a land which has a completely different culture. Some people find it very different to adjust to the Swiss culture. I've seen documentaries on Pakistan and also read some books because I love reading. Joint family system is a norm in your country, whereas it is not so in Switzerland. Swiss society is very individualistic. Everyone wants to live in his own small world. At times, they have little business even with their blood relations. My own father had trouble adjusting to the culture here."

"But he didn't come here as a refugee?" Jawad asked.

"No, he migrated from Southern Italy as he was unemployed. He had limited choice at that time because he had no job and no money. A friend found him a job as a seasonal worker. Then he met my mother and they fell in love. They got married when my mother became pregnant. However, my parents were a complete contrast."

"Like what?"

"My father was a carefree person. A little disorder around him was not a problem. But my mother was much disciplined. For the Swiss, things have to be in a certain order. So they used to have heated arguments and would get angry with each other over petty issues. They got divorced and I stayed with my mother. Even then I used to go with my father on holidays every year. He introduced me to Italian food, wine and culture. He took me to Italy many times and showed me the whole country."

"But you grew up in Zurich?"

"Yes, and the funny thing is, when I was at school, my class fellows treated me as a foreigner. They used to make fun of me and called me names but that's a long story?"

"Well, presently I've no other option. As they say, if rape is inevitable just relax and enjoy, I'm in the same predicament. Just wait and see." Jawad made his final comments.

Next day weather took a rough turn again. It was raining so Ali had a day off. He slept while Jawad spent his time watching TV. After waking up at noon, Ali took the umbrella and went to the nearby store. Ever since he started working, Jawad was buying his stuff alone. Ali soon returned with a bag full of groceries.

"Why did you buy so much food?"

"Some of the stuff is for lunch and the rest I've bought for you," Ali responded while offloading.

"You don't have to share your money with me. I'm fine," Jawad told Ali.

"Don't worry, we're friends. I haven't brought much. It's just cooking oil, eggs, tea, milk and some bread. Last night my boss told me about the bad weather today. He paid me 1000 Francs. I've never earned this much before. I'm really happy and I want to celebrate," he added, pulling out a bottle of whisky. "Let us celebrate my salary."

As they finished the second round of whisky, there was a knock at the door. It was Sonia and Jawad was stunned to see her.

"Is something special going on?" she asked teasingly.

"We're just trying to have some fun. Would you like to join us?" Ali asked her with panache.

"No, thanks, whisky is too heavy for me. Just dropped by to say hello," Sonia left soon.

"What's the matter with you?" Ali asked him when he realized Sonia's sudden arrival had silenced Jawad.

"Nothing, I'm just worried."

"Is there a problem?"

"She might not approve of my drinking whisky. I want her to have a good image of me."

"Oh god, Jawad, it is normal in this society as long as you are not drunk and causing trouble for others. We're social drinkers. I can bet you she won't even mention it the next time you see her."

After dinner, Ali and Abdul had an argument over some issue. Hussein was also there but he stayed silent. He and Abdul had become good friends lately.

"What was the matter between you and Abdul?" Jawad could not stop himself from asking.

"He was objecting to our drinking. I told him that he should mind his own business."

"What did he say then?"

"Don't worry about that."

Abdul left the room with Hussein and didn't return till midnight. Next morning it was sunny and Ali left for work.

There were many things running in his mind but Sonia was at the center of his thoughts. His position did not allow uncertainty and living on vague hopes could be fatal. Time was a luxury he could not afford though prudence required patience. He decided, for the time being, try to be close to her as much as possible. What could be a better reason than to seek her help for learning German? He should go to her as he was having some difficulty in learning the language. For this purpose he wrote some sentences in his notebook and decided to ask her for explanation. What a beautiful place this world would be once Sonia accepts him as her lover.

There was a letter for Ali and Jawad was told to inform him about that which he did.

"I'll get it from the office in the morning. I've been waiting for it any way," he said.

"But do you know where it comes from?"

"If I'm not mistaken it's my call for second interview. The interview at Kreuzlingen was the first one. Now I'll have a detailed one at the Zurich office of BFF. This is the standard procedure."

Before Sonia's next visit he attended to his language learning material. Luckily, on their next encounter, she herself inquired about that.

"Have you made any progress with the German language?"

"Not too much," he replied.

"What is the problem?"

"You know, even with the best material, I still need some guidance."

"You should keep learning it yourself," she said, flipping through one of the books.

"Could you please explain this to me?" Jawad asked while pointing out a sentence in his notebook. She read the sentence and started explaining it to him while Jawad took notes. Her command over English impressed Jawad. Soon, she was explaining him like a teacher. Once the session was over, Jawad offered her tea.

"Have you been to the central library again?" she asked while sipping tea.

"Yes, but I go to the local library more often."

"Can I ask you something?" Jawad asked.

"Sure."

"Is it possible if we could have more sessions like this every time you come here? I mean only if you have time."

"Yes we can but slowly and gradually."

"Thank you."

She then took her leave. That night Jawad told Ali the whole story.

"I think you're improving in your quest to win her over." Discussing the various strategies regarding women, they both went to sleep. It was almost five when an early morning bang woke them up. Jawad opened the door and saw two tall men standing at the door. They were policemen in civil clothes as they showed him their badges.

"Are you Abdul?" one of them asked him firmly.

"No, he is in that bed."

He asked Abdul to come out of his bed. He spoke something in French and took Abdul away. They were all stunned and frightened. Hussein seemed to have some idea due to his knowledge of French?" Jawad inquired Hussein, once the men left.

"I don't know. I think they have taken him for questioning. But the funny thing is that if they need someone from the center, they could simply ask the office people to send that person. Coming at this hour and forcing someone out of bed is not a normal practice." Hussein seemed worried. He and Abdul had become very close. Later in the day, Jawad went to the office to inquire about Abdul.

"We were also caught off guard," Martin explained his ignorance about the matter.

"What they are going to do to him?" asked Jawad.

"I don't know. But there must be a reason for his sudden arrest."

The following day Abdul called Hussein from the prison. After the call, Hussein explained his situation. Abdul claimed to be an Iraqi citizen who fled Saddam's regime, but he was originally from Lebanon. The authorities found this out as his name and date of birth were sent to other countries for inquiry. They also learned that he had previously applied for asylum in Netherlands. There he even gave his original Lebanese ID card. That ID was in the record of the Dutch immigration. After his asylum application was turned down there, he came to Switzerland. But he made a mistake. Though he changed his country of origin in his asylum application, he did give his real name and date of birth. As they found out that he had applied for asylum in the Netherlands, the Swiss authorities asked for his ID card. Which the Dutch Immigration was obliged to provide. Once in hold of his ID card, police took him to the Lebanese embassy for traveling documents. They were going to deport him back to Lebanon.

Later on Perucci came around. He showed sorrow over Abdul's deportation. He was a nihilist and possessed anti-establishment views. Soon the conversation turned to Italy. He talked about Italy and claimed it was the country of art. He was very enthusiastic about Italy's contribution to the world, first under the Romans and then during the Renaissance. In his view, the Italians made a mark in everything, Music, painting, clothing, food and architecture. For Jawad meeting Perucci was always useful and he always gained a lot of knowledge.

"What about the French?" Jawad asked.

"French cuisine, art and literature are also rich but as a nation I'm not a big fan of French people."

"And what you think about the Germans?

"My father hated the Germans because my grandfather was killed by them during World War II. My grandfather was with Italian partisans who were fighting against the fascists. Once in Italy, my father had an argument with a German and got so furious, he abused the German by calling him "a descendant of war criminals."

"But for us had there been no second world war, we might still be a British colony," Jawad commented.

"I very much doubt that, especially after the communist revolution."

"Do you believe in communism?"

"No, but some of its ideas appeal me. We, in the West, have much to thank Communism. The European elite knew that in order to avoid revolutions in their countries, they have to reform their political system. The key was to keep the workers happy because they knew that religion couldn't stop the people from becoming communists. For example Italy is the home of Catholicism but we also have one of the strongest communist parties in Europe."

"So what did the ruling class do? Jawad asked as he found the discussion interesting

"They came up with the idea of a welfare state. They promised that everyone will be fed, sheltered and provided for, working hours will be reduced. There will be perks like more holidays, insurance and unemployment benefits etc. They knew that the unsatisfied workers would revolt and there'll be blood again."

"So how is the situation now?"

"The workers are now in much better condition though the rich are still exploiting the poor. You got freedom after the British left, but in reality decolonization was only eyewash. The imperial powers left behind their socio, political, economic and cultural imperialism in the colonies before leaving. They built the United Nations, the foundation of modern hypocrisy. A friend of mine worked as a journalist in the UN. He told me that if there is a dispute between two small countries, the dispute would disappear. But if it's a dispute between a powerful country and a smaller, powerless one, the latter will disappear. And what's worse is that if there are two big powers involved, the UN will disappear."

Both enjoyed a good laugh on this irony. Perucci left after some time as it was getting late.

Finally, Jawad had made up his mind. He'll speak to Sonia directly regarding his feelings about her. The long cherished moment came when she came for work. Jawad met her once at the dining table. His throat went dry as he saw her approaching and his body stiffened, rendering him speechless. But he tried to gather his courage. He even managed to have that rare smile on his face. He stood up and greeted her warmly.

"Would you like some tea?"

"No thanks, I just had some juice. How is everything with you?"

"Everything is fine."

"How're you doing with you language lessons?"

"Not bad." He could not tell her that lately he had not been good at anything.

His mind was in turmoil. *Speak to her, tell her you want her, tell her you can't live without her and want to spend the rest of your life with her.* He wished to speak out his heart, but his tongue betrayed him and his mind disappointed him. He sat there with a blank face, short of words. His notebook and other stuff were piled up in front of him. Sonia took the language guide in her hands, opened it and explained few words to him. Jawad started writing in the notebook. For every word he would write a little explanatory note in English. After a while she courteously took her leave. Jawad sat there for a while, silently, repeating the whole scenario in his mind until Ali appeared from the room.

"How did it go?" he asked.

"I've not spoken to her yet. She didn't have much time. But she is here till tomorrow morning and I'll speak to her by then."

"I wish you luck."

Ali went to the bathroom while Jawad made some tea. Ali left for work after tea. It's now or never, he thought. He stood up and walked to the stairs, determined to face her. He knocked at the office door.

"Can I talk to you?" He spoke to her as soon she opened.

"Of course, you can," she said, offering him a chair. She seemed a bit surprised. She was studying as her books lay open.

"It all may seem very strange to you but please listen very patiently."

His throat dried up. Her blue eyes were fixed on him with a curious look.

"You may feel that I'm crossing my limits or forgetting my social position but the fact is that I like you very much and really wish to be your friend."

"But we're friends already."

"I want more than that."

"I see." Sonia said with a surprise on her face.

"I know the odds are against me but I can't control my heart anymore. You're someone very special to me."

He did not mention love directly but he made himself clear indirectly. The situation demanded clear answers. There should not be any ambiguity about his intentions.

"I understand what you are saying. I'll think about it. Could you give me some time?"

"Of course, I don't want you to rush into a decision."

Back in his room he sat down for couple of minutes as he did not want to face anyone. Once his breathing returned to normal he drank a glass of water. He did it. It was as if he had almost achieved his mission. He was glad that finally he had the courage to talk to her. She didn't say anything negative nor had she brushed him off. He had no choice but to wait till she gives him an answer. However one thing kept disturbing him. Though he was madly in love with her and she was his first real crush, but for her he might be just another man trying to get along with her, nothing so special. After all she was young and beautiful. No wonder many men might have proposed her. He might be considered one more in that long list.

He didn't hear from her the next few days. On Friday evening she came for work again. She invited him to the office and there was nobody around. First she poured two glasses of orange juice and offered him one. Silently they sipped the juice. It seemed as if she was trying to find the right words. Now it was his turn to wait and listen patiently. She rolled the glass in her hands a few times.

"I hope you won't mind if I speak frankly with you."

"I don't expect anything less."

"A few months ago I broke up with my boyfriend and now I'm living alone. We were together for three years and our split still hurts me. The thing is that I'm not ready for a new relationship. Under the present circumstances, for me it's difficult to build a new relationship. But I want to assure you that my answer has nothing to do with your present social position. You're a very nice person and I like you but I don't want to give you any false expectations. I wish you a happy and successful life. However, we can still see each other as friends and I'll be glad to help you whenever I can."

Jawad sat there speechless. He knew he was supposed to say something and after a while he gathered his courage and started speaking softly.

"For a person like me who had many unfulfilled wishes, adding one more to the list is not a big deal. But there are certain things in life which mean a lot. For me you were, you are and you'll always be a very special person. Though I regret but I respect your decision. I'm sorry for causing you any disturbance and thank you for everything."

She didn't say anything in response rather sat quietly. He walked back to his room like someone who had just lost something very precious. For the coming days he went in to a depression and even his parents were worried on the phone. They told him he was speaking in a sad tone. Soon he overcame his grief. Life was not finished with Sonia and he had to move on.

Meanwhile, the letter for his second interview arrived which was scheduled on the next Tuesday. He was asked to provide the authorities with full documentary evidence to prove that he was indeed a victim of political persecution back in Pakistan. Ali advised him as he had himself recently gone through an interview, one of the many he had.

"Don't say anything that differs from the previous interview. If in the previous interview you mentioned four policemen came to arrest you, don't say five this time; stick to the same facts and figures."

Helvetiaplatz, the venue for the interview, was located at the other end of the Zurich. He arrived half an hour before his interview time. The BFF office was on the second floor. He went to the reception.

"Yes, what can I do for you?" the man behind the counter asked.

"I have an interview at ten."

Jawad took out the letter along with his ID papers. The man checked his list and found his name.

"Please have a seat; someone will come to pick you."

Jawad tried to recall all the phony facts he had given in his last interview. One by one he rehearsed the answers of every possible probing question till he was satisfied. Although he cursed himself for lying constantly and his conscience bothered him, he realized he had come too far and turning back was not an option. Left with no other choice, he had to achieve his goals by whatever means necessary. He can't afford to live by the values and morals he was brought up with. Soon his name was called. Jawad looked up to see a middle aged man standing in the door. Jawad followed him and they entered in a room. He gestured him to sit on the chair opposite to him. Two other people were also in the room.

"My name is Rolf Schmid and I work for BFF."

"Mr. Jawad," a man of Asian appearance sitting next to a girl spoke. "My name is Haq and I'm your translator. We'll go through some formalities first. You are here because you claim that your life, due to your political views is in danger in your home country. Here you'll explain in detail, the nature of your problem. You're advised to provide all the necessary documents to support your claim. First I would like to introduce you to Miss. Zara. She is from a local NGO. She is here to make sure that you're being interviewed properly. She will also make notes of the interview. In the end she will compare the whole interview transcript with her notes. Mr. Schmid as you know is from the BFF."

After their introductions, Haq, acting on Schmid's instructions asked for documents. Jawad replied that he had none whatsoever.

"Do you have a lawyer whom we can contact in Pakistan?"

"No, I don't have a lawyer."

The interview started and his answers were being typed onto the computer. For Jawad, every answer which he gave was a lie. He told them how the rulers crush their opponents. He falsely narrated how they were arrested and beaten in the name of democracy. It was a repetition of his previous interview though this time it lasted longer. They asked him about every aspect of his life. Jawad mixed the facts with fiction at his own convenience. It took them three hours to finish. Finally a transcript of the interview was produced. Mr. Schmid handed over it to Miss. Zara who crosschecked it with her notes. All four of them signed on the last page. Jawad was once again asked to acquire his identification papers as well as the court orders from Pakistan. Mr. Haq indicated that the Interview was concluded and he may go. Jawad thanked all of them and left.

Back home Jawad told Ali all the details of his ordeal at the interview. He told him to pray to God to give him some time.

"Tomorrow the restaurant is closed because of the bad weather. So we can go out and have some fun." Ali changed the subject.

"What do you mean?"

"Let's go to disco like our African neighbors. It is weekend and we've to find women, don't you remember?"

"Yes, but who has the money for such a luxury?"

"Don't worry, together we'll manage."

"But I've never been to a disco."

"Then it is time to get started."

"But I can't even dance and I think you can't either," Jawad protested.

"Who cares? The lights there are very dim; all you have to do is move your body."

"Where are we going?

"There is a disco in downtown famous for its live music. Most women there are middle-aged. So we'll have a good chance, this I can tell you. I know you are worried about the entry charges but I'll take care of that. A beer costs five Francs, but we don't have to really buy it. Stephen told me when he gets thirsty he goes to the washroom and drink tap water. We can do the same. But once we are there, we'll only return the next morning."

"Why so?"

"Because there aren't any trams or trains after midnight and a taxi costs too much."

"Ok, I'll come with you," Jawad consented.

For the first time in his life Jawad was going to a disco. At 11 pm they caught up with Stephen and Mumba who were also leaving for the city. John Paul was not with them. Together they took a bus to Oerlikon Station and then to the central station. Though weather was not so good, the train was full of young people heading for a night out.

"Do you think Stephen and Mumba are going to the same disco?" asked Jawad.

"No, they go to the one where there are more Africans," Ali responded

The streets were busy with people walking to and fro. Crowded bars and restaurants evoked the liveliness of Zurich. They reached their destination; the name of the place "Garden of Love" was glowing from the top of the building. At the entrance a security guard frisked them and allowed them in. It was dark inside apart from the lights on the stage. Both of them approached the counter which read *Eintritt 20 Francs*. Ali handed the girl at the counter 40 Francs and she branded their wrists with a little blue stamp.

"What's this for?" Jawad asked pointing to the stamp.

"This is a proof that we've paid for our entry. If we go out of the disco, we can re-enter by showing this stamp."

The disco was something new for Jawad and it fascinated him. Around the bar counters, young men raced for more shots, yelling and laughing. No one was dancing yet.

"We must occupy some seats before it gets too crowded," Ali commented.

Men entered the hall with their girlfriends. There were hardly any single women around. A waitress approached their table and asked for an order but Ali brushed her off; he was desperately trying to find a single woman. At midnight the lights grew dimmer. The band on stage assembled. One guy picked up a guitar, another got hold of the drums and the third stood behind a big electric piano. A blonde woman stood at the microphone.

"Are you ready?" she shouted with maximum voice.

The crowd let out a loud roar, signaling to a dance beat from the musicians. They started dancing to the beat. Jawad and Ali sat at their table observing the atmosphere around them, trying to familiarize with the moves everyone made. A man sitting next to them pulled his girlfriend to the dance floor. Two other women behind Jawad watched the crowd dancing and enjoyed their red cocktails. Ali shot a smile their way. A white guy approached one of the women and whispered something in her ear and she held his hand and joined him on the floor. The woman was in her early 50's but still had a good figure, Jawad observed. *You go to a woman and ask her to dance with you but will it get you a life-long relationship or marriage?*

Another song started playing in the background. This time it was a rock song. The dance moves became quicker. Jawad and Ali felt they could join the crowd this time. But both hesitated as none of them had any prior experience in dancing. They didn't want to make fun of themselves in front of strangers. Jawad now knew it was customary that men ask women for a dance but the mere thought of a refusal was enough to dissuade him. He also noticed Ali's brimming confidence was missing too. He just sat there and watched the atmosphere in silence.

"I'm going to get some beer," Ali spoke finally.

Both were thirsty and drank in haste. The whole ambience was alien to him. *Adjusting to it would be a hard thing to do.* Ali, though silent, kept himself busy by passing smiles at every woman who passed by. The musicians took a break for a while and switched on a recorded song.

"Are we going to sit here the whole night?" Jawad asked Ali, as he saw him looking at the women at the next table.

"I don't know. I might ask someone for a dance or I'll go and dance alone. What about you? Don't you want to ask someone?"

"No. I can't give someone a chance to laugh at me."

Although Jawad enjoyed the music in the background but the unbearable volume started to daze him a bit. He regretted being unable to reach the center at this time of the night. Ali's wait soon came to an end. He went to the table next to his where a woman was sitting alone at her table. He tried his best to be a gentleman and asked her for a dance. But the woman refused and Ali moved to the dance floor. Jawad also joined him. He asked Ali what the woman said to him.

"She is waiting for her boyfriend and didn't want to be seen with anyone else."

They danced for a while but without any female company. For them the trip to the disco was a total failure. They just couldn't do what they had come to do, not even a bit of what they had planned. It seemed they had only paid to listen to music. But Ali had not given up yet. He had a bright inviting smile on his face the whole night. At 2 am the hall was full with people smoking, dancing, drinking and flirting. Jawad wanted some more beer.

"Save your money. If you're thirsty go to the washroom and drink some water." Ali advised him. Two beers did cost ten Francs so he went to the washroom to quench his thirst. He drank until his stomach could not take any more. The hall was noisier now. Jawad needed a break and he told Ali he wanted to go out.

"Show the doorman your wrist when you want to come back."

The air outside refreshed his lungs. The roads were empty. Jawad roamed around the street. They still had at least three more hours to go until the public transport starts again. Jawad didn't have the stamina to return to the noisy disco. He sat on the nearby stairs and asked a passer-by for a cigarette. However it was cold outside. Soon he was shivering and he decided to return to the hall. Ali was not present at the table. Jawad caught him on the dance floor with his eyes shut, dancing away like a drunk. At 4 am the crowd started thinning. Jawad considered them lucky to have their own cars and wondered if he could get a free ride. *Is that all they had come for? To get hell tired and spend the next day in bed?* Jawad couldn't take it anymore. At 4:30 he told Ali they should leave.

"But there is no tram or train available yet."

"I know but I've had enough for today. We can just walk or sit somewhere."

"Wait till five," he said, catching sight of another middle aged woman.

"She might be of your mother's age Ali," Jawad taunted.

At 5 am, the music stopped and people started leaving the hall. Jawad and Ali also came out and started to walk.

"I think we'll have to wait half an hour till we get some conveyance." Ali proclaimed.

"Do you think the central station will be open?"

"I think so. Let's go and check."

The streets were busy with people leaving discos and bars. Broken bottles were strewn around the streets, thrown by drunks. There were couples sitting on benches waiting for their transport. The main cafeteria at the central station was open and some of the night birds were having coffee. Train for Oerlikon arrived at 5:30. The silence was deafening as everyone was sound asleep back at the center. After having breakfast to pacify their empty stomachs, both immediately hit the beds and slept.

Life returned to its mundane routine. Ali went back to work. The center had a new night watchman, Gabrielle. She was in her fifties, thin and tall with red hair. She resembled a school teacher. One day Ali returned from work and handed Jawad an envelope.

"This is for you."

Jawad opened it to look the contents. It was a one-month pass for the Zurich transport system. Jawad can't believe it. Such a pass costs 70 Francs.

"Why did you do that?" he asked." I don't go to the city every day and every time I go, I get the ticket from the office."

"I know but I want you to go to the city every day. Meet new people, spend time on the lake and look for work rather staying here with your books. I'm earning enough and sometimes I even get a bonus from my boss. So I won't die if I spend a little money on my friend."

Jawad stood up and hugged Ali to show his gratitude. Ali also informed him about a cafeteria where the local Pakistani community frequented. Visiting there might help him get acquainted with Pakistanis living in Zurich. It was called Café Central because it was close to the Central Square. Many Pakistani expats used to come there. Jawad decided to give it a try and one evening visited that establishment. It was a mix gathering of foreigners. The Pakistanis there did notice Jawad but nobody started a conversation with him. Most of them were busy talking about Pakistani politics. He saw Mian, whom he had met at the lake with Ali, entering the café and settled with others on a table. He also acknowledged Jawad.

"Why're you sitting there alone? Come and join us," he offered to Jawad.

Jawad took his cup of coffee and moved to their table.

"I'm sorry I've forgotten your name."

"It's Jawad Mian sahib."

"Just call me Mian, and these are my Pakistani friends Mr. Nazir, Sheikh Rizwan and Abid Khan". Then he turned to Jawad. "This is Jawad, also from Pakistan. He is a new comer," Mian introduced everyone and they shook hands. Mian ordered a cappuccino.

"Have you started working?" Rizwan asked him.

"No. You see I don't have the permission to work as yet."

"Oh yes. It's difficult to find work if you don't have a permit."

"Are you guys working?" Jawad asked.

"Yes. Nazir and Abid work in a restaurant and I'm working in a carpet shop. As far as Mr. Mian is concerned, he'll tell you himself what he's up to these days," Rizwan spoke laughingly.

"I'm on unemployment benefit these days," Mian added.

"These days my foot, you're always on unemployment benefit," Abid uttered in response. The comment made everyone laugh. They discussed the Pakistan's current ruler and the rumor that he has millions of dollars stashed away in Swiss bank accounts.

"He had stolen so much money over there and put it in to the accounts here that sometimes I feel like asking the Swiss government for my share as a Pakistani citizen."

"And what about your leader" Nazir shouted.

"What about him?"

"Where did he get the money to build all those factories? After all, his father had a scrapyard if I'm not mistaken."

"At least those factories are in Pakistan, providing jobs and revenues. He didn't take all the money abroad."

They argued for an hour over their corrupt national leaders. Being a newcomer Jawad stayed out. He didn't have anything to contribute. Mian realized his situation and ended the conversation abruptly.

"I think Jawad is getting bored."

"No, it's all right. I haven't been in touch with Pakistani politics lately but I liked your discussion. Can I ask something?"

"Yes, of course," they all shouted.

"I just want to know, once I've permission to work, where should I go for my job search. Are there any recruitment agencies that can help?"

"No, I think the best way is that you go directly to the restaurants, hotels or even at the cafeterias like this one. If someone needs a worker, they'll immediately hire you," Mian explained.

"But there may be a problem in your case," Abid intruded. "Some bosses don't like to hire asylum seekers. There is no guarantee as nobody knows how long they'll be allowed to work. My boss hired two dishwashers. Both were refugees but after two or three months their asylum application was rejected and my boss received a letter from the local police to terminate their work. He now prefers people with permanent resident permits. But still there are a lot of people like you who are working. Once you get the permission to work, let us know. We might refer you to someone."

Suddenly a short sturdy man approached Mian and handed him a letter to read.

"Look at him; they'd given him the citizenship of this country even though he doesn't understand their language properly. He can't even read a letter." Mian's remarks made that man a bit embarrassed.

The guy was a cab driver and once Mian had explained him the contents of the letter, he returned to his work. Although he was a Swiss citizen thanks to his local wife, he can't read German properly, one of the four official languages. Whenever he received a letter, he'll come there and ask someone to read it to him. The letter in his hand was related to his divorce which will allow him to remarry. On Mian's suggestion Jawad gave all of them his contact details. He had no mobile phone so he wrote the number from the office. He requested them to inform him if they found any kind of work for him. Smiling lightly, he shook hands with them and left.

Coming Monday Ali was called to the office. He didn't come back to the room but Jawad could do nothing but wait for him. He returned at midnight from work and told Jawad about his ordeal. He had been kicked out of the center. He was given 72 hours to leave with a letter of expulsion. He was told to report to the headquarters of the Asylum Organization Zurich. There he'll be transferred to another center. Ali told him that he'd a heated argument with Martin.

"Did you go to the Asylum Organization?"

"Yes I went there today, however they told me to come back tomorrow. I'll get the address of the new place but I think it would be out of the city."

"What are you going to do now?"

"Nothing, living out of Zurich is difficult for me. I can share the room with a Pakistani guy. I've spoken with him and he had consented. Sadly, we won't be able to enjoy each other's company any more. But I'll come to see you whenever it's possible."

"Yes, we'll keep in touch," Jawad stressed.

The following morning Ali packed some of his stuff in bags and the rest he left with a promise to pick up soon.

"First I'll go to the office of the Asylum Organization. I want to know where they are sending me. Tonight I'll sleep at this new place I told you. My roommate works at a restaurant and comes late just like me.

But some time I'll have to sleep at the new center just to show my presence."

"All the best," Jawad wished Ali while hugging him with sadness. His heart ached to see his only friend go. Ali left for the city while Jawad headed for the language class. Now he was alone with Hussein in the room. He felt depressed as Ali was a good friend, always kind and helpful.

Next day Jawad saw more arrivals at the center. Another family arrived from Kosovo. But they were not Muslims as Jawad saw the man wearing a cross around his neck. *This is odd. The Muslims from Kosovo are blaming the Christian Serbs for their plight. What about this family? What brought them to Switzerland? How had the executers become the victims?*

He was curious so he went to see Zavet who received him warmly and offered a cigarette.

"Have you seen the new people, this new family from Kosovo?" Jawad inquired.

"Yes. What about them?"

"I mean they are not Muslims and you told me that it's the Muslims who are in trouble because of the civil war in Kosovo," Jawad questioned.

"I spoke with them briefly and the man claims that they are from an area in which the Muslims are in majority. So it is possible that Muslims had driven them out as revenge. They could have gone to Serbia but I don't think they would have been treated there as good as they are being treated here. They made a smart move. In Serbia they might have been living in a shanty village with no future. But if their asylum application is accepted here, you can imagine how good it'll be for them," Zavet summed up his thoughts.

Jawad got the answer to his question. It seemed strange that the people, who were not willing to tolerate one another's existence in the country where they had lived for centuries, were living together under the same roof in a Swiss asylum center. It's true that necessity is the mother of invention. But in Switzerland these people had learnt what they failed to do in their native lands. Live and let live, although here it was on someone else's expense.

After one week Ali came to pick up his belongings. He seemed alright and was carrying a mobile phone which he had acquired recently.

"Where did they move you?" Jawad asked him immediately.

"To Bulach, it's a small town out of Zurich. The good thing is there are no language classes, no house meetings." A beep on his phone interrupted their conversation. Afterward Ali started collecting his belongings as he was in a hurry. He wrote his number on a piece of paper and handed it to Jawad.

"Don't forget to call," Ali stressed before leaving.

"I will, don't worry."

Jawad was indebted to Ali and felt sad seeing him go but he was happy for him at the same time. Ali was earning much needed money and for that he required freedom. Here he was always sought after. From Ali's account he found out that every asylum center in the country had its own set of rules.

In the coming days he had a very strange experience. One day he went to visit the Museum Park. He relaxed on a wooden bench; he didn't notice the police car that passed him neither the policeman watching him closely. They reversed the car and stopped where Jawad sat. One of them politely spoke up: "*Ihre Ausweis bitte?*" asking him for his ID. Jawad took out his wallet and showed his ID. The couple sitting next to his bench got up and walked away. The policeman sent a message on his wireless.

"What's in your bag?"

"Nothing special," Jawad replied.

"I want you to empty your bag and put everything on this bench. Put your wallet on it too."

Jawad had no choice but to do what he was asked. People around watched him with suspicion. The cop thoroughly searched him after wearing his gloves. He reached inside Jawad's pockets looking for something. The other policeman on the wireless verified Jawad's ID and then both left without a word once they were satisfied. Jawad didn't know what to do and sat down, dazed. Gathering his courage, he headed towards the Central, to go to the café where no one would stare at him. Abid, one of the guys Mian introduced him, was sitting there with another man and invited Jawad to his table. Jawad joined them, ordered a coke but could not hide the anger on his face.

"Are you alright?" Abid asked.

"No, I'm not."

"What happened?"

"I've just been subjected to a police search. I was in the park nearby when a police car came and checked me. They searched my whole body and my bag. Everyone in the park started staring at me. I've never felt so humiliated in my life. They searched me like I was a criminal."

"There is no need to be so upset, Jawad. The police have a right to check anyone they consider suspicious. It's a matter of routine. I had a far worse experience than yours. Once, while I was having lunch at a restaurant at central station, two men in civil clothes approached me. They identified themselves as detectives from the city police and asked for my ID. Can you imagine? The place was full of people busy having lunch. Everybody started watching me. They searched me and then left. I simply paid the bill and left as well. What could one do, this is not our country."

"That's unbelievable," Jawad reacted.

"Don't worry my friend. This is one of the many prices we've to pay for living abroad," consoled Abid's friend.

Next day a Kurdish family arrived from Iraq. Hussein served as the translator as they spoke Arabic. There were eight children in all with very little age difference. It might have taken no more than 12 years for the couple to complete their herd. Hussein carried their stuff to their assigned rooms. He returned after two hours, laughing away.

"Eight children, oh my god! There are no more rooms available. I told Natasha that the couple should sleep separately otherwise they would be nine within no time."

"They should give them the T.V. room. That's the only room with enough space for the whole family," Jawad commented.

"That is a good idea. No more language class then."

"Go down and tell Natasha."

"No, you go and tell her."

They both laughed as they knew none of them was going to do that.

"Next month I have to look for work," Hussein told Jawad after they shared a meal.

"How long you've been here?"

"Four and a half months. I was in another center before. One should start searching for a job after five months because it might take a while to find one. I'll get a letter from the office regarding my work permit," Hussein explained.

It was Jawad's fourth month which meant he could also start looking for work by the end of the next month.

"What do you plan to do for your job search? I mean where will you go?" Jawad was curious

"I would look for a job in the city. Lots of hotels and restaurants are there."

Martin interrupted their conversation and told Jawad that there was a phone call for him. Jawad was surprised. Hesitantly he held the phone to his ear.

"Hello?"

"Is this Jawad?" someone asked on the other side.

"Yes, who is there?"

"This is Sheikh Rizwan, we met at Café Central. I want to talk to you about something. Call me when it's safe to talk."

"What's it about?"

"It's about some work."

Jawad knew it was not wise to ask further questions with Martin around. He wrote down the number and went to the phone booth to call Rizwan back.

"Rizwan, this is Jawad."

"Hello Jawad. I've some work for you. I'm employed at a carpet shop and on Saturday, we're having a big sale. Could you come to work then? I've spoken to my boss and he has agreed to hire you for the day. And maybe you can work some other days as well."

"Okay, but where shall I come on Saturday?"

"It's easy. Go to Oerlikon train station and take the train for Regensdorf. Ask anyone at the station about the big shopping center. It is a 10-minute walk. Once inside, come to the basement and you'll see a big carpet shop at the far end. Be there at 8 am." Rizwan spoke brief but sound.

"I'll be there. Thanks a lot," Jawad replied.

On Saturday morning, Jawad made his way to Regensdorf as Rizwan had directed. Once outside the train station, he spotted a cab driver standing next to his car.

"Could you tell me where the shopping center is?" Jawad asked him.

"Take the first right and then the second left. You can't miss it"

The shopping center was in the middle of a park. There was a big revolving gate in the front. Once inside he took the escalators going down. Soon he saw a big shop with carpets hanging in the windows. There were placards all over the window with huge signs and prices, indicating that there was a big sale on this morning. There were still 5 minutes to 8 am. Jawad knocked on the glass door, and soon a man opened up and let him in. He was middle aged, wearing blue jeans and a black sweatshirt.

"Hi, I'm here for work. Rizwan asked me to come in today."

"Yes, I know, my name is Hikmat. I own the store. Rizwan will be here any minute now." Hikmat shook hands with Jawad.

"Would you like a cup of coffee?"

"That would be nice." Jawad was glad due to Hikmat's friendliness.

He took him to the back of the shop. It had a built-in room used as an office. It was full with office appliances. Hikmat pressed the button of coffee machine. Soon Rizwan made his way into the office. He greeted both of them and also made a cup of coffee. Then he gave Jawad a run down about the work.

"Let me explain what you have to do. First, you'll clean the shop with the vacuum cleaner. In the meantime, the boss and I would change the carpets on the wall racks from the previous day. We've advertised in the newspaper and mailed out brochures around the whole area, so we are expecting a huge customers turn out. You'll show them the carpets. Sometimes a customer wants a carpet, which is beneath the others, so we've to pull out that particular out. There are trolleys at the counter and if a customer needs help for taking the stuff to the parking, that will be your job."

Jawad nodded. He went to the office, took the vacuum cleaner and started cleaning the shop. He saw Hikmat and Rizwan place the ladders on each side of a big carpet hung on the wall and brought it down. They held both corners of the new carpet and climbed up the ladder until the carpet was covering the entire wall. They then fixed the catchers and put new price tags on the bright red carpet.

"How do I clean the glass door?" Jawad had no idea so he asked them.

"You can use these tissue papers," Rizwan pointed.

He took a couple of tissue papers from the box on the table, sprayed the door with a cleaning liquid and wiped both sides of the glass. It was almost nine when a couple entered the shop with a brochure in their hands and Hikmat attended to them immediately. Rizwan took the ladder and told Jawad to pull out the carpet that the customers had pointed to. He climbed the ladder, freed the carpet from both ends, and let it fall gently to the floor. Rizwan helped him to spread it over the wooden floor for the couple to have a look and feel the material. They agreed to buy it and Hikmat went to the cash register for the payment. Jawad took the carpet and went to the parking lot with the customers. The man opened the trunk and Jawad carefully put the carpet inside.

"Wait," the man stopped him as he turned to leave.

He put a 5 Franc coin in Jawad's hand. Jawad bowed courteously and returned to the shop. The tip was almost half of his daily budget.

"Did they give you something?" Rizwan inquired.

"Yes, they gave me five Francs."

"That's good. I told them you are a student to get their sympathies. I was expecting more but five is not bad either. I hope there'll be more and in the end we can split the money between us"

"What about the boss?"

"Oh no, he is the owner. He doesn't need tips."

On the back of every carpet there was a sticker mentioning the size, origin and the price. They came from different countries like, Turkey,

Iran, Afghanistan and China. The handmade carpets were the most expensive. It was a busy morning and by eleven Jawad had 20 Francs in tips. Some customers came with brochures in their hands. They were easy to serve, as they had already made the choice and wanted a specific carpet. Jawad and Rizwan would roll out the carpet for them, while Hikmat did the sales talk, exaggerating carpet's finer points. Some customers wanted something special, something rare. Jawad did not know how many carpets they had sold and how much money the owner had made. All he knew was that he had to work till four in the afternoon, get his money, split the tips with Rizwan and go home. At 2 pm, Hikmat ordered pizzas for them, which were delivered within 10 minutes and they shared them. At 4 pm, they organized the shop and arranged the carpets lying around. Hikmat went to the cash register while Jawad went to the office. Rizwan offered him a glass of water. Jawad knew what he was expecting so he took out the money from his pockets and counted.

"How much did you make?" Rizwan questioned to him.

"78 Francs," Jawad replied.

"I was thinking about something like 100 Francs, but still it is not bad. Customers gave it even though they didn't have to. Okay, you can keep 40 Francs and I'll take the rest."

It was a fair deal.

"Wait here; let me get your money."

Rizwan put his share in his wallet and went out while Jawad stayed in the office.

"Here, these are 80 Francs for your work."

Jawad had earned 120 Francs for eight hours of work. That was not bad at all.

"Can I go now or there is something else to do?"

"No, everything is all right."

He was asked to come every Saturday till the special sale runs. Jawad shook hands with both and thanked them warmly. He was dead tired. Manual work didn't come naturally to him. He had never imagined pulling down large carpets, rolling them and taking them out to the parking lot.

On Monday after language class, Martin called John Paul in to his office. He looked dejected when he returned to his room with a letter in his hand. The envelope had red stripes on it. A letter like that was considered ominous. Soon the news was out. The authorities had rejected his asylum application. Hussein also asked Jawad about the matter. A rejection, Jawad realized, was like a severe sentence for a refugee. He went to see John Paul. Stephen and Mumba were also present in the room.

"I heard about your rejection letter."

"Yes." John Paul didn't seem worried.

"But you have a right to appeal against the decision."

"Yes but I'm not going to do that."

"What do you mean by that? You're not going to make an appeal?"

"Tell me, are you busy this Saturday?" John Paul asked him, changing the subject

"No, I guess not, but why?" Jawad had not told anybody about his work.

"I'm getting married this Saturday."

"Well, that's a real surprise. Where is all this taking place?"

"Not in Zurich. My fiancée is from Horgen and we are getting married there. They can stick this letter!"

"My god, you had this planned out all the time, Congratulations." Jawad was surprised.

"Thank you."

Since Jawad and Hussein shared a room, over time they became close to one and other. It was a strange relationship though, because Hussein prayed regularly and was often reciting the Quran. He was also disconcerted about Jawad's drinking habit. One day Jawad suggested a trip to the market square. The square was not far from the center. Shops and restaurants of all sorts surrounded it. There was a big chessboard drawn on the floor with wooden pawns and pieces. Jawad didn't know how to play chess but he was interested in watching.

"Do you know how to play chess?" he asked Hussein.

"No, it's forbidden in Islam." There was something in his attitude which showed that he despised those people.

"Tell me something Hussein. Isn't alcohol forbidden too?"

"Yes, that is why I never drink it."

"I'm sure that the people who are playing chess right here also take a drink. So if I accept your argument, then this is a country of bad people who drink alcohol and play forbidden games."

"No, I did not mean that these are bad people. What I mean is that as a Muslim I'm not allowed to drink alcohol and play chess."

"Then why did you come to this country, where the people drink alcohol and play chess. In addition, they do other *haram* things as well. Is it allowed to live on the money of people who do all these things that are forbidden in Islam?"

"What do you mean living on the money of these people?

"Come on. The money spent on us belongs to the Swiss people. It's their tax money. Of course, you know that. Why didn't you go to a place where people weren't involved in *haram* things?"

"What do you suggest then?"

"I'm not saying you should become un-Islamic or anything. All I ask you is not to consider these people inferior because of their culture or their beliefs. After all, they are helping us. Now, if you don't mind, I'm going to buy myself a beer."

Soon he was back sipping from a Heineken.

"You spoke to John Paul? Did he tell you about his wedding this weekend?" Hussein spoke after a long silence.

"Yes he did."

"He told me he was going to invite us to the wedding as he doesn't have many friends."

"Do you want to go?" Jawad asked.

"I'm not sure. You see, it'll cost too much money. A train ticket plus you're not expected to go to a wedding empty handed."

"What excuse will you give then?"

"I've only known him for a few weeks. I'm sure he'll understand."

"I don't think I can go either." Jawad did not mention the work on Saturday.

Later, Jawad went to Zavet to get some cigarettes who gladly gave him a full packet. He had always plenty.

"Hey man, did you find a girl?" Zavet asked him.

"Not yet. What about you?"

"I've my sweetheart back in Pristina. She calls me some time. I plan to marry her once we get our freedom."

"What if you don't get your freedom?"

"Then we'll wait. But I'm sure we are very close."

"I see. I'll catch with you later. I've to make a call, thanks for the cigarettes." Jawad left afterward. He went to the phone both to call his family. Lately his contact with them had been a phone call once a week. It was expensive to call to Pakistan for a person of his resources. He always gave them satisfactory answers to their questions. No body made any demands, as they knew he was learning the language before he gets a job. His folks had been mostly worried about his wellbeing. He never called any of his friends or even Ahmad due to lack of money.

On Friday evening, he met Sonia at the stairs as she was coming in accompanied by a Kosovan family. They exchanged greetings and went inside.

"There is something I would like to tell you," she spoke before going to office.

"Go ahead I'm listening."

"I've found a new job."

What sort of a job is that?" Jawad pretended to be happy for her.

"It's at an orphanage close to where I live. Last week I had an interview and today I received the confirmation letter. It is related to my studies and I'm so glad that I've been selected."

"Congratulations," he tried to smile.

"Thanks. By the way, have you been to the Longstreet festival?"

"Which festival, I had no idea that there is a festival in town?"

"It's called *Langstrassefest*. It is celebrated once a year."

To Jawad *Langstrasse* was a district of Zurich where prostitutes and drug dealers plied their trade. He had never heard of a festival connected to it.

"How long does this festival last?"

"It's on till Sunday evening. I intend to go there tomorrow evening."

"Is it possible that I can also come with you?" he asked tentatively.

"Oh yes, of course. I'm working till tomorrow evening so we can go together."

They both agreed to leave at six in the evening.

Jawad was working next day, which meant he would be tired by the end of the day. But he didn't want to miss an opportunity to be with her at the festival. Jawad spent the whole day at work thinking about the time he would spend with Sonia. The work at the carpet shop was the same but this time he made 130 Francs altogether. Hikmat was also happy as they sold more than the last Saturday. Jawad was tired from work. Back home, he relaxed a little then went for a hot bath which improved his condition. At six, Sonia came out of her office and Gabi, the other night supervisor, took over the charge.

"How was your day?" she asked him while they walked to the bus stop.

"Good, I visited Ali and we had lunch together. What about you?"

"Boring, but I studied most of the time. I saw Mumba and Stephen going to the wedding."

"Oh yes, did they ask about me?"

"No. They were too busy looking for a camera to take wedding pictures. We have a Polaroid in the office but it's not good for a wedding. I told them to go to any kiosk and buy a disposable camera. "

They boarded the bus, which was already full of passengers, presumably going to the festival as well. Soon they were at the festival. It was still daylight and the place was crowded.

"Let's go and sit somewhere."

They went to a built-in bar.

"What would you like to drink?"

"Some white wine?"

Jawad ordered two glasses of Aigle. As he took out his wallet to pay Sonia stopped him and paid for the drinks. Jawad felt a shiver run through his body as her hand touched his. Sonia wrapped her hands around the glass, which was as cold as the liquid inside. They sat silently, enjoying the drink and savoring the atmosphere.

"The next drink is on me," he told her while throwing the plastic glasses in the bin.

The area around them was buzzing with people having a good time. They got up and made their way towards the center of the festivities. It was hard to walk at a steady pace. He wanted to hold her hand but was afraid that she might not be willing. Food stalls were set up all around the place selling Chinese, Thai, Caribbean, Swiss and all sorts of cuisine from around the world. A handicraft shop caught Sonia's attention. She checked out handmade clothes probably made in Africa. Jawad saw people hanging around and getting drunk even before the evening had properly started.

He was more interested in Sonia than the festival. She seemed interested in handicrafts and the colorful clothing displayed on the stalls. She would look at an item and feel the texture with her finger wondering where it had come from and how it was prepared. The festival was a source of inspiration and knowledge for her, Jawad thought. He found a drinks stall and asked her what she would like.

"Wine is ok."

"I want to try something new. What would you recommend?" Jawad asked her.

She looked at the list with the prices of different drinks.

"Try gin with tonic. I'm sure you would like that."

The drinks worked as an appetizer and he soon felt hungry. At noon, he ate pizza at work. However, he wondered if he could afford to pay for an expensive dinner. He looked at Sonia and thought that the mere fact that she was born in Switzerland meant her life was free of basic problems; people like Jawad were inundated with. She was earning, studying and living a respectable life. Her worries might only consist of where to spend her free time or which country to go for her summer holidays. On the other hand, Jawad didn't even know where he would be living or what he might be doing in years to come. He could be stateless for years, moving from one country to another until he gets an opportunity to settle somewhere.

They continued wandering around and enjoying the atmosphere, and soon reached at the end of the street. There was a huge platform with a live band playing and lights flashing. The music was loud and hundreds of young people were dancing to their hearts content.

"Let's go to Kaserne Park. We can come back here later."

They crossed the street and walked towards the park opposite. Jawad had never been there before, and the scene there was like another dimension of the festival. Along with people of almost every ethnic origin, there were stalls selling every conceivable thing from all around the world. The music was as loud as it could get. The place was suffocating because of the huge crowd. On Jawad's proposal, they sat on the grass like many other people around them. The sky was as clear and there was a slight breeze.

"This is the most colorful festival I've ever seen in my life," Jawad confessed.

"You should wait till August."

"What happens in August?"

"Zurich had been holding one of the biggest street parties in the world for the last couple of years. It's on the second Saturday of every August, over at the lake area. People from all around the world come to see it."

"Is it like a carnival?"

"You can call it that. They expect one million people to attend this year. There are street discos, massive parades and huge musical events. It is something you'll never forget."

"To you, this festival must be nothing compared to that."

"No, this one has its own attraction. It's very multicultural and you get a glimpse of Zurich's diversity. Did you see that most of the people who own the stalls are foreigners; they are living, working and enjoying life in Switzerland."

"True, could we go back to that open disco? I found that place much more interesting," Jawad proposed.

"Ok, let's go."

Jawad stood up and put forward his hand to Sonia. She held his hand and stood up. He saw a rare brightness in Sonia's eyes as she started swaying to the music. She knew the lyrics of that song and started lip-syncing. Rather than live band, there was a DJ on stage. He held the mike and shouted: "Put your hands in the air if you love this music."

The crowd roared and danced to the new song. Together they joined the crowd. Sonia started dancing with her bag bouncing on her shoulder. The music picked up. Jawad felt overjoyed due to dancing with Sonia, something he could hardly have imagined just a few days ago. Jawad decided to hold her hand as the couples around them did. The DJ knew exactly when to slow the music down so that people could relax a little. When the music switched to a romantic beat, Jawad took Sonia's hand and delicately placed it on his shoulder. He felt relieved that she did not reject his gesture. Jawad placed his hand on her waist and they both swayed to the music. It was the first time that he ever danced with a girl. He was on cloud nine; her smile made him want to freeze the moment in time. He wanted to hold her close and engulf himself with her beauty. Their bodies touched. His heartbeat was faster than it had ever been and Sonia's presence in his arms made him tremble. He didn't want this moment to end. After dancing for a while, they sat down on an empty bench. The man from the nearby bar came over.

"Do you want some beer?"

"Are they cold?" Sonia asked.

She touched the bottles to make sure beer was cold and asked him for two. When Jawad tried to pay, she said, "There is no need for that. This one is on me."

She paid the man and handed one beer to Jawad.

"I'm tired but still I enjoyed it," she spoke, referring to the dance.

"Me too, As a matter of fact this is the most fun I've had since I moved here."

"Jawad, tell me what do you plan to do in future?" he was surprised at her question as it was an entirely different subject.

"I'm waiting to get a work permit and then I can start job hunt. Therefore, if I get lucky, I'll be working as a dishwasher in the coming months. However, I don't mind. Any job is better than sitting idle all day."

"Dishwashers are also human beings and there's no shame in that. But you're an educated person who likes reading, so you may find it harder than others to wash dishes and clean floors."

"I know that will be a big blow to my aesthetic sense but I'm ready to do anything right now. What about your studies?"

"They are going fine. Once finished with my studies, I would like to go on a world tour. Then I'll come back and look for a job."

Jawad realized she had no room for him on her trip. However, he felt a difference in Sonia's speech; she was one of those people who become vulnerable even with small quantities of alcohol. She would suddenly pause in the middle of the conversation, stammer and then rephrase her sentence. Jawad felt fine but he could not control his hunger. At the first opportunity, he confessed that.

"I'm hungry, what about you?"

"Yeah, me too either. I've got an idea. My room is only three bus stops away from here. Why don't we go and dine at my place? I'd eaten a couple of times at your place so why don't we do the opposite today?"

How could he deny such an offer? They took a bus and soon reached her apartment. There was no lift so they walked up the stairs to the third floor to her room. The stairs were so quiet that Jawad could hear the echo of their footsteps. She unlocked her door and invited him in. She switched on the lights and both took off the shoes. The room was large enough with an in-built kitchen. Opposite to the kitchen was the toilet with a shower. On one side was the bed neighboring a wooden bookshelf with a television and a computer. She had a two-seat sofa. Sonia went to freshen up and asked Jawad to sit. When she came out, Jawad went to the toilet. He looked at his reflection in the mirror and felt lucky to be there. Suddenly, out of curiosity, he opened the mirror cabinet very softly, knowing he was doing something immoral. There was a blue perfume bottle and an array of lotions. However, one distinct item caught his eyes. It was a small red-colored packet. Jawad opened it and saw two unused condoms. Perhaps, leftover of a love that was once there but now gone. He put the packet back in its place and closed the cabinet softly. He came out of the washroom and sat on the sofa. She switched on the TV and stopped at a documentary channel. Jawad liked the program so she didn't change the channel.

"I need to change my clothes," she said.

She went to the washroom and returned wearing a black tracksuit. Her white skin was in contrast with the black dress, which added to her beauty. He was mesmerized; yet he remained silent. He didn't want to ogle at her and make her feel uncomfortable.

"What would you like to eat?" Sonia asked like a good host.

"Anything will do, except pork."

"I don't have it anyway. I think I'll make some seafood risotto. It's easy to prepare. As far as the taste is concerned, you may judge it yourself. Would you like some wine?"

"I wouldn't mind some."

"Sure."

She opened the cupboard and pulled out a bottle of red wine. She also opened the door to the balcony to let in some fresh air. Jawad went to the balcony to catch a view of the street below. From the balcony he watched her making dinner.

"Jawad, why don't you pour some wine?"

He felt the sweetness with which she called his name out.

"You see the wine needs fresh air to improve its taste."

Jawad poured the wine in her glass. His intention was to fill the glass but she stopped him.

"First just a little, to try," she picked up the glass and tasted it.

"It's good, very good actually."

Jawad poured her some more. She went back to the kitchen to stir the food and returned.

"The weather is really nice outside and it'll be great to have dinner on the balcony."

"Yes, we can dine there," she consented gladly.

There were two chairs and a small table in the balcony. Sonia checked the risotto on the stove. She prepared two plates of salad and handed Jawad some bread to cut. He sliced the bread in equal size while she mixed olive oil and vinegar to make a dressing.

"I prefer homemade dressing."

While she placed the bread in the basket, Jawad arranged the chairs on the balcony. Soon the table was ready.

"*Bon appétit.*"

"*Bon appétit,*" he responded while tasting the salad.

"I like your home made salad dressing."

"Thank you," she smiled while emptying her wine glass.

Wine was good and after finishing his second glass of wine, he felt really relaxed. He didn't want to leave. All he wanted to do was to sit there and watch her. He watched her playing with her long beautiful hairs. Jawad imagined her ex-boyfriend must have sat at the very place. How he might have caressed her after dinner. They might have danced, kissed and made love. Jawad tried to stop his thoughts from going too far. He wasn't her boyfriend and he had already acted out of character by looking in her cabinet. Sonia got up and removed the empty salad plates. She prepared two more plates with risotto and returned to the balcony. Jawad noticed a distinct redness in her eyes. The effects of the wine were becoming apparent. She seemed to be having problems maintaining her balance. May be Shakespeare was right when he said that true character comes out when one drinks a lot.

Knowing that it'll be discourteous to leave immediately after dinner, he kept talking to her even though she seemed to be having difficulty keeping up with the conversation. She picked up her wine glass and went to sit on the sofa inside.

Jawad had better control over his body; he didn't let wine distract him from these precious moments. When he went and sat next to her, she did not object. Their bodies were almost touching. She switched the channel to MTV, leant back and closed her eyes.

"Are you tired?"

"Not really. I feel strange; it's the drinks I think," she said opening her eyes briefly. They were red. Jawad didn't want to leave her alone in that condition. In addition, he realized that he would probably never be in this situation with Sonia again. There was nothing more in this world that he wanted than to lie beside her and feel her warm body next to his. He knew it was now or never. He put his arm around her tentatively, and to his utter relief, she did not twitch. He softly caressed her shoulder and she moved closer to him. The wine seemed to have expended the usual energy from her mind and body. She was almost motionless and for a few moments, Jawad had control over her. Wanting to make love to her for just once in his life, her lack of reaction to his advances encouraged him to go further. He kissed her softly on the neck; when he looked at her, he sensed there was a subtle invitation in her eyes. He kissed her on the lips. He felt his own body shivering. It was the first time that he kissed a girl. He never imagined that his first kiss would come from a beautiful Swiss girl. Life had been full of surprises lately. He quickly removed his lips out of fear of her disapproval, but just as he pulled away, she cooed softly, "Oh la la!"

He kissed her again and this time she kissed him back. Then just as suddenly, she pulled away and stood up.

"I've to go to the washroom."

When she returned, she had something in her hands which she placed on her side table. It was the pack of condoms. She was careful even when drunk. Jawad stood up, removed his shirt and joined her on the bed. She welcomed him. The formalities they had a few moments ago, were gone once they removed their clothes. It took Jawad twenty minutes of intensive lovemaking to lose his lifelong virginity. Afterwards, she just rolled over and lay on her side, lost in deep thought with her eyes partly open. Jawad had no idea what to do now. This was all unfamiliar territory for him.

"I think it's getting late and I better leave now," he mumbled.

"Okay, I'll lock the door later," she said without getting up.

Jawad unlocked the door very quietly and took the stairs down. He wondered if this was a once only encounter, or a prelude to long-term relationship. *Would she change her mind and accept me as her new partner in life?* This morning he didn't have the slightest inkling that the day would end with a dream coming true.

Jawad was afraid to think that everything that had happened was without any meaning or substance; deep down in his heart he knew this all would have strong repercussions in the coming days. Sonia might come over to the center tomorrow and scream at him, or she might just call and talk things over.

He didn't have to wait for very long. Two days later Martin handed him a letter. He knew it was from Sonia. He wanted to read it without any disturbance. But he couldn't find a place where he could sit alone without being disturbed. He went to a nearby street corner with a beautiful water fountain. He sat on one of the benches and took out the letter from his jacket. The place was quiet; there was no one around. With trembling hands, he opened it. The letter was hand written. He had no idea what it might say.

Dear Jawad.

It is with regret and mixed emotions that I'm writing this letter. I could not wait to see you again and there were things, which I wanted to express immediately. First, I thought of calling but could not find the strength to do so. All that happened between us the other evening was a big mistake. I think that the festive atmosphere and the drinks carried me away. The thing, which I regret the most, is not merely the shamefulness of being carried away but the fact that it might give way to false hopes and expectations in your mind.

You are a lovely human being and I respect you very much. I was already sorry that I had hurt you because I realized that my denial meant a lot to you. My encounters with you in the last few days were just to show that I had no hard feelings against you, but I was not ready for another relationship. I didn't want to be torn between the lover and the love I had just left behind. The mere thought that you might think that I used you for an evening's pleasure is hurting me the most. Please forgive me for everything that happened and I do hope you'll keep this matter a secret.

Sincerely,
Sonia Laibacher

P.S: As I told you that I'm only working at the Center until the end of month, will you be kind enough to return my library card?

Jawad finished reading the letter with a heavy heart. She had explained herself well. Jawad realized that her heart was more sensitive than he had previously thought. Her intention to keep the whole matter secret was fair. He should write to her and console her, to assure her that he would keep their brief affair a secret. If she had not wasted time in expressing herself, he'll do the same. He decided to write the letter in the library where he could concentrate. He took his notebook, went to the corner cabin and sat down. He read her letter again and closed his eyes for a moment. Once he had made up his mind, he began to write.

My dear Sonia,

Please do not feel bad for what happened the other evening. I respect you and I know things slipped out of hands that evening. For me it is satisfactory that I surrendered my body to the person, whom I had already surrendered my heart to. I think the pleasant evening, the festival, the music, the food and the drinks led things to that end, and there is nothing to regret or feel guilty about. So don't worry, discretion on my part is guaranteed because there is no point in telling others about something which was intensely personal and private between us. I think no further discussion about this matter is necessary and I hope we can continue to be the friends that we used to be.

Sincerely,
Mohammad Jawad

P.S. I'll return your library card without owing any books before you leave the job.

He re-read the letter, picked up his bag, and went to the post office. After posting the letter his heart felt better. He went back to the library and watched a movie to distract himself from the thoughts that engulfed him.

The following day Hussein showed Jawad a letter of recommendation for his job search. The letter was issued a month earlier so he could start his job hunt. They went to the city together because Hussein wanted to see a certain Mr. Markus at the Asylum Organization. Mr. Markus was responsible for the placement of refugees and to help them in their job hunt. It was a crowded building in downtown Zurich and it was crammed with refugees who needed help. They found Mr. Markus who, after a brief interview, copied all of Hussein's credentials. Markus told him to be patient; he also promised to get in touch in case of a vacancy.

"You know Jawad, I'm fed up here," Hussein proclaimed once they were out.

"What do you mean that you're fed up? You've hardly been here a few months."

"Back home I had a small business of my own. I worked as an electrician. I knew some relatives who were abroad and earning much better than I did. I wished to earn some money and return so I could expand my business and employ people. I sold everything and even borrowed some money from my relatives. God knows what I went through to get to Switzerland. I'm sure you've heard plenty of horror stories around here. Crossing jungles and starving for days."

Hussein's story reminded him of Khan whom he had met when he arrived in Kreuzlingen. Jawad considered himself lucky to have flown in directly with a visa on his passport. He realized that not everyone was so lucky.

"Don't feel so bad, things will change Hussein. You'll see."

"Thanks for your encouragement but things aren't easy. I pray to God that if I can just earn the money I spent to come to here, I won't complain even if they send me back," Hussein spoke disconsolately.

Later that day, Hussein went to see Martin in the office and when he returned he looked worried.

"What's the matter?" asked Jawad.

"Martin just told me that this morning police took Zavet away."

"But why, what might have he done, he can't even walk properly?"

"I don't know, but police told Martin that they were taking him for questioning."

"I'm shocked," said Jawad.

That day Jawad saw Mian in Café Central, coming with someone he had never seen before. They entered and came straight to Jawad's table. Mian introduced his new friend.

"Jawad, this is Mr. Jatinder Singh from India. He also lives in the Oerlikon area."

Singh warmly shook hands with Jawad. He was a short but well-built man in his late 20s. His skin was darker than Jawad's. Unlike other people of the Sikh faith, he was not wearing a turban and no beard either. However, he did wear the metal *karra* on his wrist.

"You want to drink something?" Mian asked to him but Jawad replied that he was fine.

"What's the progress?" Mian asked.

"Soon I'll have my work permission and then I'll try to find a job."

"What about the other thing?"

"What other thing?"

"Did you find anybody?" Mian asked with a wink.

Jawad smiled but didn't answer.

"Keep trying, you'll succeed someday. You should also go to the lake to try your luck with the women there. Mr. Singh had also tried there but with success. Am I right, Mr. Singh?"

"Shut up you." Singh said with a smile.

"Where do you live in Oerlikon?" Singh asked Jawad.

"I live in an asylum center."

"Where is it exactly?"

Jawad explained the address.

Jatinder Singh was an auto-mechanic who had finished his work early that day because of his appointment with the doctor. Jawad smiled that though India and Pakistan were always at each other's throats, here in Switzerland, they were talking like close friends. The fact that they were living in a distant land had brought them together.

"It's getting late, I've to buy some supplies," apologized Mian after finishing his Espresso and left.

"Are you going to Oerlikon?" Singh asked Jawad.

"Yes?"

"I can drop you. I'm also going that way."

Jawad was grateful for a free ride and jumped into Singh's blue Volvo. They spoke about some mundane things, as it was their first meeting.

"Jawad, do you have something important to attend to?" suddenly Singh asked him on the way.

"No, why did you ask?"

"Actually I'm alone this evening as my wife has gone to see her parents. Why don't you come over to my place and after dinner I'll drop you off at your place?"

"That's very kind of you." Jawad realized that Singh was inviting him to kill the boredom. But a denial could be impolite. They spoke same language and belonged to a similar culture. Singh has a flat with three rooms, newly carpeted and clean. At the entrance, they removed their shoes and put the spare slippers on. On the lounge wall there were various religious icons belonging to the Sikh faith.

"We should not forget our roots, no matter where we go," he told Jawad who was looking at the icons. Singh guided Jawad to the TV lounge and left. Then he returned after changing his clothes and placed a DVD in the player and soon the room was alive with Bollywood music.

"That's the picture of my wedding day," Singh told him pointing to a portrait hanging above the TV. Jawad looked the picture keenly while Singh went to the kitchen. His partner though seemed of same age, was almost a double in weight. However, she had an innocent face, quite similar to Singh's, which probably meant harmony in their married life.

"What should I cook; actually I'm not a vegetarian?" Singh confessed

"There is no need to worry, anything will do. Can I help?"

"No, you're my guest. By the way, do you drink?"

"Like a fish." Jawad responded laughingly.

In an hour, Singh brought freshly cooked rice with shrimps curry and a bottle of red wine. Over dinner, Singh narrated his journey from India to Switzerland. He worked as an auto-mechanic in Dubai for five years but he always wanted to settle in Europe or America. His older brother had settled in France many years ago. With the help of his brother and the money he saved, he managed to get a visa for France. However later he decided to leave France and came to Switzerland and asked for political asylum. After nine months, he received his rejection letter. He had worked for only three months. Luckily, a friend offered him a place in his room without rent. Then he met his future wife, Stephanie at the lake one day. She was trying out her new camera and Singh offered to take her photo. They gradually started talking. She had been to India and loved the food and culture. Singh thought inviting her over for dinner might be a useful idea. After many spicy curries and biryanis, with suitable wines, Singh moved into her apartment and her life. Six months later, they got married. Jawad liked Singh's open and friendly attitude. There was nothing pretentious about him. He felt at ease listening to him. He showed him the picture of his family back in India. Like Perucci, Singh too was easy to befriend. And Jawad knew they'll be just that in the future. Jawad realized it was getting late so he asked for permission to leave.

"No problem. I'll drop you," Singh got up and both came out of the house.

They exchanged contact details for further interactions. Back at the center Jawad went straight to Zavet's room. He was sitting on the chair with his leg straightened on the small table. Mehmet was busy reading some Albanian newspaper. Zavet smiled sheepishly when Jawad asked him why the police took him.

"They said that I was collecting money from the Kosovans for my organization. They told me I can't use my stay here for collecting funds to support the war back home."

"What did you say?"

"I denied everything."

"What are they going to do now?"

"I don't know, they have warned me not to break the law."

"You didn't break the law, did you Zavet?" Jawad asked him smilingly.

"Never, just my leg only," laughed Zavet. Jawad realized Zavet was not telling the truth.

He asked Jawad to help himself to a drink. Jawad declined and left for his room after a little. They were not friends but somehow Jawad felt attached to him. Zavet was courageous and smart. Jawad realized that his phase of life was confusing regarding relationship. People may come in his life and for a time being they'll be very important. However, they may also disappear suddenly, never to meet again. There was no need to be worried. Only thing permanent was his family. Other people may come and go during the course of life but that's the way life is. He had no contact with his friends back in Pakistan or even Ahmad. He might see those people again or he may not. Life is like a stage, people come and play their parts and go behind the curtain. He remembered the divine words of Shakespeare, that world is a stage and people are mere the actors.

———————

Winter was around the corner and it had already started to rain constantly. Jawad had phoned Nasir to send his clothes but he advised Jawad to find a private address. Nasir was very busy and had no time to visit him. Jawad desperately needed to get a full time job. He would visit the café every other day to inquire if there was a vacancy anywhere, but there were none. One day, while it was drizzling, he decided to visit the library. The temperature had gone below ten. While waiting for the bus, he saw an elegant elderly woman standing under the shed. She noticed Jawad move to the corner of the shed to avoid the rain and cold. She came over to him.

"You should wear enough clothes young man, it is very cold," she spoke like a mother.

"Yes I know." Jawad.

"Do you live at that house for refugees?"

"Yes, for the last few months."

"Are you from India?"

"No. I'm from Pakistan actually."

"You could catch cold you know. You really need to be careful." She offered motherly advice. Just then, the bus came and they both went their separate ways. When he returned to the center later in the evening, he saw a note on his door. It was a message from Muller, requesting him to come to the office. He went immediately.

"It was on my door," he said showing him the message. "I was at the library."

"Someone left a package for you." Muller went inside and brought back a folded plastic bag. It contained clothes, tied with a string; along with it was a small envelope. Jawad was surprised to see that.

"Who left this for me?"

"I don't know. It was here before I arrived. Natasha asked me to give it to you."

"Thanks a lot."

Jawad came to his room and opened the package. There were two jackets, one made of blue denim and the other of high quality leather. He wondered who had sent them. He opened the envelope and read the note inside.

Dear Sir,

I met you at the bus stop today. These jackets belonged to my son who had moved to Australia. I'll be very pleased if you take them. If you don't like them, please give them to someone else.

With kind regards

Monika Mathieu

Tears welled up in his eyes as he finished reading the note. His heart filled with gratitude. He wished he could bow down in front of her and thank her for the kindness. Yet at the same time, he felt belittled. *I've fallen so low. A proud man back home but now reduced to living on charity, a man to be pitied.*

That evening Hussein returned with some good news. He had found a job at some restaurant as a dishwasher. As an employee he could also rent a room upstairs.

"Can you imagine? The room will cost me only 300 Francs," he told Jawad proudly. "I'll have to work one day as a trial and if they are happy, I'll be hired."

That Saturday was the last day of the sale at the carpet shop and they made many changes in the layout. However, for some reason, that Saturday was not so busy. Jawad didn't have to carry much to the parking. Hikmat's wife came in at lunchtime, bringing with her a pot full of meat stew which they all shared. Hikmat seemed a bit disappointed as he was expecting a lot of business on the last day. Jawad had not made much from the tips that day. Altogether, it came to 30 Francs, which he put on the office table once the work was finished.

"You can keep them all," Rizwan told him when it was time for closing.

"What, won't you take your share?"

"It is not much so you can have the lot."

He also handed over Jawad's wage of 80 Francs. Again it was a big plus to his finances.

"Wait," Jawad stopped Rizwan as he saw him going back to the shop front.

"I need a mobile phone. An old one will do just fine, any ideas?"

"You can try at the flea market. Today it's late, better try next Saturday."

"Are they reliable? I don't want to buy a stolen one."

"You can ask them for a receipt, but wait, let me ask the boss."

Hikmat was busy talking to his wife. Rizwan went up to him and spoke for a while. He came to the office and opened a drawer. He pulled a mobile and a charger. It was an old model. He plugged the charger in and attached it to the phone. It blinked and seemed to be in working condition.

"Will this do?" He asked Jawad.

"Yes of course but how much is it?"

Hikmat laughed and then started thinking as to what to say.

"Look, fifty Francs will cover it. It's an old phone. Is that okay?"

"More than okay," Jawad paid him fifty Francs.

"Where shall I go to buy a sim card?"

"Just upstairs in the electronic shop but you should hurry. Leave the phone here to charge."

He went upstairs and bought the sim card for his first ever mobile phone. Now he'll have a contact number like everyone else. He switched on the phone; the battery was running low but was still enough to register the sim card. He gave his number to Hikmat and Rizwan. They were still smiling about his prized possession when he left. Back home he charged the battery to the maximum.

It was Sonia's last weekend at the center. Jawad felt sad and depressed. He went to the lake to ward off his thoughts. The sky was partly cloudy. He thought about the story of Jatinder Singh. *How the lake had changed his life forever.* Are these meetings destined or just chance meetings. Maybe these kinds of encounters needed much better weather, he finally concluded and returned to the center. Hussein was not in the room. Jawad prepared dinner and half-heartedly hoped Sonia would come to say goodbye. He watched the sky from his room window, covered with clouds and threatening heavy rain. He heard a knock at the door. It was Ali. Jawad was overjoyed to see him. He desperately wanted a friend to talk to.

"Good to see you. Tell me, how's everything?" Jawad asked.

"Everything is fine my friend."

"What about your work?"

"I'm working at the same place."

"But your time is up; can't you apply for legal work now?"

"Yes, but I like it that way."

"You mean you don't want to work legally. Why is that?"

"That's the way it is. I get 314 in benefits from the state plus the health insurance. Nevertheless, by working somewhere legally mean I'll be on my own. After all the required deductions, I'll be left with much less money than I make now. Presently I only pay rent because I want to stay close to my work otherwise I can sleep at my center."

His argument made sense. One could make more money by working illegally. Jawad made some food for Ali and after a long chat walked with Ali to the bus stand. Ali stored his contact number. When he returned to the center he met Sonia near the office. She smiled at him.

"Hi Jawad, how're you?"

"I'm fine, what about you?"

"I'm okay as well."

"Did you get my reply?"

"Yes, I did," she nodded positively.

"So you understood what I wrote. I didn't think I was very articulate"

"Of course I understood. I think I know you well enough by now."

"So we can still be friends?"

"Yes, always."

He returned the library card to Sonia. They smiled, and Jawad thanked her for her kindness. After a big farewell hug, they went their separate ways. Back in his room, he felt downhearted and sad. The next day he called his new friend Singh to give his phone number. Singh made a prompt suggestion.

"My wife and I are going for a drive. Would you like to come?"

"Where're you going?"

"I don't know, not too far. Perhaps Rapperswill or Zug but not any further than that."

"Do you think it's a good idea? It is the weekend and your wife might prefer to be alone with you."

"That's not a problem. I'm sure you'll be good company."

At around eleven, Singh pulled up at the door of the center. Mrs. Singh sat on the front seat. They both jumped out of the car to greet Jawad.

"Stephanie, this is Jawad."

"Hello Jawad. Please to meet you."

Jawad was surprised at her command of English as she had a pleasant accent.

"Where shall we go?" Singh asked her.

"I don't know. Let's just drive along the lake till Rapperswill and then we can decide." Stephanie suggested.

They were soon out of the city and driving along the lake. They passed the villages spread along the lake. The sky was partly blue and the boats were out in the lake – it was a beautiful scene. From a distance, Jawad saw an old brown-bricked castle at a hilltop.

"What's that?" he asked Singh pointing to that building.

"It's Rapperswill Castle. Let us go there."

They drove in the streets of Rapperswill. After parking, they walked towards the castle, which was on a steep hill. It was not a huge castle and its terrace offered a stunning view of the lake. The vineyards on the slopes of the surrounding mountains looked enchanting. Just down the terrace was the final stop for the passenger boats coming in from Zurich. Jawad sat on the bench at the far end of the terrace, taking in the scene. Singh joined him.

"I love going out on Sundays," Singh spoke while settling on the bench.

"Me too either. Tell me where did your wife learn so good English?"

"I could ask you the same question. No, she lived in Australia for two years. She got her accent from there. And she can also speak French, Spanish besides Swiss German."

"That's wonderful, four languages."

"You're right. Actually I must confess she is a very decent person, and I'm not just saying that because she is my wife. When we got married, my family was hesitant because she wasn't slim and tanned like the girls there. Nevertheless, I told them I'll marry her with or without their consent. They had no choice but to agree. Back in India, my folks lived in quite a small place near Mohali. While we were there on holidays, she accepted Indian culture without any problems. She is one of a kind I feel lucky. Where would I be without her?" Singh acknowledged, looking over to his wife. She simply smiled in return, not understanding what they were talking.

"Let's go to the city now," she proposed.

They drove for a few minutes, through the wide boulevards spread between magnificent old mansions. Jawad was glad that he had come along for the outing. For the time being at least, he could forget issues that were more pressing.

"Are you hungry?" Singh inquired.

"Not really, I just had breakfast at the center when you came to pick me."

"We'll eat at Zug then."

They drove to Zug, which was a nice city. They had a pleasant lunch at a Turkish restaurant. Jawad felt as if he was a member of a new family and he felt blessed. They drove back but this time around the other side of the lake. At around 4 pm Singh dropped him back. Stephanie invited Jawad for dinner to which he politely declined. He already felt indebted to them.

"If you need anything just give me a call," Singh poke while leaving.

"I will. You don't know what this day meant to me," Jawad said to both of them. "And it was a pleasure to meet you Stephanie," she smiled sweetly back.

Before going to his room, he called his family. They all seemed fine, asking about his situation in Zurich. Then he made his first ever call to Ahmad who was glad to hear from him at last. Jawad excused and told him the true picture. He asked him to think twice before leaving for abroad. His phone card finished and they did not talk much.

In the evening, Hussein returned to his room with a huge grin on his face. It was his trial day at the restaurant. He came over to Jawad and gave him a bear hug.

"I got it, I got the job!"

"Congratulations. Tell me, how did it go?"

"First I met the head cook and he showed me the kitchen and told me what I had to do. My job is washing and helping in the kitchen. They have an automatic system. When I'm not busy with the washing, I shall be cutting the salads and vegetables in the room next to the kitchen."

"Do you like the place?"

"Well, it is a bit hectic and I'm not used to that kind of work. But it's okay."

"When would you start?"

"Next month."

"How much is your salary?"

"Around 3000, minus the rent and other taxes, I'll get about 1600 Francs every month. But the good thing is that I can eat in the staff room for whole month." Jawad congratulated him on his luck.

The coming week, Hussein packed his things and moved to his new room. Now Jawad was alone in his room. His transfer was due soon unless he found a job. He had no idea where will they send him. He missed Sonia deeply. She remained in his thoughts constantly. The memories of her and the precious little time they had spent together were too strong. They were his hidden jewels, to treasure until his very last days. Jawad desperately waited for the month to be over when he could finally receive his work permit. There would be no more language classes or meetings; he would concentrate on finding a job. One day, as he was ironing his clothes, Martin knocked at the door and told him to come to the office.

"What's the problem?" Jawad was a bit surprised.

"Frau Christina wants to see you. It's about your transfer. You know you are entitled for transfer soon."

Jawad went to see her in the office.

"Hello Jawad, please do come in," she greeted him warmly and told him to take a seat.

"I've good news for you. Due to the situation in Kosovo, we are expecting more refugees and we may need all the space we can get. I've talked to the head office about your transfer. The staff here speaks highly about you and I think you deserve a reward. I know that a place away from the city would limit your library visits. A vacancy is available in the city in one of our buildings. There is only one occupant for every room, with common bath and kitchen. That house belongs to our organization though rules are different. Since you are not working, you don't have to pay any rent. What do you think?"

Jawad could not believe his ears. He was going to get a room of his own. There wasn't much to think.

"I'll be lucky to have my own room. Thanks a lot."

"My pleasure, Martin will give you the address and the person you need to contact. You'll have to come to get your money here until the paperwork is done. Please let us know when you'll be moving. We could use that room for housing a family."

The next day he went to see Mr. Vanoni in the city, who was the in-charge of the house he was going to move in. He was a short, thin man and looked extremely confident and clever. Jawad introduced himself.

"Yes, Frau Christina mentioned your name yesterday," he told opening a thick file.

"Okay, first the rules, no drugs, no loud music or TV, no illegal guests," he spoke to Jawad in a tone free of any emotion.

"All right sir," Jawad replied, saluting him jokingly. Vanoni looked at him blankly and continued.

"The rent for the room is 360 Francs which will be paid by the Asylum Organization. However, once you get a job you'll have to pay it yourself. You'll get three keys, one for the front door, one for your room and one for the letter box outside."

"I understand everything sir." Jawad wondered if Vanoni could comprehend that, he was probably just as well educated, but only in less fortunate circumstances.

Vanoni took him to his room upstairs; it was at the far end of second floor, next to the bathroom – room 14B. It was a medium sized room, clean and pleasant enough. Room was furnished with a single bed, a closet, two chairs and a table. There was a door opposite the entrance, which opened in to a small balcony.

Good God, I've my own balcony, and a room with a view!

A treetop almost reached up to the balcony. Finally, he had a place where he could live without disturbance. A fresh start and like everyone else, he too had moved on.

Back at the center, Jawad asked Martin to let him take his pots and utensils, as there was none available at his new place. Martin agreed on that. He also promised to send his letter of recommendation to his new address for job search. That letter was to serve as a temporary work permit. The employer was supposed to send it to the police department to get a real one. Everybody wished him luck as the word got out that Jawad was leaving. He had mixed feelings about the place. It had given him beautiful memories and new friends, but also made him aware of how helpless and vulnerable a human being could become. His heart ached whenever he saw children sitting with their parents in one room. Children who probably wondered why they are not living like normal families, like they did back home.

Jawad phoned Singh to ask if he could help him move his things to the new place. He told Jawad that he'll be at the center in the evening. It was Friday. They carried everything from the room and piled it in the trunk. There was not much stuff any way. At the new place, Singh helped to unpack and place things as best as they could be. Singh liked the place, but he noticed there was no television. He promised to bring an old set he had in the store the next time he came to see him. Once Singh left, Jawad went for a walk in the neighborhoods to get his bearings. The variety of different people and businesses in the area surprised him. There were Turkish meat shops and kebab shops, Indian *sari* houses alongside Tamil handicraft shops. The various restaurants and selling every conceivable food of Arabic, Thai, Chinese origins added to the multi ethnicity and faces in the area.

Singh arrived the next day carrying a portable television set. It does not look too bad, Jawad thought.

"We're going to visit my in laws and Stephanie is waiting in the car. I thought I better drop this off on the way." Singh seemed to be n hurry.

Jawad asked Singh to write down his home address so that Nasir can send his clothes there. Singh did that happily. Jawad thanked Singh and went downstairs with him to say hello to Stephanie. He called Nasir immediately, telling him the Singh's address. Nasir promised to mail the parcel of his clothes. First letter to arrive at his new address was from Martin who had kept his promise. It was for his job search. Jawad informed Ali about his room. Coming day, he went to see Mr. Markus at the Asylum Organization. Markus did not find a Job for Hussein but he may help Jawad. He filled out the form and Markus made copies of his credentials. Markus had a look at his papers.

"Okay, I've got your phone number and I'll call you if something comes up," said Markus. Jawed thanked him and left.

He decided to meet up with his friends at the café to see if there was any news about a job. It was the usual story. He also looked for jobs in the newspaper but there were ads mostly for white-collar jobs. Ali called him the next day.

"Could you do me a favor?"

"Yes, what is it?" Jawad was a bit surprised on his question.

"I told you about the guy whose place I'm living at these days. His name is Kazi and he is getting married."

"Okay," Jawad wondered what was coming.

"It's actually just a sham marriage but obviously he'll have to show that it's the real thing. Therefore, he needs people to come to the ceremony to make it look realistic. All we have to do is dress up and join the procession and pretend to enjoy the occasion."

"What day is it?"

"It's on coming Thursday at ten in the morning. We've to turn up with flowers and nice clothes at the City Hall. After the ceremony and the photos everybody may leave including the bride."

"Sounds like fun, I think I'll come along and wish the new couple well."

"Wonderful," Ali seemed delighted.

"So what's the plan on Thursday?"

"Could you meet me at the central station at half past nine?"

"I'll be there."

"Any luck with your job hunt?"

"No, but I still have time. What about you, are you still happy there?"

"Yes, it's fine. Listen, I've to go now. I'll catch up with you on Thursday, bye?"

Thursday was suitably cloudy to welcome the sham celebrations. Luckily his clothes did arrive from Nasir. Sing delivered them to him on Wednesday evening. Jawad wore his 'Made in Pakistan' black suit. He wondered if black was suitable but he had little choice. He met Ali at the train station on the given time. Ali wore a brown suit with a blue bow tie. They joined Kazi's friends at the Central Station.

"Here comes the bride groom." Someone shouted, and they looked at the man who was in reality doing a rehearsal for the real thing on another day. Kazi was dressed in a light blue suit with a matching tie fixed with a gold pin. He carried two flower bouquets in his hands and was accompanied by his so called wife-to-be and another woman. He shook hands with all of them but surprisingly did not introduce anyone to the women. Meanwhile, Ali took the bouquets from the bridegroom, kept one and handed the other to Jawad. They all took the next tram and stepped off near the City Hall. Before entering, they posed in front of the entrance for a group photo.

"Have you taken the day off?" Jawad asked Ali.

"No, I've to start at eleven. I'm sure we would be finished by that time."

The Zurich City Hall resembled a rich medieval castle. Kazi went to the information counter with the bride. Soon they were all standing in front of the marriage office. An elegantly dressed woman ushered them all into the appointed room where an official was waiting at the large table with papers in front of him. Kazi shook hands with the official while everyone else stood, looking slightly lost. Kazi handed him some papers along with two ID cards of the people who were to be the witness. The official spoke as politely as he could under the circumstances. Soon the ceremony started. The couple took their vows and exchanged the rings. Everyone looked on with interest, wondering if they would be going through this process in the near future. The official read a few lines from a book, and then followed the signatures. It was a solemn event and lasted about half an hour. *Thirty minutes to change a person's life.* They were pronounced man and wife. They did not even kiss each other. Some in the audience would have deemed it as committing adultery. The flowers, the flash of cameras, the handshakes and hugs added some reality to the occasion. The couple seemed pleased enough with everyone's performance. Kazi looked relieved that it was all over, and smiled like a genuine groom while proudly holding a small red book in his hand.

"What's the red book?" Jawad wanted to know.

"That contains the marriage certificate; it's called the family book. It is why we are all here this morning. Kazi has to take it to the immigration office and they'll issue him the residence permit. That's the whole point." explained Ali.

After the photo session, everyone started dispersing. There was no invitation for lunch, not even for a drink. They had served their purpose and it was time to leave. Kazi and his bride walked towards the lake, apparently for some more photos.

"He is one lucky guy Kazi. Now he can go to Pakistan with presents and pockets filled with cash. He can travel to any place he likes. Way to go Kazi," Ali tried to put on a brave face.

Jawad continued with his job hunt. With so many eateries in his new neighborhood, he could afford to be fussy. He decided to go for direct shot in his job hunt. He chose a large elegant Swiss restaurant to try his luck. The manager was sitting behind the bar talking to a customer as he walked in. Speaking in English was out of the question as it may create a bad impression and lessen his chances of getting a job. He greeted the manager courteously, speaking whatever German he could.

"Hello, what can I do for you?" the man asked him politely.

"I'm looking for a job. Is there any vacancy here?" Jawad took out his work permit and ID papers.

"What kind of job?"

"Anything would do. In the kitchen, washing, cleaning," Jawad couldn't believe his own ears.

"Sorry, we've no job at the moment," the man tried to sound sympathetic.

Jawad didn't lose hope and entered another nearby restaurant. A girl was cleaning the table near the entrance door. Jawad asked her if he could speak to the manager when suddenly a man appeared from behind the counter.

"Yes, what can I do for you young man?"

"I'm looking for a job sir." Jawad told him nervously.

"Sorry mate, I've nothing for you. Things are quiet these days," he said while walking away, without waiting to hear what Jawad might have to say.

Jawad tried a couple of more places and then, feeling deflated; he went to the Café Central. His friends there were busy with their own problems and they could only offer him their sympathies. They were always talking on same issues. If it was not Pakistani politics then they were talking about cheap flights, cheap flats, cheaper phone tariffs and how to increase their income. They were fortune hunters like Jawad who wanted to break the deadlock of poverty. He returned home down hearted, hoping that next day might bring him luck.

However, nothing materialized after a whole week of trying. At last, he received a call from Mr. Markus.

"Could you come to my office tomorrow morning?"

"Yes, at what time?"

"Be here at 9 am."

"But what is it about?"

"I think I may have something for you, but we'll talk when you come here."

Jawad was delighted to receive the call. He imagined himself working. Surprisingly, he no longer felt bad about working as a dishwasher, although he could never imagine washing dishes back in Lahore. His sisters would never have believed it. He vowed never to tell them.

Next morning, he went to meet Markus.

"Okay Mr. Jawad, I may have good news for you," he spoke, his eyes still on the computer. "There is a restaurant downtown and they need somebody in the kitchen. Language is no problem but they need a hard working person. It's a very popular restaurant and you'll be working in the kitchen. I have spoken to the woman who is the HR manager there, and she told me they have a modern washing system. What do you say?"

"Oh that's fine with me."

"Look, I'm not forcing you but this is the best I can find. It's in the center of the city and the HR lady is really good. Her name is Eveline Smith but do call her Frau Smith to show your respect. She has no issues in hiring a refugee. If you haven't found anything yet you should give it a try," insisted Markus.

"Okay. When should I go over?" Jawad tried to sound blasé.

"You can go today. She promised to give you a chance. Here is the address, and the name of the person. Go over and mention my name and she'll take care of you."

"Thanks for your help Mr. Markus. I'll go there this afternoon and let you know the outcome."

"Okay, good luck."

That afternoon Jawad took the tram for Paradeplatz and searched for the restaurant named *Zughaus*. It was located in a wide alley in Zurich's downtown. A tall leafy tree and two Swiss flags welcomed guests in the vast courtyard of the three-story building. Jawad entered through the main door. It was lunchtime and place was busy.

"Can I see Frau Smith?" Jawad asked the nearest girl.

"What is your name?"

"It's Jawad. Mr. Markus from the Asylum Organization sent me."

The tables were decorated with white tablecloths, with expertly placed knives, forks and napkins ready to serve the valued guests. The girl went to a corner, pulled the telephone from the wall and spoke for a while.

"Go to the second floor and knock on the door facing you. Frau Smith is expecting you." The girl told him after speaking on the phone.

Jawad thanked her and went towards the stairs. There was a lift but it looked busy. On the second floor there was a large door barring access to the floor. The woman, who opened the door, was the tallest he had ever seen.

Must be more than six feet tall.

"Hello, I'm Frau Smith." she sounded pleasant enough.

"My name is Jawad. Mr. Markus sent me."

"Yes, he spoke about you. Do come in? Did you find our place easily enough?"

"Yes I did. Thank you."

She motioned him to have a seat and walked round to the other side of her large concave desk.

"Okay, about this vacancy. One of our employees in the kitchen had to leave a couple of days ago without giving us much time. From the beginning of next month we need someone on a permanent basis to take his place."

"No problem. I can start on that date."

"Do you have any experience of such work?"

"No, but I think I can manage."

"I'm sure you can. Mr. Markus assured me you're a capable young man. I promised that I'll give you the opportunity to prove us both right. Can I please see your documents?"

Jawad handed over his *Ausweis* and the letter of recommendation.

She copied both and returned the originals.

"Do you have a contact number?"

"Yes," Jawad wrote his number on a notepaper and gave it to her.

"I'll call you in a couple of days to arrange a trial day. Is that okay?"

"Yes, of course."

"Good. Let's go downstairs and I'll show you the kitchen where you will be working."

The kitchen was huge and elaborate. *This looks more like a space capsule than a cooking area.* It was gleaming, loaded with all kinds of machines, large ovens, grills and gas stoves. Cooks were busy preparing multiple dishes and their assistants were cutting and slicing meats and salads. There were refrigerators stored with beef, ham, chicken and frozen vegetables. In one corner were two massive industrial dishwashing machines with a conveyor belt to move the dishes through the scrapper, power wash, and the rinsing unit. They were capable of washing and drying hundreds of dishes in an hour. One to wash plates, dishes and utensils and the other was for large pots and pans. Frau Smith checked a couple of trays of food that were ready for serving, and spoke to one of the staff. Jawad stood and took in the scene in front of him.

"Felix," she called out to a goateed man wearing the tallest white hat that is peculiar to chefs.

"Coming Madame," Felix shouted, closing the door to a red-hot oven and walking over.

"This is Jawad. He'll be replacing Sami. I've told him to come for a trial soon."

"Hello Jawad. It'll be good to have you on board. I am Felix, the head cook," both shook hands warmly.

Frau Smith motioned to Jawad and they walked over where two men were loading plates into one of the machines.

"Jawad, this is Khalil, and this is Galli. You'll be working with them," she said. Jawad warmly shook hands with his soon to be fellow workers. Then she led him to a door, which opened to a back alley.

"This is the door used by the staff. The uniform lockers are on the first floor, which I'll show you next time. We provide the uniforms here, so no need to worry about what to wear when you come for the trial. I'll call you soon for the trial. Do you have any questions?"

"No, everything seems fine."

"Good. Okay I'll show you out."

Once out in the courtyard, he called Markus and informed him about his visit.

"Give it your best shot," Markus advised before he hung up.

Later in the evening, Jawad went to the café and told his friends about his upcoming trial.

"They'll be watching your performance. If the head cook is satisfied, he'll recommend hiring you. I was also hired like you and now I'm working as a waiter at the same place. I worked hard and now I'm earning more than double when I first started," Ejaz, one of his compatriots told him proudly.

The cost of staying abroad kept getting higher. Slowly he was coming to terms with reality. This was the price he had to pay for a better future. Jawad knew that the job would bring not only more money but also some self-respect back into his life. The following Monday, Frau Smith called him about his trial which was scheduled in two days' time. Getting out of bed on Wednesday, Jawad wasn't particularly nervous. Indeed, he felt odd that, with a Master's degree in his possession, he was to be tested whether he could place dishes properly into a washer, and then stack them onto drying racks without breaking them.

They never taught me stuff like that at the University, he thought.

Making himself look presentable, he left to catch a tram to *Zughaus*. He entered the restaurant through the staff door as advised by Frau Smith. When he entered the kitchen, Felix was busy whisking cream at the nearest table. He shook hand with Jawad and called Frau Smith.

Soon she came downstairs and greeted Jawad. She took him to an adjoining room where two women, Maria and Mona, were busy washing clothes, napkins and aprons. Maria handed Jawad blue trousers and a blue sweatshirt. Frau Smith took Jawad to the first floor, where the lockers were.

"Once you start working regularly, you'll also get a key for one of these lockers. Now change your cloths, I'll be waiting outside."

Jawad hung his clothes in an empty locker. They went downstairs to the kitchen. Frau Smith called Khalil who walked over to them, smiling at Jawad.

"Jawad will be working with you today on a trial basis. Explain his duties and everything about your work. And don't be too hard on him?"

"No problem, I'll do my best."

"Okay. Jawad, I'll leave you in Khalil's good hands. He hasn't broken a plate to this day. Take care."

"Thank you Frau Smith, I'll try my best."

Galli was also there. Once Frau Smith left, Galli also came over and shook hands with Jawad. Khalil took Jawad over to a huge sink with a metal base almost three meters long. The area was partitioned, from the rest of the kitchen with cabinets used by the cooks for storage. There were also two large stoves, a big grill and a large silver fryer adjacent to the stoves. Everywhere, there were racks full of plates, dishes, pots and pans. A window with two sliding glass panels served as the link between the kitchen and the restaurant. One was being used for delivering the food, while the other was for returning the dirty utensils. Jawad watched as Galli opened one of the washing machines. Clouds of hot steam poured out. Khalil showed him how to operate the machines, and which warning lights to look out for. Inside were plain plastic trays with holes used for washing spoons, knives, forks and other steel utensils. There were lines of grips to hold the plates. Once set up, the machine was mostly automatic, the sensors and the computer chips making the adjustments required in the washing. The clean plates and utensils would come out from the other side. There were plenty of racks for plates. The spoons, knives, and forks were sorted separately in grey colored trays.

Finally, Jawad was ready to carry his first load. *At least it is less heavy than the carpets, he thought.* Khalil helped him with loading the machine until it was full. He told him he had to be careful, and to check that everything was in exact order before closing the machine door. With a broad smile, Khalil asked him to start the machine.

The cooks were busy preparing different orders; the salads and desserts were prepared in a neighboring small room. At 11 am the staff had a lunch of chicken wings and boiled potatoes. Jawad noticed there were equal numbers of males and females in the kitchen. Everyone had lunch together, the cooks, the service staff. The women from the laundry joined them too. It was like one big happy family. Within thirty minutes, everybody finished eating and it was back to the grind. Jawad was founding it funny to communicate. Some time, trying his German and sometime he would communicate in English. Trouble was that not everybody in the restaurant spoke English. He could understand a bit German now, but was not able to speak much.

"How many people work here?" he asked to Galli.

"I don't know exactly, maybe twenty."

"I didn't see Frau Smith or other managers at lunch."

"No, they eat later in the dining hall on the corner table next to the kitchen. They never lunch with us."

Soon the service managers started guiding guests to the tables. A small printer in the kitchen ejected the orders. Every order slip had the table number on it and the surname of the server.

Jawad noticed Felix walk quickly over to the kitchen door as an imposing tall man in his sixties came in. He patted Felix on his shoulder, and said a few words. Soon they both walked over to where Jawad was working with Khalil.

"Hello, my name is Meier and I'm the owner of the restaurant," he said, shaking Jawad's hand.

"Morning Mr. Meier, I'm Jawad."

"Is everything fine?"

"Yes sir," Jawad replied with a big smile.

"Okay, I just wanted to say a quick hello. Frau Smith told me you're here for the trial." Meier left soon.

By noon, the printer was running furiously. Felix looked anxious, and began speaking loudly at everyone. The cooks were rushing around at speed. Once the order of a table was complete, Felix would put everything together as decoratively as possible and place it at the window. From there the service staff would take over, noting the details on the slip of paper on the tray.

Later in the afternoon, Jawad told Khalil that he knew exactly what to do.

This isn't rocket science, thought Jawad.

The plates being brought back mostly had food leftovers. He emptied the food in the bin, placed the plates in the trays and pushed them. Jawad was thankful for the machines because he couldn't imagine washing thousands of plates all day himself.

They all took a break around two in the afternoon. By then the fourth member of their team Carlos had arrived and it was time for them to leave.

Khalil and Galli were both Iraqi Kurds. From his chat with them, he found out that there were not many chances of a promotion for them. There designation was *Officemitarbeiter.* Khalil had been working there for last 18 months.

Good God! I can't imagine myself staying here for the next one and half year.

The job was the lowest in that establishment but everybody treated them well. They had two timetables. First shift, started at 10 in the morning with a break at 2 pm. They would resume work at 6 in the evening till closing time. The second shift would start at 2 pm and would work until closing which was 11 pm.

Jawad realized that in his afternoon break he could go home for rest. His first day had been tiresome. He went home and returned for staff dinner at 5:30. There were less people in the staff room. After dinner, they went to their respective posts. The printer picked up speed at 6 pm. It was time for the big machine to start its work. Soon it was business as usual. Felix started assigning the cooks for different dishes who in return began to run around and put ingredients together for the said orders. Smells of different foods wafted all around. Only after 9 am, it slowed a little and at 10 am, it all came to a grinding halt. Everybody drank something for a little refreshment. Once the kitchen was empty, they started washing the floor. They cleaned everything in the kitchen and left. As they left the kitchen, Jawad saw Mr. Meier and the two managers sitting on the big round table in.

"What am I supposed to do now?" He asked Khalil once they were out.

"I've to tell Frau Smith about your performance but she'll also ask Felix. I'll tell her that I liked your work. I'm sure she will call you soon to make an agreement."

"Thanks a lot."

"You're welcome."

"Where do you live?"

"I live close to Wiedikon train station."

"Khalil, tell me what happened to the guy who left. Did he resign?"

"He had a fierce dispute with a cook. But I think he did it on purpose."

"Why on purpose?"

"So he could claim benefits because he is not working."

"What happened to the cook?"

"Nothing, he is still working because he was innocent."

Jawad left after thanking once more. Next day after lunch, he received a phone call from Frau Smith. He had not expected her call so early.

"Hello Jawad, this is Frau Smith. I'm happy to tell you that you've got the job. Will you be kind enough to come to Zughaus again?"

"Oh thanks, shall I come today?"

"Yes, or tomorrow as you like."

"I'll come this afternoon."

He was delighted to sign the agreement as Frau Smith instructed. She was kind enough to explain the different clauses. It was then that she told him that she was married to an American. Well, Americans are adventurous and do like big things. He was scheduled eight and half hours work day with two days off weekly. Then there were 5 weeks holidays annually. Monthly pay was 3,100 Francs and after the deductions, he'll remain with 1,800 Francs. Out of that, he had to pay for compulsory health insurance and rent. Jawad was completely satisfied with the arrangements and once out, he had only one thing in his mind. He could not wait to break the good news to his family. His brother answered the phone and said his father was not at home for the tuition classes. He asked his brother to bring his mother on the phone.

"Mom, I've some really great news."

"*Baitay*, as long you are healthy, it's always good news."

"Mom, I'm healthy and soon going to be wealthy," he replied with melancholy.

Excitingly he disclosed the news to his mother. She did not ask how much money he'll be earning or what kind of job it was. She was happy that her son had a job and he was moving forward in his life. However, his brother was curious about the nature of his job.

"What kind of job is it Jawad?" the young man could not refrain asking.

"I'll be working at a super store," Jawad knew that soon the news would be around.

He lied to him because he knew his family would be bitterly disappointed if he told them that he was going to work as a manual worker. But he was happy to break the good news to his family. Next, he called Ali and Singh to tell them about his job.

According to his work schedule which he got through mail, he was starting from the beginning of October. There were still few days left to start his work. Until then he decided to enjoy his time reading and watching TV. One day he felt bored and decided to go for a long walk at the lake. He strolled along the river and came across the City Hall Bridge, close to Fraumunster Abbey; he had to climb a couple of stairs because the bridge was higher than the riverbank. Jawad climbed the stairs. There was a small wall to restrict access to the river. The wall was wide enough and people often used it as a bench. Jawad noticed an elderly man coming downstairs. Suddenly the man's ankle twisted and he fell forward. Jawad moved quickly to save him from falling. He was a thin but a tall man and as Jawad grappled him, he let out a painful cry. Putting his hand on Jawad's shoulders, the man balanced himself and sat on the stairs

"Are you okay?" Jawad asked him in English.

He moaned, "Yes, thank you."

The man rolled up his trouser and removed his shoes. He rubbed his ankle and stared at Jawad, who looked down at him with concern. Had Jawad not been there, he might have fallen badly, hurting himself.

"Shall I call a cab for you?"

"No, I think I'll be able to walk again in a while. By the way I'm Hans Graf and you are, Sir?"

The man spoke in English. One can guess the surprise, which Jawad felt as nobody until then, had ever called him "Sir". The way he spoke, Jawad knew he was going to be ok.

"My name is Jawad."

"Jawad," he repeated his name.

"Are you a tourist?"

A harmless lie seemed appropriate for the occasion but then the thought of the guilt, which would feel later, he decide to go for the truth.

"No, I'm an asylum seeker," he told the man.

He looked at Jawad in disbelief but did not say anything. Maybe it was the first time he had seen such a person. He put his foot back in his shoe and stood up. He shifted his weight off the troubled ankle and took a sigh of relief.

"You feel ok?"

"Yes, I think so."

"Wish you a nice evening, Sir," said Jawad as he intended to leave.

"Mr. Jawad, have you got some time?"

"Yes, I think so."

"Can I invite you for a drink?"

Jawad realized that he wanted to show his gratitude by inviting him for a drink. The dress, personality and demeanor of Mr. Graf were a sign that he belonged to the upper class gentry. He wondered what could be the basis of their conversation. However, denying his offer seemed rude, as he had already told him that he did not have any pressing engagement. So Jawad agreed to his offer. Graf was waiting for a reply.

"Ok, where would you like to go?" Jawad asked him.

"Right there," he pointed to a nearby bar with the chairs outside.

They walked over and found an empty table. The waiter came for an order. Jawad ordered a beer while Graf asked for a Martini.

"Young man you saved me from an injury."

"There is no need for that, it was a natural reaction."

"May I ask where you come from?"

"I'm from Pakistan."

"Are you working these days?"

"I'll be starting next month."

"But you live in Zurich?"

"Yes, I live in the city."

"Well, I live in Zollikon," Jawad knew that area. It was close to the lake and was called 'Gold coast' because only rich people housed there.

"Do you work in Zurich?" Jawad put the first question.

"No, I'm my own boss. I had worked in different banks in Zurich and the USA but now I work privately." Graf took a sip for a pause. "But you get financial support while you're not working?" He asked in an assuring way.

"I get state help."

"How much is that?"

"It's around 300 Francs."

"For one month?" Graf asked disapprovingly.

"Yes for one month".

"But how can one live on such a small sum of money?"

"It's all right; it's not that bad as you think. They also pay for room and the health insurance."

"Well listen, I'm glad I bumped in to you. Some friends had invited me to dinner at a Spanish restaurant. Would you care for another drink?" Graf asked him politely.

"No thanks. I think I should leave. Your friends must be waiting for you," Jawad reminded him.

"Indeed you're right, but can I ask your phone number?"

"Yes, but what for?"

"Maybe I might have some work for you."

"What kind of work?"

"I live alone and there are a few things in my house I want sorted. And I need someone to help."

Jawad gave him his number, shook his hand and left. He didn't care much for that incident.

Later in the evening, Jawad received a phone call from him.

"Is this Jawad?" Jawad recognized his voice immediately.

"Yes, Mr. Graf?"

"Oh, I'm glad you remembered me?"

"Good to hear from you, Sir?"

"But please don't call me Sir unless the queen of England bestows that honor on me. You can call me Graf. How are you?"

"I'm fine."

"I wanted to know if you are busy tomorrow."

"Not really, but why?"

"I told you I had some work to do at home. I need an extra hand. I'll be much obliged if you could spare some time. Of course you'll be paid for your work."

"Ok, where should I come?"

"Could you come to Tiefenbrunnen tomorrow morning at ten? I'll come to pick you up."

"All right, I'll be there," Jawad knew that place.

Next morning he reached Tiefenbrunnen 15 minutes earlier than agreed. There was a half-empty parking lot in the rear of the train station. After 10 minutes, he saw a silver Mercedes entering the parking lot. Jawad recognized the driver, crossed the street and walked towards the car. They shook hands and Graf invited him into the car.

"Did you have any difficulty in reaching here?"

"No, I knew this place already."

Graf's flat was in a multi-story house surrounded by a beautiful lawn. They reached the fourth floor through an elevator and his host went ahead to open the door. The flat had three rooms and a big lounge. The house seemed full of antiques. The sofas, divans and even the dinner table reflected owner's rich taste and wealth.

"Would you like something to drink?"

"No, thanks, I'm fine."

"Okay, let me explain. There is a lot of stuff in this house, which I want to dispose of. I've spoken to a chap who owns a second-hand shop in the city. He is ready to take all the stuff. We just need to pack everything and I can drop it at the shop in my car. Most of the stuff is in the basement."

"Should we begin here first?" Jawad asked.

"That's a good idea. Nevertheless, keep one thing in mind; if there is anything that you find useful just tell me."

"Thanks, I'll keep that in mind."

One by one, they filled the cartons with books, shoes, crockery, clothes, and other stuff. Jawad did not ask for anything. Once a box was full, Jawad would seal it with a thick brown tape. After the cartons were full, they went downstairs to load them in to the trunk. They then went to the basement and moved a lot of stuff from there as well. Graf had folded the back seats and there was enough space for everything. It took them almost three hours to finish. Jawad also helped him to manage his cellar a bit orderly.

"Is there anything else to do?"

"No, I think it's all done except one thing. May I invite you to some wine and cheese?"

"Well, I'm not that hungry." Jawad wanted to leave.

"But you won't mind a glass of wine or two."

"That will be nice."

Graf went to the kitchen and returned with a tray containing cheese, a bottle of red wine and two glasses. He poured wine in both glasses.

"Please, help yourself," Graf pointed to the cheese.

"Do you live alone?" Jawad asked to start the conversation.

"Actually I'm a long suffering patient of Insomnia. I can't sleep more than four hours a night. It has ruined my marriage. My wife and two children live in Geneva now. How could one live with a man who is awake most of the night?"

Jawad listened to him but he didn't respond.

"Well there are also some positive sides to it; one can acquire knowledge, especially in my field of finance," Graf continued.

"Oh yes, you mean reading the latest magazines and books."

"Not only these. Through the Internet, I remain in touch with the stock markets around the globe. I do a lot of online trading."

"You must've worked really hard."

"Yes I did. I went to the USA after my studies to work at Wall Street. I was lucky that I found a patron. He was a Jewish broker who taught me about share trading. It was a bumpy road but I survived. It's a story I'll tell you another day. What about you?"

"Sorry. What about me?" Jawad was lost for an answer.

"I mean you told me you're an asylum seeker and soon you'll be start working."

"Yes, that's right. But there's not much to tell really." Jawad felt a bit nervous.

"There is a lot of fuss about asylum seekers these days. I've got friends who are members of the Swiss People's Party. They are against foreigners in general and asylum seekers in particular."

"Why is that?"

"You see, we were running quite a clean show on our own. But the economic boom made us rely on foreign workers. When foreigners came, they brought their cultures, languages and a different set of problems with them. Afterward the asylum seekers crossed our mountains and lakes and sought refuge on the basis of some treaty Switzerland signed back in the 1950s, which hardly people remember now. They flocked in in their thousands, which put a huge hole in our treasury. According to my figures, last year it did cost us about three billion Francs. My insomnia has led me to become an observatory of useless knowledge. So you'll have to excuse my eccentric facts and figures."

"Knowledge is never useless Sir," Jawad said politely.

"But excess of everything is bad, even if it's knowledge." Graf laughed at his own self-justification. "Anyway, personally I'm not against giving refuge to a person whose life is in danger. It's part of my Christian belief."

"I see, are you a Catholic?"

"No, I've been blamed for many things but never been called a Catholic. I'm a just a humble Protestant."

"Forgive me sir; I don't know much about Christianity. Is there a big difference between the two, the Catholics and the Protestants?"

"Yes, the Catholic belief is based on submission but Protestantism is based on discussion. You've raised a very important point on which I can speak for hours. But I'm not a fanatic Christian and my beliefs are based more on intellectual grounds rather than on anything remotely practical."

"Ok, now I understand," Jawad tried to share in the camaraderie.

"Good. Tell me, what was your education back home?"

"I did my Masters back in Pakistan."

"I knew that the moment I met you, even when I was falling. Surely, you don't seem remotely like a typical refugee. There was something in your manner, and that English accent of yours."

"Thanks for your kindness."

"Tell me Jawad, have you heard of the dark ages?"

"Yes, I've read something about it."

"What broke that cycle, that mental blockage in civilization?"

"I don't know, may be industrialization," Jawad responded thinking hard.

"You're partially right, but there was something else, something which broke many taboos in society. That was the Christian reformation, made possible by Martin Luther and many others. Industrialization was the natural outcome of the Christian reformation because people were not bound to the church for knowledge anymore. They sought knowledge for themselves from wherever they could, which led to modernization. Today, the most economically developed and stable countries are those where there is a majority of Protestants. A German philosopher Max Weber had written on this issue."

"But then why are the Catholics still in majority?" asked Jawad tentatively.

"That's due to Latin America. From the very beginning, it was a Spanish and Portuguese colony. As they say *Cuius regio, eius religio,* "Whose realm, his religion". They are Catholics because their masters were Catholics."

"Then same applies to the Europeans, are not they Christians because their masters, the Romans, were Christians?"

"Yes, but you see, at that time the whole known world followed Rome. So no wonder our forefathers flocked to the Holy Cross."

Jawad could have mentioned Japan, South Korea or Singapore. These were also developed countries without protestant population. But he remained silent to give his host a sense of superiority. He began to see the irony of his own situation. He was drinking wine sitting on a balcony overlooking the lake with someone who belonged to a society completely in contrast with his. In the coming days, he'll be washing dishes and boiling potatoes in a restaurant which might not even appeal to his host for a meal. The thought made him feel uncomfortable. He finished his wine and decided it was time to leave.

"Okay. I'll be going for a walk soon and then finish reading the newspaper. Later I've to meet friends at Savoy this evening." Graf spoke, handing Jawad an envelope. "This is for you."

Jawad folded the envelope and shoved it inside his jacket. He didn't even check the contents.

"If I could be of any assistance, don't hesitate to call me," Graf told him. Although he insisted on dropping Jawad to the train station, latter denied his offer. He knew car was full with cartons and things. Although the front seat was free, he preferred to walk. Jawad shook hands with Graf and parted. Before returning to his room, he went to the post office and opened an account to get his paycheck. Jawad was pleasantly surprised that Graf had paid him 150 Francs for few hours' work. He deposited the money and took the tram home.

His co-worker and mentor Khalil welcomed him on his first day. Jawad put on his blue uniform. He told Jawad he could have coffee from the drinks buffet to refresh him before work. Jawad went there and saw another brown-skinned worker of about his age moving crates of drinks. He was wearing a cross around his neck to show his faith. He stopped as Jawad approached.

"I'm Denni, are you the new guy in the kitchen?"

"Yes, I'm Jawad."

"I'm from Sri Lanka. Khalil told me you're from Pakistan.

"That's right."

"What would you like?"

"Can I have a cup of coffee?"

"Okay," Denni pushed the crates on one side so Jawad could pass and walk to the coffee machine. When he returned with his cupful, Khalil was busy working at the big machine. As usual, the real work began around 11:30. Never-ending orders meant never-ending washing. As the pace picked up, Felix's yelling dominated the sound waves in the kitchen, making everybody work at full speed. Galli had a day off.

At 2 pm, he and Khalil went for a break while Carlos replaced them. The evening was busy even though it was a Tuesday. Dining out, it seemed, was a Swiss custom. As dishwashers, they knew what they were supposed to do, and they did their duty with due care. After all, it paid for everything in their humble lives. The next time he went for drinks at the buffet, Jawad spoke with Denni and soon the talk turned to Bollywood movies. It was something that most people from the south Asia could share.

"You see that girl over there?" he said pointing to a waitress. "She is my girlfriend. We've been living together for the last 6 months. Her name is Daniella." Denni told him proudly.

"That's fantastic, Denni and Daniella," Jawad commented.

Soon Jawad became used to his routine. Five days passed quickly and his co-workers had been supportive of him. By Saturday evening, Jawad heaved a sigh of relief when he finished work for the week. He knew he had the next two days off and he'll be able to rest. He could stay in bed as long as he wanted to. Sunday morning he was still lying in the bed when his phone went beeped. It was Hussein asking his address. Jawad explained the directions; Hussein wanted to see him immediately. Within half an hour, he showed up, looking worried.

"What's the matter? Is everything alright?" Jawad looked at him.

"Actually I've a problem. I too came from Lebanon, but I applied for asylum as an Iraqi."

"Have they found out?"

"Yes, I received a letter yesterday."

"But how did they know?"

"Before coming here, I was in another country. They found that out from some fingerprint database. These bloody computers, I wish nobody had ever invented them."

"What will you do now?"

"That's why I'm here, I've to leave by 15th of November. I've spoken to my other friends who advised me to leave. I want to go to Canada."

"How'll you manage all that?"

"I know a person who is an expert in such matters. He'd promised to meet me today."

"And do you want me to come with you?"

"Yes, if it's possible. All of my friends are working. "

Jawad realized the gravity of the situation. Soon they were on their way to the central station. They went to a nearby café and waited for Hussein's contact. He came within ten minutes of their arrival. He introduced himself as Yousaf, also from Lebanon. Hussein began to talk about his situation immediately. They gradually began speaking in Arabic. Jawad could see reflections in Hussein's eyes. First it was despair, then questioning, then confusion and to despair again. Eventually, Yousaf shook hands with both of them and left.

"What did he say?" Jawad asked but Hussein seemed puzzled.

"He said it will cost 3,500 Francs, but there is no guarantee."

"And what will he do for that money?"

"Once I pay him the money and my picture; he'll give me a fake Italian passport with my picture on it the next day. I would fly to Canada from Geneva. He'll give me a shirt with the logo of some famous Italian football club, which I'll have to wear on my journey. The last man he helped to reach Canada traveled with a Greek passport, dressed as a Greek monk. That trip was delayed till the man had a full beard."

Jawad was amazed at Yousaf's expertise on this matter. However Hussein had one advantage. His skin color was fair enough that he could be misunderstood as an Italian. And he always shaved his head. Jawad wondered how Yousaf could possibly disguise him if he needed his services. *A British gentleman, a Spanish businessman* or *perhaps as a Catholic priest?*

"So, what are you going to do now?"

"I've no option but to do as he suggests."

Jawad told Hussein to think twice before making a decision. Hussein left after an hour, leaving Jawad worried for him. However, he knew Hussein had to make a quick decision. Time was not on his side. Hussein called him after three days telling that he was set to leave on Friday and assured Jawad that he'll remain in touch. Jawad could only wish him luck, though he didn't think he would get very far with his plan.

Life turned into a routine. He was becoming used to his work. The month was ending and he was eager to call home to inform them that from now on he'll be supporting the family. He planned to send the money over using the *hundi* system at the local Pakistani shop. They would transfer the money to a local moneychanger in Lahore. Jawad could imagine his father, walking proudly into the moneychanger's shop, telling the cashier his name and the amount of money. It was a landmark in his life.

Surprisingly Jawad didn't hear from Hussein again. That's the way things had been lately. Jawad assumed that Hussein had reached Canada. Had he failed, he might've called for sure. Meanwhile, Jawad had an addition in his social circle: Denni, the Sri Lankan at Zughaus. He was a good person to be around, always ready with a smile and advice. Jawad's routine was to travel to his workplace by tram, reading something of interest on the way. Over the weeks, he had earned the respect from everyone at work. They liked the cheerful quirk chap who spoke like a Brit and never gave anyone a reason for complaint. Some called him a bookworm while others named him professor. One day Jawad found a copy of *The Economist* on the tram, which someone had left behind. While he was reading it at recess time in the staff room, Michael, Mr. Meier's assistant manager walked in.

"Are you looking at the pictures in there?" Michael spoke in a teasing way.

"No, there are some interesting articles," Jawad responded in kind.

Soon they were talking about the contents of the magazine and other similar ones like *Time* and *Newsweek*. Michael was interested in one of the articles in the magazine on China. They had an interesting chat and Michael liked Jawad's general knowledge. Jawad forgot about the conversation and went back to work.

Next day at 2 pm, Jawad was called to the office. Frau Smith was sitting behind her table with Michael on her right side, while Denni sat next to the door.

"Please have a seat Jawad. We would like to discuss a small proposal," Frau Smith began.

"Please go ahead, I'm listening," Jawad answered.

"We've been looking for an extra worker for our drinks buffet and bar. A girl left work a week ago due to maternity leave. After some discussion, we've decided to ask you if you could move there. Denni is in-charge there and he believes that you can handle that job. So if you agree we would like to transfer you to the drinks buffet," She concluded.

Jawad could not believe his ears. He looked at Denni, who just smiled back.

"What about my colleagues in the kitchen. They might get annoyed at my sudden promotion?"

"Leave that to us. We're used to deal with these kinds of things all the time," Michael assured him.

"From next week you can start working with Denni, if you wish," Frau Smith spoke conclusively.

"I don't know what to say. I never expected this." Jawad looked around.

"I appreciate people with talent. When I spoke to you yesterday, I thought you're in the wrong job," Michael tried to encourage him.

"It would be my pleasure, of course."

Jawad thanked everyone and left the room with Denni.

"Thanks buddy," Jawad said to him on the way out.

"For what, I didn't do much. It was Michael who proposed your name, and I agreed. He is very impressed with you."

Jawad was overjoyed at his promotion. His new title was *Buffetmitarbeiter,* responsible for all kind of drinks. It seemed like a miracle. Meanwhile a Somalian guy replaced him as dishwasher. He learned his new job fast. They had a printer attached to the ordering machine. Every time it ran, it printed a small order chit for the drink with the quantity required. All he had to do was to put the drinks together for the service staff. Apart from the alcoholic beverages, there were also two coffee machines and one for making tea and hot chocolate. One places a cup below the valve, press the relevant buttons and let it pour. During the first couple of days, Denni told Jawad to work with the liquor and beer orders only. As the orders came through the printer, Denni would place the chits in front of him. Along with them were two Spanish women, Margareta and Celia. They made a good team, and were a fine example of a staff dedicated to their work. Over time, he learnt that Denni came to Switzerland eight years ago due to the civil war in Sri Lanka. A year ago, his asylum application had been accepted. He was very confident regarding his job because the management respected him for his work. At times, he would use overtly strong words if any of the service staff annoyed him. But he always treated Jawad like an equal as he considered him well educated and from a decent background.

His job at the restaurant was providing Jawad with plenty of food and drinks as well good money, things that were a thorny issue just a while ago. The impending New Year in a few weeks' time made Jawad reflect over his life. He thought about Sonia and his heart filled with pain. How was she? What was she doing nowadays? He wondered if she ever thought about him. He didn't really want to celebrate the New Year and just tried to appear as cheerful as he could at work.

It was business as usual when he returned for work on the first working day of the New Year. While Denni was off, Jawad had to go downstairs to fetch the drinks as required at the bar. He loaded up the trolley in the basement to refill the fridges and the coolers. Out of the lift, he moved the trolley to the bar.

"Can I have a cup of coffee please?" he turned and saw a pretty girl in her mid-twenties, with long hair and a pleasant smile.

"Sorry, I didn't notice you," Jawad was surprised.

"I just came in. I'm Carla, the new waitress."

"Ah, now I know. I'm Jawad. Pleased to meet you," he offered his hand.

Carla was of middle height and had stunningly beautiful eyes. She wore a gleaming white service uniform and looked keen in her new job. He made a cup of coffee quickly and slid it towards her with panache. She smiled at his neat style. Jawad liked her in a way and always tried to talk to her. Denni was quick to note the staff addition when he returned from his day off. He spotted Jawad speaking with Carla in earnest. He introduced himself to Carla who was as pleasant as possible to him. As she left with her order, Denni walked over to Jawad.

"I see you've got a new friend," he spoke smilingly. "This could be your lucky break."

"Easy my friend, you're jumping to big conclusions within thirty seconds," Jawad laughed at Denni.

"Seriously Jawad, you should make your move before someone else does."

"What do you suggest?"

"Invite her to a drink or lunch when you both have a day off. Love alone won't get you very far. As for her, start finding out more about her," Denni advised.

"Yes boss. Is that an order?" he joked. Denni nodded while laughing.

Jawad started to get to know her. Some time he would ask a direct question, other times he pretended he was teasing her. Soon he had a broad picture of her background. Carla was an Italian who had migrated to Switzerland twenty years ago with her parents. She was fluent in Italian, Swiss German and her English was not bad either. Most important of all, she was single. She mostly came across as a happy go lucky person, innocent and fragile. Jawad felt attracted to her personality and her innocence, but at the same time, he was afraid that one wrong move could mess up his job. He decided to take things as they came. He was still trying to get over Sonia.

Winter had firmly taken a hold, and the temperature dropped to below zero for the next few weeks. The snows became a permanent feature, and over the weeks, turned into thick ice.

One bitter, cold day, Jawad finished work and began to leave for his afternoon break. He and Denni mostly worked with a recess.

"Where're you going?" Denni asked.

"Home, it's too cold to think about anything else."

"Why don't you come with us? Daniella and I are going to Movenpick, and we've also invited Carla. It'll be good company."

Hearing Carla's name and that she was also coming along, Jawad agreed. Movenpick restaurant was not so busy when they arrived. They took a table near the window and ordered hot drinks to warm themselves up. Soon they were all talking like old friends. Daniella was just as friendly as Denni, and soon mixed in. She went to refill her drink and called Denni over to show him something on the notice board. It was a flyer about the movies being shown at the nearby cinemas. Jawad was alone with Carla.

In their new environment, both felt shy and were quiet. Jawad pretended he was busy thinking. In a way he was, of Sonia. Then others returned to the table and everyone began to chat again. Afterwards it was time to return for work.

"How was it?" Denni asked him as soon as they were in the changing room alone.

"It was okay. Well' we didn't speak much."

"You're some guy Jawad. We left you alone so that you could weave your charms on her."

"But I know she is single and open to suggestions. So I've time."

"Yes, but she doesn't know that you've got any suggestions to make," mocked Denni.

"There is always a next time brother," Jawad tried to justify.

He noted his feelings for Carla when she didn't show up for work. He decided that whenever she returned, he'll try to show his interest in her. Though he still had a tender spot for Sonia but he realized she was his past and a painful one. Carla might be his future. Denni always told Jawad to take her out for a romantic evening. Finally, he made up his mind. When she returned to work, he caught Carla watching him from the wooden partition. She smiled shyly, like a child caught stealing. He decided he would ask her out no matter what. First, he checked the timetable; she had Monday and Tuesday off. Ironically, Jawad had work on both those days. Denni on the other hand had Tuesday and Wednesday off, so Jawad decided to ask if he could change with him.

"First you should ask her. I don't have a problem if she agrees."

Jawad plucked up courage went up to Carla in the afternoon.

"Carla. Could we speak for a moment?" Jawad initiated.

"Of course, what is it?" Carla looked at him.

"It's cold, isn't it?"

"Yes, it is absolutely freezing outside."

"Actually, there is something I want to ask you?"

"You want to know if I want a coffee. Is that it?" she seemed puzzled.

"No, are you working on Tuesday?"

"That's my day off, why?"

"I'm also off that day."

"Ok?"

"Would you like to have dinner with me on Tuesday?"

"Where do you want me to come?"

"We could go to the city in a restaurant of your choice."

"I'll have to check a few things. I'll let you know by tomorrow."

"Of course, I'll be waiting."

"Thanks for asking," she smiled and walked to the service area.

The next day, Jawad told Denni that he had asked her out at last.

"So, did she agree?"

"I don't know yet," Jawad was just as uncertain.

"Actually we would have to ask Michael for the change in our timetable. Frau Smith is off for the weekend."

Carla was busy all morning while Jawad waited for his moment. Eventually things calmed down and she came over for a quick coffee. Jawad felt it was the hardest thing to do, but he knew he had to know one way or another.

"Carla, I'm still waiting for your answer," he plucked enough courage.

"Yes, I'll be happy to come," she confirmed shyly.

Jawad was overjoyed and smiled broadly. He couldn't wait to share the news with Denni.

"Guess what! She is coming," he blurted out when Denni came to him. Together they went to Michael and asked him for a change in the timetable. He agreed and switched their workdays.

"Carla, what time shall we meet?" he asked her that evening.

"Give me your number and I'll call you on Tuesday. Let's first meet in the evening at the central station and then we may decide where to go."

"Okay, here it is," Jawad wrote his number on a piece of paper and gave it to her.

On Tuesday, he woke with a smile on his face, and sought out his best clothes from the wardrobe. Recently, he did buy some stuff. She called at around 2 pm and they agreed to meet at the central station at 5:30. He reached the station and posted himself at the meeting point. Jawad instantly saw her walking calmly with a tweed shoulder bag at her side. She wore a red hat with a velvet jacket and a pleated black trouser. They both smiled.

"Thanks for coming," he said.

"You're welcome. So, where would you like to go?"

"I want to try some Italian food," Jawad told her. "Shall we go to the Niederdorf Street first, and then we may decide where to go?"

"Could we go to Santa Lucia? It's a fine Italian restaurant," Carla proposed.

"Okay, where is that?"

"It's not far. The food is good and it might not be very busy because it's not the weekend."

They reached there in 10 minutes. The place was finely decorated with only a few tables occupied. Jawad selected a table at the far corner for the privacy. A waiter brought them two menus.

"Will you like a glass of champagne?" Jawad asked Carla.

"No thanks, I prefer Prosecco if that's okay."

He ordered two glasses. They clinked and sipped slowly, savoring the moments.

"Will you order for me as well?" requested Jawad. "I'm not sure with some of the dishes."

He also told her that he didn't want any pork in his food.

"Of course, I guessed that already. So are you a good Muslim?" She asked teasingly.

"Fifty-fifty, I drink but don't eat pork."

She laughed at the selective following of his faith. After some mutual consultation, they ordered some salad as starters and pizzas for main course. She handed the wine card to Jawad. He glanced at the card, and decided against Barolo and Amarone, both vintages and expensive. He opted for a bottle of Chianti. He thought how this dinner could be the prelude to a romantic relationship with her, only if he said the right things. But that was not easy, as they didn't have much in common. Nor did he know much about Italy that he could talk to her about.

Lie you should and lie you will.

As the drinks began to melt the ice, Carla asked him about his education and his country. Jawad answered as briefly as possible. He tried to skirt along without being sucked into the issue about his status in the country. But Carla had done her homework; she knew exactly what to ask.

"You are a refugee, is that right?" she asked while eating salad.

"Yes, that's right. I hope you won't walk out on me now," he tried to joke. She laughed. They were talking in English and German alternatively.

Mentally Jawad cursed his circumstances. His whole personality with all its manhood was lost as soon as the word refugee was mentioned. He wanted to leave the table immediately. To go to some unknown place where no one would point at him and call him a refugee. It was so demeaning. But it was also the truth, which he had to carry around like a cross. Meanwhile they were finished with the salads and waiter arrived with hot pizzas. He tried to change the subject slightly and asked Carla about her family.

"My brother lives in Lugano with his wife and son. My father had passed away and my mother is retired and lives in Italy. Her pension is more than enough if she resides in Italy."

"Where do you live?"

I've a two room flat in Oerlikon." Jawad was surprised, she too lived in Oerlikon.

"I see."

"How about some dessert or may be some ice cream?" Jawad asked once they were done with the main course.

"What about you?"

"I'm not really fond of sweet things."

"We can share a Tiramisu."

"Good idea."

She told the waiter to bring a Tiramisu with two spoons.

"I make it at home but only if I have guests," she informed cheerfully.

Later, Jawad ordered two cappuccinos. On the foam topping of the cappuccino, the waiter had drawn heart shapes with chocolate cream. They both smiled when they saw the hearts. Jawad complimented the waiter's sense of humor and asked him for the check. She insisted on sharing the bill but Jawad told her that she was his guest.

"Next time I'll pay," she insisted as they left the restaurant.

Once in the street, his eyes caught a man selling dark red roses on a pleasant little stand next to the restaurant. Carla was busy looking at the window of a shop, selling designer wear.

"Wait here Carla. I'll be right back." Jawad returned with three roses and presented them to Carla.

"Oh thank you. That's so sweet of you," she beamed.

She took the roses carefully and with a smile. The smile, which surfaced on her lips, gave Jawad hope that he had succeeded in planting something in her heart. They stopped almost in front of every shop, passing comments on their way back. Jawad bid farewell to her at the door of the train, exchanging a kiss on the cheeks.

"Thank you for a beautiful evening." She waved from the train door while Jawad stood there until the train left.

On their next encounter, Jawad told Denni about his date.

"Why didn't you kiss her on the lips?"

"How could I kiss her when we were out together for the first time?" Jawad argued.

"I took mine to bed on the very first date," Denni confessed proudly.

"I'm not as clever as you are."

Soon Carla was spending afternoons with Jawad. They would go to some café to spend their free time. Still nothing serious happened between them. One sunny afternoon they decided to go to the nearby river during their break. They walked until they found an empty bench on the riverside. Behind them was Urania Park. He could see a kind of softness in Carla's eyes. Jawad decided it was time. He put his hand on her shoulder and softly kissed her. She did not resist.

"I love you," he said looking into her eyes.

"Yes, I know," she replied in an affirmative tone.

Her tone made him want to kiss her again, but this time a bit more passionately. She kissed him back. Suddenly he remembered similar moments spent with Sonia. She put her hand behind his head. Their relationship took a whole new turn in the next few moments. From friends they became lovers. She lay on the bench watching Jawad with her innocent eyes, as he gently ran his fingers through her hair and kissed her on the forehead. Her approval of him took away all of Jawad's worries. She had accepted him despite all the differences and shortcomings. They returned to work still holding hands. Before entering, Jawad kissed her again, and reluctantly they went to change for work.

"I did it," he told Denni excitingly.

"You did what?"

"I kissed her."

"Congratulations, that's great."

"I owe it to you."

On Saturday, Jawad called up Singh and told him about his new found love. Singh was delighted for him and started giving fatherly advice.

"Bring her to our house as well. We'll be delighted to meet her."

"I'll try. Let me work something out."

Carla always had first two days of the week off. Jawad realized that in order to win her heart he ought to stay with her as much as possible. He wanted to have the same two days off, so that he could spend more time with her. He decided to go and talk to Frau Smith about his wish.

"Why do you want the first two days of the week off?"

"Actually on Mondays I've to clean the floor where I live and on Tuesdays it is my turn to do the washing." Frau Smith told him that she'll do her best to accommodate him but sometime it might be difficult.

Nobody took much notice of their relationship. They were always together whenever it was possible. Jawad had not moved any further from kissing. He decided to be patient. And they had not been to each other's homes yet. Jawad had repeatedly told her about the invitation from Singh. The last Monday of the month was a public holiday and they decided that they would visit Singhs that day. Carla told him that she'll come to pick him up so he wrote down his address. Jawad informed Singh who welcomed the news.

Monday afternoon, Jawad waited for Carla on his balcony. He had cleaned every inch of his room to impress her of his clutter-free living. He opened the door and kissed her gently when she arrived. He took her overcoat and hung it behind the door.

"This is a nice place," she commented after looking around.

"I'm glad that you liked it. It's not always so tidy though." he smiled.

"I can imagine. But I like it anyway."

He offered her juice and opened the door to show her the balcony.

"It has a wonderful view. You must enjoy living here."

"Yes, it's better than the previous one and easier on the pocket too."

Soon it was time to leave. Carla stepped out as Jawad followed. She had parked her car on the street opposite to the building. It was a light blue Twingo which matched Carla's personality just fine. They reached Singh's place. Singhs welcomed them at the door and both seemed happy to see Jawad and Carla. Carla had brought a bottle of wine packed in a gift bag as a present. They all settled comfortably in the drawing room.

"We would love to help in the kitchen. Please don't think of us as formal guests," Jawad declared to Mrs. Singh.

"There is nothing much to do. The chicken is almost done in the oven along with potatoes and veggies. Food could be at the table at a short notice."

On Carla's insistence, she and Jawad both readied the table. They spoke for a while and then it was time to eat. One by one, they brought in the food along with wine. Stephanie served salad on everyone's plates along with Italian dressing. The marinated chicken with vegetables was delicious. After the meal, Stephanie showed Carla her wedding pictures.

"They are wonderful," Carla loved the colorful images of the India.

"We had the time of our life in India."

"I can imagine. Look at you in that gorgeous sari," exclaimed Carla.

Jawad and Singh went to the kitchen to prepare coffee.

"Have you been to her place?" Singh asked discreetly.

"Not yet."

"First step, visit her place. Go to her home and go to bed with her. She is European and knows that eventually this will happen. If all goes well, the second step is to convince her to live with you" Singh advised.

"I think that might be risky at this stage."

"It's the time Jawad that you should take risks."

"Okay. What else do I need to do, mister expert?"

"Be nice to her, become a part of her life. She should feel her life is incomplete without you. So the day you ask her to marry, she'll accept like that," he said clicking his fingers. "I did the same. It's good that you've brought her here today. She won't feel that she is the first one to fall in love with a brown man. She needs to be convinced that you are a decent man," he continued in his friendly manner.

Mrs. Singh and Carla, it seemed, were getting along well on their first meeting. They had similar perspectives and were partners of two men from similar backgrounds. In a way, they had become kindred spirits. Stephanie spoke well of both the men. It was getting dark and Jawad and Carla soon got ready to leave. Their hosts too had a busy day ahead.

"Do come again. It was such a pleasure to meet you," Stephanie warmly told Carla before they left.

Jawad decided to follow Singh's advice after giving it some careful thought. He knew that time was not on his side, and eventually, he'll have to settle down with someone. Carla had been nice to him and seemed to accept him just as he was. On the way Jawad told Carla that he was going to the Oerlikon library the next day and would love to see her while he was in the neighborhood.

"What time are you going there?"

"Tomorrow afternoon."

"Then you can help me to shop as well if you have any spare time."

"Where do you shop?"

"I mostly go to the Oerlikon Complex for shopping."

"All right, let's meet up at two in front of the shopping center. See you there." He kissed her warmly before coming out of the car.

Of course, Jawad's library visit was just a cover to see her place. He was waiting for her outside when she came. Carla had a list of things to buy and they went to the supermarket. They grabbed a trolley and filled up with groceries as they walked up and down the vast aisles. Then Carla led the way to the beauty shop where she bought some creams, and soon they were in the underground parking and loading up the car. She asked Jawad to take a seat and together they went to her flat. She lived in a three-story building. Tall trees everywhere made the area look pleasant and green. She parked the car in the blue lane and walked to entrance. Her flat was on the second floor and was accessible only by the stairs. They struggled up with the bags of grocery. The windows of the living room had white silk curtains. It was a comfortable room; a leather sofa faced a wide screen TV and a drinks cupboard full of multi colored bottles. The adjoining bedroom was decorated in subtle pinks and pastels. The living room also had a dining table and four chairs, and a mahogany shelf behind it was laden with dishes and crockery. Her little house was intimate and attractive. Just like the owner, thought Jawad

"Will you like to drink something?"

"Some beer, if you have any sweetheart?" he tried to be blasé.

Carla brought a beer for him and some soda for herself and sat next to him on the leather sofa. They talked for a while about different things. Jawad knew he had to make a move and quick. He waited a while until he had absorbed the atmosphere of the house. Impatience could be risky. First, he held her hand and felt the warmth. After caressing and rubbing for a while he gently pulled her to his side. All the vows of patience stored in his subconscious, evaporated into thin air. It was like some flood gates had just opened. Jawad realized he could not, even if he wanted to, control things. She let him explore and exploit the hidden pleasures. They both knew where they headed. Soon they moved to her bedroom. Jawad was now lying topless. He put the condom pack on the dressing table to show her that he was a responsible partner. It was the first he ever bought. She switched off the room light and turned on the bedside lamp. Jawad did his best to satisfy his body's urge, not forgetting Carla's. But he realized she was hesitant and shy. He could never imagine doing something like that in Pakistan. Soon the foundations of their physical bond were complete and he kept kissing her to solidify it. Jawad felt peace lying close to her. He felt as if Carla was taking the place that Sonia once occupied in his psyche. He also felt pure love for her and her silence gave Jawad a sense of belonging. He was sure he had found his life partner and it wouldn't be long until he could ask her hand in marriage. She was lying with her head on his arm, her long silky hair spilled onto his cheeks, and everything seemed in perfect harmony. She was a beautiful, gentle, loving soul. What more could he possibly want from a mate? They both lay there, sometimes silent, then kissing, caressing and teasing each other. He decided not to spend the night at her place, as he didn't want to be too possessive. After a quick meal and a glass of wine, he took his leave.

Once at home, he felt completely transformed. He felt like someone new, not like the old, shy boy from a lower middle class Pakistani family. He was becoming slowly westernized in many ways. Transformation, he realized, was the key to success for migrants like him. Who knew that the Algerian man driving the taxi was a respectable teacher in his homeland, or that the Portuguese waiter was a tourist guide with his own boat back in Algarve. But they had transformed themselves, forgetting what they were when they arrived in Switzerland. They forgot their occupations, their lifestyle and some even forgot their families. Jawad still cared for the values he had learnt in his homeland. He knew his parents would never approve of him sleeping with a woman outside marriage. It was a sin with capital S. He decided never to share this fact with his family. He would hide it like he hid his drinking habit, and God knew what else.

The days became warmer and the evenings longer. Beautiful spring sunshine outside reflected his radiant inner self. The change Carla brought in his life was immeasurable. He no longer seemed depressed. He became optimistic and smiled much more easily. What vibrancy a woman's love can bring in a man's life! One day Carla told him that she had informed her mother about their relationship. Jawad did not ask what her mother's reaction had been. Now, it had become a routine to spend their days off together. They would go to the shops, to the cinema and sometime just drive around. Jawad would sometimes stay the night at her place, helping her, caring her, loving her. One night, they went to sleep once their appetite for love and food had been satisfied. Jawad looked at her face. Sleep had doubled the innocence on her face. Could he ever betray the person who had opened her heart and her home for him? *Spending the rest of my life with her is surely my destiny.*

Six months had passed since he'd started working at Zughaus. Now he would be entitled for unemployment benefit if he loses his job for some reason. From the grapevine he knew that once he is entitled to unemployment benefit, he could ask for some vocational training. That would help him to find a better job. He needed some advice about the best options open to him now. One Sunday he went to the café to meet his acquaintances. They were busy discussing the sub-continent's politics as usual. Back home, things were as dire as ever. One of the chaps who worked as a waiter seemed an authority on this matter. He told Jawad that he should learn a new trade. The unemployment office offered courses in waiters training. In his view, it was a good job; as a waiter, he was earning about 1500 Francs in tips alone, and this was tax-free. Jawad knew this fact from Carla's experience as well.

"But my biggest problem is how to get dismissed from my present job," Jawad confessed.

"You must have a good heart," said Raja, his new mentor. "You don't even know how to get yourself fired?"

"No, what should I do?"

"Well, you can start a fight, or turn up at work completely drunk. You may also send them a certificate that you are sick."

"But I'm not sick."

"My very simple minded friend, science hasn't invented a gadget which can detect an invisible back pain. Go to your doctor and stay off for a week or two, that's all."

"How can you be so sure?"

"I had been fired from four different places," Raja told him proudly.

It was his seventh month at Zughaus. He would have to work for another month after his termination notice. However, he did not want to do anything that would jeopardize his relationship with Carla. He felt he should tell her the truth. He explained to her his plan to move on. He told her that he detested the work he was doing at Zughaus. The first thing was to get himself dismissed so that he could go on benefits, then he would be entitled to attend a language school or get some sort of vocational training. She didn't agree with him about leaving his job at first, but came round to the idea as he pressed his case in broken German and perfect English.

Anyway, she could see that Jawad had already made up his mind. He said he needed more money, and for that purpose working as a waiter was ideal. Once he overcame a few hurdles, he could easily try his luck at better jobs. For that he might have to spend a year or two at a university and get some education for a job of his choice. He, who was desperately looking for a job just a few months ago, was now looking for ways to give it up so he could make more money. What a contrast.

Jawad chalked out different plans to get him fired: a fake accident, backache, getting drunk at the workplace or constantly showing up late for work. One day when Denni was off, Jawad grabbed a bucket and went to the cellar to fetch a load of ice cubes. The lift was busy, so he took the stairs. When he was returning upstairs, an idea came to his mind. Go for it Jawad, This could be the way out. With a loud clang, he let the bucket fall on the stairs. As it bounced off the steps, the ice cubes spilled onto the stairs and the floor below. Jawad let his left foot slide and then landed with a loud cry of pain. He made sure that he did not get hurt in reality.

"Help, is anybody there?" he shouted in apparent distress.

One of the cooks, Jose rushed to the stairs and helped Jawad up, who seemed in immense pain. Michael too arrived at the scene and asked Jawad what had happened. He explained that he had slipped on the stairs. He was dripping wet with water.

"How bad is the pain?" he asked anxiously.

"I think I may have fractured something," Jawad said clutching his leg and back.

"In that case you should better go to the hospital. I'll drive you there," he said with a worried look.

Soon Jawad was taken to the Emergency at the University Hospital Zurich. A nurse took him inside and told him to change into a hospital gown and allotted him a bed. Soon a doctor came in and Jawad told him about the accident. The doctor sent him for some x-rays.

"See you after the x-rays."

The nurse gave him two pills for the pain, which Jawad pretended to swallow. Another nurse took him for the x-ray and helped him to stand up in front of the plates. He was x-rayed from different angles for a better diagnosis.

"You'll have to wait till the result from the x-ray comes," the nurse brought him back to his bed.

Within an hour, the doctor appeared with the negatives in his hand.

"Apparently there is no fracture, which is good news. The pain you have is probably due to falling on the stairs on your left leg and back, causing tissue damage. I'll write you some medicine and if you don't feel better, you can go to the orthopedic ward for outpatients. But I'm sure you'll be feeling fine soon."

Jawad didn't want to feel fine and he had no intention of getting better soon. He'll feel better only when he'll get his termination letter.

"Do you need a sickness certificate for your employer?"

"Yes, I do actually," he appeared nonchalant.

The doctor took a form from his table and filled it in. He advised a three-day rest and prescribed some medicines. Soon Jawad was on his way home. He limped out as best as he could, feeling guilty for wasting everyone's time. Carla called him and came to visit him in the afternoon at his room. She smiled knowingly when she saw him in the bed with a pained look, with the medicine on the side table.

"What a waste of expensive pills. These I can give to my mother," she said, taking the packet of painkillers.

"Take them all and give them to your dear mother. Now, come to bed and rub my poor back," he said meaningfully.

"No time for mischief. I've to go to work soon, unlike you. Everyone was talking about your fall in the cellar. What an actor you are?" she laughed loudly.

"I used to be the hero in our school dramas you know. Now come to your Romeo, O Juliet," he put out his arms in jest.

"No, it'll ruin my clothes and everybody'll know what I've been up to in my break."

"Just for a little while."

She fell into his arms and he kissed her. She gazed at his face and into his loving eyes, wondering what was in his mind.

"Only God knows how much I love you my doll," he said.

"Oh amore, I love you too." (They were no longer calling each other by name rather just spoke "amore" mutually. Italian language perhaps best suited to the lovers). Her response was quick and firm.

She stayed until 5 pm and then left. Jawad stayed home for three days and Carla would visit him during her break time. She gave his sickness certificate for sick leave to Frau Smith. On the fourth day, Jawad went to the orthopedic department where the receptionist checked his card and told him to wait. After half an hour he was directed to a certain Dr. Hessler's room. Jawad went in limping from his left leg and showing signs of pain. The doctor read his reports, pressed, and probed. He checked his reactions with a small rubber hammer and tapped it on various joints and points. Nothing looked conclusive.

"It might be one of the spine discs, but I can't be sure without MRI."

He wrote another prescription and recommended complete bed rest for one more week.

"If it doesn't improve, I'll send you for an MRI," Dr. Hessler informed him.

Jawad limped out of hospital. He knew that the restaurant could not fire him while he was on sick leave. Therefore, he showed up for work after seven days. He kept complaining about the pain. After few days, he made another visit to the hospital and asked for physiotherapy because he did not want to go for an MRI. Luckily, it was a different doctor, who agreed.

"Go to this address and give them my prescription. They'll give you the appointments."

The doctor, to Jawad's disappointment, did not give him any medical certificate barring him from work. Jawad immediately went to the address and asked for a set of appointments with the physiotherapist. Four of the sessions were in the early morning while three were in the afternoons, the times of which he notified at his workplace. In the coming days, he did not do much work and complained of severe pains. Everyone knew he was having physiotherapy. The other staff had to shoulder the burden of his incapacity.

On the last Monday of the month, he received a registered letter from Zughaus. Jawad opened it with excitement and trepidation. It seemed that either their patience had run out. Or they were taking precautionary measures against any trouble, which he might make in the future. He had been dismissed from work with a one-month notice. He took the letter with him to Carla who explained it to him in detail.

"Congratulations, you got what you wanted," Carla told him with a sly smile.

"Now I can go to school to learn German. If I succeed in my devious plans, they will send me to gastronomy school for waiter training."

Carla went to the kitchen and Jawad thought about what he had just said.

I'll be a waiter that is all. Did I leave my country to become a waiter? What about my degree and all the knowledge that I acquired. Would I be ever able to use that knowledge?

He brushed such thoughts aside. What had he accomplished with all the books he had read and all the exams he had taken?

Go on boy, be a waiter and a good one too, make some money and forget the dialogues of Hamlet you spent learning in your university days. Transform yourself, and do it quickly, so that you too can become a moneymaking machine, just like your fellow countrymen here.

When he went to meet Frau Smith, he pretended to be upset at his dismissal. She responded that it was difficult to manage things with his irregular attendance.

"I'm sorry. We're a small establishment and can't afford the luxury of hiring temporary workers all the time. We've to be sure about our staff's attendance," she explained her position.

Denni, though he had to work more due to Jawad's absence, did not like that he was leaving.

"What do you plan to do now?" Denni asked with a sad tone.

"Do I look like someone who has plans?"

"You know you can claim benefits, right?"

"Yeah, I think that's what I'll do actually," he pretended to realize.

"Listen Jawad, try to find a job as soon as possible. Women here don't like a man who sits around all day."

"I will try my best," replied Jawad.

Meanwhile Carla informed Jawad that she was expecting her mother over for a brief visit. She had taken a week off for her. Jawad was surprised by this sudden news. Perhaps she was coming to evaluate and judge what kind of a man her daughter was currently spending time with. It was hard for him to leave Zughaus and the last day of his work was emotional. He shook hands with everybody and in turn, they wished him good luck. Denni gave him a small gift. It was a corkscrew set in a wooden box.

"Every time when you'll open a bottle of wine, you'll recall our time together," he said.

With a promise to keep in touch, he took his leave.

It had been almost 15 months since his arrival in Switzerland, and with the passage of time, he was moving ahead. His family was happy to receive regular money from him. He had returned the money he had borrowed from them and they were satisfied with his apparent progress. What they did not know was his liaisons with Carla. Eventually he had to bring this up with his family, but only when Carla agreed to marry him. He could not tell his family unless he was sure of her commitment. In addition, before that, he had to go through a scrutiny of Carla's mother. *I hope she is not a xenophobic. More tests, more examinations. Life seemed to be full of them.*

Jawad knew how important it was that Carla's mother should approve of him. Nevertheless, he realized that he had to look relaxed and not appear stressed out and give out wrong signals. On the morning of her arrival, he went with Carla to receive her at the train station. Her train was due at noon at platform number eleven. Jawad had bought a small bouquet of flowers as a welcome gesture. Carla searched for her in the crowd of people emerging from the train compartments and walking towards the exit. Jawad noted the broad smile on her face as she spotted her mother in the crowd. She rushed to her as Jawad followed, wondering who his possible future mother in law would turn out to be. Soon Carla was hugging a smartly dressed woman with white hair, carrying a handbag and pulling her luggage. Jawad handed her the flower bouquet. She smiled back and took the flowers with a big *Gracias*. As Carla had instructed him beforehand, Jawad kissed her on cheeks. She seemed pleased with the gesture and showed no visible reaction to his foreignness, so far.

"Mother this is Jawad, my friend. And Jawad this is my dear mother, Isabella," Carla beamed. She was speaking German for the convenience of Jawad who took her luggage and together they walked to the exit. Jawad opened the car door for Isabella and placed her luggage in the trunk. She did not speak much German and no English at all, which was a relief for Jawad as there was no danger of getting a direct grilling. Her only way to know about him was through Carla and most mothers have a habit of having a soft corner for their daughters. Carla drove and chatted cheerfully with her mom in Italian, which was pleasing for Jawad to hear. Back home they all settled in the drawing room. Isabella explained to Carla her medical problems and the treatment she was currently receiving. Jawad realized this as she showed her medicines one by one, as if they were her prized possessions. Italians had a strange appeal for Jawad, as they seemed like distant cousins of his own people. They were very different as compared to the Swiss. Italian language had a musical quality to it and the speakers often found it necessary to use their hands while conversing. Soon Jawad was the topic of discussion; this he found out from their gestures. Isabella observed him like a teacher looking at a new pupil. She said something and then Carla nodded positively looking at him. Jawad pretended to be nonchalant and feigned ignorance about the discussion.

He felt bored, a fact that Carla soon realized. Suddenly, she stood up and went behind him and massaged his shoulders; Jawad did not say anything. He knew that she was doing it as a reward for his patience. She had made the arrangements for a special dinner befitting the occasion. Her mother loved fish. So to welcome her mother, she had planned to prepare salmon with potatoes. Jawad went to the kitchen with her as she was placing the fish in the oven tray surrounded by potatoes. He looked at the fish, lying next to one another like martyrs after a battle. The tray was pushed in the oven. Three creatures alive a few days ago were lying in that little hell, waiting to satisfy human appetite. To honor the arrival of a lady who came from far away to watch what kind of a man was sleeping with her daughter, Jawad arranged the table and opened the wine. Carla brought the hot tray and placed it in the middle of the dinner table. Carla's mother was not so keen to drinking wine due to her medication. He poured a little in her mother's glass. He wanted to give Isabella the impression that he really cared about Carla. After dinner, he helped Carla with the dishes. Jawad decided to take them out for their dessert. They went to a nearby café for that purpose. Both ladies ordered crème caramel while Jawad settled for Tiramisu.

Since Isabella's arrival, Jawad and Carla had little time to spend together. Carla spent most of the time with her mother. Isabella had a lot of old acquaintances in Zurich. It was the daily routine to visit some old friend. Those visits cheered her up and Isabella was having a good time. Jawad also kept up appearances. Soon it was time for Isabella to return to Italy. They both went to the train station to bed farewell. Jawad helped with the luggage while Carla held her mother's hand and took her to the seat. Isabella seemed upset at leaving her daughter and did not speak much; Carla too seemed close to tears. She hugged both of them and kissed Carla on the cheek. Soon the goodbyes were over and the whistle sounded. As they waved the train off, Carla was wiping her tears. Jawad put his arm round her shoulders.

"Thanks, I'll be fine," she said.

"What did she say about me? I mean did she like me?" Jawad asked her while walking towards the car.

"I didn't ask her about that. It's my life," she proclaimed.

Jawad was convinced that her mother had made that journey to form an opinion about someone who might become a family member.

"Actually, I didn't tell her that you're seeking asylum. And all she cared about was that you live in Zurich and we worked together. I told her that you'll be going to language school and that you are a nice man. I think she also likes you."

"How do you know that?"

"The way she said farewell to you, that says something."

They went back, and Jawad asked to be dropped off at the Café Central. He wanted to visit his friends to inquire about the process of registration at the unemployment office. All the usual suspects were there as it was weekend. Once Jawad told about his problem, suggestions poured in from all of them. There were few things to do and then there were few things not to do. He had to be careful while dealing his unemployment counselor. They all briefed him well as every one of them had been to that situation at least once.

Zurich had a number of unemployment offices, each responsible for a designated district. The one responsible for his area was not far from his home. It was on the 3rd floor of a big office building and Jawad reached the registration counter, following signs as best as he could. A pleasant lady greeted him with a smile on her face.

"I've just lost my job and I want to register," he spoke to the lady in plain English.

His friends had told him to speak English rather than German. It would increase his chances of getting admission into language school. Once he was in language school, it would reduce the burden on him.

"Can I see your ID?"

He presented his *Ausweis*. She disappeared inside and returned with his documents after few minutes.

"Okay, there is an information brochure here for you but it is in German. If you please have a seat someone will see you in a while."

Later, another lady gestured Jawad to follow her into the next room. She had a computer in front of her on a small desk. She asked Jawad basic questions about his stay in Zurich and where he had worked before. She inquired about his educational background, language skills and his work and why he was dismissed. Jawad spoke politely and in simple English, and showed her his dismissal letter.

"We're almost done here. You'll receive mail from us regularly. First you'll get an invitation for a day-long information lecture. Then you'll receive a letter from your employment counselor. It is he who'll have final word over you and his decisions can rarely be challenged. He'll help you in your job hunt and would also look into the matter of schooling. This is the form which you'll have to submit every month giving the details of your job hunt. You'll be explained about that in the info lecture but till then you are obliged to keep searching for job, any questions?"

"No, everything is fine."

Jawad had no questions and even if he had one, better wait till that information lecture. He looked at the form. It contained empty spaces with hints like where had he applied, for what kind of job and what was the result. His friends had advised him to get a phone directory. All he had to do was select the names of some bars, restaurants and hotels and split them in to different dates but no weekends. That was all. He could mention that there was no job available and even if there was one, he was not selected. Every month, he'll be receiving unemployment benefit which was almost equal to his last salary. Though he could be sent to work but the chances were not high due to his poor performance of the German language. One weekend Singh called Jawad and asked him to come over. His wife had a company dinner and Singh was alone so they drank and ate without any female company.

"What is your next move about Carla, I mean when do you plan to marry her?"

"I don't know. I've not thought about it much."

"What are you waiting for?"

"What do you mean?"

"Look Jawad, you know the marriage process in this country is not so easy for people like us. There is a lot of documentation involved and then everything is triple checked."

"What do you recommend then"?

"Simple. Get marry as soon as possible."

"Actually, I'm afraid because we have not been together for so long."

"I know, but at least you could convince her to start thinking. I think you should try some emotional blackmailing. That's what I did."

"Why don't you tell me what you did, maybe I can do the same."

"I assume you are behaving like a gentleman and she is in love with you, correct?"

"Up till now, yes."

"And you have been sharing her bed regularly?"

"Yes." Jawad felt a little uncomfortable. This was turning into a grilling.

"Now you should arrange a really romantic evening someday. You should have dinner together and afterwards a nice walk. You return home and it'll be time for bed. After making love, gather your emotions and promise your everlasting love for her. Tell her how lucky you think you are and that it is impossible to live without her. Tell her that you're always worried that your asylum application may get rejected and you would have to leave the country anytime. And if that happens, you don't know how you'll live without her."

"Why can't I simply ask her to marry me?" Jawad tried to argue.

"Yes, you can. But you see people in this country can live their whole lives together without marrying but, in your case, I'm afraid you don't have many years. You'll have to give her a reason why you are interested in marriage."

"You mean this reason will be enough for her?"

"Well, it worked for me. You have to assure her that it's only because of this reason you want a marriage, otherwise you are happy the way things are now."

"What if she refuses me?"

"I don't think she will. You are both living like husband and wife anyway, and she seems to be deeply in love with you."

"But what if she just said no?" Jawad insisted.

"Well, then we should look for other options."

"And what are those options?"

"Some other woman or even a paper marriage, you know about that, don't you?"

"Yes, I even attended one," Jawad remembered the sham marriage he attended not long time ago.

"Good. But don't worry. I'll tell Stephanie to talk to her as well. My wife is quite fond of her and I think Carla feels the same."

That night he returned at Carla's home where he was mostly lodging lately, engulfed in thoughts and worries. He was double minded. Next day something happened, which changed the situation completely. He was still asleep when his phone beeped.

"Hello Jawad. How are you and sorry for disturbing you." It was Ali on the line. They have not spoken for a while. Last time when he called, mostly they talked about Carla as Ali was inquisitive.

"Hi Ali! I'm fine, and what about you?"

"I'm in trouble. I'm actually calling you from the airport prison."

"You're in prison, what happened?"

"It's a long story and I'll tell you when you come here." Ali gave Jawad the number for the prison office to make an appointment to see him.

"Do you need anything?"

"Not really, Khadim, the chap I used to work with will come today. I've told him to bring some telephone cards."

Jawad called at the prison office and made an appointment for the next day. The lady reminded him that he could not bring anything illegal. He bought three phone cards and some chocolates for Ali. Next morning, he took the train for Rumlang, a village close to the airport. From there he took bus, which stopped near a gate with no signs or windows. There were cameras at the gate. As Jawad approached, the gate opened automatically. He entered the compound and walked towards the prison entrance. A stern looking guard signaled him to move into an enclosure. He was given a strict security check, similar to the ones at airports. The guard returned his things and led him to the room reserved for visitors. It looked like a normal waiting room with chairs and round tables. The thing which surprised Jawad the most was the presence of glasses on every table. They were filled with condoms. A door opened and Ali walked in few minutes later. Jawad smiled and gave him a hug.

"My dear Ali, what happened? What're you doing here?"

"I think I told you that this was my second asylum application," Ali looked apologetic.

"Yes, I know that."

"Then I received a letter that I should give some proof that I left Switzerland and returned to Pakistan before coming again. But I had no such proof. The next letter told me that my asylum application had been rejected and I shall leave the country within a month. I discussed the matter with Khadim who told me to stay in hiding. He advised not to tell anybody about this."

"Ok, now I got it why I was unaware," Jawad added.

Yes, that's why I never told you as well. I had almost managed the money required for a sham marriage and Khadim was looking for a woman for that purpose. But then my luck ran out. One day I was coming back from work late at night and a police car passed by me. They turned around and asked me for my ID, but I had none. It had expired and it can't be renewed as my application had been rejected. They arrested me and a deportation order was arranged and now I'm here. They took me to the Pakistani embassy where I denied that I was a Pakistani. They had no proof of my origin anyway. Then they took me to the Indian Embassy, where I spoke Arabic."

"But you don't speak Arabic!"

"No man, I just recited some verses from the Quran, that's all. They told the cops to take me away and try their luck at the embassy of some Arab country."

"And what they goanna do now?"

"Actually, I too made a mistake. When I applied for asylum I gave my correct address in Pakistan. Now they have emailed my photo to the Swiss embassy there and soon someone will go to my town, and find out everything. I'll be deported as soon as they got the proof of my origin. Pakistani Embassy will have no choice but to issue travelling documents for me."

"How much time will it take?"

"I don't know, may be a month or so."

"What will you do in Pakistan?"

"I don't know. Khadim had assured me that I'll get every penny back from him."

"At least you can start your own business in Pakistan."

"Yes I can, but who said I want to live in Pakistan."

Jawad felt sad for Ali. He did not like Pakistan and Switzerland did not like him. He gave him the chocolates and phone cards.

"What about you and your Italian girl?" Ali asked.

"We are together but that's all. Who knows where it will end."

"Look at me. I was caught just when I had the money to go for a sham marriage," Ali repeated his sorrow. Jawad did not respond to that. He was afraid too. With a heavy heart, he hugged Ali and promised to keep in touch.

He felt terrible for his friend, who after years of trying his best had ended up in the prison, awaiting deportation. What a sorry end to a gallant effort to improve his life. He wondered of his own future. Would it end the same way? At the moment, Carla seemed his savior. But to become Carla's groom, so much had to happen. Her consent was the most important, and the most difficult. Then there was the red tape and a lot of formalities to be taken care of. Singh was right. He had to talk to Carla as soon as possible.

Monday was her rest day. They had their breakfast at her place and afterwards left to buy groceries. Jawad decided to talk to Carla in the evening. Proposing was tough for him. He realized that he had not even introduced her to his family. Though his parents, seeing the prospects may allow him to marry her. But he didn't have the courage to tell them that he had a girlfriend. He was sure that they would approve of the marriage because it would mean a permanent stay for him, which means financial support for the family. That evening, after dinner, they went for a stroll. Once back home, they went to bed and Jawad made love to her with an extra vigor. Afterward, it was time for her favorite TV program, *Big Brother*. Jawad waited till it was over. He sat silently, putting his hands around her.

"I need to talk to you about something very important," he at last plucked up enough courage. He was finding it difficult to convince that innocent looking girl to marry him.

"Oh, is everything all right amore?" she muted the program and turned to him.

Jawad told her that he loved her more than anything in the world and he wanted to stay with her the rest of his life. From the very first day of their relationship he'd never hidden anything or lied to her. He'd spoken to his family about her. Though they still had not spoken to her or met her, thought well of her. But he had his concerns. He was always worried that his asylum application could be turned down and he'll have to leave. Jawad spoke German as well English for the most important conversation of his life. In order to ensure their lives together it was necessary that they should marry. Carla listened as he spoke with passion about their future together. He assured her that he was doing it only to make sure that nothing could take her away from him. He even mentioned the visit to the prison where his friend was waiting to be deported. What would happen to both of them if something similar was to occur? He could leave the country, but he could never leave her. He said this fact was eating him up, keeping him awake at nights. Jawad made it clear that he could not imagine a life without her. He asked her to think of everything before giving an answer. He hugged and kissed her repeatedly to reassure her. She hugged him back but remained silent.

"Please don't make your decision just to save my skin. Only say yes if you truly believe that our future is together. I'll understand if you say no but you just have to say it sweetheart," he said finally, leaving her looking completely bewildered.

"Whatever you decide, I'll always love you," he turned and left, feeling every word he spoke.

He returned to his place and could not sleep much that night. Next day he got up with a heavy heart and a head full of conflicting thoughts. He had to attend the lecture at the unemployment office. He got ready, skipped the breakfast and reached there within forty minutes. First he was to hear a lecture. The speaker was an unemployment counselor, who spoke English with a French accent. There were 16 people in the class. The purpose of the lecture was to guide them to fulfill their duties as unemployed individuals. This ranged from filling in lots of forms and showing up for appointments. They were advised to comply with all the rules otherwise they'll be penalized, which meant deductions from there benefit money.

Then they took a language test supervised by a panel of three. Jawad didn't pay much attention and wrote his name and address where it was required. He merely ticked a few answers and left the rest empty. It was a trick taught to him by his colleagues at the café. A poor performance would ensure that he'll be sent to a language school. Once in school, it'll reduce his responsibility because his counselor would know that he was busy learning the language. When everyone had handed in the sheets, they were advised to wait outside. They were called in individually to discuss the results. Jawad was called half way through.

"You didn't pass the test, which means that you should be sent to a language school. We would send our recommendations to your counselor," a lady from the panel told him.

Afterward he was allowed to leave. From there, rather than going to his room, Jawad returned to Carla's place and found her watching TV. They did not speak on the issue of marriage again. Jawad wanted her to think it over.

Her answer came few days later and in a strange way. She went to work and Jawad promised to meet her so that they could spend the afternoon together. It was quarter past two when she showed up. After the welcome kiss they walked towards the river. They sat down as usual, she was quiet, looked out at the river. Suddenly his anxiety arose, why still no answer. He saw his future disintegrating; not only marriage, but he also might lose her. Perhaps she also realized what he was thinking. Eventually she turned and spoke in a serious tone.

"A few days ago you asked me a something and you must be wondering about my answer."

He nodded nervously.

"I don't have the courage to tell you my answer, to be honest," she continued. Jawad was ready to break up, his head spun.

"I can't say anything; this may give you my answer," she said solemnly and handed him an envelope. *Her last letter?*

He opened the envelope and looked inside with his heart-thumping, ready to bust out of his chest. It was a leaflet from the City Hall. It explained the procedure to follow for marriage, the documents required and the rules and regulations. Carla had probably gone and picked it up for free but for Jawad it had his future printed on it. He gave her the most passionate and the longest kiss since they had met. It took her breath away.

"Easy, what will people think?"

"They can think what they like."

He could not believe his luck. She had consented in such a peculiar way. Rather than saying a direct yes she went to gather information regarding the marriage process. Jawad didn't need any more information, he had everything. Since he had her consent, he realized that world had become more beautiful.

What a stroke of luck, the girl and a permanent stay in Switzerland, two birds with one stone.

For the asylum seekers the course of getting married was a lengthy one. It took Jawad and Carla five anxious and long months to set up their big day. A great deal happened during this time. If a life changing "No" from her would have caused him a great deal of pain, the process of implementing her "Yes" was not less demanding. He'd never imagined that to realize the dream of getting married, there was a lot to do. It didn't help that both of them were living so far from their respective families, who could do little to help in their sacred quest. Back in Lahore, the women of the house might've managed most of the wedding arrangements. The paperwork usually consisted of a few lines in the Mullah's register, and a handwritten *Nikah* certificate. Since, most weddings there were arranged by the parents and the final nod of approval usually came from the groom and the bride. In this instance, Jawad had to seek their approval about his choice of partner. Keeping in mind the religious inclinations of his mother, he knew it'll be tricky to get her onside. After all, the bride was a Christian, which also raised the possibility that her grandchildren could be Christians. Jawad wondered, whether Isabella harbored such fears for her daughter's future? She might be probably more concerned whether he would make her daughter happy, and if he was marrying her out of love or for more ulterior motives. In addition, he knew if one of his sisters were to do what Carla was doing, she'll be facing severe consequences. In a boy's case, it was usually tolerated, with a few conditions attached. Jawed wondered what his father's reaction would be. He'll probably be more pragmatic.

Jawad had never been in this situation before, and was dreading the direction that the conversation may take. He needed some guidance, and suddenly remembered that there was someone who had been in this very situation before. He needed to seek his advice. Therefore, he called his cousin Nasir, who was surprised to hear about Jawad's progress in securing a partner. Jawad told him about his dread of talking with his parents. Nasir explained to him that a chance like this doesn't come along every day and his family's misgivings should be secondary.

"You know how people back home think. They want best of both worlds. That I should settle abroad for the livelihood of the family, but also hold onto my roots, and my values," Jawad moaned.

"I know that and I'll try and explain it to your parents. Don't worry Jawad; I went through same problems when I wanted to marry over here," Nasir confessed.

Nasir assured him that once he had spoken to them, it'll be easy for Jawad to ask their consent. Jawad was still nervous. It was well known that whenever a son left for the west, the parents dreaded that he might marry a western girl.

Next day Nasir called and told him that he had had a lengthy talk with his father. Nasir presented himself as an example. He was married to a German girl, and his family had no complaints about it. Then he mentioned the list of problems Jawad was facing in order to continue residing in Switzerland. Moreover, to resolve most of these issues, it was necessary that Jawad should marry. He had met someone and they were both in love. Nasir also portrayed the other side of the picture. Failing to acquire a permanent stay in Switzerland meant Jawad would be returning home soon, empty handed. His father said that he would speak to the family about the matter.

"I've done my best buddy. A lawyer couldn't have done a better job. I told them how you are madly in love with her and that they might lose you if they didn't agree," he told Jawad who thanked him warmly.

Still, Jawad decided not to call immediately. It was an important matter and he decided to give his folks sometime. When he called, his father asked why Jawad hadn't talked to him directly.

"I didn't have the courage, so I asked Nasir to make the first call," he confessed.

"What's her name?" his father asked abruptly.

"Her name is Carla and she is Italian. Nasir must have told you all that. She is a girl of good character, Dad."

"No problem son, I'm more concerned about your mother's feelings."

Soon it was his mother on the phone. She asked about her character and beliefs. Did she drink? Would she stop eating pork and would become a Muslim before they married? Jawad gave the answers, which he thought would satisfy his mother. Then it was his father again. He wanted to know about the technicalities. They had surely discussed the matter in details, Jawad realized. Finally his parents told him that there was nothing wrong in allowing their son to marry a girl who was white, foreigner, and a Christian. His father took note of the documents that Jawad required, and assured him that they'll be on the way soon. Then it was the turn of his sisters. They wanted to see pictures of Carla as soon as possible. Jawad promised to send them soon. Luckily, his brother was not home. Once the call was over, Jawad sighed and slumped down in relief. He'd covered another milestone.

Next, he needed his passport which he'd left with Nasir in Germany. He knew getting the passport through the post could be dangerous. Yet without it, his dossier was incomplete. However, having a passport at all might be problematic, as he had previously denied having that. He decided to speak to Singh on the matter. Jawad called him and expressed his fears. Singh told him not to worry, as marriage process had nothing to do with the asylum process. He consoled Jawad that it was a matter of some other department. Jawad was relieved to hear that. When he called Nasir again, he mentioned the chat he had with his parents. Nasir was happy to hear that they had given him their blessings. When

Jawad told him about his passport problem, Nasir told him he'll try to find a solution.

The solution came in the form of a Turkish truck driver, who drove regularly to and fro between Germany and Switzerland. His job was to deliver meat to various Turkish restaurants. Nasir said that he would receive a phone call from the Turk in the next few days.

"Just go wherever he asks and pay him 200 Francs. He'll give you the passport."

Jawad had to wait ten days before he got a call from someone who spoke German in a strange dialect. He told him to come to a Turkish restaurant in down town.

"Your cousin has sent some books for you," the person informed. Jawad hurried there and found a tall, thin man smoking in a corner. The man recognized Jawad from his features. They shook hands and spoke for a while. Jawad brought out his wallet and paid him the money.

Suddenly the man got up and took Jawad in to the kitchen. Nobody took notice of them. The chap opened a drawer and gave Jawad an envelope. It was a fair deal and Jawad checked his passport in the envelope. It was there.

———————————

While Jawad was getting his documents together for the big day, the people at the unemployment office had forgotten neither him nor their job. Their duty was to help him find a job. He had attended the info lecture and now he can't give any excuse about the paper work. On his first meeting, Mr. Stauffacher, his employment counselor came to receive him in the waiting room, like a doctor receiving his next patient. It was ten in the morning and Jawad greeted him in plain English. Mr. Stauffacher checked Jawad's details on his computer and pulled a file from the rack behind him. On his part, Jawad assured him that he was doing his best to find a job. Mr. Stauffacher read his CV and told him that he felt sorry that Jawad was working at such a lower position but he had no power to change the rules. He informed Jawad that he'll receive a letter from a language school.

"To get a reasonable job, you must learn the local language first," he emphasized.

He asked Jawad few questions regarding his job hunt. After half an hour, his host escorted him outside and bid him farewell. He told Jawad that he'll send the new appointment by mail.

"Good luck for your job hunt and work hard in the school," he shook hands with Jawad and returned to the office.

Jawad was happy with the proceedings. He'll go to the language school and try to learn German, the language of Goethe, Schiller, Marx and Thomas Mann. Carla was also glad to hear the news. Meanwhile he asked her for a couple of pictures and posted them to his family. As a formality, Carla had informed her mother and brother about her decision to get marry. No one raised an objection. Within two weeks, Jawad received the documents he needed from Pakistan. He paid 200 Francs to have them translated into German.

Finally, both of them had all the documents needed. Equipped with a bulging file containing papers to satisfy the bureaucrats who were more concerned with the law than the human beings for whom the laws were made, both went to the City Hall. Once they handed the documents over, they had to wait. Soon the clerk told them that their documents were complete. Jawad's documents would be copied and send to Pakistan for verification. Once the Swiss embassy in Pakistan sends a positive reply, both will get an invitation to come and discuss possible dates for their marriage. They returned home, feeling relieved.

In his country, there was a saying that every good deed had a return, in this world and the world hereafter. Now Jawad counted all his good deeds, which might have helped him to earn that wonderful country and a beautiful kindhearted girl. In the evening, he called Singh, who was delighted to hear about the progress and congratulated him. He told him to tell his family to be careful because soon someone will come to verify the documents. Singh told him that in his case, the man who went to his village in India had taken his photo with him and showed it to the people in the neighborhood, asking whether he was already married. Jawad had no fear of that sort. *Married? He was not even engaged.* But he decided to tell his father to be careful anyway. Someone might say the wrong thing that would be enough to jeopardize everything.

On the first day of the following month, he received a letter from his new language school. Jawad was glad that there were no books or other material to buy. On his first day there, he noted that his class had a fair balance of age, gender and nationalities. Their teacher was Frau Gattiker, a woman in the final years of her profession. Jawad took his classes very seriously. He had to master the new language if he didn't want to remain a dishwasher for the rest of his life. He was not an executive of a company who could do without knowing the local language; at that level English was the *lingua franca.*

One day after the class, Jawad went to meet Carla at home who had called him to inform about the arrival of her brother. She introduced him to her brother. Jawad greeted him in Italian. Paulo too, like his mother, spoke very little German and no English at all. He was in Zurich because he had bought a used car on the Internet. He told them that he had to drive back with it and the sooner he started his journey the better. He spoke very little with Jawad due to the language barrier. Together they drank coffee with some cake. Paulo looked at Jawad with inquisitive eyes. Jawad kept playing the innocent. He picked the empty cups and brought them to the kitchen and did some other things like that. He wanted to show Paulo, he was a part of his sister's life. They were both conversing in Italian and Jawad didn't understand anything.

"Was he inquisitive about me?" Jawad asked as soon Paulo left.

"Not much, but he asked about the kind of marriage we would like."

"What did you tell him?"

"Not much. I told him that I'll prefer something private. Not too many people. First to the registrar office and after the signing ceremony we may go for some drinks, followed by lunch."

"Did he like the idea?"

"Actually on his wedding there were more than 100 people with music, food and plenty of wine. He spent a lot of money and it brought him nothing. All what's left of that day are few photo albums which they can't even remember where they put."

Jawad agreed with Carla. Something grand would cost hefty money. He was already finding it difficult to cope with the expenses, though he never showed any worries to Carla. He wanted to give her the impression that he can cope with the responsibilities without putting any burden on her. Getting married was an expensive business. He was still reeling from the expenses at the marriage office and rather liked Carla's idea of a simple ceremony. How could he possibly disapprove, considering his financial position?

As Carla was soon to become a member of his family, it was necessary that she should be acquainted with them. He had already told her about his folks in Lahore, painting as rosy a picture of them as possible. He decided that at least his family may talk to Carla on phone. He told Carla about his intention and planned the day and the time for a call. Thousands of miles away his family lined up anxiously to talk to their future daughter in-law. Jawad told Carla that it was his sisters who wanted to speak to her first. They spoke for a while. Carla tried to sound as friendly as she could, and was surprised by their fluency in English. Then his father came on and in a somber voice he spoke to Carla about the feelings of his family. He told her that everybody was looking forward to meet her in the near future. Once all the hurdles were over, they should visit them in Pakistan. Next it was his mother who said a few words in broken English. Carla was touched by her kind tone and words of love spoken in familiar inflections. Carla could hear a lot of whispers in the background. Finally, she gave the phone to Jawad. His mother told him that the news that Jawad was marrying a foreign girl had spread like wildfire in their extended family. Some had expressed surprise and others showed jealousy, she told him. Jawad informed his father that he won't be able to send over money for a while. He needed money so that he could pay for the wedding expenses. His father told him not to worry.

At the end of that month, he went to visit Mr. Stauffacher in response to the letter he'd received. Jawad updated him on his job hunt and that he was still unlucky and tried his best to satisfy him. He was again instructed to concentrate on learning German. Meanwhile he passed the monthly exam at the school. Jawad tried to learn the words, which had some similarity with English. Carla also helped him with the exercises at home. German grammar was something that Jawad found difficult to grasp. He was finding it hard to cope with the three articles, Der, Die, Das, which represented "The" in English. Der was used to denote masculine things, Die for feminine, and Das denoted neutrality. His teacher, Frau Gattiker, was a very patient woman and always tried to do her best to help Jawad when he had problems understanding the nuances of the new language.

There was still no news about Jawad's documents. He'll call his family twice a week but always got the same answer. No one had come to make an inquiry. He asked his colleagues at the café and they told him it could take months. At the end of the second month in school, he passed his second level. Fluency in German was important for him to get ahead in life. But German was not English which he started learning from early childhood. He'd learnt that language as easily as his own mother tongue, Urdu. Once done with the language class, Jawad decided to implement plan B which was to ask for some vocational training. He realized that it'll be feasible to become a waiter for the time being. He tried to convince Mr. Stauffacher that it was pointless, especially after his newly acquired language skills that he should go back and work as a dishwasher.

"What do you want to do?" he asked while looking at his school report.

"I think after my experience as a barman, I want to work in the front, as a waiter. But for that I need a diploma," Jawad replied somberly.

Mr. Stauffacher took a deep breath and looked at Jawad.

"I'll see what could be done in this regard."

He kept his words. A letter from the Zurich School of Gastronomy arrived soon. It contained information regarding an orientation day. Jawad went to his new school, along with 50 new students. The receptionist collected their registration letters and handed them their badges. They were taken in to a hall where three people occupied the podium. One introduced himself as the cooking teacher, the other as the director of the school, while the third, a short and stout figure, was the service teacher. He introduced himself as Ricko. First, they were lectured about rules, timings, and discipline of the school. Then they were divided into two groups according to their trade. Jawad and his group followed Ricko upstairs, while the cooking students headed towards the kitchen with their teacher. Ricko distributed a Service book to his group. The book contained every conceivable illustration required to serve a table. He informed them about their lecture timings, starting from 9 am in the morning with a short break at 10.30 and lunch at noon. Every day five different people from the group would serve as waiters for practice. At the end of the term, they had to take an exam. Their performance report would be sent to their counselor. The class was a mixture of Serbs, Tunisians and Turkish students. Jawad and a Swiss were the odd ones out in Ricko's group. Their uniform was a white shirt with a black trouser. The cooks wore chef jackets.

Jawad realized that the school operated in a very intelligent way. Downstairs was the cooking department. The cooking students would learn as well as cook for almost 60 people till noon. Every day they would try different dishes. At lunchtime the service students would arrive in the dining room and learn to serve the meal. Ricko would advise them how to present food. The people sitting on the tables were to be treated as real customers and there was no room for being nonchalant. A major part of the dining experience was wine. Swiss took their wine very seriously. The class was not able to use actual wine to teach the norms. Each day service students would fill the bottles with water and then seal them with the cork machine. While serving lunch, the bottled water was to be served as wine, following strict rules. Sometimes, the atmosphere would become surreal. Still, Jawad enjoyed the eccentricity and marveled at how somber the serving of a soup could be.

Dressed like a waiter with dreams of a university student long gone, Jawad went to attend the first day of his Gastronomy School. The lectures were in German. He prepared the notes and tried to memorize things just like he used to do when he studied English literature at university. Sometimes he would say to himself, *what a fall from grace! From Shakespeare to spoons, from Twain to* champagne*! How would Oscar Wilde describe the irony of it all?*

But he would console himself by the vague promises of money which he would earn after finishing that course. Jawad was impressed by the technical facilities in the classroom. It was equipped with a large projector screen. It was linked to the computer and a remote, which Ricko wielded like a sergeant major's stick. Ricko taught them how to decorate a table for a multi-course dinner and how to arrange the wine glasses according to the client's order. On his first day, Jawad watched as Ricko prepared a table for four and told his group to finish the rest. Within twenty minutes, they had arranged the dining room for seventy people. Then all the students sat down except the five chosen to provide the service. Ricko took a bottle of water and showed them how to serve the wine. Then he stood aside and watched his students replicate his precise instructions. Ricko emphasized that theirs was a respectable profession, and that the person serving the food was as important as the food itself. An establishment with poor service and personnel could ruin the business, no matter how highly it was rated otherwise. The staff should look like gentlemen and act like gentlemen while serving the guests. Only the woman staff was exempt from this rule, he would add with a chuckle.

For Jawad it was a small step but an important one to solve his short-term financial problem. He planned to apply for higher studies and work in a proper profession once he had settled down and resolved his financial problems. Right now, he looked forward to the completion of this course and finding a job, which shall pay well. *One step at a time.*

Carla had never been to a Gastronomy school. She'll read the service book with great interest, comparing it with the real world. She told that some of the stuff they were taught was more for show and to give an illusion of a superior establishment.

Back at the school, Jawad had a new friend, a Serb named Goran. He had worked at various jobs, but always for a very short period. Now his employment counselor had sent him there to learn the skill and find a steady job. He was tall, strong, with blue eyes and blond hair. His wife worked in a hotel and they both had many connections in the food business. Jawad often accompanied Goran for a smoke during their breaks or at the end of the day. Goran spoke little English but his German was better than Jawad's. He seemed to be an interesting person, always commenting on the women around. He commuted to the school with car and always dropped Jawad home at the end of the day. However, before that he'll always stop by some bar. After couple of pints and some loose talk, they would resume journey back home.

Jawad was now permanently living with Carla. On Singh's suggestion, he had given up his room. Mr. Vanoni told him there was no need for the usual months' notice as the room shall be occupied in no time. Only problem was that Jawad needed a fictitious new address; he didn't want to give Carla's address until they're married. He was sure Singh would agree to register his place as Jawad's new address. Singh didn't let him down. The following week, he called Jawad about a letter from the Asylum office. Jawad dropped what he was reading and raced to Singh's place who handed him an envelope with red stripes.

Red stripes oh my God.

He remembered seeing the red pattern on John Paul's letter. Jawad opened it with dread. There were various forms inside and a very official looking letter. He skipped most of the top half of the letter, and jumped to the middle, which was in bold and underlined.

Though he didn't understand all the details, he found out that his asylum application had been rejected. He was required to leave the country within two months.

"That's just what I feared the most." Jawad said, looking aghast. Singh put his arm around his shoulder and tried to reassure him that it wasn't the end of the whole affair.

"I know how you feel *buddy.* We take a torturous path when we leave our house and family. However, the strongest always survive. We'll get there yet my friend," Singh spoke philosophically.

Were all my efforts in vain after all? Jawad wondered.

They waited until Stephanie returned home; she could explain the contents better. She went through the whole letter, and once finished she clarified as best as she could. First, she told Jawad that he still had a chance for an appeal within thirty days. He was also required to provide some evidence in support of the claims he had made in his interview.

"And where am I going to get this evidence?" Jawad looked beaten.

"The first thing you should do is not to lose your nerves. Let's see now. Okay, although I got myself a lawyer, I don't think that's very useful in your case," Singh expressed aloud.

"Why do you think so?" Jawad asked in a worried tone.

"Because you don't have any proof to support your claim. All you can do is try to argue and reshuffle your last interview. We need to write a letter in response, defending your situation. Stephanie can help you to write it. It'll buy you some time. I hope that by then you'll be married. But if you have a genuine political situation back home, it's best to get a lawyer," Singh suggested.

They decided to buy as much time as possible and write the letter three days before the deadline for his appeal. After a glass of wine with Singh, Jawad left. Once home, he tried his best to hide the bad news from Carla, though she seemed to notice that all wasn't well.

Next day he received a phone call from his father. After inquiring about his wellbeing, his father told him that someone came to the house from Islamabad. He asked questions about Jawad. His father assured Jawad that everything went fine and the man left after a short interview. Jawad immediately called Singh.

"Now the Marriage office will send you the letter to come and choose a date. We're not finished yet my friend." Singh reassured him. Jawad wasn't totally convinced.

He tried to keep his mind occupied and read as much of the course material as he could by the help of a German - English dictionary. At the school, Ricko did his best to make professional waiters out of them. Tunisians, the biggest demographic group in the class, considered Jawad as one of them. Seven out of twenty-five students were Tunisians. It always surprised Jawad that so many from that country had ended up in Switzerland. To satisfy his curiosity he asked one of them; the answer was very simple. They had all worked in the tourist industry back in Tunis, which was a favorite destination for European travelers. They charmed, befriended and married European women who were on holidays there. Those women fell in love with these Tunisian Casanovas and brought them home, like a hunter brings back a trophy from a distant safari. Jawad wondered who the predator was in this case, and who the prey was. On the other hand, maybe it was a win-win situation for all those concerned.

Jawad knew that soon he'll be searching for a job and Goran could prove a good connection in that regard. They were spending the weekends together due to the occupation of their respective spouses. The five weeks at the school passed quickly. Jawad and Goran both passed easily and received a certificate from Ricko, who said they should value it like a university degree. Ricko wished them the best of luck. On the last day they were served lunch. This time by real waiters hired for the occasion. Afterwards, Goran drove Jawad home for some celebration drinks. As usual, he was great company, though he seemed always to be economical with the truth when relating stories and describing events of his past.

Jawad realized that he was running out of time. He should be married as soon as possible. Once a deportation order is out, police might come to look for him at his given address. He remembered what happened with Abdul and Ali. But his worries were lessened as Carla received a letter after almost four months of submitting their papers. They went to the city marriage office very next morning. After checking the register, the lady at the counter gave them possible dates on which they could marry. They decided for September 14. Next thing was to go through the guest list. Jawad invited the Singhs, Denni, Daniella and Mr. & Mrs. Goran. He didn't invite any of his colleagues from Café Central. Nasir excused because of his trip to Pakistan. Carla invited a few friends from Zughaus. Her mother would join them on the wedding day along with her son Paulo and his family. In Pakistan, he informed his family about the wedding. They were all excited though little disappointed due to their absence. He didn't tell any of his friends in Lahore, as he had hardly been in touch with anybody other than his family. Friends that took oaths of eternal friendship had disappeared with time and now were oblivious to each other's lives.

Jawad also went to do some shopping with Carla. First item was the wedding rings. Both looked for something modest and not too expensive. After some window-shopping and deliberations, they chose what they thought was just right. It turned out to be simpler than they had imagined. They were offered free engravings, which they thought was a nice touch. They selected a couple of words to engrave for each other, which they hoped to live up to until their senior years, or senile years as Jawad called the golden age.

Next on the shopping list was what to wear for their big day. After much consideration, Carla bought a light blue dress with stunning silver pearls on it. Jawad selected a cream-colored three piece suit with a silk tie. Paying for everything was less of a problem as they had budgeted beforehand. *Now I just need to make sure that I'm still in Switzerland on my wedding day.* Stephanie told them that she'll take care of the flowers. *Sorted, Jawad thought.*

The wedding was to take place at eleven in the morning and then an *Aperitif* and lunch. A friend of Carla's late father owned at a restaurant on Niederdorf Street. They went there and discussed different options. Finally, they agreed on a three-course menu, first soup, then salad and finally main course of beef along with multiple side dishes, followed by a wedding cake. Now everything was falling into place and they began the count down to their grand day. Carla's mother was to arrive with her son on the morning of the 14th. She didn't want to burden them by coming early though Carla insisted. Jawad liked the idea; with their two rooms flat it might be difficult. Goran confirmed his attendance but informed that his wife won't be able to attend due to her work. Denni also confirmed his attendance with his girlfriend. Singhs were to join them at home on the wedding day to help with the preparations. Mr. Singh was to be the official wedding photographer, though Jawad had not seen anything in his portfolio to be overly impressed. Meanwhile Stephanie helped Jawad with the letter to the refugee office. He knew it would be considered as an appeal. With the wedding day in sight, he felt much more confident about his situation. He decided to contact the immigration office immediately after the wedding, to submit the necessary documents for a permanent residence permit.

On the eve of their wedding, Jawad and Carla had the car washed, cleaned the apartment, drew money from the bank. They did not want anything to go wrong the next day, and Carla went through her tasks list and ticked off things one by one. By late evening it was slowly dawning on him the almost unbelievable fact that he was getting married to a beautiful girl in Switzerland, something he had never imagined in his wildest dreams back in Lahore. By nightfall, they chatted, nervous and excited and clinked two glasses of wine to their health and good fortune the following day.

"Your last day of freedom, from tomorrow you can't look at any other girl," joked Carla.

"I can't see anybody, my eyes can only look at you," Jawad sang in return.

They woke up early the next morning and enjoyed a hurried breakfast. It was time to get washed, groomed and to look their very best. Carla began to transform herself from a pretty maiden to a stunning bride.

Mr. and Mrs. Singh arrived at nine as planned. Carla emerged from the bedroom, and Stephanie ran up to hug her. She'd never looked so beautiful. Jawad glowed with pride while Singh began to capture the moments on his expensive looking camera. Isabella and Paulo, accompanied by his wife and son arrived shortly; after the hugs and kisses it was time for more poses and portraits. Singh was savoring his newfound role as a wedding photographer, and was gleefully ordering everyone around. Carla's family found the whole situation highly amusing. Stephanie told Singh not to take himself too seriously, and let everyone relax.

Jawad left the room to call his family in Lahore. His father had taken the day off and they were all together for the special day, waiting to hear updates from Jawad. He heard his sisters talking excitedly in the background. His mother showered him with blessings and wished she was there to see her eldest son, and the first of her children, getting married. Listening to her sweet voice, Jawed tried his best not to break down. Suddenly it dawned on him just how far he was from his beloved family; he felt his stomach tightening, his eyes welling up.

Come on, be brave. You're supposed to be the pillar of the family, remember.

Thankfully, his sisters cheered him up with their frantic comments on how handsome their brother must be looking on his big day. There were more requests for lots of photos of the day's proceedings. Finally, he said he had to go or else he'll be missing his own wedding. He hung up and went back into the living room. At last, everyone walked towards the waiting cars which were arranged neatly in a row. Jawad and Carla sat with Stephanie while Singh drove their car. Paulo took some shots of them leaving home on his video camera. Soon the whole entourage was on their way to the City Hall. Thankfully, it was a pleasant and mostly sunny day and the memories, both in mind and on film would be bright and cheerful.

As they arrived at the hall, Singh and Paulo got out and rushed ahead, to film the couple getting out of the car and entering the venue. After posing for a few group photos they went upstairs to the marriage office. The staff was different this time. The lady in-charge of the ceremony welcomed them and asked for two witnesses to accompany the couple. As planned, Stephanie and Singh stepped forward.

A door to the adjoining room opened and a young girl asked the wedding couple and witnesses to enter. Carla also took her mother along, and asked permission for Singh and Paulo to do the photography. The girl explained the procedure and showed them the marriage certificate. She read a small poem, asked them to take their vows. Soon she declared them husband and wife. After the rings, there was a long kiss to show their determination. Jawad was given his marriage certificate, a prized possession. Comparing this to the ceremony and the proceedings of weddings in Lahore, to Jawad it seemed trivial. Back home, festivities usually last up to three days, with meals for hundreds and the celebrations costing a fortune. The whole ceremony took less than half an hour.

The couple came outside and crossed over to stand in front of the river for some romantic poses. Everyone hugged and congratulated the newlywed couple. It went on until noon and then the wedding party proceeded to the restaurant for lunch. The manager there greeted the couple warmly. They all settled around the designated tables. As the guest satisfied their thirst, Jawad warned Singh not to show any hints of alcohol in the photos. Lunch started on time at 12:30; it was most appetizing, and the guests seemed to be enjoying the occasion and the ambience. Jawad thought the wine was delightful and Goran offered him toast after toast. He held Carla's hand to cut the cake, more for guidance than tradition as his head was getting heavy with the wine. The wedding gifts were piled on a corner table. With the cutlery clinking, along with the sound of laughter, everyone seemed relaxed and jolly.

After having their share of the wedding cake, the guests started leaving. Denni and Daniella were the first to say their goodbyes and best wishes. Carla's mother was beaming with joy and invited the couple to Italy. Her brother asked them to come to Lugano first. "They have accepted me as part of their family", thought Jawad. Though Carla asked her mother to stay a little longer, she insisted on leaving with Paulo. They too decided to leave, and asked for the bill. They paid with a large tip, and complimented for good food and service. The staff helped them to put the gifts in the car, as Singh took some final snaps. Stephanie told them that she'll prepare the dinner and get it delivered by her husband. Singh drove them back, and they found themselves at home, now officially man and wife. A few warm kisses, another celebratory drink, wishing each other a happy future, both went to bed for some rest. From now on, they owned each other, officially.

Jawad called his family later in the evening, after drinking some strong coffee. It seemed they too had been celebrating. Everyone wanted to know how the day went and how marriages take place in the west. Some of Jawad's relatives were also there and he also heard music in the background. Jawad answered their never-ending questions as best as he could, making up certain facts to suit the occasion. They were happy with his guileful answers, and asked to speak to Carla. He told them she was tired and taking some rest. As he was finishing with the call, the doorbell rang. He guessed it might be Singh and opened the door. Singh handed him a large bag and disappeared as quickly as he had arrived. Jawad opened the bag in the kitchen. It contained roast chicken, rice, potatoes with *chutney,* and a bottle of Moet Chandon champagne.

"Dinner time sweetheart, courtesy of Stephanie and Singh," Jawad shouted to Carla.

"Oh, how sweet of them," she cooed.

She went to the kitchen and looked for a few candles to put on the table. It was their first dinner after marriage. No mischief was avoided and none of the childishness spared. Chilled champagne was perfect with roasted chicken and spiced rice.

Next morning they opened the presents one by one. There were all kinds of gifts, from decoration pieces to bottles of wine; a scarf for Carla and a tie for him and some perfumes as well. Then they went to change Jawad's address in the local municipal office. From there they drove to the immigration office where they presented their marriage certificate and applied for Jawad's residence permit. It could take four to six weeks, the clerk told them dryly.

He also informed Mr. Stauffacher about his wedding who smiled and congratulated him. Days passed quickly and soon Carla was back at work. Jawad was spending most of the daytime alone. His only companion was Goran. They were both looking for jobs. Thanks to his new friend, Jawad was drinking more. Goran knew many people, mostly Serbs who had settled in Switzerland. One Saturday Goran invited Jawad to the inauguration of a bar in his neighborhood. The owner was a fellow Serb and one of his friends. He asked Jawad whether he'll like to come. Jawad was finding it hard to say no to free drinks and company of pretty chicks. Goran came to pick him up in his car. The bar owner welcomed them with two cocktails. The place was pack with young couples. They danced, smoked and drank, as did everybody. It went on until midnight. Jawad was worried about Carla waiting for him, but Goran seemed oblivious to his concerns and went on enjoying the party. Eventually, Jawad got a call from Carla. He quickly went outside the bar to take the call. He knew he'd to give an excuse. He told her that Goran brought him along for an opening ceremony and both were helping the proprietor who needed extra people.

Jawad felt a strong guilt in his mind. He lied to her, although not for the first time, but that day he felt different. However, the display of liberties inside pulled him. They returned very late. Goran avoided the main roads to avoid police. When Jawad entered the bedroom, Carla was sleeping. Jawad tried to sober up as much as was possible. He gargled with a strong mouthwash, trying his best to kill the smell of alcohol. Thankfully, Carla was in deep sleep and didn't notice his arrival.

In the meantime, Jawad was trying to transform himself into a proper husband. He had played the part of a lover and now it was time for further advancement. He helped her in the home whenever he could. He tried to give her the intimate company she might be looking for in life. The only intrusion was Goran, his booze companion. Though Jawad liked his company, he avoided him when she was at home.

Carla got four days off from work in May. They planned to visit her brother in Lugano during that. They started early in the morning. The scenery along the route stunned Jawad. They reached Lugano and took the road along the lake in the middle of the city. Her brother lived in the suburbs. He had a four-bedroom apartment and one of them had been transformed into a guest room for the couple. Paulo and his wife welcomed them warmly. Their five-year-old boy hid behind his mother. He said something in Italian in a very endearing way. They had lunch and rested a while in their room. Soon Jawad dozed off, and when he woke up he heard Carla talking to her brother in the adjoining room. Afterwards she returned to the room.

"Is everything all right?" Jawad inquired.

"Yes, I was telling my brother not to wait for us at dinner and that made him a little angry. Actually I want to go to the city and we can eat there. We're on holidays."

They drove to the city and parked the car. That part of the city surrounded the lake. There was a long winding road, which enabled one to walk from one corner of the boulevard to the other in a semi-circle. There were mountains on the either side of the lake and clouds capped the mountaintops. Even in Lahore, people often spoke of the snowcapped Swiss mountains, comparing them to the sights in Kashmir. Jawad found it difficult to decide which was more stunning. They walked to and fro holding hands. Once, got tired, they settled on a bench. After a while, Jawad left Carla on the bench and went to nearby shops. He bought a bottle of red wine, roasted chicken and olive bread. The sales girl gave him utensils and two plastic glasses. Carla laughed when she saw him carrying the bag. She got up and went to a nearby restaurant to uncork the wine. To grace the evening, soon a full bright moon showed up. Lights on the boats sailing on the lake added to Lugano's wonderful scenery. Rather than sitting at a dull table in a restaurant, they were enjoying the meal sitting on the lake. Jawad looked back at his life and wondered how his fortunes had turned. He'd seen some lows, perhaps it was time for some highs. He realized that life often threw up surprises when you least expected them.

Next day they went to visit Lake Maggiore on Jawad's request. He had a special desire to see the place. It all came from when he read Hemingway's *A Farewell to Arms* in his university years. It was written by that tragic alcoholic who fanned his suicidal tendencies with wild hunts and cocktails. Jawad never imagined that someday he'll visit the lake which provided the backdrop for an important scene in the book. Though Jawad admired Hemingway, he never did understand why he committed suicide. May be it was the success that unleashed the demons within him and which eventually destroyed him. Carla had not read the book and all she knew was that he wanted to visit another lake. While they stood there, Jawad imagined the imaginary scene when the two tragic characters, Frederic Henry and Helen Ferguson rowed towards Switzerland. On the other side was Italy. Milan was less than an hour away but he had no visa for Italy.

They stayed in Lugano for two more nights and visited all the popular sights and scenes in their surroundings. Paulo and his wife were wonderful hosts who cooked great Italian food and served the best wine. Their son never bothered them, played when it was time to play and studied when it was time to study. He was in his first school year. Carla spoke to her mother couple of times as well. The couple returned to Zurich on the fourth day, full of fine memories and a carton of Merlot di Ticino, one of the renowned local wines. Next day Carla left for work as usual. Jawad checked the pile of mail. He'd been waiting for something. It was a letter from the local municipal office. He was informed to bring along his passport and a payment of seventy Francs. Finally, his resident permit had arrived. Once he stepped out of the office and on to the pavement, Jawad paused. He pulled out his residence permit to have a second look at it. There it was; the fruit of his efforts, the fulfillment of his mother's prayers, and the symbol of his success. First, he called his parents to break the news. They were overjoyed. Their son seemed to be doing well. Then he called Singh and Goran. In the afternoon, he went to collect Carla as she emerged from the Zughaus for her break. She too was delighted for both of them. He was no longer an asylum seeker; rather he was now a resident husband of an honorable Italian citizen. In addition, the chances of getting a job were now much brighter.

On his next visit, Mr. Stauffacher copied Jawad's new residence permit and put it in the file.

"I've something for you as well," he told Jawad, handing him some papers.

"What's this?"

"There is a place close to the Zurich airport; it's called Conference House, a big establishment with large halls and a restaurant. It's mostly used for conferences, meetings and concerts. Many of the guests are foreigners and English is widely spoken there. I've spoken to their HR Manager about you and she seems positive. All the details are on the sheet I've given to you. You may call Miss. Luis Hansen, the HR Manger and mention my name."

Jawad thanked Mr. Stauffacher and called Miss Hansen as soon as left the office. She was quick to recognize the purpose of his call.

"When is it convenient for you to come?" Miss Hansen asked.

"I can come today if you like."

"What about tomorrow at ten in the morning? I'll speak with Mr. Bollinger who is our restaurant manager. His consent is also necessary for the new staff in the restaurant."

Jawad was satisfied. Thanks to the language school and the help he got from Carla, his German was much better now. Things were moving in the right direction. Carla too welcomed the news. She gave Jawad many tips for his interview. She advised him to stay there after the meeting and try to work for lunch hours to impress the potential employer of his determination. She ironed his clothes and checked his file. That night, Jawad went to bed optimistic, but that didn't stop him from thinking what lengths he had to go through just to find a job as a waiter. Next morning, he was determined to be positive about things as he set out for his interview. He had to take a bus from the airport as advised by Miss Hansen. His destination, the Conference House, was a big building. He went to the reception and asked for Miss Hansen. Five minutes later, Jawad saw a young woman approaching him. She was a rare type of beauty that Jawad had seen in Switzerland; possessing the seductive looks that one only imagines in fairy tales or sees in Hollywood movies. She had a tall voluptuous body, with long golden hair and deep blue eyes. Jawad tried hard to overcome his awe and shook her hand as nonchalantly as he could. She introduced herself as Luis Hansen, the HR Manager of the establishment. She took him upstairs, opened the door of a small office and offered him a seat. Jawad handed over the copy of his credentials. After quickly leafing through the file, she stood up and copied his documents at the photocopier in the office. She kept the copies in a file with Jawad's name on it.

"Mr. Bollinger is waiting for us," she said going towards the door.

The restaurant was in the rear of the building with a garden. Two waiters were busy arranging the tables for lunch while a girl was watering the flowers in the garden. The restaurant was beautiful and had modern lighting and beautiful paintings, which further enhanced the beauty of the place.

Bollinger was standing behind the bar. He was dressed in a business suit and looked more like a banker. They sat on a corner table for their little assembly. Miss Hansen handed over Jawad's file. He opened it with intent.

"No experience?" Bollinger seemed irritated.

"Yes sir, but how could I have any experience if nobody gives me a job," Jawad pleaded.

"You got a point. How is your English?"

"Excellent, as you can see in my CV, I did my Masters in English."

"What, then why are you looking for work as a waiter?" Bollinger asked with surprise.

Jawad politely explained that his degree was not acceptable in Switzerland and he had to take up some other profession. He didn't forget to mention that he'd recently got married and needed a job urgently. Jawad also told him that his wife was in the same profession He was not strange to the field either as he had worked at Zughaus. Once Jawad had spoken, Miss Hansen stood up.

"I'm leaving you with Mr. Bollinger and he'll explain the nature of your job. Once finished, you're free to go. There are some other candidates for the same job as well. But we'll contact you in any case."

Bollinger introduced Jawad to the two men who were working there. They were Mark and Niccola, one German and the other Italian. Then they went towards the kitchen which was huge. Bollinger explained to him that one section of the kitchen was for the restaurant and the other for parties and functions when hundreds of meals had to be served. Behind the kitchen was the staff dining room. Then he showed him the service area. Bollinger also explained the automatic system for ordering meals and drinks. A slim girl was working behind the drinks buffet.

"This is Nada, she is responsible for the drinks," he introduced the girl.

He took the menu card and explained its contents to Jawad. It was a combination of French, Italian and Swiss cuisine. The introduction finished in half an hour. Bollinger made some final remarks and shook hands with Jawad.

"Can I ask you a small favor?" Jawad asked politely.

"Of course you can," he seemed surprised.

"Is it possible that I can stay for the lunch hour to work today?"

Bollinger was silent for a few moments.

"I think you can, but I'll have to ask Miss. Hansen," he replied thoughtfully.

He went to the service area and picked up the phone. Jawad waited patiently.

"I've spoken to Miss Hansen and she had consented. I'll attach you with Mark who can guide you."

He called Mark over and explained what he had to do.

"Mr. Jawad is here to work with us for lunch hours. I'm putting him under your supervision."

Jawad followed Mark and together they prepared the tables for lunch. Mark also explained the nature of the work. Then it was time for the staff lunch. Mark introduced him to Sandra, Sasha and Petrovic, three female members of their team. They were a team of five working 100%. For the busy evenings, Bollinger was at liberty to seek help from other workers of the house.

At 11:30, they returned to the restaurant. Bollinger gave a few instructions about the lunch menu and told them their duties in the restaurant. Mark and Jawad were assigned to the tables on the right side. The work wasn't new for Jawad as he had seen it all at Zughaus. The guests here were different than Zughaus. Mark ushered the diners to their tables while Jawad brought them the menu cards, asking them about drinks. There were daily menus and the regular restaurant card, then a separate card for wines and one for the desserts. Bollinger was everywhere. Jawad smiled at his guests, taking orders politely and serving them with his utmost care. He wanted to make an impression and demonstrate that he was not a novice in this work. A small group of British arrived for lunch. Mark told Jawad to take care of them. Jawad asked them to follow him and offered them a quiet table in the corner. Jawad explained the in house specialties and took their order. Out of the corner of his eyes, he noticed Bollinger watching him intently from a distance. He served them lunch with confidence and panache, knowing well that he was under observation. All went well and after the lunch service, Bollinger told Jawad that he could leave. From his tone, Jawad knew that he'd made the grade. He'd shown his ability as well as flexibility to fit in with the rest of the staff.

After two days, Jawad received a call from the Conference House. Miss Hansen informed him that he had got the job. He'll receive the contract through post and could start working next month. Once she had the signed agreement, he'll receive his timetable. He informed Carla about the good news. The next day he received two copies of a two-page document with all the details regarding his work, salary, holidays and etc. His gross monthly pay would be 3,800 Francs. It was subject to a raise after the completion of his trial period, which was three months. He signed the document and Carla wrote a request for rest days similar to her. Jawad's workplace was at some distance. It meant they won't be spending the afternoons together but they'll have to compromise, keeping in view of their financial needs.

Jawad prepared himself for his new job. He bought a new uniform and a special wallet to store the change. He also bought an extra pair of shoes with comfortable soles. He was ready to embark on a new and promising career. He planned to work at that place as long it required, to fulfill his obligation, which he owed to his family. Four to five years of hard work might be enough for these things, and then he planned to study further. He would love to work as a teacher or work in an office environment. He met up with Goran the next day who gave him a few tips regarding making extra money at work. "If you've an American customer, tell him that service is not included in the bill. Americans give at least 10 to 20% tip. Take care of the Russians and always recommend them the expensive stuff. They feel pride in paying more. Most of the Russians coming to this country are millionaires, otherwise they won't be here. Don't bother about French or Japanese, they don't give tips," he advised.

Jawad wondered that how could his guests know that their generosity was paving the way for the prosperity of his family thousands of miles away in Pakistan? They should like the cheering fellow who never leaves them unattended and gives them good vibes. He realized that the money he was going to earn every month was beyond anything that he or his family had ever earned. The more money he saves, the sooner he'll be able to pay off his obligations.

Mao famously once said that a journey of thousand miles begins with the first step. For Jawad his new job was a small step towards his long cherished dreams of prosperity. Something which had until now eluded him.

The person who greeted him on his first day at the Conference House was Niccola. He told Jawad to prepare the tables for lunch. It was all ready when Bollinger arrived. He acknowledged Jawad and others and went into his office. Jawad had not seen Miss. Hansen and missed her majestic presence. Jawad was working with Niccola. Sasha and Petrovic also joined them at the staff lunch, as did Mark. Sandra had a day off. Afterwards, Bollinger explained the duties for the day and assigned the tables. Lunch hours began and everybody moved to his or her post. Jawad observed his colleagues trying to place as many guests as possible on their designated tables. The more customers meant more tips

Jawad held a tray under his arm like the others most of the time. There were times when he used to carry the books at that place. He took orders, served meals, cleaned and arranged the tables. At 2 pm, only he and Niccola stayed behind while others left for their break. Afternoon was not busy and he spent the time learning the ins and outs of his work. Niccola was kind enough to explain to him how to use the order machine.

"Hello Jawad, I hope you're settling in perfectly," someone said as he was talking to Niccola.

It was Miss. Hansen. Jawad tried to keep his composure, though he realized that looking at her was some kind of nourishment for the soul. She'd come a long way from the office to welcome Jawad on his first day of work. Jawad felt indebted and asked if she would like a coffee or something. She told him not to hesitate to contact her if there was any problem. *You are my main problem.*

"How was your first day?" Carla asked him when he returned home.

"It was fine, but very demanding," Jawad answered with sleepy eyes. He kissed her and soon dozed off.

On his fourth day, Bollinger told him that he can work independently. Jawad would have his own tables in the restaurant and an electronic key, to use on the electronic register for ordering. At the end of the their work, everyone from the service staff had to fill a form and deposit the money and the credit card receipts in a leather bag provided by the management. What pleased Jawad the most was the approval of his request for the rest days. He was off on the first two days of the week just like Carla.

First shift started at 9 am. In the morning, they only had to serve coffee and snacks. At lunch, people mostly ordered one of the four menus, which were changed every day. The magic moment came when he placed the order for his first table. Jawad had his first tip from a couple, who were probably workmates out for lunch. The man paid the bill though his companion insisted on sharing. He gave him a three Francs tip and Jawad thanked him with a slight bow. First week at work passed and he felt relieved as nothing disturbing happened. He enjoyed every minute of two days off with his wife. Next week his shift changed and he worked with a break at 2 pm. On his first break, he asked Niccola where he goes for break.

"To the airport, it's not that far."

Jawad also went with Niccola to spend the recess. It was not a bad place to spend some idle time. There was a big recreation area just like every other international airport. They sat near the viewing gallery and Jawad began reading a book he had brought while Niccola browsed an Italian newspaper. They drank coffee, and then browsed around the gift shops until it was time to go back.

Over time, Jawad realized that their boss Bollinger was actually a very decent man. He'll run around, making sure everything was in order when the restaurant was full. He wanted the customers to get their order precisely and immediately. On concert days, the place was exceptionally busy. The guests had time and money to enjoy an evening, which was to serve as a prelude to the rest of the week. There were people like Hans Graf, who were without any financial worries and would spend as they pleased. On evenings like these, the restaurant made up to triple the normal sales and the service staff got more tips. People would be in a hurry to go to concert. Once the restaurant was empty, they could relax a little. Some guests would come back after the concert for a late night snack or a drink. By 11 pm, it was time to close.

In three weeks, Jawad had made almost 900 Francs in tips. It was four times more than what he used to earn while working for Mr. Malik. The thing that he noticed was that when he was working, he seldom spent money. He had given up smoking a while ago because Carla disliked the smell. Meals and drinks were provided courtesy of his employer and charges were nominal for that. He felt his financial burden lifting and sensed a sweet smell of success around him.

In Pakistan Jawad had often heard a saying, "If you want to know someone, either travel with him or dine with him."

Some guests would ask for every detail about food. What were the ingredients? Where did they come from? How the dish was prepared? At times, he had to run back to the kitchen and ask questions from the chef to satisfy a diner who won't eat without knowing all the details. A few of his workmates joked that these guests were from lunatic asylum. Some guests would declare that they had given up the pleasures of the flesh, at least the eating part of it. Jawad had to be extra careful with the sauces, as some of them contained meat extracts. One thing he hated the most was opening a wine bottle. In rush hours when someone ordered a vintage wine, the guest expected a ritual. First, he had to clean the imaginary dust from the bottle and present it to the esteemed guest, who in turn would verify the name and the year of the wine. Then he had to take the glass, pour just a sip, and give it to the guest to try. Some would approve it just from the smell; others would take a sip and move it around inside the mouth before giving the nod. During this process, precious minutes would be lost, minutes in which he could take a couple of orders or serve a meal. However, it was all part of the service, and anyway there was no such thing as free meals in life, he realized.

The chemistry among the service team was a bit complicated. If someone had served fewer tables, he was resentful of others and vice versa. Then there was rift between the cooks and the service staff. The cooks would claim that the guests were regular customers because of them. If they didn't cook so well, there would be no customers in the establishment. They considered themselves the backbone of the business. The service people, in their opinion, were doing nothing but placing and removing the plates from the tables. The cooks never missed an opportunity to insult the service staff, and neither did the staff in return. Service staff had a pride of its own. They considered themselves the face of the restaurant and a beautiful one too. They argued that if they didn't take care of the needs of the guests, they won't return. It was their cheerful mannerism, the sense of servitude, which they offered to the guests and that compelled them to come again. But perhaps the real driving force of the establishment was Mr. Bollinger. He was everywhere, the omnipotent and the omniscient. In his presence, things would run smoothly even though Jawad never heard him raising his voice. Whenever there was a problem or a complaint, he knew exactly how to handle it. He made the whole place tick like clockwork.

On the 26th of his first month, he received his salary out of which he sent 2,500 Francs to his family in Lahore. As the situation of his finances improved, his urge to visit his family increased. He had heard from his Asian friends about their first journey back home. A period of four years was considered normal. Then there were people who returned home after a decade or so of listless wandering. However, they still considered their ordeal worthy, their tribulation a quest of an ultimate success. Anyone returning within a couple of years was considered lucky. However, the first visit back home was like Caesar returning to Rome. The later visits were routine but the first one was the special one. It was a proof of success and evidence that "one had made it." But it was normal that a trip like that required considerable thoughts and substantial cash. He'll have to buy gifts for every family member, not just ordinary gifts. Jawad tried to make a list of shopping and expenses required for his trip home. It seemed daunting. First three months were his probation period and it was impossible to take holidays during that. The fourth month might not be suitable as well. Two weeks of holidays seemed sufficient and he needed to start planning his journey. He decided not to take Carla along on his first trip. If she came along, Jawad knew it would be difficult for both of them to feel free. It was not a liberal open society where she could travel as she pleased. Either he'll have to accompany her everywhere or she would have to stay home most of the time.

Meanwhile, his performance at work improved day by day and Bollinger seemed happy with him. Jawad was also pleased to be there. He always longed for a glimpse of Miss Hansen who rarely showed up in his work area. His only contact with her was through his pay slips, which bore her signature. Nevertheless, he knew he would see her at the end of his probation period. In the last week of Jawad's third month, she congratulated him on the successful completion of his probation period. She also told him that from then on he was a permanent member of the staff of Conference House. Jawad thanked her for the help and the trust she had shown in him.

"Do you want to say anything?" Miss. Hansen asked at the conclusion.

"Yes, there is something I would like to ask. I need holidays to visit my parents in Pakistan."

"This is something you would have to discuss with Mr. Bollinger."

He thanked her and left the office.

He went to speak with Bollinger. Jawad explained to Bollinger that it had been years since he'd seen his family. He admitted that he'd not been at the Conference House for long but only recently did get his immigration papers. As now he can travel, he requested if he could have two weeks off at the start of his fifth month. Bollinger noted it on a sheet, but didn't give him a definite answer, though he said he'll try his best to work something out. Jawad was satisfied with his conversation and went to join Niccola for some company during the break. He eventually found him sleeping on a chair, with a newspaper on his face at a coffee shop at the airport.

Although Jawad was confident that Carla won't object to his trip to Pakistan, it was still tricky because he had to tell her that he planned to travel alone. The following night, Jawad mentioned his desire to visit his parents. He told her that he was not taking her along this time, for sound reasons. But next time they would go together. She seemed slightly surprised but didn't raise any objections. Jawad explained that he'd not seen his family for years and assured her that he'll be back within few days. Carla told him that she understood absolutely though her eyes betrayed her sadness. Jawad made her clear that next time they would go together.

On Wednesday, Bollinger told him that he'd checked and Jawad could have his two weeks holidays in the beginning of next month. Jawad wasted no time in handing him a note with the dates written on it, with the first day of his holiday starting on a Wednesday. In that case Jawad could also use Monday and Tuesday. Bollinger indicated that there were no problems and he could go as he planned to the country he was once so anxious to leave but now missed badly. Perhaps it was because he was sure of his stay in Switzerland now and could think of issues beside immigration. The fourth month of his work was ending, and it was time to make arrangements. Singh gave him the number of a travel agent. Jawad called that guy and gave the dates of his travel. Soon he got an email with the reservation. He'll be flying to Dubai with Emirates Airlines, and after a brief stopover, onwards to Lahore. Jawad visited the travel agent and picked the ticket. The guy told Jawad that he was getting the best offer.

Singh told him that it was better not to inform his local acquaintances about his visit; otherwise he would be overwhelmed with requests to take gifts and gadgets for their own families back home. Singh also told him to take Swiss chocolates with him, according to his experience it was something people of every age liked. Carla also mentioned her own ideas about what to buy. His first purchase was Swiss watches for every member of the family. He knew his brother would love to have a video camera. He decided to buy perfumes and colognes from Dubai airport duty free. A week before his departure, he went with Carla to a chocolate factory. It was famous for selling chocolates to tourists and locals at a reduced price. They bought 15kg of the finest Swiss chocolates of different types of fillings. Once he felt he was all prepared, Jawad broke the news to his family of his visit. They were surprised and delighted with the news, though little disappointed that they won't be meeting the new bride. His mother's voice was quivering at the sudden news and she said she'd spent many a nights worrying whether she'll ever see her son in her lifetime. They all wished him a safe journey. When he asked if they wanted anything from Zurich, he was touched to hear that they just wanted to see him again. He decided to hang up before tears engulfed and suddenly realized how much they all meant to him and how desperately he wanted to see them again. In the following days, his heart was no longer in his work His mind constantly flashing images of his arrival at Lahore airport, and seeing the whole family waiting anxiously for him. He wondered how they might have changed over the years. His siblings would certainly be mature, and probably more serious and wiser. From his phone calls, he noticed that at least they hadn't lost their sense of humor.

Sunday evening he bade farewell to his fellow workers who in return wished him a safe and enjoyable trip. His flight was due next day and he'd to be at the airport at 12:30 pm. Carla made him a big breakfast but she was mostly quiet. Jawad tried to cheer her up, joking with her, hugging, and kissing her. However, nothing would lessen the pigment of sadness in her blue eyes. He reminded her it was only for two weeks. After a few more hugs and kisses, eventually they towed his luggage downstairs to the car. Everything was double checked, the passport and the ticket etc. Jawad was glad while Carla stared ahead, mostly in silence. Thankfully, he'd to unload quickly at the "pick and drop zone", as he too was getting emotional at leaving her. It was their first separation since their official union. A last wave as Carla drove away and Jawad went towards the check-in. Ahead lay tiresome lines, much waiting and security checks. His flight to Dubai was six hours long, and then another three hours to Lahore where his family would be waiting anxiously for his arrival. He was the savior of the family, the one who had taken it upon his head and considered it his utmost duty to provide for them. He was returning home to them with pride and honor.

During the flight, Jawad was disconcerted that some of his fellow countrymen could not curb their curiosity and asked him all sorts of strange questions. Some of them he knew from Café Central. How was it that he was travelling so well if he had been a refugee? How did he manage to get married in Switzerland? If he married without money and only for love, then what was his trick? Jawad tried his best to pacify them, telling them that such questions were not suitable for such high altitude and require some earthly consideration. Rather than wasting too many words on them, he put it all down to *lady luck,* his fate written in the skies above. They looked at his wedding ring and nodded in admiration. Jawed closed his eyes and thought of the coming hours which were now almost within sight. Dubai airport was a magical world. It was a big tube full of shopping malls, restaurants and lounges. Jawad went to the Duty Free and bought some cosmetics, perfumes and couple of handbags. After three hours, he was checking into his last leg of the journey in a different plane. He was surprised at the decline in quality of the service and the change in general demeanor of the flight crew. It was the same airline but now they didn't seem to be as professional or as concerned. Two hours into the flight, the monitors showed the plane entering the airspace near Karachi, just where the Arabian Sea met the sub-continent.

After circling a few times, the plane landed at the new Lahore airport, named after the country's national poet. It was 4 am in the morning. Just like everybody else, he went through the custom and immigration hurdles. He soon found himself outside. The heat seemed to hit him like when he would open the huge ovens and machines at the Zughaus restaurant. In the arrivals lounge he spotted his father and brother who were anxiously waving to catch his eye. Much hugging and backslapping followed. His brother introduced Jawad to his friend Mr. Baqir. It was his car they were using to pick him up. They loaded his luggage into the car and drove home in haste. Faraz phoned ahead that they were on their way home. Jawad looked out at the scenes that were whizzing past him. Though he had lived in this city most of his life, right now it seemed somewhat alien. The intense light, the heat, the throngs of people, the dusty roads and the chaotic traffic had a strange effect on him.

The car slowed and pulled up outside the house. Everything was same. There was almost a commotion as the rest of the family rushed out to greet him. His sisters clung to their long lost brother who had returned as a successful man. He turned to his beloved mother who was waiting patiently. She kissed his forehead with tears in her eyes. Jawad could no longer hold back his own tears as he hugged her. She hadn't changed as much as he'd feared and was looking as elegant and wise as ever. His sisters looked much taller than and twice as pretty as when he'd left them. Typical girls, thought Jawad, always in hurry and growing up much quicker than the boys. He was glad to see the house and the memories came flooding back when he entered his room. They all gathered around the dinner table. It was laden with the most exotic foods he had seen for years. There was a whole buffet of the traditional eastern cuisine and to Jawad the smells were heavenly. He ate with relish and answered many questions. Everyone realized he needed a rest and he was excused to sleep. It'd been a long journey, one that had stretched his nerves to breaking point. He couldn't even pour himself a glass of wine as he normally would "back home". *Where was back home actually?* Wondered Jawad as he walked into his room.

Before lying down, he called Carla and assured her about his safe arrival. She seemed distant and still sounded sad. *What a sweet girl she is.* He told her to keep busy and invite friends over or go out with them. She said that she was fine. Jawad made some jokes and finally he heard her sweet laughter. Afterward he hung up and went to sleep. Jawad slept until early evening and when he awoke, his mother wasn't around. She had gone to visit a shrine with his brother to offer her gratitude for the safe arrival of her son. When Jawad found out he thought it might've been better to thank the Emirate's crew instead of a saint long gone, someone who had never seen a flying machine in his lifetime.

His father had taken leave from work and was sitting in the veranda. His mother returned soon and asked Jawad how he was feeling. Jawad assured her that he was fine. He wandered over to where his sisters were studying, and they quickly put down their books and pens. He told them he'd brought gifts for them, and some special Swiss chocolates.

They jumped up in delight and shouted to the others to come and see the Swiss goodies. Soon, they surrounded him like children around a juggler waiting to watch his next trick. One by one, he showered them with gifts. Everybody was trying on his or her watch and delighting in seeing objects from a distant land. Once finished with the gifts he put the chocolates on the table. He saw the happiness in the eyes of the young and pride in the eyes of his parents. All his efforts and hard work seemed to worth it. He felt exonerated. He also called some of his old friends and told them that he was in town, inviting them over. They were delighted to hear from him and welcomed him back to Pakistan. The neighbors too came round and treated him like a star, looking at him with awe. His mother and sisters tried their best to take care of him in every way and protected him like a fragile object. He reminded them that he was still the same person who had lived there a few years ago.

In the coming days, everybody slowly got busy with routine life once again. Jawad's father went to teach, his sisters sat their various exams. His brother had recently started working as a trainee in a finance company and he was worrying about his prospects of getting a job. His mother who commanded the position of an elder in the family, decided that Jawad needed to visit some close relatives. He agreed rather reluctantly as he knew this meant more grilling and interviews. He also wanted to see some of his old acquaintances first.

First, he went to meet Mr. Sheikh, the person responsible for sending him abroad in the first instance. Sheikh was delighted to see him. They spoke for a while and Jawad gave him a bottle of cologne. Next he went to see Ahmad and his first ever employer at Money World. Ironically, Ahmad was sitting on the other side of the partition serving some customers. Jawad decided to surprise him. The guard outside the shop was not the same as when Jawad worked here. He pulled out some Swiss Francs and went to the counter. Ahmad was still busy with counting money and Jawad waited his turn. As the counter became free, he thrust forward the money: "Excuse me sir, would you please change these." He spoke like a regular customer while pushing the money through the hole. Ahmad seemed to recognize the voice and looked up. His eyes widened with surprise.

"Oh my God! I don't believe this!" he dropped the notes onto the counter.

The loud exclamation alarmed the security man but he soon realized that everything was fine and it was just harmless greetings of old friends. Ahmad opened the door and soon Jawad was sitting at his old place of work. A few more customers arrived and Ahmad was busy serving and talking simultaneously to Jawad. His wallet soon became heavy with rupees that Ahmad handed over. Jawad could see a look of envy in Ahmad's eyes.

"So, how are you doing my old buddy?" Jawad asked him.

"Fine, I'd given up my plan of leaving for abroad. My mother had made it clear that as long as she is alive, she won't allow me to leave. I tried my best to convince her but in vain. I don't want to break her heart; she is so dear to me. But the good thing is I'm starting my own business very soon. My father had given me some money and I also have some savings of my own. Mr. Malik is helping me to open a travel agency. These days I'm attending an evening school for air-ticketing course. What about you? You called only couple of times and now you're here all of a sudden. I hope you've not been deported."

"Do I look like a guy who had been deported?"

"No but I asked because people usually don't return that early."

"Well, I was close to deportation but an angel saved me."

"What kind of an angel?" Ahmad asked in surprise.

"A very beautiful angel, her name is Carla and she is my wife."

"What, are you trying to tell me that you are married to a *gori*?"

"I'm not trying, I'm telling you."

"Wow that's great. And how is she?"

"She is a very nice and kind person."

"But did your parents agree to the match?"

"Of course they did. That was the only way that I could stay there. Now everything is settled. I've a job, a wife and a residence permit. I'm here only for two weeks."

"You had done well *buddy*! So what kind of a job do you have over there?"

"I work as a salesman at an electronics shop," Jawad tried to keep a straight face.

Soon, Mr. Malik arrived. He was surprised at the sight of Jawad sitting behind the counter and gave him the traditional hug. Then the questions followed and Jawad read the script once again. He was becoming sick of the probing questions and the inquisitive nature of his fellow compatriots. Malik too wanted to know every single detail of his story. He told Jawad that he was trying to send his son to England for higher studies.

"The sooner he gets out of this country, the better." Malik concluded.

Before leaving, Jawad gave Ahmad a perfume and some chocolates. To Malik, he gave few chocolates for his children. Ahmad's role had been very vital in his life though they lost touch.

The grilling, which he faced visiting his relatives with his mother, was even tougher. Many sought his advice so that their boys could also join the lucky ones living abroad. Jawad tried his best to explain to them that life abroad was not a bed of roses. But his mother later advised that he should not tell the difficult aspects of migrating abroad. "People may think that you've done alright, yet you're telling them not to send their boys abroad."

"What do I care if somebody goes abroad or not?"

"I know, but these people may consider that you are jealous as their boys might achieve what you've achieved," she tried to reason with him.

Meanwhile, Jawad realized that things had changed in his social circle. His old friends were all busy, some with jobs, others got married and some had gone abroad. He didn't have the time to meet all of them. Agha Sahib had moved to a bigger house with an even bigger lawn. His business had now expanded to the Far East. He'd become a telecom tycoon.

Jawad called Carla every single day, sometimes more than once. She missed him. Jawad missed gazing into her eyes, the odor of her body, her gentle voice and touch. From afar, she seemed like something ethereal. Living with her on a daily basis, he'd gotten used to her angelic face, blue eyes and her noble personality. He vowed never to take her for granted. She was beyond precious. He remembered the vows he had recently taken.

The excitement of visiting Lahore soon began to wear off and within a week, Jawad began to feel bored. Though seeing his parents and siblings again was a pleasure beyond measure, his bland daily routine and lack of social life soon began to take a toll. The lonely nights without Carla were becoming more and more unbearable. During the day, he would go out to buy the groceries, do small chores for his mother and read the local papers to pass the time. Then his mother would take him to some relatives for a visit. His mother would sing his praises in front of them and would tell them how the son's virtues hadn't been corrupted in the West. He hadn't changed a bit. Jawad was glad that she didn't knows how many lies he'd told and how much alcohol he'd consumed since he left. His premarital relationship with Carla would have been one of the highest moral sins in the eyes of his mother had she actually known. Jawad heard her pray that her daughter-in-law should embrace Islam soon. She had even planned to ask for that at her next visit to some shrine.

Jawad had a wish to see his old friend Ali Akbar but he didn't have his number. He knew his town but going there and looking for him without an address was not a practical idea. The days passed and he didn't have much time on his hands. The money he had sent so far was not all spent.

His parents had saved it carefully and told him they were thinking about redecorating the house. Jawad assured them to go ahead.

"There is something else I'd like to discuss with you. It's about your sisters," his father told him one evening.

"About my sisters, what is it?" Jawad asked, looking concerned.

"This is their final year of graduation and soon they'll have their final exams. One option is further study at the university. But only the youngest can qualify for that. Other one has no such intention. Your mother and I were thinking that the sooner we marry them off the better it will be. There is a very suitable proposal for that."

"Who are those people?"

"There is a distant relative of mine who lives in Kuwait with his family. He has two sons who help him to run his business there. They also have some property in Lahore but they are happy in Kuwait and have no plans to return in the near future. He was in Pakistan last month with his wife and they visited us and asked us for the hands of your sisters."

Jawad had heard about that family but never actually met them.

"Did you say yes?" Jawad asked, sounding responsible.

"Not yet, we wanted to ask you first. They also asked us to consider a couple of things."

"And those are?"

"They want both the sons to be married simultaneously. There'll be no dowry because the girls will be moving to Kuwait. They don't want the hassle of transporting the furniture and things to over there. They just want a simple ceremony, preferably sometime next year. But as they are not asking for dowry, we want to give at least something to your sisters. We can't just send them off empty handed like that."

"Of course we can't," Jawad understood.

"Well this is the situation; your mother and I are both happy with this match. Now what do you think son?"

"What can I say? I'm in favor because both of you are."

Jawad knew that he can do anything for the happiness of his sisters and the honor of the family. He'll help his parents to give the girls some land as a gift where they could build their homes whenever they returned to Pakistan. Unlike migrants to Europe, Pakistanis never get nationality in almost all the Gulf countries, even the generations which were born there. Eventually, when their skills were no longer required, they were sent back along with their descendants.

Jawad asked his mother whether she had asked the girls about all this. His mother assured him that she had. The girls responded that they knew their parents wouldn't decide anything which was harmful for them. They would consent to any decision that they made. Jawad was relieved because he knew that mostly girls were not consulted about the most important decision of their lives. They were only informed once everything had been decided for them. Then, they had no other choice but to accept the decision even if they don't agree with the match

One thing Jawad had to get for himself while in Lahore was a driving license. It would help him to get a Swiss driving license on his return. And thanks to the corrupt ways and the local modus operandi, he didn't have to do very much. He went to the license office, where there were so called intermediaries roaming around looking for clients. The man he happened to speak turned out to be perfect. He was an ex-policeman who was dismissed for corruption, a rare occurrence as corruption was the norm in this country. The procedure and the amount of money were soon agreed upon and Jawad paid him half of the amount. Rest was to be paid on the receipt of the document. Within two days, he was issued a brand new computerized driving license. There was no theory test, no practical, only a test of his means. Money here not only talked or walked, it even drove. Now he could even go and drive in Switzerland. All he had to do was to get an appointment for a half hour driving test. If it was found to be satisfactory, he'll get his Swiss driving license in a matter of no time.

On the eve of his departure, while he was packing, his mother came in to his room. He was surprised to see that she was holding a red velvet box."

"This is for Carla and don't come alone next time. Bring her with you as well."

Jawad opened the box and saw that it contained a beautiful gold necklace with matching earrings, studded with pink pearls.

"Mum, why did you spend so much money on that?" Jawad protested.

"Nothing is too much for my daughter in law," she reassured him. "Anyway, I didn't spend much money. There was some old jewelry that my mother gave me when I got married. I took it to the goldsmith who fashioned it into something that can be worn even by a European. You've a very beautiful wife," she spoke with pride.

Jawad was touched by the love his mother portrayed for his wife. He could just imagine how overwhelmed Carla would be when he'll give her that box. His sisters did their part too. They gave him two beautifully embroidered dresses for Carla and some gift cards with all kind of zany things drawn and written on them. There was also a videocassette, produced, directed and mostly acted by his sisters.

Jawad called Carla and gave her the details of his return flight. She said she would come to the airport, regardless of her work. He bought some local sweets and delicacies. He gave to his father most of the money he brought with, keeping only what he needed for the journey back. He owed them plenty and he knew that money will be spent on more important things here than in Zurich. Jawad had an early morning flight and nobody slept that night. Everyone was trying to get the last words. His siblings joked about childhood incidents, which always turned out to be refreshing. As the morning dawned, he saw sadness in the eyes of his mother. His brother and father were more pragmatic and wanted to know about his plans in Zurich. While there seemed so much to discuss and share, it was time to leave. Laden with their love and prayers, he left once again for the airport, looking at his mother and sisters standing at the doorstep as the car pulled away. Baqir drove them to the airport.

This time he left Lahore without the element of uncertainty. Officer at the immigration desk didn't bother much and waved him through. Overall, Jawad was satisfied with his trip. He enjoyed the honor and importance his family had shown to him. His visit also made him more aware than ever of the differences in the two societies that he shared.

The flight to Dubai was spent mostly reminiscing about the people and place he had visited. His stopover in Dubai seemed shorter when he met two of the regulars from the Café Central. They invited him for some Lebanese food in one of the outlets at the airport. Jawad relished the food, especially because he could now compliment it with some suitable liquor. A few times in Lahore, he felt he could have upped his sagging spirit with some alcohol, particularly when he had sorely missed Carla's company. Soon it was time to catch the flight to Zurich. He was thinking about Carla only, absence does indeed make the hearts grow fonder, he thought.

It was raining when the plane landed in Zurich. Rushing thorough the immigration and quickly collecting his luggage, he soon found Carla waving excitedly in the arrival lounge. They hugged and he gave her a long passionate kiss. He couldn't keep his eyes off her; she looked even more divine than ever. When she asked if he kept well during his trip, he had to tell her that he had hardly ever slept without her. Carla jokingly asked who he had slept with then. They both laughed, two souls united again.

Back home the table was ready for the meal. He enjoyed the meal but what he enjoyed even more was her company. After they were finished with the meal Jawad, opened his bags and took out the gifts. First, he gave her the jewelry set from his mother. She looked at it with amazement and immediately tried it on. The eastern adornment seemed even more delightful on her European features. Carla couldn't believe how many presents his family had sent her. She asked him to play the tape his sisters had sent her. It was the first time she had seen all her in laws in their surroundings, and found it hilarious when girls read out funny poems for her and posed in their *saris,* dancing to a raucous Bollywood song. Carla was almost speechless and wanted to visit her new family that had showered with such gifts and shown her so much love.

"I promise Carla, I'll take you along next time," he tried to pacify her.

"Are all Pakistani girls as sweet as them?" she eventually asked, looking at his sisters on the screen.

"Lahore alone must have a million like them. But these two are my little angels," he said.

"Mine too. Is it true that you could not sleep without me, amore?" Carla asked teasingly.

"I slept sometimes. You know, I found it so strange that I had slept in the same bed, in the same room for so many years of my life. Then, the same room seemed so empty without you. Yet, you'd never even been in that room Carla. How could a room not seem to have someone in it, if that someone had never been near the room in the first place? I couldn't figure it out. That kept me awake even more," he tried to explain.

"If it makes you feel any better, you weren't the only one awake at nights," she confessed looking into his eyes.

"Oh my sweetie, I didn't know," he seemed perturbed. "Let's go and catch up with some sleep."

Back at work, he received a warm welcome from his colleagues at the Conference House. Jawad was now a member of the team, on equal terms. He was no more a hesitant beginner who had to check twice what the guests wanted. He had covered another milestone in his journey of transformation. Others in the team had already done that. Of course, the monetary reward of that change was immense.

Yet there was something he could not give meaning to. At times, his work mates would have melancholic smiles on their faces. Sometime he would see them talking but when he came closer they would become silent, or walk away as if they didn't want him to hear their private little chat. He knew that there was something going on but he'd no idea what it was. Jawad also noticed a few times that some of his colleagues were serving the drinks without any ordering slips. Slowly it all clicked. He realized that they were stealing and they didn't want him to know. It was obvious to Jawad that this was only possible because it was a very busy establishment. The restaurant had sales of six to ten thousand Francs a day. Bollinger or the management could not check every transaction, especially when the place was full. When Bollinger had a day off, there was a part time female substitute from the office. She was a middle aged German and didn't bothered much. Jawad wondered how to react. In the beginning, he thought that he should discuss the matter with Bollinger. However, he soon dropped the idea. Firstly, he had no proof and second, it was none of his business. He was not doing something wrong, at least presently.

He decided to take the direct action and talk to Niccola what was going on, but first he'll observe and learn. He began to see a pattern. Sometimes there were guests only for coffee or drinks. He saw Niccola serving the coffee to such customers, charged the money without touching the ordering machine. Instead of the order being registered, it was pocketed by the staff. It wasn't difficult to understand. Jawad was amazed that if he could figure it out in a few months, how come that Bollinger was unaware of this. Or maybe they have an accomplice. He decided to have a word with Niccola about this.

"Niccola, can I ask you something?" They were spending there recess hours at the airport cafeteria.

"Yes, of course."

"How do you get the stuff without ordering at the electronic register?"

"What stuff do you mean?" Niccola asked while looking around.

"Oh come on, I've seen you serving and charging the customers without even touching the ordering machine."

Niccola was silent for a while. He looked like someone who'd just been caught stealing.

"It's simple. Even you can do it," he confessed eventually.

Jawad had no such intentions but he wanted to know who else was involved. Niccola explained that almost everyone in the service staff was stealing. Moreover, he was right; they had an accomplice and a very clever one. Nada was responsible for drinks. People in the kitchen were not so keen in cooperating. However, at rush hour one was at liberty to play the tricks. Especially with soups and salads which were in the open for the staff to take at their discretion.

"When you are serving about hundred people within two hours of time, few coffees, two or three salads or soups don't make a big difference. At the end of the day you have more money and at the end of month much more. Mr. Bollinger is a very straightforward person and he could never imagine that such a thing was going on below his nose. The service team is used to deal the regular customers and they know their paying habits. Some never bother with the bill and pay whatever the amount is. They hardly look at the bill, only at the sum. We pay Nada at the end of the day and there is no criterion. Sometime she complains and we pay her more."

Niccola explained the rules of the game but he was nervous, like all the thieves are. Jawad consoled him, telling that he would keep that secret. Jawad realized that those rascals earned much more than him. He wondered whether he should join them or stay out it. That evening was very busy. He saw Niccola serving two glasses of wine at one of Jawad's tables. The customer paid and Niccola gave the money to Jawad who took the money hesitantly.

"Now just don't register it on the machine. It's all yours, but give something to Nada as well."

Jawad could've denied, protested or gone to Bollinger but he did nothing. He considered himself someone who had started his journey on foot. On the way he found new ways and means, some means accelerated his progress. However, what started as a slight mischief soon became a full-fledged engagement. His salary, along with tips and the money he made from stealing, added up to more than six thousand Francs a month. This was beyond his wildest imagination. His honest, hardworking father didn't make as much in half a year, even as a senior lecturer in a college. Indeed, his father was a little worried when he sent a particularly large payment to Lahore that month. Jawad assured him that he worked overtime. At home, Carla had no idea about what was going on.

During their rest days, Jawad and Carla kept themselves busy. They would go on a long drive, and eat out or watch a movie. However, deep in his heart, Jawad felt strange. He wanted a change in his life and start afresh in a new profession. Although his job paid him well still his heart craved for something else. He never imagined that he would get disenchanted with it so soon. Then, developments at the Conference House changed the situation dramatically.

Criminals are usually considered to be half-witted but those who think they could never be caught are probably the most witless. Now that all of them had become involved in stealing from the business, it was causing losses of thousands of Francs to the House every month. Perhaps, Jawad had joined in the gang's unsavory activities at a bad time. Nevertheless, nobody had forced him. He had himself to blame for his poor judgment and moral failing. The first sign of trouble was the sudden disappearance of Nada from her job. Then they were told to collect their soup and salad orders from the kitchen while before that stuff was left on a side table for the service staff to fetch. The opportunity to interfere with those vanished.

When Jawad went to work next Wednesday, he was told to report to the office along with others. They assembled in the lobby outside the office. Bollinger was stomping in and out of the room and no longer looked like his pleasant self. They noticed the house director going into the office shortly after. First Niccola went inside. He came out after 15 minutes along with Bollinger, who motioned him to leave the building quietly. Jawad had little difficulty in understanding what was going on. They were all being confronted about the stealing. But what Jawad feared the most was the legal action that may follow. That could result in serious consequences. Then it was Jawad's turn to face the music. He knew he'd been caught and didn't want to argue with Bollinger who seemed to know their guilt anyway. All Jawad could do was to accept his fault and ask for leniency. The office had been turned into a courtroom. The most embarrassing moment was when he noticed Miss. Hansen sitting next to Bollinger and the director.

"You know why you are here?" She spoke, trying to hide the anger in her eyes.

"Not really," Jawad tried to pretend ignorance but perhaps it was too late.

"We had a signed statement from Nada, detailing how you guys stole money by charging customers through unregistered sales. Do you admit to this allegation or is she lying?" Hanson pushed the charge sheet towards him.

Jawad had a sudden sinking feeling. Never in his life before, had he been accused of such base behavior. Only a few weeks ago he had been received as the savior of his family in Lahore. If his parents could witness the scene now, they would probably die of shame. His throat became dry and he desperately tried to get his voice back. After mumbling incoherently, he decided to remain quiet. He couldn't look in to their eyes. They had been so kind and supportive of him, and this was how he had repaid their trust. There was an eerie long silence.

"I take your silence as a yes to the allegation," Miss. Hanson eventually broke the hush.

Jawad realized that staying mute was more useful than speaking and he sat with his eyes fixed on the table, looking grave and guilty.

"We've spoken with our lawyer. For your information, we're not pressing any criminal charges presently. But your contract with this company has been terminated with immediate effect. You'll get your salary for the month but consider yourself an ex-employee of Conference House. Just to show that we mean no ill will, we won't be mentioning anything in your reference letter. People who trust you in their establishment will be doing so at their own risk. Is that all understood?"

"Yes," he barely whispered.

"Now please read this and sign it if you agree. It's your termination letter."

Jawad signed the document without even looking at it. There was no room for any arguments. He handed over the keys to Bollinger.

"You'll get all the necessary documents in the mail soon. Do you want to say something?"

"I'm so sorry for letting you and Mr. Bollinger down," he spoke, finally looking up.

"We are sorry too for trusting you but your apology is noted," she moved her eyes away from him and started typing on her computer. Bollinger gestured him to leave. Jawad left the building without saying a word to his colleagues. When he reached the bus stop, he saw Niccola waiting for bus. He didn't know whether to blame Niccola for getting him into this mess or to just let it go.

"Niccola, what went wrong in there?"

"It's all Mark's fault. He began arguing with Nada about her cut from the money. What they didn't notice was that Bollinger was also around and he heard everything. When he pressed on Nada, she told him that we were all in it."

"And how do you know all that?"

"Mark told me. They had already arranged the new staff last week."

"Now what's next?"

"The world doesn't end with the Conference House. We can always look for another job. But first I'm going to rest for a while. They're paying this month's salary anyway," he seemed unconcerned.

"It might be simple for you, but for me it was difficult enough to find my first job. And I blew it."

"Don't be so hard on yourself. I'm sure you'll find something. You're a smart guy after all."

Niccola tried to raise his spirit.

They exchanged their contact numbers with a promise to keep in touch. Though justice had been swift and applied clinically, he liked the Swiss style of justice. It was strong of head but soft of heart. In addition, they hadn't tried to demean or disparage the staff, despite being cheated and deprived of tens of thousands of Francs.

Jawad returned home with a heavy heart. In the morning, he had left home with a smile on his face and a well-paid job, and now he had lost it all. He wondered how he'll explain this all to Carla. He couldn't tell her that he'd been involved in stealing and pilfering. Eventually he made up a story. He decided to tell her that some of the team members were caught stealing and management took it for granted that they were all involved. He could tell her that he was not experienced enough to do such a thing but management made no exemptions and the whole team had been fired. He knew it'll be difficult to sell his story but hopefully she'll believe him as she always did. However, before that he decided to talk to Goran who was also working in the same field. He phoned Goran to discuss the matter. He wanted to test whether Goran is convinced with his lie or not. Then there was the issue of finding a new job. They met at Letzipark Center, which was convenient for Goran. They found a window table and ordered drinks.

"So what is it you want to tell me, Mr. Groom?" Goran asked to him.

"I've lost my job Goran," Jawad said after a brief pause.

"Oh God, that's bad news!" Goran was taken aback. "But how did you lose your job?"

Jawad decided to tell him the same story he had planned for Carla. He told him about his innocence, while putting the blame on the old cadre. Goran bought the story and called his superiors as pigs who fired Jawad even though he had done nothing wrong.

"So, what are you going to do now?"

"I don't know. I've got to find a new job and the sooner I get one the better. I've responsibilities here and a family in Pakistan to support. Carla is working and doesn't need help from me. I can go on unemployment benefit but that won't be enough," he looked beaten.

"Yes, you are right. Once you are used to earning money and spending it, it's not easy to pull back," Goran professed.

"But if I don't find something soon, I may ask for unemployment benefit," Jawad proclaimed.

Goran was quiet for a while.

"Listen Jawad, my boss is planning to expand. He's making a small fortune from the restaurant and wants to branch out into a different line of work. He wants to open a disco. These days, he is finalizing a deal to rent a place in Schlieren. The place needs some renovation. He told me that he wants me to work there. But he'll be looking for more workers. However, it'll open only at the weekends, which means two nights of work a week. Rest of the week I'll be doing stuff like advertising and fixing the place. I can talk to him about you if you like."

Jawad liked the idea. The club might be an interesting place to work. Jawad thanked Goran for his consideration.

At night when Carla returned Jawad pretended to be asleep. He decided to talk to her in the morning as she might be tired after work. Next morning, he was waiting for her at the breakfast table, still in pajamas.

"Amore, do you have a day off today?"

"No, actually there is a problem," he looked serious.

"What kind of problem amore?" Carla couldn't understand.

"I've been fired from work," he decided to come to the point.

"You are kidding!"

Jawad rubbed her hands gently. He was warming her up to listen to his story and to believe his lies. As he had planned, he put all the blame on the others, stressing his own innocence. She didn't question him and looked at him with sympathy. She tried to reassure him that everything will be fine and that she still had a job which is enough for them both. He breathed a sigh of relief when Carla left. *A few lies in a long life of good deeds were not such a big deal.* To make himself useful, he took charge of the household. He cleaned the house, washed the clothes and bought some Knicks knacks to brighten up the place. He fixed a few things in the kitchen and the bathroom which had been long overdue. He wanted to prove his resolve and worth to Carla.

Jawad also phoned Singh to tell him about his job loss. He also informed his friends at the Café Central about his unemployment. He had not been there for a while and they updated him about things which he missed due to his absence. After everyone poled in with their stories, he told them he intended to find work quickly but needed their help. Jawad called Goran for an update on the possibility of starting work at the club. Goran told him that it might take a few weeks for some progress. Jawad realized that if things kept going the way they were, he might have to register for benefit after all. He can't live without income for long. That month he received his salary as usual with his letter of recommendation. It was well written and Miss. Hansen had kept her word. He was stated as hardworking, punctual and a friendly person. Flexibility was the hallmark of his work. The reason of his job termination was blamed on the seasonal drop in turnover and the cutbacks at the company. Jawad felt another bout of guilt.

He checked the newspapers and the internet for any suitable jobs. He couldn't rely on other people anymore. Though Goran was always in contact with him, telling him that things were moving in the right direction and he need not to worry. Carla contacted her friends in the gastronomy branch and they promised to inform her if there was a job available. Jawad also tried to look for a job in language schools where he could teach English. However, those schools were already crammed with teachers, qualified from the UK and USA. Who would like to hire an inexperienced teacher who didn't even have an internationally recognized degree? Then Jawad got a break, one he didn't even expect though it was for a short time.

One of Goran's acquaintances, Alex Cetkovic had migrated to Switzerland from Belgrade some twenty years ago. He'd been working in various restaurants since then. For some time he wanted to open an establishment of his own. He was stunned by the success of some of his fellow compatriots, whom he considered inferior in knowledge and expertise to him. He described to Jawad that he'd completed compulsory army service in Yugoslavia under Marshal Tito's rule. He even once served Tito when the former came on the inspection of his regiment. Later he had pursued a career in acting. He even learned English for that purpose, in case Hollywood shows some interest. He claimed to have worked with Richard Burton as an extra when Burton came to Yugoslavia to film "Sutjeska". He cursed the day when he came to his country, a move which deprived the film audiences of another Burton. He was a close relative of Goran's wife. It was she who recommended Jawad to him and arranged a meeting. Alex told Jawad that as the place he was starting up was still under construction, he needed an extra hand to help with the preliminary work. His brother who was supposed to do that work was stuck in Belgrade due to a visa problem. Later he drove Jawad to show the place of his dreams; a place which he professed would make him rich and successful. He seemed a bit strange to Jawad; he pretended to possess an imaginary aristocratic aura, for which Jawad saw no real cause. Alex had named the place "Little Italy" and intended to offer Italian cuisine in his new restaurant. As Alex led him in, Jawad saw that the place was still in the early stage of renovation.

"The people who are working here have other jobs to finish as well, so they come whenever they can. Actually they're m**y** friends. There'll be a dining hall big enough to house more than eighty people." Alex explained.

On one corner, there was a U-shaped bar, which Alex claimed would've all kinds of liquors and beers on taps.

"Here I want to construct a lounge," Alex spoke, tapping the floor with his shoes.

"I'm looking for some nice sofas and teak tables for over there. This part would be mainly used for drinks," he mentioned.

"Here, this is for you," Alex gave him a set of keys. "From tomorrow on, you'll open the place every day, except on weekends, at around ten in the morning and stay till the evening. I'll also come here every day at different times. I want the door to remain open all day. If someone comes to deliver something or to do some work, let those people in. I also need you for buying the stuff for the restaurant as you can see there is still lot to do. The only inheritance, which my predecessor left for me are few bottles of brandy." he concluded.

Jawad was surprised at the sudden turn of events and pocketed the key. Alex went behind the bar, filled two glasses of brandy and offered one to Jawad. They stood in the future lounge and Alex continued chatting. Jawad still had no idea about the salary, and dropped a hint.

"I can't pay you much, so if you agree I think 2,500 Francs would be a reasonable sum." Alex replied. Jawad bargained a little and finally they agreed on 3,000 a month, plus the drinks which Jawad was at liberty to consume provided he didn't get drunk. Once the restaurant starts running, Jawad will be working as a waiter. However, both the parties were at liberty to depart at a short notice.

Next day he opened the soon-to-be restaurant. The first man who entered "Little Italy" in the morning was a short and strange looking guy. He was just over five feet tall with a double chin. His round protruding belly made him look comical. He introduced himself as Rosso, the head cook. He was followed by an assistant cook cum dishwasher named Salvatore. Then the pizza maker Joaon arrived who was Portuguese. Rosso told Jawad that he was from Naples and came to Switzerland 30 years ago. He claimed that he was one of the best footballers of his time in Naples. He compared his style of play with Maradona. Looking at his physique, Jawad ignored his lofty claims. They held a long meeting in the kitchen. To pass the time in the garbled and half-done place, Jawad always came to work with a few books.

Following morning, some men arrived to fix the ventilation system which probably needed replacement. Next week, the floor was almost ready, though it still needed a thorough cleaning. The furniture arrived at the weekend, and Jawad helped Alex to arrange the tables after trying different angles. Within two weeks, the place looked entirely different. The kitchen was upgraded, fitted with new utilities. New lights were installed and decorations hung from the ceiling. Alex planned a big party for the opening but there were still few things to be done. Alex and Rosso were busy preparing the new menu cards in Italian and German. At the end of the third week, everything was almost in place. Jawad helped Alex with the shopping. They went to all the local second hand shops and bought paintings and antiques to create the right ambience. Alex, with his aristocratic airs finally declared that the restaurant was definitely going to be a roaring success.

"My friend, many people spend a million Francs on a new business but avoid spending a penny on publicity. In this case, you'll see ads on local television, radio and in the newspapers. I've even contacted a columnist to write a feature on this place. That's the way to start a business professionally," Alex made his plans clear.

With his fancy new utensils in the kitchen, Rosso started experimenting with the cooking. He'll prepare a meal from the proposed Restaurant card and then ask their opinion. Soon the cards arrived with their leather covers while the wine dealers began to come with their samples and deals. Alex wanted Italian wines only and for this purpose selected just one of the suppliers who was obliged and showed his gratitude with a bottle of Grappa. It was duly sampled and approved by everyone at the end of the long day. Carla was busy working and every evening Jawad told her the proceedings of the day. On the last Friday of the month, the work at Little Italy was all but complete. Alex selected a Monday for the opening ceremony. Invitations were distributed to the whole street and Alex personally went to some of the local offices to invite people. It was decided that there would be free pizza, snacks and drinks for all those who came to the opening. Alex told Jawad to invite his wife as well. He asked Goran to be the bar man, and his own wife, Denka, was to be the hostess at the door to welcome the guests.

Monday morning, Alex picked up Jawad from home and they both arrived early at the restaurant. Rosso joined them along with the rest of the kitchen staff who were all on edge with a busy day ahead. Alex formulated and explained the plan of action to everyone. The pizza maker demonstrated his talents with four different pizzas which everyone shared for lunch. Goran appeared in the afternoon and got busy at the bar. He decorated it with a multitude of decanters and glasses. The official time given to guests was five. Many of the arrivals were supposed to be future customers and Alex was anxious that they were especially catered for. He told Jawad not to let anybody leave without a drink. Jawad liked his generous attitude. The journalist with the cameraman came first and both settled down with their martinis. Rosso had made some snacks, while Joaon laid out slices of various pizzas onto large trays. Carla soon came too and posted herself with the hostess at the door. Music played softly in the background and everyone was soon busy talking, drinking and singing the praises of the new place. Jawad moved back and forth with a tray full of drinks. Alex offered snacks and pretzels to every newcomer. Brochures of the restaurant were handed to the guests and Alex ensured that nobody left without them. At its peak, the place was buzzing with excitement and the drinks. Cameraman showed his talent by taking pictures for the newspaper. By 10 pm, people started leaving. Slowly, sanity was restored; the music too was toned down. They all began to clean up so it would be ready for business the next day. Women took charge of washing and drying the dishes and the glasses. Men removed the decoration and re-arranged the tables and the furniture.

Everybody seemed to have had a good time. When Jawad eventually met up with Carla, she gave him a strange description of Alex and his wife. She had the impression that they were the kind of people who love a lavish lifestyle but could not really afford to have it. Expensive cars, expensive holidays and designer clothes were what Mrs. Alex spoke to Carla about all evening. Jawad considered that people like Alex make many assumptions and if they fail, they never accept the responsibility. They'll deny the fact that it was they who had assumed unrealistic hopes.

Next day Jawad drove to work with Alex, who was strangely talking to himself. He kept saying "to be or not to be" repeatedly, and seemed to be under the spell of Richard Burton. Jawad came dressed as a waiter while Alex looked smart in a black suit with a purple tie. Mrs. Alex was also there to help wherever it was needed. Rosso rushed around, trying desperately to organize for the lunch hours. The pizza maker, Joaon, went off to the cellar where he was to prepare the dough for lunch. Finally, it was time when the customers were supposed to arrive. The big white board outside highlighted the four menus 'Little Italy' offered that day. The first customers were three Italian construction workers. Alex informed them that as the first customers they were entitled to free drinks. Though everybody was welcome, Alex told Jawad that he preferred Swiss customers.

"The Swiss had money and they like to spend it", he said. A few students arrived for coffee. The big moment came when four middle aged Swiss men in business suits entered the restaurant. Alex took charge of them. He told them how lucky he felt to welcome such valued customers on the first day of his business. Their arrival changed the atmosphere. They were seated at a window table with the best view in the house. Rosso was told to take extra care of the order. Alex offered them free Grappa after the meal but it was declined, as they had to work. There was some left from that bottle they had been given free. Everything was done to make them feel special and the food was exquisite. More people arrived and soon the restaurant was half-full. Alex repeatedly asked every customer about the food quality and the service.

"Not bad for the first day," he said when almost everybody had left.

In the evening only four tables were busy and at 9 pm, Alex let Jawad go. He seemed a bit disappointed. On the third day, a fight broke out between Rosso and Joaon. Rosso asked him to do something which he refused. Alex took Rosso's side which infuriated Joaon even more and he left immediately. Alex sat on the barstool with his head in his hands. As a precaution, he told Jawad to remove the pizza list from the cards. He also told Rosso to find another pizza maker soon. He tried to blame Rosso who in turn claimed that Portuguese should have not been hired in the first place.

"The only thing they are good at is working on building sites," he exclaimed.

Rosso realized the gravity of the situation. The loss of Joaon increased the pressure on Rosso who let it out on Salvatore.

Meanwhile Goran called Jawad again and told him that it was just a matter of days when he'll be called for the new job. He inquired about 'Little Italy' and Jawad told him about the problems. It took two days to get a new pizza maker. He was an Italian which satisfied Rosso but Alex doubted if things would really change. He still cursed Rosso for the fight, reminding him that he had taken personal and bank loans to open the place and he had no desire to go back and work as a waiter; especially now that he had acquired the taste of being an entrepreneur. By the end of the week, Alex's smile had vanished. Surprisingly, the second week was better in terms of sales. As the weather changed and it rained constantly, people crammed into nearby restaurants. Little Italy was attracting more and more diners and every new arrival was a big boost for the owner.

The following week Goran took him to show the club where Jawad hoped to work one day. Its name was Club7, located on the ground floor of a multi-story complex with plenty of parking space in front. Being an office area ensured the building would be empty on weekends. There was red velvet on the walls and the lighting arrangement looked sensational. Club had two VIP rooms behind the stage for private use. There were two bars at the both sides of the hall. The cellars were large enough to store a multitude of beer tanks and bottles, some of them refrigerated. Jawad had just been through a restaurant opening but this one might be different. Carla didn't like his working in the club. However, she gave no specific reason but it was evident from her tone that she didn't approve. Jawad had to charm her a little and said it was the only job available for the time being. He knew she was unhappy because she'll be alone at the nights of his work. He assured her that as soon as he finds a suitable job, he'll leave that place.

Jawad again went to the club on Monday to meet the owner. He was a Macedonian, named Ivan. He was a tall tough looking man, but there was a strange kind of uprightness and melancholy in his eyes. He had a flattened nose which was regarded a dangerous trait in Jawad's country. Ivan did not like to waste time on formalities. He checked Jawad's credentials and pulled a sheet to take a few notes.

"Look Mr. Jawad, I want honest people and that's the most important thing to me. Of course everyone works to his potential but I won't tolerate dishonesty," he warned in a very frank tone.

"I assure you that you won't have any problem about that," Jawad made himself clear.

"Not everything can be checked at a place like this and a lot depends on the staff. I'm not the type who gets angry because someone goes for a smoke or offers a free drink to a friend. My problem begins when someone starts filling his own pockets." Ivan stressed.

Jawad had a bad experience before and that humiliation was still fresh in his mind. He took a secret oath that never again would he go through that ordeal again even if he had to starve. Jawad reassured Ivan of his complete honesty and that time shall prove that. Goran also joined the meeting and nodded in agreement. Goran and Jawad had to work on Friday and Saturday with Sunday and Monday off. They were to return on Tuesdays and go through the stock and make sure that everything was ready for the next weekend. They were told that if there were some hours left from the weekly mandatory time, they could compensate it by working at his restaurant. Ivan too had fancy publicity plans. He was putting faith in in the growing population of Balkan youth in Zurich. They were the club's target segment. There would be Western beats, Balkan beats, and Turkish and Arabic nights.

Goran drove Jawad back home. He was excited about the booze he'll be having and the girls he might be flirting with at the club. He played the music even louder than usual. Jawad did not like that but stayed quiet. Goran enthused that this job was something, which he really looked forward to and was sure, would be real fun. Jawad told him that there'll be someone watching them all the time.

"You mean Ivan?" Goran wanted to know.

"Yes, he is not hiring us to act as the play boys in his business."

"Don't worry about him; he is an easy going guy. Moreover, the reason he is opening this club is to have some fun. He was married for 16 years and now he is single and with money. He wants to enjoy his life as much as possible. And anyway we'll be careful."

Jawad realized that his friend had become a Casanova who might easily blow it like he himself had messed up at the Conference House. Ivan seemed friendly but he won't tolerate Goran's extra curriculum excursions at the club. That evening Jawad told Alex that he'll be leaving Little Italy at the end of the month. Alex knew about the opening of the Club 7 from the grapevine. He wanted Jawad to stay a little longer as his brother had still not been able to get a visa. Jawad told him he needed a secure job and not a temporary one. At the end of the second month, Jawad bid farewell to Alex, and wished him luck.

Next day he went to the club. Goran was already there arranging the things. They were there for a meeting. The four barmaids arrived in the meantime. All the girls had exceptional good looks and physique. On top of it all, they wore tight fitting cloths. One by one, Ivan had an introduction session with them and he explained them their jobs. The girls were Hilda, Violeta, Angie and Malka. Hilda was German while other three girls were Serbs. Goran and Jawad were responsible for supplies, service and to act as assistants to the security in case of any trouble. Any unruly customer will be notified to the security. Ivan came well prepared and opened his briefcase to begin. He gave them all a work agreement and explained every clause carefully. Goran and Jawad were the only ones to be employed as full time staff at the club. The girls were hired on hourly basis and were obliged to work at the restaurant as well if required. All of them signed the agreement. The tips were to be distributed among the six of them equally. For the security of the club, he had contacted a security firm. He showed them the advertisements he had arranged for in the local newspaper. Ivan suggested they meet again on Thursday for the final preparations. On Friday, they should take as much rest as possible and come in the evening. He advised them to have a big meal so that they wouldn't feel hungry in the middle of the night. However, they could help themselves to the sandwiches available for sale at the bar for the public. It was Tuesday and Carla waited for Jawad to return. She seemed quiet, although Jawad could not discern why. She asked him a few questions about his meeting with the owner and other things about the club. Jawad could sense that she wasn't happy. Perhaps she felt insecure. She talked about the drug culture and people having sex under the influence. There were also stories of people catching all sorts of diseases due to unsafe sex. Indirectly she made him aware of the possible consequences of working in a club and Jawad understood her point. He kissed her gently and assured her that he'll stay clean.

Jawad had a stable sex life with Carla but the barmaids seemed to be a potential challenge to his manly urges. Jawad knew that for men, more was merrier which he now saw as a real curse. Why men always want more, not necessarily better but always more, he couldn't comprehend. Women on the other hand seemed to be quite strong in this respect. To make matters worse, Ivan had gone out of his way to recruit the most attractive looking barmaids possible. Jawad felt that his own taste had reached at a stage where experimenting with some new adventure seemed almost like a necessity. But he knew that Carla will never tolerate a thing like that. The mere thought of causing any pain to her made him feel ashamed. That evening while walking in the street with her, they came across an advertisement poster on the bus stop. It showed a few half-naked girls dancing on a stage and announcing the opening of a new club called Club7. Jawad quickly took Carla away and walked in the other direction.

On Thursday, it was their day for the final preparations. They all assembled at ten in the morning and started working. The cleaning staff had done a fine job and everything was spick and span. The girls took charge of the bars. The counters looked immaculate and the cabinets were shining in the spotlights. Jawad and Goran brought the drinks up from the cellars. A technician checked the sound system. Ivan was in the office room amid files and papers. Goran was already teasing one of the barmaids Malka, who played along with him. Jawad checked the cocktail list and made sure that everything was in place. Once, on the way to the cellar, Goran told Jawad that he found Malka attractive and he wanted to make out with her.

"Don't you think it's a bit early?" Jawad asked.

"What do you mean?" Goran looked puzzled.

"In my country it is said that the thieves should wait till the new village is inhabited. We haven't even started yet and you are already pulling at the leash."

"My friend, when it comes to a beautiful girl, I truly believe in a pre-emptive strike."

Jawad thought about Malka. *Does she know that Goran was fantasizing about her?*

Soon Ivan declared that everything was ready and he offered drinks for everyone. After a while, the staff left while Ivan went back to his office. It was still afternoon and Goran proposed the idea of going to the lake with the girls. Though one of the girls, Angie excused herself, everyone else thought some fresh air and relaxation would be a good idea. Goran proudly led them to his fancy car. Jawad sat in the front and the three girls piled into the back, complimenting on the car's jazzed up interior. Goran smiled broadly and turned on the music. He drove till Burkliplatz and parked across from the lakeside. It was a sunny day and the grassy lawns were crowded with people enjoying picnics and children playing all sorts of games. Goran led the way across and soon they were sitting on the grass. Jawad felt relaxed and happy though he realized that Carla was working only a few hundred yards away. They were all talking hesitantly and in short questions and answers. Hilda didn't say much and just looked around. Goran was at his usual best trying to charm the women. He bought ice cream for everyone and did most of the talking. He asked the girls whether they were in a relationship. This question put the girls in an awkward position. Accepting that they were in a relationship might deprive them from any future favors, as men don't care much for a woman when there is little chance of any meaningful return. Saying they were free and single could be even more problematic as it would mean they were open to suggestions.

Haltingly, Hilda and Malka said they were currently single while Violeta told them that she was married and her husband worked in a local factory. Then Malka asked Goran and Jawad the same question. Goran replied that they were both married. Nevertheless, he also added that their marriages were doomed because they had married only to get residence in Switzerland. He even explained them the process of sham marriage. This angered Jawad but he kept quiet. Goran proposed that they should go in the water, as it looked nice and warm. Soon they were all in the water up to their knees. Jawad looked at Hilda, who was taller than him. She was not thin but not fat either. She had golden hair and blue eyes, a specimen for whom the Third Reich was supposed to last a thousand years. Goran called Malka to the side to show her something he'd found. Hilda was rubbing her feet and sprinkling water on her long arms. Her beautiful limbs shone in the water and her blonde hair radiated in the sunlight. A remarkable sight, thought Jawad. Soon they were all splashing water at each other and having a good time. The lake visit broke the ice between them and they felt more relaxed as they walked to the car. Back at Burkliplatz, the girls said they would make their own way though Goran had offered to drop them home.

Next day Jawad and Goran were at the Club by 8 pm, as was most of the other staff. Ivan was busy talking to the two security men. He greeted the duo with a smile. Jawad went to the cellar and brought ice cubes from the ice machine. The house DJ was checking his mikes and the sound system. His professional name was DJ Capo and had played in most of the clubs in Zurich and even a few in Germany. DJ Capo didn't talk much but he soon had the place rocking with his music. Jawad and the rest soon found themselves moving in harmony with the rhythmic beats coming from all directions of the hall.

By 10 pm, swanky looking young boys and scantily dressed young girls started gathering outside in the parking lot. Most already seemed high in spirits and few were busy smoking things besides cigarettes. Ivan was charging 15 Francs per person for entry. As they trickled in, the security at the entrance stamped indelible ink on their wrists so they could go in and out freely for the rest of the night. Within an hour of opening, the club was more than half-full and most were jigging to the lively beats of music. As the night wore on, the lights got dimmer and the music got louder. By midnight, there was only elbowroom, the place heaved with young breathless bodies. There was much shouting, crazy dancing, even crazier drinking, and lots of kissing and frolicking. However, it was all good spirited and there was not much for security to worry about. Not all the visitors were youngsters. There were a few who were swinging in their 30's. Jawad was impressed by the spirit and energy of the people around. By two at night, there was barely enough space in the club for the staff to do any work. Most of the drinks were being sold on self-service basis. Jawad and Goran were busy removing the empty bottles and glasses from the hall. Sometime they'll go out one by one for some fresh air and relief from the noise. In the ground outside, youngsters continued to feed their insatiable passions, to smoke joints and drink from unbranded bottles they had procured from their fancy new cars. Jawad saw a couple offering Goran a puff or two, who was obliged. Once inside, he offered Jawad a few sips from his large coke glass as well. Jawad knew it contained multitude of liquors which he witnessed Malka was regularly topping up for him. Jawad could not refuse Goran's tempting drinks for very long; though first they both made sure Ivan was not around. Jawad found the ambience more and more to his liking and the barmaids looked stunning in the club lights. He tried to talk to Hilda a few times but the music was too loud for any meaningful conversation.

It was almost three in the morning and everything was going smooth so far. Then Jawad saw something unusual happen. He was outside when he heard some noise at the door. He saw the security carry out a young man whose eyes were closed and his arms dangled from his body. Others, possibly his friends, followed them. The security gently put the young man on the stairs while his friends gathered around. They tried to arouse him but, though he was breathing, didn't react much. Soon an ambulance arrived and they too tried to revive him, without much success. Eventually they put him on a stretcher and drove him away. Jawad returned inside along with most others. Later he found out that the youngster had taken a pill which was popular among the club goers. Those pills were notorious, putting people in some kind of ecstasy. By 4:30, the people started leaving. Soon the staff was busy cleaning up after the partygoers had left. The dance area littered with plastic glasses and junk of all kind. Jawad and Goran went to every corner of the club and filled the large bin bags with the discards, collected the valuables that were left behind while the owners had other things on their minds. Jawad decided not to get involved in any unsavory ideas that Goran might tempt him with while picking up the mobile phones and the credit cards. He made sure they were left in Ivan's office for safekeeping. The empty bottles were dumped in the cellar and the glasses returned to the bar tops. Ivan told them to finish as quickly as possible. Everyone was tired and wanted to leave anyway. The security people left as the last of guests staggered out of the hall. Ivan collected the money and went to office. Goran helped Ivan to count the cash and tally it with the printouts from the registers while Jawad helped the girls with the clean up behind the bars. Ivan had earlier told them they had to be there same time the next evening. The girls left after a chat with Ivan while Jawad waited in the hall for Goran. When he didn't show up, he went into the office. Goran was standing while Ivan was sitting on his executive chair. Jawad noticed something unusual on the table. On the glass top there was a line of white powder. Ivan was holding a small white pipe made from a rolled paper and sniffing that powder. Jawad did not react. *If Ivan is a cocaine addict, it's not my problem.* He was tired and sleepy and the last few hours had been punishing for his mind and body. Goran was saying something to Ivan in his native language. Ivan put the roll up to his nostril and took a long sniff. His face became red and soon a smile appeared on it. The tension seemed to drain from his body and he seemed much more relaxed. Jawad looked at Goran who was smiling. They didn't seem to mind that Jawad had walked in on the scene.

The day was almost breaking when Goran dropped him at home. On the road, they both had a light breakfast from a gas station. Jawad went straight to bed. Carla was sound asleep and he tried his best not to wake her. Jawad had no idea when she left for work. He slept until late but in his dreams, he was still at the club. The music still thumped in his head, and the lights bedazzled his closed eyes. Finally, he got tired of the dreams and woke up. He had no inclination to cook so he fried two eggs, wrapped them in bread and swallowed it all with a glass of milk. It revived his worn mind and body and he was able to take a shower. He lay in front of the TV, still half-asleep until the afternoon. Carla came home for her break. She asked a few questions and Jawad tried to avoid going into much detail. Most aspects of his new job would have been unpalatable to her innocent ears. Before leaving, she cooked dinner for him. His mind disorientated after his first ever night in an ear splitting, drug crazed club scene. The most he had ever experienced in Lahore had been a couple of raucous weddings. This had been on a different level. He stared blankly at the screen, ate his dinner and waited for Goran. Back in the club, it was business as usual. The place was ready for another night of madness. After the final touches, they waited. Jawad was still curious about the office scene of the night before. He had been too tired to ask Goran as they drove home and now saw his chance while they were waiting.

"What was Ivan sniffing in the morning?"

"It was cocaine man, don't you know that stuff?" Groan replied nonchalantly.

"Yes I know what cocaine is, but I just wanted to make sure."

"Why, do you have a problem?"

"No, I was just curious."

"Listen mate, what Ivan does is not your problem. He is an easygoing fellow and didn't even hide his little secret. Anyway, that stuff is not so bad. I've tried it myself."

He had seen Goran smoking hashish and cannabis joints but the fact that he also tried cocaine was a surprise for Jawad.

"And how do you feel? Jawad was curious.

"You feel like flying," he said breaking into a laugh.

Jawad came from a country which had huge heroin problems. He had seen families destroyed and lives cut short even before they had matured. In his neighborhood, he watched addicts lying unconscious on the street after a session of collective abuse. He was surprised to witness similar scenes in such an advanced society which had so many other sources of entertainment.

That night was not different than the previous one. Goran never missed an opportunity in chatting up pretty girls, even dancing with them. Though he was married, Goran wanted more. Jawad had spent most of his life in a closed society, women seldom mixed with the opposite sex there. As they were mostly invisible in society, they became a rare sight and something very special in a man's eyes. Any thoughts of premarital sex were dismissed, as even the slightest contact with a girl could be fatal. Girls too were very sensitive about their honor and chasteness. Any girl who failed to produce the "rose of honor" on the wedding night was considered immoral. However, he saw that here in the west, there were no such taboos. So a night in a club culminating in sex afterwards was normal, almost obligatory. Jawad was amazed when Goran told him stories of his one-night stands. When he couldn't remember how he'd ended up in somebody's bed, and what had transpired during the night. Groan said this would be true for many of the clubbers by the end of the night. He reasoned that the chicks in sexy outfits causing trouble in his pants, was not his fault at all. Beauty in such open abundance would make any hot-blooded man horny. For once, Jawad had to agree with Goran's interpretation of the facts in front of him. The girls were so beautiful and sexy that Jawad felt his heart missing the odd beats. Given the chance, he was sure he won't hesitate in bedding some of them dancing in the hall.

That night, Goran seemed less energetic than normal and he kept venturing outside. Perhaps in search of some free joints, thought Jawad. In the hall, the music was roaring unsparingly. Jawad decided to use the ear blockers to reduce the sound; otherwise, he figured he would end up permanently half-deaf. Hilda called him a couple of times that night for help, as she constantly needed something or another. All the barmaids wore skimpy little clothing, and Hilda's athletic tall body was more alluring than many of the beauties in the hall. Even without Goran's encouragements, Jawad drank more than the previous night. And due to his drunkenness, Jawad tried to work on the motto of "look busy and do nothing." In an electric atmosphere like this, he soon realized that things, if left on their own, automatically take their own course. Jawad spotted Goran standing outside with Malka. He seemed to be improving in his quest for her.

Back home, it took him some time to sleep and when Carla kissed him goodbye as she left for work, he could only mumble in his sleep. The next two days he had off and that would give him an opportunity to get some rest. Sunday was spent all day in bed and that meant he can't sleep during the night. He knew it would take some time until he got used to his new routine. Carla came home for her break and prepared dinner for him before she left. She was always serious about her matrimonial duties and made sure Jawad lacked for nothing. She had no idea about the thoughts which her husband was lately having about the opposite sex. He slept more or less all day and later felt bored. Perhaps Goran too was having same thoughts as he called him late in the evening. Jawad had just finished his weekly call to his family in Lahore. Carla was supposed to return at around midnight. Goran told him to get ready as soon as possible. Once in the car, he told they were going for an evening out. Jawad had no idea where were they going. Goran told him that he had called Malka and Hilda and both of them were coming along too. They had spent the whole day in the bed and a little exterior almost seemed compulsory. Jawad was surprised when he heard about Hilda. He thought her a bit different.

They picked up both the girls and went to the far end of the lake. They settled in the comfortable lounge of the Casino Restaurant, sitting near the windows which opened towards the lake. Being a Sunday evening, the place was not that crowded. Malka seemed to be teasing Goran. When he tried to speak with her in their native language, she told him to speak German so the others wouldn't feel left out. That evening, after a few drinks, everyone began to open up. Hilda seemed more talkative than normal. She spoke about the unemployment problems in her native part of East Germany, and complained about the discrimination she felt from fellow West Germans. Her ordeal finally ended, when she found a job in Switzerland and now she did not intend to return to her native land. Meanwhile Malka and Goran went to smoke outside, probably something more than a cigarette thought Jawad. He deduced that it was just a matter of time before he'll get her into the bed. He sat alone with Hilda but had no idea what he should speak. His chronic shyness, thanks to his culture, was becoming a real problem in a society where everyone mixed freely and openly. At the same time, he felt strongly attracted to Hilda and was keen to befriend her. However, he was not devious by nature and didn't want to spin stories or lead her on. Therefore, he just remained mostly quiet until Goran and Malka returned.

"Why don't you guys go out and try this?" Goran said while giving Jawad a joint. Jawad knew smoking that thing was illegal. When Jawad hesitated, Goran told him not to worry, as it was nothing but tobacco mixed with a little something to refresh the mind. Hilda also seemed hesitant but then she stood up slowly, looking sheepishly at Goran. Jawad didn't intend to take any kinds of drugs but he decided to go along with Hilda.

"I'd not tried anything like this for almost a year," Hilda confessed. He was bemused to realize that whatever was in the cigarette most probably was a common practice in that country. That thing reminded him of Perucci who offered him a joint for the first time. It was something that he'd never even seen personally in Lahore, though he'd witnessed the effects on others. Was this another taboo that he was about to shatter today. He wasn't quite sure as they went outside and found an empty bench. "Ladies first" he spoke, handing Hilda the damn thing. Hilda took out a little pink lighter from her purse and lit the roll up. Jawad could smell an odd stench in the air, even as she inhaled. She took one more puff and gave it to Jawad who hesitated before following suit. He could taste the lipstick where her lips had been a few moments ago. Though he inhaled a couple of times, he couldn't see what all the fuss was about. He didn't feel any different; unlike after a strong drink, when he would instantly feel warmth and the subtle effect on the mind. After few more puffs, he handed the joint back to Hilda and indicated that he wasn't interested in it anymore. After a couple of more drags, she felt the same and they returned inside

They ordered some more beers. Jawad felt a bit dizzy, maybe drinking after that smoke was a bad idea. He noticed that everyone round the table were looking lightheaded and wore strange smiles as if they were drunk already. Suddenly Goran grabbed Malka and kissed her on the cheeks, she pretended to resist, but was soon laughing. Jawad looked at Hilda who was smiling at their antics. The music in the restaurant was romantic and the lights were dim. Outside, the lights around the lakeside and the boats moving serenely in the water presented a majestic view. Feeling giddy, Jawad turned to Hilda and asked for her phone number. She gave it gladly and Jawad gave her his number. He wanted her to know that though they hadn't interacted much, he was interested in her.

It was getting late when they returned. First, they dropped Hilda at her address in the Wipkingen area. Jawad was next and then Goran went to drop Malka. Jawad could see that there was malice in his eyes as they drove off. He knew that after a few more drinks, Goran might have another of his infamous one-night stands, if not the first of many. Carla was not yet home and he changed his clothes quickly. He didn't want her to smell the drink and smoke from him and he had no intention of telling her about his evening out. He felt guilty deep in his heart, and when he made love to her the next day, it was like redemption for staring lustily at all those bodies, which had been occupying his mind lately. One thing he could not refrain from doing was comparing her with Hilda. However, he'd not seen Hilda in her natural state but she possessed some kind of exoticness. While Carla looked like an angel, an innocent girl, Hilda had a strange erotic attraction, one that drives men crazy.

Tuesday he and Goran went to the club in the daytime. The place seemed strange now that it was empty of hundreds of heaving bodies. However, it was neat and clean and everything was shining, thanks to the cleaning people Ivan employed. They held a meeting with Ivan who seemed satisfied with the weekend's efforts but told them there was still lots to do. They discussed the strategy for the next week. Soon Ivan returned to his office while Goran and Jawad went to the cellar. They had to sort out the empty bottles which they dumped randomly other nights. It took a while and when they finished, Goran told him to stay back for a while. He opened two beers and even took time out to make a large joint. They were supposed to check the stock and to make an order list. For that, Goran had a simple strategy. Both simply counted how many empty bottles there were in the respective crates and wrote them down in the order forms. Therefore, ordering simply what they had sold. They finished their beer and made their way upstairs. In the office, Goran faxed the order to the supplier. Ivan was on his mobile and did not take much notice of them. While they waited for the fax sheets to go through, a courier arrived with flyers for the following week. Together they went through the flyers and made three equal bundles. Jawad and Goran left immediately to distribute them at different bars and restaurants in the vicinity. First, they had lunch at a Turkish takeaway and then began their tour. Their strategy was simple; Goran would stop the car in front of a bar or restaurant and Jawad would go inside. Mostly such businesses had a place for flyers. Usually it was a stand or a soft board on the wall. At the end of the day, Goran dropped him home. He told Jawad that he was going to see Malka. He mentioned she and Hilda were working at Ivan's restaurant that evening, but Jawad was not tempted.

"You should go home to your wife sometimes Goran," he advised.

"Look man, my wife is the queen of my heart and my house. No one can ever take her place. However, Malka & company, they are great to flirt with and to keep me young. One needs to have some variety in life. You can't eat the same meal every day," Goran explained his philosophy.

Jawad gave him a patient hearing, but felt like asking him what if his wife had the same feelings for other men. Jawad imagined in that scenario, considering his east European background, Goran would judge differently.

Carla was watching TV when he entered. There was a twinkle in her eyes and Jawad wasted no time in kissing her passionately. Since he had started working in the club, there was a strange look in her eyes. Jawad can't give any meaning to that. It was as if her eyes were questioning him. In order to avoid that Jawad tried to have less eye contact with her lately. He knew that women had an instinct and could figure out such things faster than men could. Wednesday was not much different at the club. Rather than dealing with the empty bottles, they stacked the shelves with new ones. Once the work in the cellar was over, they decided to distribute some more flyers. Ivan was sitting in the office checking the invoices for the drinks. Jawad went to the bar for a drink when a man entered. He acknowledged Jawad and told him he was there to see Ivan. As he entered the office, Goran came out.

"Shall we go now?" Jawad asked him.

"Wait a minute. I want to see that man," Goran responded, nodding towards the office.

When the man came out, Goran accompanied him to the parking lot. Jawad could not make much of the coming and going. Perhaps the man was a mutual friend and Goran went out of courtesy. Soon Goran was back and they drove out. Once they had distributed all the flyers, they decided to visit the girls at the restaurant that evening. But first they went to the club. Driving back, Goran spoke about his domestic life. His wife wanted a baby but he wanted to wait a while. Having a child would mean that she won't be working and it was difficult to survive on one salary. Jawad knew that this was a dilemma for many migrants. They wanted to have kids but due to their meager incomes, they had to wait or abandon their plans. In addition, because of the cost of living, couples mostly opted for one or two kids at the most. Jawad had not given it much thought and his strategy was to wait until the right time.

Back at the club, Goran went straight to the bar and poured two drinks. Ivan's office was empty. Drinking his shot in one gulp, he offered one to Jawad. It was Bacardi with cola and very strong. Jawad poured some more cola in it. Goran pulled a small plastic bag out of his pocket. Jawad knew it was cocaine, and was surprised at Goran's audacity. The zigzag table around the bar had a glass top. Goran poured that powder in a line shape on it, rolled a paper and started sniffing it. A strange voice arose from his throat, and then he smiled. Jawad could not comprehend what was happening to him. Soon he seemed ok. Rather, he seemed energized and cheerful. He took another snort and looked at Jawad with a melancholy expression.

"How you feel?" Jawad asked him.

"Fine, but did you think I was going to die. It's not poison man, it is something which make you feel real good," Goran defended his habit.

"But where do you get this stuff from?"

"You remember the guy who came to see Ivan earlier?

"Yes."

"He was here to give Ivan his dope. I bought it from him for almost next to nothing. He was offering me to sell it in the club, but I said no way dude," Goran looked at Jawad as if he was too clever to be tempted.

With a twinkle in his eyes, he nodded at the line of powder on the glass top. Jawad was hesitant at first, but then he decided to try it. If he didn't like it, Goran can't force him to try a second time. He put the paper to his nose and sniffed hard. The first thing he felt was a strange euphoria, a kind of energy. Then he thought he saw some clouds, but they soon started thinning out. He heard Goran calling him slowly but Jawad thought he was somewhere in a rainbow. He leaned forward and put his head on the table. Goran didn't disturb him and went to make another drink, Jawad told him not to make one for him as he didn't want to pass out altogether. It took him a while to come out of his state of ecstasy and return to his senses. He felt numb and the one thing that disturbed him the most was the lights which he wanted to turn low. After a while, Goran returned and said it was time to leave. Both of them washed their faces and tried to look as normal as possible. They went to the restaurant owned by Ivan. It was not busy and Ivan was standing at the door. Hilda and Malka were working inside. Goran told Ivan about the proceedings and went to fetch some water. Then Hilda came over and asked if they would like something to eat. Jawad didn't initially like the idea of going there for eating but slowly he was becoming comfortable.

"He was dying to see you, so I brought him over," Goran teased Jawad.

"Don't listen to the idiot. He had a bit too much to drink."

Hilda looked at Jawad and their eyes locked for a few moments. She smiled and then went back to her job.

"What's the matter with you? I'm trying to help you and you call me a drunk," Goran sounded hurt but there was no resentment in his voice.

Jawad looked inside and saw Ivan was now sitting with a rough looking guy who was accompanied by a beautiful blonde.

"Goran, who is this guy sitting beside Ivan?"

"He is a pimp, I know that. What he is doing here I've no idea." Jawad did not need any more explanation. Ivan had drug dealers and pimps at his disposal to satisfy his needs. Jawad still felt quite high from the cocaine. Rather than feeling dizzy or tired, it had a different effect. *But what about all those junkies who had given up all other aspects of life to get their regular kick?* Jawad had seen some of them with stoned eyes, with nothing else on their mind except the next high.

Hilda brought them two pizzas. After the meal, as a pretext to stay there, Goran started helping behind the counter. Jawad also joined him. Hilda came and talked for a while with Jawad. They stayed till 10 pm; the girls had to work till midnight. On their way back, Goran told him that the coming Sunday was going to be special. He'll go to visit Malka at her place. Jawad was surprised that he hadn't already and wished him luck, though he doubted the sincerity of his own comments.

Friday evening the club was more crowded than before. Ivan was constantly in the company of the girl Jawad had seen the other day sitting with him in the restaurant. Perhaps he had come to an agreement with the pimp and the girl. At around 2 am when the party was in full swing he disappeared into the office with the girl. Goran saw his chance and asked Jawad to cover for Malka at the bar. He told him he was taking her to the cellar, to teach her how to change the beer tank. Jawad knew what that meant. They returned after a few minutes and Goran told Jawad that she was a great kisser. It was business as usual. The music got louder and the dancing got even more frantic. Couples would cling to each other and some would lock lips while they danced. Once exhausted, they would return to the bar for more drinks.

Practically he and Goran were working two full nights, and the rest of the week was not so stressful. In the weekdays, he and Goran would put everything into place for the weekend. Ivan was happy with their work and his new venture had a great start. He didn't bother with the petty things and knew well that the staff would be taking liberties behind his back. Both of his businesses were running well and he was reaping the rewards of hard work. Goran told Jawad that Ivan had a lifelong dream of building a hotel in his native country and for that he needed money. Money that he intends to earn in Switzerland but will be invested somewhere else. Jawad doubted if his business ventures would be as successful back home. Jawad's own earning at the end of the month was just over 5,000 Francs. He was back on track and could smell success again.

Looking at Ivan's success, Jawad was also having thoughts about some business. He could save some money and open a place of his own, not a big place but something reasonable to start with. Perhaps he was also becoming a victim of the syndrome which plagued many migrants before him. They were not content with their slice of the cake and wanted more. Those who were successful with their ventures were earning beyond their wildest dreams. However, he knew there was a lot of distance between the cup and the lips: saving money, convincing Carla and finding a suitable place.

Next time when he called his father, he had a long conversation with him. His father told him that there was an offer for early retirement based on new government regulations. He'd been working for more than 28 years and could retire with a good pension. But he'd no intention of leading a retired life. He was planning to open an academy with modern facilities like computers and audio-visual systems. It was a booming business and he'll be doing what he enjoyed most. Jawad told him to do some fact finding and assured him of his full cooperation. He also told his father his intention of starting a business of his own in Zurich. In return, his father assured him that once his plan materialized, he'll try his best not to burden him any further. Jawad realized that in order to move things forward, he'll have to take some action. Until now, he was sending money regularly but payments differed. He decided to do something he had never thought of before. After some mutual consultation with Carla, he went to his bank and asked for a loan of thirty thousand Francs. He did all the paperwork that they asked for and filled in the various forms. The bank seemed pleased to see that they were both working and owed nothing. This meant a good credit rating. Within ten days, the bank deposited the money into his account. His father was a bit surprised when Jawad phoned to tell him about the money. That amounted to a small fortune in Pakistan. He told Jawad the sum will go a long way. From now on, all Jawad had to do was, pay the monthly installment to the bank, which was less than seven hundred monthly. There'll be no more imbursement to Pakistan for some time, and he could save from his salary to start his own business.

Meantime Carla seemed to have accepted his work routine and no longer showed any resentment about his job at the club. It was also because whenever they had a day off together, Jawad spent every minute of it with her. He played the part of a loving husband perfectly. As for Hilda, he liked her but feared that one wrong move may destroy his marriage. Though he sometimes fantasied about Hilda's body, he knew that to get a girl like that into bed, one had to play with fire. Once Goran told him that she asked him many questions about Jawad and was curious about his marriage. Goran reassured her that both of their marriages were just shams and they were both living with their wives to keep the immigration people at bay. Goran told her that they were not even sleeping in the same beds as their wives and it was only a matter of time before they'll be free to live as they pleased. But until then, he reasoned, they still had their male instincts to tend to. Jawed thought he might have made a good politician back home.

As for Hilda, Jawad felt a conflict brewing in his mind. The more time he spent at the club, and watching everyone around him, behaving in a decadent manner, the more he thought it was only natural to desire extra. Then Goran told Jawad about his rendezvous at Malka's place the previous evening. She had asked him about some CDs and Goran promised to bring them around. Along with the CDs he took along wine and some roses. They listened to the music and drank wine. On a highly romantic song, Goran asked her for a dance and soon she was in his arms. Goran convinced Malka that he was madly in love with her. He told Jawad now that he had tamed her; he intended to spend as much time as possible with her. Goran celebrated his conquest with cocaine and offered some to Jawad to share his happiness. Since their first experience together, they were taking it at least once a week besides smoking joints frequently. For Jawad it was becoming difficult to control the urge when he was at home. He felt he could do with a joint whenever he was feeling low but he realized that such addictions cost money. He can't always accept them free from Goran who seemed to have a constant supply. He never asked for money and only took whatever Jawad gave him.

Jawad's odd hours at the club were having an impact on his social life as well. He hadn't been to the Café Central for a while to see his Asian friends; neither was he seeing the Singhs like before. However, he would speak to Singh on the phone regularly. Monday he would spend all day with Carla and on Tuesday would rush home as soon as he finished. He realized he was doing that only because of his love for her, to provide her company.

Hilda continued to rankle his mind with her good looks and her teasing smiles. Sometime Jawad wondered what she might be thinking of him, if she ever did. Then the situation changed further when Goran told Jawad that he should bring his own car to work. He was supposed to pick Malka on a permanent basis. He told that he found it difficult to pick Jawad and Malka as both lived on opposite sides of the city. Jawad had acquired his Swiss driving license and he was driving whenever he went out with Carla. He had no trouble in bringing the car. But the change would offer a window of opportunity as far Hilda was concerned. He can offer her a ride to and from work. On Friday morning, he sent her a message that he'll come to pick her for work. She replied in the positive by texting her address. Jawad had been there only once. When she came out of her building, Jawad was waiting outside, leaning on the passenger seat door. He opened the door for her and she sat down smiling broadly. It was the first time that he'd opened the door of the car for a beautiful girl, other than Carla of course. He thought about her at that moment. How she might view him being extra courteous to his beautiful work mate? She made no objection on Jawad's taking the car but had no idea that he'll be offering his services to some other girl. They reached the Club and Jawad jumped out of the car and opened the door for her. He was acting like a perfect gentleman, and Hilda found it most amusing. She appreciated that Jawad probably wasn't aware that this sort of chivalry was mostly frowned upon nowadays. Obviously, he was of the old school. Goran was there already and going through the stock. They had all become used to their job and it didn't make any difference what kind of music was played, or which DJ would be running the show. All they knew was that the club should be full and they had to sell and sell. They were paid to sell and they sold to be paid. Every drink they sold made Ivan richer. Goran had his own priorities and his innovative nature seemed to know no limits. He was asking the youngster for marijuana. Some gave him little while others made fun of him. At the end of the night, Goran had a modest stock of his own. He made few joints out of that stock. He even gave one to Jawad. That morning when he left with Hilda for home, he still had that joint with him. He and Goran drove simultaneously out of the club parking, Jawad with Hilda besides him while Goran had Malka on his side. Perhaps they were all trying to adjust to their new roles as part-time lovers. Jawad didn't drink much in the course of the night as he knew he'll be driving in the morning. Any encounter with the police while driving under the influence would be most problematic.

Driving through the almost empty streets of Zurich, they reached the house where Hilda had a one-room apartment. Jawad stopped the car in front of the entrance, stepped out and opened her door.

"Would you like some?" He asked Hilda showing her the joint. At first she seemed to be unsure but then nodded.

"But not here, we better go upstairs," she suggested, looking apprehensively along the street.

He parked the car and followed her upstairs. She opened the door of her room, which was on the first floor. It had no balcony. She had left a window open and room was filled with a fresh morning breeze. There was an ashtray on a small table with a lighter though Hilda was not a strong smoker. The room reminded him of Sonia and her room. Lately he did not think much about her. What caught his eyes was a guitar. Hilda disappeared with some clothes to the washroom. When she returned, she was wearing a sleeping suit. Her beauty was even more radiant in the casual gear. Jawad knew she was sleepy like him so he wasted no time and lit the joint. When he exhaled, the smell of marijuana engulfed the room. He handed it to her who took it with a smile. The joint was strong and presumably of good quality. Jawad took his turn and felt its impact. Feeling unsteady, he sat on the sofa and handed the joint to her.

"I've to drive so you can enjoy the rest," he spoke in a slight daze. She closed the door as he left but not before a big hug. He was there alone with her and he was surprised how he had controlled himself. Being alone with such beauty was a rare privilege for him. However, he knew time was on his side and the visits would be regular, only if he played his cards right. *Blow as the wind blows.* At home, it was business as usual. First thing he did was clean his teeth. Then he kissed Carla as he entered the room; she kissed him as she left. She returned during her break and Jawad was still sleeping. It was his strategy, to have a big breakfast and then go to sleep. He got up just before it was time for her to leave for the evening shift. He showered, ate and left soon after.

"How is everything?" Goran asked him in the evening as they both went to the cellar to fetch the crates. There was a smile on his face.

"Fine," Jawad knew where this was heading.

"And did you do it?" Goran got to the point immediately.

"Do what?" Jawad pretended ignorance.

"You know what I mean, with Hilda?"

"First tell me about yourself." Jawad teased him.

"I had her for my breakfast today, and I hope tomorrow as well. God, it's so satisfying to share her with milk and honey in the mornings. Now tell me, what happened when you drove her home?"

"That was all, I drove her home."

"Did not she ask you to come inside?"

"No, I just dropped her and drove home."

"That was all?" Goran seemed shocked.

"Yes, were you expecting something else?"

"You're a fool. Malka didn't ask me in when I first went to drop her. I pretended that I want to pee and then she had to let me in. I stayed there for an hour, though we only talked that day. Next time I went to give her CD's. She knew exactly why I was there. Enjoy the forbidden fruit my friend, you live only once."

"You're bad influence, you know that."

Goran laughed on the verdict.

Ivan however seemed to follow Goran's philosophy on life. No girl was on his side for more than two weeks. In addition, the new one will be even more stunning than the previous. Sometime he'll disappear into his office with his new companion. His absence always provided them the chance to relax a little. Gradually, like Goran, he too seemed to be on his way to becoming an addict. Instead of a glass of wine when he was at home, he'll rather smoke marijuana. And without it he felt nervous and angry sometime. He realized it was like a monster he was trying to keep under control and knew little where he would end up in the future. Moreover, beyond marijuana, there were the random sessions of cocaine as well. Right now, Goran was buying it only seldom because of the high price. Over time, Jawad began to pay for his share as it didn't seem right not to. What started a joke was becoming troublesome. Luckily Carla had no knowledge of his addictions and Hilda only knew about the random cannabis inhales.

Next Sunday evening, Carla left for her evening shift, reminding him about the food in the fridge. Jawad had no intention to eat at home. He wanted to meet Hilda. He quickly bathed, dressed and looked at his watch. It was almost 5:30 pm, time for some action. When he drove to the shops, most were close due to Sunday. He knew where he ought to go and drove to the local gas station. There, he bought a bottle of Amarone, cheese, some peanuts, bread and a packet of condoms. He also picked up two plastic glasses, forks and knives for a little picnic. Jawad smiled at himself when it occurred to him that all this could be a complete waste of time and money. He had not even spoken to Hilda yet. From the parking, he called her. He heard the ring on the other side, and like a good German she didn't say hello, rather uttered 'Ja'. Jawad knew he should tread carefully.

"Hi there, how're you?"

"Fine Jawad, and how're you?"

"Fine as well. So what are you doing?"

"I was watching TV but why did you ask?"

"Do you have something against a little picnic?"

"What do you mean?"

"Actually I was feeling lonely so I thought maybe we could go out together."

"When would you like to come?

"How long will it take you to get ready?"

"Let's say half an hour?"

"Ok, I'll be there in half an hour and then we'll decide where to go," so far so good he thought.

There was time to kill and he decided to call Singh. Jawad blamed his work schedule for not seeing him lately. Singh responded that it was okay. Both had different rest days and that made it difficult to meet up. They spoke for a while and then it was time to ring her bell. She hugged him warmly at the doorstep. Jawad opened the front door for her. It was a pleasant evening; she was wearing a stylish pink dress and high heels. Jawad drove along the lake till Zollikon and pulled over next to an empty bench. There was hardly anyone around as Jawad opened her door and took out the shopping bags. Hilda smiled when he took out the wine and opened it. He took the glass and poured a little for her to test. She nodded in approval. They toasted, looking in each other's eyes.

"It's beautiful out here. We should have some music I think."

She took out her mobile phone and tapped on the screen. She could not have selected better music as it played Marvin Gaye's *Let's Get It On*. Jawad felt that those words somehow reflected what he felt in his heart. But he was no Goran and his shyness hindered any sudden advances. He had no drugs. The wine and her presence might be enough to get high tonight. She was silent in the beginning. From his short experience he knew that it is after the second or third glass that people felt at ease. Wine with bread and cheese was a great combination and they began chatting about work. Still, he felt awkward and hesitant. He knew she was strong and he was weak due to his experience and background. The music changed. They were drinking slowly and both knew there was no hurry. Jawad had until midnight to return home, she had the whole night.

Hilda seemed relaxed and there was no sign of any concern on her face. Jawad knew that being a beautiful European girl; things were completely in her favor. Jawad could not force her for anything. Any sexual advances would've to be on her terms. Jawad poured more nectar from the bottle as they looked at the lake view. Meanwhile, she loosened her hair and now her long golden locks were gracing her cheeks and tumbling onto her shoulders. Was it some kind of a signal or was it just out of habit, Jawad could not decide.

"Tell me, is it true that you and Goran are not really married but it's just a sham to get a residence permit here?" Jawad was surprised at her directness.

"Yes it is true."

Though he answered easily, he felt heartache inside. He was betraying the person who had been the most kind to him. He was confused for a moment. On one side was Carla who made him what he was today. On the other was Hilda, a dream girl, and having her was like compensating for all the sexual shortfalls of his previous life.

"What about you, do you've a boyfriend?"

"I had one, but a couple of months ago he moved to Canada. I didn't want to move again, so we separated."

There was a brief silence. They were like two chess players thinking about their next move. Then Jawad took the initiative. He told her about his life and family. He also mentioned to Hilda that she didn't know how lucky she was. She didn't have to apply for asylum or arrange a sham marriage to stay in Switzerland. Perhaps he was trying to justify his actions and gain her sympathies. She asked some probing questions and Jawad tried to bluff as best as he could. He had fooled people before in far more perilous situations and this was another lying session. Both glasses were empty again and they had eaten almost half the food. Jawad looked out at the lake. Far away, he could see a ship crawl away from Zurich towards Rapperswill. The sun had set and there was redness on the sky in the eastern side. Jawad took her right hand and started examining it like a palmist.

"What're you looking at?" she asked, surprisingly.

"Nothing, I just want to check whether my name is written somewhere between these lines."

"And did you find it?"

"Oh yes, it's right there but not everybody can see it."

She laughed and Jawad let her hand go, rubbing it gently. He filled her glass but not his own. He told her he had to drive back and needed a clear mind. She did not object as she knew that. Then they were silent again. Jawad felt frustrated and the absurdity of the situation was slowly dawning on him. He had come as a hunter but now felt like the prey. She was sitting close to him with all her sexual superiority. He thought about driving back and to forget everything. But when he looked at her again he changed his mind. He had come so far, what was wrong with a little patience. She was not in a relationship and she needed someone in her life. He was in a relationship but still needed someone else in his life. He stood up and went behind her. He put his hands on her shoulders and massaged them a little. She moaned slightly and looked up at him.

"I can do a really good Indian head massage you know," he claimed.

"Hmm, that would be nice. But not here," she smiled.

He returned and sat beside her but this time much closer. He circled her soft cheek with his fingers and squeezed it as she seemed to blush.

Holding her hands, he slowly pulled her down onto the soft grass, making sure her head rested on his arm and shoulder. He kissed her softly on the cheek, and she moaned lightly. Next kiss belonged to the lips. They kissed for a while and he ran his fingers thorough her beautiful silky hair. Soon he was all over her. However, they knew this was not the place to take things any further. The foreplay had served as an appetizer but they realized that the main course had to be consumed somewhere else. To resume the pleasures of the evening, they had to return. He kissed her again and helped her getting up. Grabbing their things from the bench, they hurried back to the car.

"Don't drive too fast," she spoke teasingly.

"That's easy for you to say. Try being in my shoes right now," he responded soundly.

To maintain the ambience, he put some romantic Indian music on the car stereo. She seemed to enjoy its exoticness, though not understanding the lyrics. Soon they arrived at her apartment. She didn't ask him anything and he didn't tell her anything. Both fell onto the bed, entangled. She was very open in her sexuality and for Jawad it was the first time that someone else was leading the way. Her physical grandeur gave her an upper hand over him. She knew how to exploit his desires, something he found most intriguing. She was arousing his desires while stopping just short of satisfying them. With her sexual aggression, she could be the dream girl of half the globe. Her physical attributes were even more abundant in bare skin. For a while, he felt he was drowning in her musky body, and clung to her intimately. They had harmony in their timing and finally both lay quietly, breathless. She went for a shower. Jawad lay still, unable to believe how wonderful she had been. She came back, her hair dripping, her body naked from the waist up. She sat on the bed, toweling her hair, while he watched adoringly. He could watch her like this forever. Both felt hungry. She made some pasta quickly and they dined together. Then, making sure he looked as normal as was possible, he kissed her lovingly and left.

In his country, there was an old saying that if a lion once tastes the blood of a human, he won't eat anything but human flesh. He loved Carla but when it came to lovemaking, she was no match for Hilda. Carla's body and servitude was no comparison to what he had experienced with Hilda. But Carla was precious to him in so many other ways. He could never wish her any pain. If there ever came a time when he had to choose between Carla and Hilda, he knew the answer. It'll always be Carla. However, he had tasted the sweet nectar, which was Hilda, and knew it'll be difficult to control his desires from now on.

But what if Carla develops a relationship like he had, what would be his own reaction. Knowing the answer, he felt a deep sense of guilt and even shame. *Why do men always want their women to be faithful while never missing a chance to commit adultery themselves?* Jawad realized he had no answer.

He had to share his thoughts with someone who could understand his dilemma. After he promised not to divulge, even to Malka, he decided to tell Goran the whole story. It was their rest day. Goran laughed at first, and then he took Jawad for a long drive in his car. They drove to Rheinfall while Jawad gave him the intimate details of his evening with Hilda. Goran struggled to keep his eyes on the road as Jawad slowly revealed what he'd been hiding from him all along.

"So, you took my advice about eating the forbidden fruit after all," he howled.

"But how do I get over the guilt I feel about cheating on Carla?" Jawad protested.

"That's another art I'll teach you my very naive friend," he laughed.

They talked about different things and it seemed as if they were laughing at the trusting nature of their wives. After couple of beers and some more backslapping, they drove back.

From now on, his Sunday and Thursday evenings were reserved for Hilda. He'll visit her flat, using public transport so that he could drink as much he liked. They'll prepare something for dinner and smoke joints. Jawad discovered that she was a serious drinker, and it was not just wine, rather preferred Vodka and Bacardi mixed with energy drinks. She liked his company and the stories of his early years and his trials and tribulations after arriving in Zurich. Sometime they'll go to the cinema or watch movies on television at home, listening to the music, cooking and doing all those things that lovers do. However, Jawad avoided venturing out too often, fearing that he might bump into someone who knew him and Carla. The mere thought was enough to send a shiver thorough him. At times Hilda would have her girlfriends over for a visit or a meal. Jawad always helped her in the kitchen. He made exotic cocktails and served at the table while the girls gossiped and joked. He was doing it to justify his presence there and he loved the atmosphere that slowly evolved as they drank late into the evenings. But Jawad had no illusions about the fragile nature of his relationship with Hilda. She was a European girl and she had already been through various relationships. One more break up won't devastate her life and she'll move on just like before.

What worried Jawad most was his slow addiction to drugs. His life had been divided in work, drugs, his wife and his mistress. He was not the same innocent asylum seeker who had arrived with such naivety a few years ago. Slowly he was integrated into the Swiss society, but he was also picking the most negative aspects. He had come a long way and often he thought about his past. A few years ago, he might have never imagined that he'll be leading such a different life. All he wanted to do then was to work hard and support his family in Lahore. *How far he had veered from such simple ideals?*

Meanwhile health authorities issued the warnings of a flu epidemic that was particularly viral. There was talk of bird flu and swine flu, which terrified people. Some went so far as to stop eating poultry. Some even avoided handshakes which could transmit the germs. Despite her precautions, Carla came down with the virus. What started as a few sneezes and runny nose transformed into a full-fledged flu. By the third day, she was burning with fever. Jawad took her to the doctor who advised bed rest for a few days. On Friday evening he went to pick up Hilda as usual, she too was sniffing and sneezing. On reaching the club, they found Goran standing outside, talking on his mobile. He seemed a bit perturbed. Jawad realized that there was something wrong. They waited until he finished his call.

"Did you hear the news?" he asked Jawad.

"What news?"

"Last night Ivan's father passed away and this morning he took a flight home. I dropped him off at the airport; he was taking it pretty hard man." Goran was uncharacteristically somber. "He made me in charge while he is away. I spoke to a friend who'll help you with the work. I'll be covering the entrance and the office," he explained all in a hurry.

Jawad realized that there was no time to waste. He immediately went to work. Soon Goran's friend Dragan, who seemed to know his way around the bar, joined him. The DJ had started his routine and the club was in full flow once again. The scene was similar but the staff felt like a ship without a captain. Goran was doing his best to fill Ivan's shoes. He was running around making sure things were in order. Due to the fear that something may go wrong because of their inexperience, Jawad and Goran stayed extra alert. Their only consolation was few cocktails. Jawad called Carla in late evening, and she told him that the worst seemed to be over and she was feeling fine and watching TV. Jawad knew that she didn't want to worry him at his work and decided to go straight home when they finished for the night. He dropped Hilda and advised her to visit the doctor before it's too late.

Back home he found Carla in a deep sleep. He touched her wrist to feel the fever, which still seemed high. She opened her eyes and Jawad was stunned. They were red and there was something in her eyes which he felt to be like torment. He turned his eyes away from her, just as thieves do when caught stealing. He made some breakfast but Carla told him she had no appetite. He gave her two more antibiotics with a glass of warm milk and lay next to her. She snuggled unto him and soon fell asleep. He woke up in the afternoon and checked his mobile. There was a message from Hilda. She had been to her GP who advised complete bed rest. Jawad worried about the lack of staff, and that too for Saturday night. They were already without Ivan and now with Hilda in bed they would struggle. He called Goran who told him not to worry. There was a music festival in Luzern that evening. Goran figured that a lot of people would go there instead.

Just as Jawad was getting ready to leave, Carla took a bad turn. First, she vomited and then she complained of dizziness. He touched her forehead and it was burning. He was about to call Goran but then thought he'll be overwhelmed. Carla assured him that she'll be fine and he should go ahead. He stayed with her for a while, and sent a message to Goran that he might be late. He tried to cheer her up as much as he could. He left food and drinks next to the bed, kissed her forehead and left with a heavy heart. On the way to the club, he wrote Hilda a message, wishing her well.

Goran was right regarding the number of people who came to the club that night. But it was still half full and they were wary of being stretched. Goran stayed at the front door in the beginning but as he felt that no more clubbers were showing up, he relaxed. Soon he was sitting in the office and Malka joined him. Jawad felt strange that day. He was constantly thinking about Carla. Her sickness was not a big deal but he couldn't stop thinking that she was suffering due to his sins. Seeing her sick in bed, he realized just how deeply he loved her and that he would be utterly devastated if something were to happen to her. She was such a loving person, and yet he'd reciprocated by cheating on her. This was not the Jawad he'd known all his life.

It was three in the morning and Goran started his drinking spree. Jawad felt that his heart was not really in it tonight. He drank couple of vodka shots halfheartedly and then excused himself to go to the washroom. Once out of sight, he went down to the cellar. He wanted to be alone. There was a wash basin for the workers in the corridor. He looked in the mirror and saw himself standing there drunk and shaking without his customary high.

A time comes in one's life when some serious introspection becomes important. Jawad felt that his personality had been split in two.

Look at you. What had become of you? From a humble and simple person you've become a liar, a thief, an adulterer, an alcoholic and a potential drug addict. What a transformation. You even cheated on the person who was most loyal and accepted you as her life partner.

There, standing in front of the mirror in the cellar, he took an oath. He'll quit this job and everything that came with it. He'll look for another job, any kind of a job but he won't work at this damned club. By leaving, he would get rid of Goran and his addictions and also Hilda and her seductions. He'll return to Carla, his true soul mate.

Better now before Carla finds out and regrets her decision to fall in love with you.

There is an old saying that when character is lost, everything is lost. Jawad wanted to keep whatever was left of his character. He washed his face and returned upstairs, feeling lighter. The crowd was thinner and Goran realized that there was something wrong with him.

"What is the matter with you man? Hilda will be back soon," he said tauntingly.

Jawad smiled halfheartedly. He wanted to show that everything was normal. Soon the hall was empty and the security people left along with the DJ. Now there was only staff members left. Goran emptied the cash registers and locked the money in the office drawers. Jawad wanted to leave then but they all pushed him to stay a while longer. It was still dark outside and nobody seemed to be in the mood to leave. Jawad was fighting the urge to do something. Maybe his body wanted something else, something like cocaine or cannabis. Whatever urge he was having, he was fighting against it. He was having flashes in his mind. He realized that the sooner he left the better it would be. He wanted to speak to Goran and tell him he'll be leaving and won't be coming back. He'll tell him that there is no need for an argument as he had made up his mind.

He was feeling unwell but didn't know what was wrong with him. The only thing which came to his mind was that the lack of drugs was causing all that. He decided to talk to Goran some other time and left, though they were all still shouting at him to stay. Slowly he came out of the parking lot. He knew he had to be careful because of the drinks. His mind wasn't quite right. He seemed to be the only driver on the road at that early morning. He concentrated and kept his eyes on the road, but it was impossible to stop the flow of thoughts. While driving on the desolate Zurich road his thoughts were with Carla. Is she paying the price of my sins? He also visualized his folks eating a Sunday brunch and enjoying their day off. Meanwhile he was getting the shakes and withdrawal symptoms. He again felt flashes in his mind while driving home, drunk, at five in the morning. As he was mentally back home, seeing his family relaxing in the living room. His mother and sisters making the traditional *parathas*, he didn't realize that he had veered onto the left side of the road just like in Lahore. There was a diversion due to road works and he had to pass below the bridge to cross over. Mentally disillusioned, he took the wrong turn and drove onto a one-way road. Going around the corner, it was only when he saw the truck from the Swiss Post coming point blank from the opposite direction, that he realized his fatal mistake. However, it was too late by then. The big monster slammed into his puny two doors Twingo. Last things he heard were the sound of crunching metal, and his car screeching off the road barrier. He went into a coma even as they cut him free from the smashed car. It was a blessing in disguise as it saved him from seeing many ugly things. Police cars, the ambulance, fire engines and the rescue crew arrived at the scene. All were trying to pull him intact from the crashed car. It took him three days to come out of the coma. When his eyes slowly focused, the first face he saw was none other than Carla's. Tubes, wires and machines surrounded him. A monitor showed that he was still alive.

Heavily drugged and in a haze, he saw Carla looking nervously down at him. He tried to move his hand but realized he was unable to. His mind was not fully awake and he felt pain, immense pain. It was as if his whole body had turned in to a giant ball of pain. He noticed that he had plasters and bandages all over him. Doctors, in their noble duty of saving lives and mending the bones and flesh of the unfortunates, had tried their best. His death might have been a terrible loss not only to his family but also to the insurance company. Under strong medication, not a lot made much sense to him. Carla was quick to call the nurse, to tell her about Jawad regaining consciousness. By the time she came back, he was half-asleep and could only mumble obscurely in broken sentences. The nurse reassured Carla that it was a good sign. Once she had left the room, Carla held his swollen hand and whispered something to him. He could only flutter his eyes and then fell asleep. Next morning, he was in a better condition, and was able to speak coherently. Carla hadn't arrived yet but the duty doctor came to see how he was feeling. Jawad asked if he could have some medicine, as his back was agonizingly painful. The doctor told him that he would get the pills at the fixed time. Jawad asked him what injuries he had. Doctor advised him to be strong and rest. When Jawad insisted, doctor told him that he had a broken rib, a head injury and some damage to his back. He asked Jawad to move his legs and he felt enormous pain in the lower part of his body. He told Jawad this was because of the trauma to his spine, but he was fortunate as he was not paralyzed.

"You're lucky to be alive, young man. We were quite horrified at your injuries when they brought you in."

The doctor tried to raise his spirit. However, Jawad felt anything but lucky at that moment.

"My wife, what time she comes?" He asked weakly to the duty nurse.

"She comes every afternoon. She hardly left your side in the first two days. Eventually we warned her about you catching the flu from her. That's why she'd been going home for the nights. You're a lucky man to have such a kind and caring wife."

Jawad nodded and closed his eyes. A lone tear ran down his left eye. It was both for Carla and at his perilous condition. *I had it all, and threw it all away. I should've seen this coming.*

He suddenly remembered his family back in Pakistan. They might have no idea that he had almost died. What would have happened to them and their dreams for the future? It was agonizing to even contemplate what his parents and especially his beloved sisters would have had to go thorough if he had perished that night. This was the result of his selfishness and lack of control of his unending desires. The mental pain was almost as excruciating as the physical injuries. He waited patiently for Carla to arrive. He needed her more than ever, to ask for her forgiveness and share with her the mental torture he was feeling for having been utterly self-centered. He was in tears when she walked in with flowers in her hands. She had a delightful look when she saw him awake. She held his hand and gave him a very gentle kiss on his cheek. Jawad tried his best to stop himself from sobbing at her unrequited love. She may have imagined that the tears were due to pain which was so far from the truth. It had taken a truck to stop him and to make him realize of his total disregard for those who had loved him and supported him in all his highs and lows. He motioned for Carla to come close to him, and when she did, he held her tightly. She felt his chest heaving and slowly pulled away.

"Are you in pain amore?" she asked disconsolately.

"Yes," he cried in anguish.

"Jawad, please don't blame yourself for the accident. It can happen to anyone." She held his hand again and gently touched his face. Jawad looked away. *If only you knew my angel. Perhaps the truck had been a blessing in disguise.*

"I've slept so many days," he looked into her eyes. "Did you think I won't wake up Carla?"

"No, such a thought never came to my mind."

She also told him that she had informed all his close friends and his family. It was police that notified her as they found out from the registration. She kept her hand on his forehead. Her mere presence besides the bed was enough to raise his spirits. The door opened and the nurse walked in with some pills and a glass of water.

"Mr. Jawad, time for your painkillers."

"To be honest sister, I don't think I need them. My pain is much better now," he spoke while looking at Carla as she was the reason of his improvement.

To cheer him up, Carla began to read some book for him which she had brought with her from his stock. Jawad kept his eyes fixed on her. She read English in an Italian dialect, which he found amusing. Though it was difficult to turn his head, he found solace in her soft voice and her unbounded love.

"Mr. Jawad, there are two policemen who want to speak to you," nurse informed them. Carla left along with the nurse and the two out of uniform officers walked in and introduced themselves. Jawad knew what the issue was, but he was determined to face up to them. After all, he had admitted his guilt to himself, now it was time to pay the price. They informed him that the alcohol level in his blood was twice as high as the legal limit. In addition, the accident was his fault entirely and there'll be consequences due to his negligence and driving under the influence. Fortunately, the other driver had not suffered any injuries but there were damages. Now it was between Jawad and his insurance company to sort out the costs. Charges had already been filed against him but they'll wait for further action until he was reasonably healthy. They took a detailed interview and noted the circumstances surrounding the accident. Jawad knew it was better to come clean and not make things complicated. He was not overly worried about the financial costs. Luckily, on the day of his accident, he didn't use any drugs.

They don't hang you in this country if you couldn't pay the bills.

Jawad realized that he should try his best to save two things, one was his health and the other was his relationship with Carla. Alas, for him, the repentance was too late. The officers left after a while, advising him to contact their office when he left the hospital. At least they weren't out to bruise my feelings, he thought. When Carla came and asked what they were, interviewing him about, Jawad took a deep breath and told her the truth.

"I've been drinking at work that day."

"Oh amore, what is going to happen now?" she asked.

"I'll have to pay for my deeds I guess. It'll probably do me good in the long term."

He apologized to her for all the agony he was putting her thorough. Though she forgave him easily, she asked him to promise never to put himself in similar danger again.

"If it's any consolation Carla, I don't think I'll ever drive again," he reminded her. He soon felt drowsy and slept. He had few visitors. Some of his old workmates from Zughaus showed up including Denni and his girlfriend.

The only person who came every day, besides Carla, was his dear friend Singh, sometime accompanied by his wife. He always tried to cheer him up. Goran also came one afternoon, carrying a bouquet of flowers. He smelled of spirits. Jawed had to smile at the irony. He couldn't change Goran and others but he could certainly change himself. Goran asked what had happened and Jawad avoided blaming anyone but himself. However, he knew it was also time to change the company that he kept. To Goran, it was clear that his buddy won't be coming to work again. Hilda also came at the weekend and was horrified to see his injuries. Jawad was thankful that Carla wasn't present. He didn't say much and perhaps she understood why he wasn't talkative. When she came the second time, Carla was also there. He was asleep and Jawad had no idea what they spoke about, but she never showed up again. Carla did not mention the conversation they had between them. He prayed that Hilda kept their secret and didn't cause any more grief to Carla.

As Carla had informed his parents, when Jawad called for the first time from the hospital, it all became so emotional to bear. His mother cried on the phone while his father told her to stay calm. She cursed the day when she allowed him to go abroad. But his father was pragmatic as usual and said that an accident could happen anywhere. They did not know that he was driving under influence and that he may never work again. It was a painful conversation, Jawad felt for his family's helplessness.

They couldn't even visit him and console him, or be there in his hour of need. After two weeks, he was discharged from the hospital. With his back injury, he was not able to move much but it was a big relief to be at home again. Every day, during her break, Carla would take him to a nearby clinic for a two hours therapy session. Slowly his back and the lower part of the body were healing with time. Doctors advised him that an operation was risky and might not be successful in any case. It seemed that part of his nervous system might never recover and he might be using crutches to walk for a long time. It all depended how his body reacted to the medications and the physiotherapy. Jawad knew that even if he healed physically, he'll never fully recover emotionally.

Next thing was the legal process, which was entangled, and the most aggravating. Everyone seemed to be looking for a part of him and their share of the compensation. The date for his court appearance arrived and he was banned from driving for the rest of his life. The license that he'd just procured had to be given up. Jawad was in no shape to drive both physically and mentally any way. His insurance company paid most of the costs. But he was liable to pay his share, which amounted to 30,000 Francs. There were also unpaid bank installments.

After three months, he was able to walk better with the aid of a cane. It was to support his right leg which limped along as he walked. It was only then that she informed her mother and brother. Both came to visit them and were angry that they were not informed earlier. Carla argued that she didn't want to disturb them. Her mother stayed a whole week.

Carla was trying her best to cope with her work and Jawad's condition. She was busy, calling different offices, pleading for time to make the various payments. They were constantly receiving letters demanding ever-increasing payments. Jawad knew he'll have to do something or else they might lose everything that was left. By combing through the brochures and booklets that Carla and Singh had brought in, he finally found an NGO that may help him. He contacted them and made an appointment. After assessing his situation, they advised him to contact a debt settlement company who may help reach a deal with the companies he owed to. In addition, they advised him to join a hotel receptionist diploma course as he could no longer do manual work. They told him that they would also pay for his course and assist him in his job hunt. Jawad was relieved that things were moving on at last, and may change for the better.

Within weeks, he was sitting in the classroom of a technical school, the only student with a handicap. Some of classmates looked at him with sorrow and they were all sympathetic with his situation. Over the weeks, he learnt the necessary skills required for reception work. It also helped to keep his mind occupied and raised his spirit.

Goran called a couple of times but Jawad didn't show much interest in his calls for going out and relieving his misery with therapeutic herbs. Over time, Goran stopped calling and perhaps eventually got the message that Jawad was no longer interested in his ideas of having a good time. Jawad found it disconcerting how both their world's had changed almost overnight. Only a few a months ago, they felt invincible and the world was their oyster. Now everything seemed so uncertain. By the end of November Jawad had completed his course. He had passed the relevant exam, which was relatively easy for a man of his credentials. Back at the NGO office, they asked him to keep in touch and advised to look for job vacancies. They assured him that they would keep him informed of any developments.

Winter was upon the city and it began to snow. There was a lot of excitement as it was the last year of the millennium. To welcome the new millennium and the century, everybody was up to something. He spoke to his folks almost daily. His father told him that the family business was doing well and Jawad should only be concerned about his health.

The first fortnight passed since he finished his course and there was no progress in his job hunt. Jawad knew it was difficult. Who would like to hire a disabled receptionist? What he didn't know was that the kind old woman at the NGO was working tirelessly on his behalf. And her efforts finally bore fruit. A few days before Christmas, he received a phone call from her. She asked him to note the details of a hotel in Affoltern. He was to contact the manager, Mr. Thilmann immediately. He called the guy. Mr. Thilmann advised him to come for a visit the next day. Jawad kept the news secret from Carla and went the along with Singh who had a day off. The hotel was a nice looking building at the foot of a hill. Thilmann was a young man of around Jawad's own age and welcomed him warmly. He asked Jawad about his credentials and questioned his physical condition. He told Jawad about the vacancy of the night receptionist and that they would very much like to hire him. It seemed that the kind woman had already sown the seeds of sympathy in Mr. Thilmann's heart. Together they visited the whole premises. Jawad followed his potential boss, walking with the help of his cane. Singh waited in the cafeteria.

As they wandered into the hotel restaurant, it reminded Jawad of his past jobs. Thilmann told him that he'll be working as the night receptionist as that was the least busy time and required little physical effort. All he had to do was to take the phone calls and stay on watch. If there were any late check-ins, he'll have to deal with the customer's details. Mr. Thilmann also introduced him to the other staff and he was welcomed warmly. Whether his physical disability played a role in that he did not know. Working hours were to be 11 pm until 8 am so he'll have to adjust his own sleeping hours. Jawad felt that he had rested enough. Thilmann asked him for one night trial to see if he can handle the job. Then he saw them off at the hotel gate. Jawad looked forward to breaking a bit of good news to Carla.

She was happy for him. He'll be working again. What else she can desire. The extra income would help with the repayments. On the night of his trial, she drove Jawad to the hotel in the late evening. George, the guy at the reception that night greeted him with a smile and explained everything from the computer to the security issues. He also told him that it was a good place to work and one could catch up with reading and going online, though the access was restricted. That night was a quiet one and nothing much happened. Some guests returned late after attending a wedding and asked for the keys and direction to their rooms. George showed him a list of guests with instructions for early morning calls. In the morning, George picked up the phone and started calling their rooms. Some had appointments to reach and others had flights to catch. There were some early checkouts and George explained how to handle the payments. Almost everybody who paid their bill also gave generous tips. Then there was a rush of guests at around eight when the lodgers came down for their breakfast. Thilmann also appeared and took Jawad to his office.

"Well, what do you think, could you handle it?" he asked Jawad in a friendly tone.

"I'm sure I can," Jawad assured him.

"Good. I'll send you the work agreement through the post. Sign it if you're satisfied and post it back. And don't forget you are entitled for a nice breakfast every morning," he reminded him.

"Great. Then I won't have to cook when I get home. Thanks for everything Mr. Thilmann. You've been most kind," Jawad was genuinely indebted. He left after breakfast and took the bus home. Carla was preparing to leave for work as he arrived. Jawad told her the good news and that he was happy with his new job. They visited the Singhs on Christmas day and enjoyed a special dinner. Everyone was happy at Jawad's recovery and thankful for his narrow escape that night. It almost felt like a Thanksgiving meal.

The euphoria of the approaching millennium night was at its peak. People considered the turn of the century and millennium, a truly historical event. *Mostly they would celebrate it by an orgy of drunkenness and sex.* Newspapers and the media were adding to the frenzy and a general feeling of exultation. Men of God had their own agendas and special prayers were organized in various churches, celebrating two thousand years of Christian calendar. Jawad was not keen to be part of the mass hysteria. Like most major cities, Zurich too had a tradition of firework on New Year's Eve. As it was the millennium night, spectators were assured that the firework would be special and on an exceptional scale. Though Jawad was not interested, Carla didn't want to miss the opportunity for some fun and celebrations. She asked Jawad to join her at the celebrations on the 31st of December. Jawad promised her that he'll meet her at the entrance of Fraumunster Abbey around 11:30. From there they can walk to the Bellevue.

It was a bitter cold evening and Jawad felt a bit arthritic. He covered himself well as the temperature was expected to be around minus ten at midnight. Thanks to his limp and the cane, he was always offered a seat in public transport. The trams were jam packed that evening. From Paradeplatz, he walked slowly to their meeting point. The abbey was open and there were some people singing Gospel inside. More and more people were arriving and every one was keen to find the best place to view the fireworks. Carla came on time and eventually found him standing at the door, looking a little lost. They walked to the Bellevue. No traffic was to run in the area that night. There were colorful notices posted everywhere that celebrations would begin with the fireworks on the boats, waiting in the lake. Most people were carrying bottles of champagne, some were already drunk. Carla had brought a small bottle of Prosecco. She told Jawad that he'll get only a sip to celebrate. As the seconds ticked towards the final minute of the millennium, church bells began to ring and after the cheers that rang round for miles in the night, the fireworks began. Carla looked euphoric with excitement and gave Jawad a celebratory kiss. She opened the bottle and handed him a glass. She kissed him with vigor.

"Happy new year amore", she spoke, looking radiant in the light from the colorful illuminations.

Jawad looked at her; slowly tears came to his eyes. He thought about the predicament that he'd put everyone thorough, including himself and the way Carla had faced the crisis. She'd truly stood by her man.

"Happy New Year," he replied and kissed her gently back. "Amore, I want to say something this special night," he spoke while looking into her beautiful luminous eyes.

"Yes sweetheart?" Carla turned to him with concern on her face.

"I just want to say thanks and please forgive me."

"For what?"

"For everything."

In response to his plea, she kissed him passionately. A huge explosion high in the sky took her attention away but Jawad was still looking at her. He could see the reflection of lights in her eyes. She looked at him with a smile on her lips and love in her eyes. Jawad kissed her again tenderly and he could feel her infinite love, her ceaseless energy. He felt that she alone had made his long journey worthwhile. Thousands of miles away from his humble home in Lahore, he had found his soul mate. He wondered if his family back home could see the same side of moon that was above the Zurich sky. The crowd was cheering at the finale, the conclusion of a journey of a thousand years. A new day, a new year, a new century and a new millennium had begun. He wrapped himself around her to save her from the cold. Both turned to look up at the sky, which seemed infinitely full of lights and colors.

The End